Arnolfini ART Mysteries 3

Rich DiSILVIO

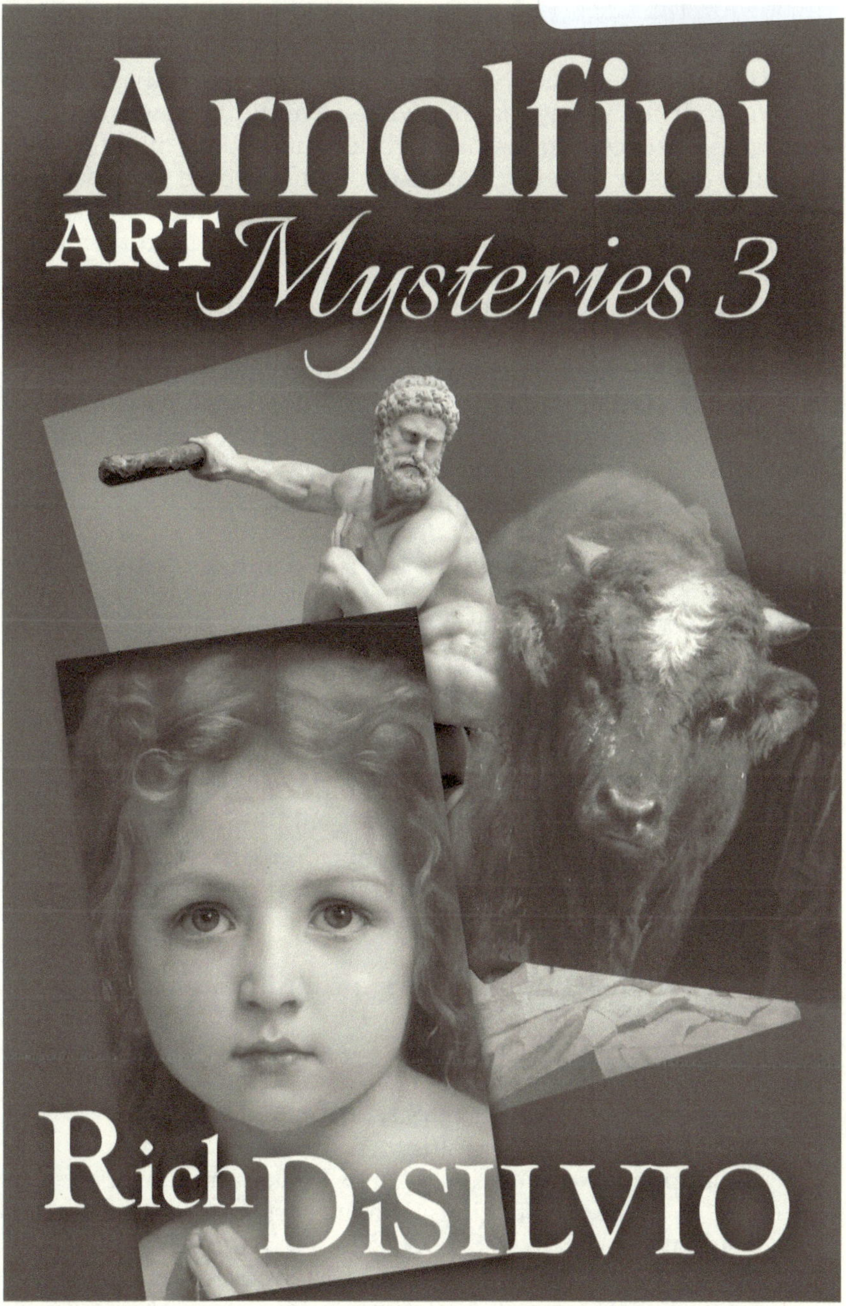

Published by DV Books, an imprint of Digital Vista, inc.

 Names of notable people, such as Rosa Bonheur, Jackson Pollack, Alain de Boissieu, and others were utilized in a fictional context and in the last case used fictional dialogue. Some actual quotes by or about such notable figures were used, and information about the looting by Hitler, Goering and Alexander Langsdorff were factual. All other acting characters herein are fictional, and any coincidence to actual people with similar names is purely unintentional. Any fictional characters working at actual museums or galleries mentioned do not officially represent their organizations in any way and are fabrications of the author.

Cover art design © Rich DiSilvio. Interior paintings/artwork, *Blue Jay in Winter, Heronry, Tanager, Old Whale's Tale, Moby Dick*, and *White Whale Attacking The Essex* by Rich DiSilvio. *Preliminary Study for Weaning the Calves* created by Rich DiSilvio using Rosa Bonheur's original *Weaning the Calves. The Horse Fair* and *Weaning the Calves* photos (public domain) are courtesy of the MET Museum of Art. *Apollo & Daphne* photo by Architas. Photo of *The Georgia Guidestones* by Dina Eric. Photo of *Hercules & Cacus* by Jebulon. Photo of *Villa Medici* by Niccolo-Rigacci. Photos of historical artwork are in the public domain, courtesy of Wikipedia. Additional photos/illustrations purchased via FreePik.

Author's Website: www.richdisilvio.com

- - - - - - - - - - - - - - - - - -

Names: DiSilvio, Rich
Title: The Arnolfini Art Mysteries 3
Description: New York, USA: DV Books, an imprint of Digital Vista, inc.
Identifiers: ISBN 978-1-950052-15-8 (paperback) | ISBN 978-1-950052-14-1 (eBook)
Subjects: Short Stories | Art Crimes | Mysteries, Thrillers | Private Investigator | Artists, Composers | Detective Stories
Illustrations/Photos: 40

Contents

An Old Whale's Tale

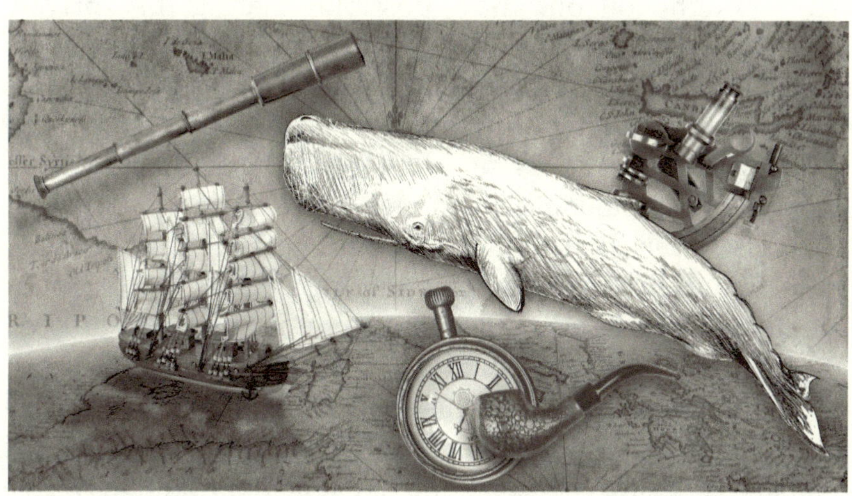

Armand Arnolfini looked at his daughter, Artemisia, lovingly, as thoughts of his intriguing case twelve years prior came streaming into his mind. The Amnesia of Artemisia case, as it was dubbed, was how his wife Andrea and he were inspired to name their first child Artemisia, after the famous Baroque painter, Artemisia Gentileschi.

Meanwhile, sitting at Artemisia's side in the den was her little brother, Jacque, named after Andrea's Parisian father, yet whom they called Jack. Jack was ten years old, and often made his voice heard, regardless of whether or not anyone cared to hear it.

The topic of conversation was about the historic Gardner Museum heist eight years prior, in 1990. As Artemisia tried to ask her father another question, Jack trampled her words, as he blurted, "Hold on, Arty!" as he called her. "Dad said the stupid museum guard let the robbers in. So, the guard must have been part of the plot. I say he walked away with some of the booty."

Armand smiled. He loved having these sessions with his children to spark their sense of reasoning and inquiry. The thought of one day possibly sharing his private investigations with one or both of his children was appealing, even if not particularly a wise decision. He was well aware that children have their own unique DNA and their own passions. As such, no good parent should force their will on a child and crush their inner spirit.

However, both children loved hearing their father's tales about his many fascinating cases, whether they be about art forgery, art thefts, architectural mysteries, or even the grisly murder cases that inevitably fell in his lap.

Armand gazed at his son. "Well, Jack, as I've mentioned, the Gardner Museum heist was the biggest art robbery in history. It is estimated that approximately five hundred million dollars worth of art was stolen."

As his kids' eyes widened, he continued to explain that the two guards on duty that night were college students. As such, the museum administrators were woefully negligent about security. As he pointed out, to entrust college kids with a museum that housed billions of dollars worth of art, and have an inadequate alarm system to boot, was pure incompetency. He finished by stating, "However, the young guards were interrogated and found to be innocent."

Artemisia shot her brother a condescending glance. "I told you they had nothing to do with it, Wacky Jacky! But you can never— "

"Oh, shush up, Arty farty! You think you're—"

"All right!" Armand cut in. "Enough of the bickering. It's imperative to keep a cool head when you're investigating a crime. You don't want to be like an angry bull distracted by a red cape, it can lure you into making a fatal mistake."

Jack swallowed hard as he envisioned a bull charging headlong to its death. "Jeez, I don't wanna end up dead!"

Armand laughed, even eliciting a chuckle from Artemisia. "Yes," he said. "Focus on the issues at hand, without being distracted." Playfully, he added, "Discuss. Don't make a fuss."

Jack giggled. "Okay, Pops. So why did the guards let the robbers in?"

Armand reached over, grasping each of his children's shoulders, and drew them in. He looked down into their young, innocent eyes, and said, "The robbers were dressed as policemen. And quite simply, the young guards were gullible. That's why it's imperative to be alert at all times. Never be fooled by a façade. Always dig down through the veneer to uncover the truth."

Artemisia squinted. "But they looked like policemen. How were the guards to know they were imposters?"

Armand leaned back. "Well, I'll agree, the robbers had a very good plan in place. But taking on the role of a professional guard means being alert and diligent. So, they should have contacted police headquarters to verify that there was in fact a call about a disturbance, which was the ploy the robbers had used. A more seasoned and well-trained guard would have questioned their motives, especially since the museum didn't have a security system in place to acknowledge the disturbance."

Just then, Armand's wife walked into the den. The trio looked over, as Andrea looked at Armand. "We have a visitor."

"And whom might that be?" Armand inquired.

Andrea placed her hand on her forehead and playfully closed her eyes. "Hmm, can you guess who our mystery guest is?"

Armand laughed. "Ah! Yes of course! Send Shirley in."

As Artemisia and Jack looked at each other, befuddled, Shirley Taylor, the famous TV psychic and dear friend, walked into the den.

Armand rose to his feet and walked over. The two embraced, giving each other a peck on the cheek, as the kids smiled and offered cordial greetings. Armand stepped back. "So, what brings you out to Westport, Connecticut?"

"The question is, what brought you out here to Westport?" Shirley said. "Why didn't you stay in Manhattan?"

"Well, I had used that apartment as my office for several years, but finally gave it up." He gazed out the rear sliding doors at the sprawling patio and built-in pool. Beyond that was a bulkhead with his 45-foot Owens cabin cruiser sitting peacefully upon the rippling waves of the Long Island Sound. "So, what's not to like about that gorgeous view?"

As Shirley gazed out upon the panoramic vista, he added, "Besides, one of my idols had lived in Westport for several years. So it can't be all that bad."

"Oh, no, it's not bad, not at all," she said with a smile. "In fact it is gorgeous. Perhaps I'm jealous. Living in that cement canyon has its good points for sure, but it can't compare to this." She squinted, then looked back into his eyes. "What idol?"

Armand laughed. "You're the psychic, you tell me?"

As Artemisia and Jack each ventured to blurt out the name, Armand raised his finger. "Shh! Let's give the famous psychic a try."

Andrea shook her head with a smile. "You're always teasing her. You know Shirley can't see or know everything, honey."

"Yes, but it is fun to test her abilities. One never knows what pops out of her mystical head."

Shirley smirked. "Well, on this one, I'll never know if you don't tell me."

Armand glanced at the DVD & CD shelf unit. "Well, I'll give you a hint before it's twilight, it's in that zone, somewhere."

Shirley laughed as her eyes landed on the *Twilight Zone* collection. "Of course, Rod Serling. I should have known. You speak of him often enough."

Armand nodded reverently. "Indeed I do. Serling and his team created a masterpiece." He rubbed his chin. "Well, since your visions enter the Twilight Zone," he added, "I would have expected you to be a fan, as well."

"You make a good point, Armand, because a TZ vision is what brought me here. You see, I've been having these strange, recurring dreams."

Armand pointed to the couch. "Have a seat."

As Shirley complied, Andrea asked Artemisia and Jack to help her in the kitchen.

Armand sat beside Shirley. "So, what vision is it this time?"

Shirley blinked and shook her head slightly. "Well, it's really more of a premonition. It's about a stolen piece of art or possibly an object. I'm not really sure." She paused, then added, "Somewhere in Massachusetts."

Armand's eyes widened! "Massachusetts?" His mind immediately envisioned the Gardner Museum in Boston, and the stolen art that had never been recovered. He swallowed hard with anticipation, and near elation. "Could it be in Boston, by any chance?"

Shirley paused in thought, then shook her head. "No. It's not a big city." She glanced at the *Twilight Zone* DVD collection. "Actually, I've been seeing glimpses of another famous writer." She looked at Armand. "Herman Melville."

Armand's shoulders wilted, somewhat disappointed. The loss of art from the biggest heist in history was a private eye's greatest challenge. He blinked and gazed into her eyes. "Herman Melville? What piece of art or object could be associated with him? Other than a pricey, first edition novel?"

Shirley's lips twisted in befuddlement. "I'm not sure, exactly. All I saw were visions of a seaside village…with whaling ships and whalebones. After all, Melville did write *Moby Dick,* right?"

Armand nodded. "Yes. In fact, *Moby Dick* took place in Nantucket."

Just then, Andrea and the kids walked back into the den with trays of finger sandwiches, raw vegetables, and cups of tea.

As they all gathered around the coffee table and distributed the plates, Armand looked at Andrea and said, "Well, honey, we've been trying to decide where to take the family on vacation, and I think Nantucket Island would be a great place to go. What do you say?"

As Andrea pondered the thought, Shirley's eyes widened, as she exclaimed, "Armand! Are you seriously thinking of taking your whole family on a wild goose chase?"

Andrea's eyes veered slyly toward her husband. "So, a vacation of work, is that it?"

Armand chuckled. "Ah, come on, it's not really work, darling. Shirley has no clue as to what was actually stolen or who might be involved. That's if anyone is involved at all. As I said, she's not sure of much, but I do know that Nantucket is a beautiful island, with a lot of history, as well. I've heard they have a nice whaling museum. So we can enjoy the beach and ocean while also adding a bit of culture in the mix."

Andrea sighed, as Shirley took a sheepish sip of tea, then said, "I'm sorry, Andrea, I had no idea Armand would jump on this hazy premonition of mine, especially with your whole family."

Jack and Artemisia glanced at each other, excited, then looked at their mother, as Jack begged, "Come on, Mom! Dad always has all the fun. It will be cool for us to join him on this case."

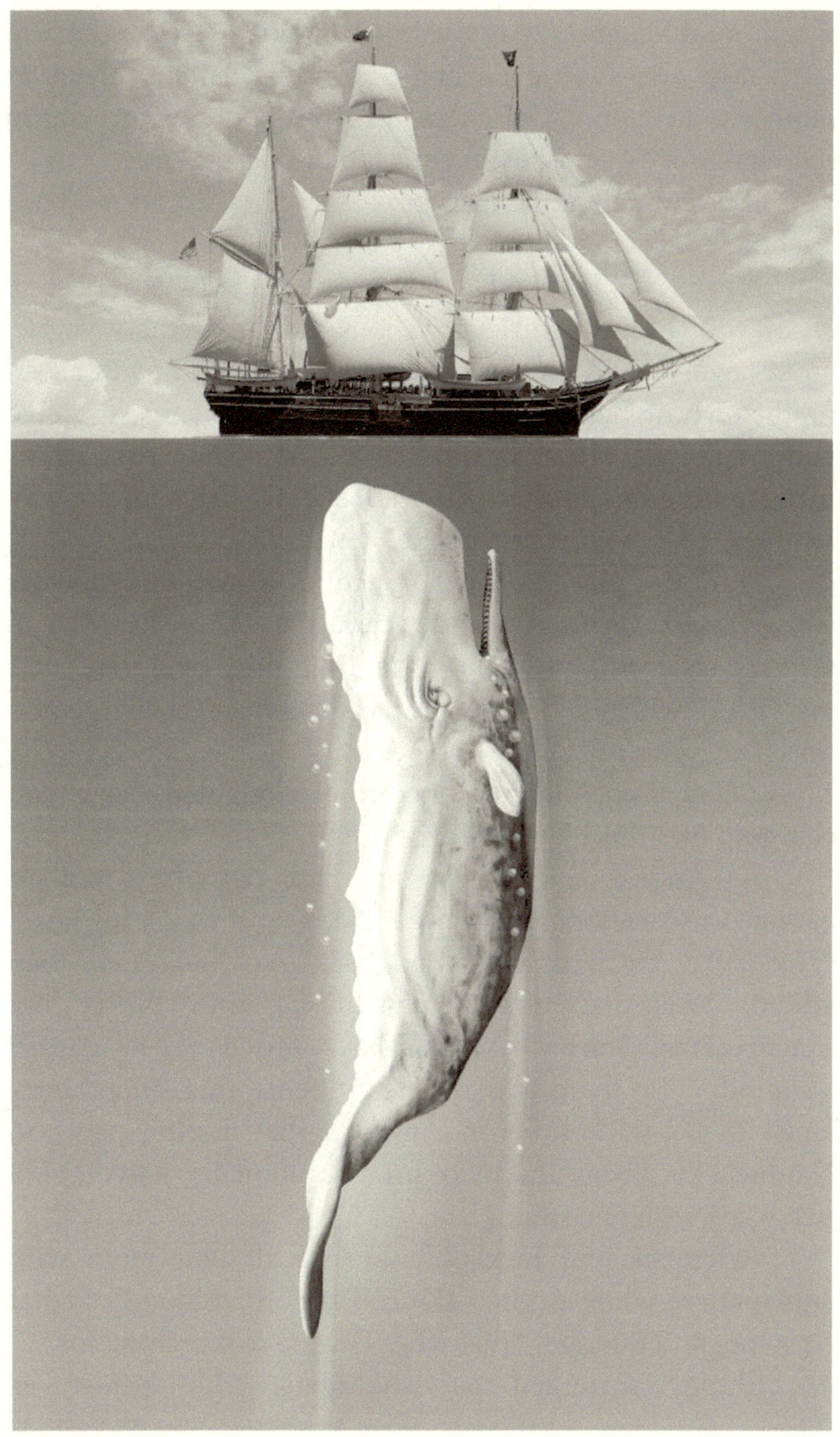

"Yeah! I agree," Artemisia seconded.

"My sweet little darlings," Andrea said to them in motherly fashion. "Do either of you know what you're searching for? As it is, even your father doesn't know."

Jack jumped at the response. "Yeah, a wild goose chase or some kinda crazy hunt."

As they all laughed, Armand interjected, "Now listen, all of you. I know Shirley's visions were extremely vague, and I never would have entertained this idea if I hadn't seen firsthand how her previous vision led me to solve the Five and Dime case. She does offer some compelling reasons for investigating this further. After all, she did drive all the way out here, to Westport, to tell me."

Shirley placed her teacup down, somewhat embarrassed. "Well, Armand, actually I was on my way to visit my sister in Mystic, but figured I'd drop by. I'm sorry if my vision, which is quite unclear, is making you charge into this."

"Hey, Pop!" Jack interjected. He giggled. "Are you charging into this like that silly bull!?"

As Andrea and Shirley squinted, not privy to their earlier conversation, Armand chuckled, and shook his head. "No, Jack." He paused, leaned back into the couch, then added, "Well, perhaps in a conventional sense, but no, not exactly. First, Shirley's visions have proven to be correct quite often. So there is plausible evidence that something's amiss in Nantucket. Second, even if that doesn't pan out, Nantucket is a beautiful place for a vacation. So, why not kill two birds with one stone?"

Artemisia and Jack each looked at their mom with anticipation, while Andrea glanced at Shirley then looked at Armand, and queried, "Just what is it we're searching for?"

Shirley shrugged her shoulders, still unclear, as

Armand said confidently, "A piece of art or an artifact that was stolen from someone or someplace in Nantucket. I suspect the Whaling Museum would be the first place to investigate."

Shirley rubbed her chin, impressed. "I imagine that would be a good place to start. It seems you have a clearer idea of what's going on there than I do."

Jack sprung to his feet. "So! Is it settled? Huh? Are we going?"

Andrea looked at Jack, then at Artemisia, who nodded excitedly. Andrea pursed her lips, then smiled. "Very well, Nantucket it is."

Armand looked at Shirley. "Would you like to join us?"

Shirley rose from the couch. "Thank you, but no. As I said, I'm heading to Mystic to spend a few days with my sister."

"Very well," Armand said. "I'll keep you informed if anything arises." He turned toward the children. "Well, shake a leg! Pack your bags. We'll leave in the morning."

By the afternoon of the next day, the Arnolfinis arrived in Nantucket in their new 1998 Lincoln Navigator. On the CD player, *Me and My Big Ideas* by Tears for Fears played, prompting Andrea to look at Armand. "This song sounds like you, honey."

"Very cute," Armand said as he shoved the gearshift into Park. "Just you wait, I still think my big idea will yield something."

After getting settled in the motel, they drove through the quaint village. The kids stuck their heads out the windows as the wind blew through their hair. The streets were lined with weathered houses, clad with cedar shingles, and old buildings, and eventually they arrived at the

Whaling Museum, situated on 13 Broad Street. Jack and Artemisia jumped out of the car and ran toward the entrance, while Andrea smiled, grasped Armand's hand, and walked toward the ticket booth.

Moments later, they strolled into the museum, with its fine array of nautical artifacts, while Armand slipped away and headed for the administration office.

Meanwhile, Jack and Artemisia stopped to gaze up at a huge skeleton of a sperm whale.

Jack's eyes widened. "Wow! Look at the size of this freakin' fish!"

Artemisia rolled her eyes. "Whales are mammals, you boob!"

Jack smirked. "Yeah, yeah, I knew that."

"No you didn't!' She retorted.

"Now, now!" Andrea interjected discreetly, yet firmly. "No arguments. Is that clear?"

As the two children smirked and nodded begrudgingly, Armand returned with an elderly woman by his side. "I'd like to introduce you all to Janet Harnett," he said. "She's the museum curator."

As they each made their introductions, Armand gazed at Janet. "Well, as I was saying, we're curious to know if you have any art or artifacts related to Herman Melville?"

With that, Jack's eyes bulged as he peered back at the colossal skeleton. "Hey! Is that Moby Dick?"

Janet laughed. "No, son. But it *is* a sperm whale, just like Moby Dick."

Artemisia pouted as her eyes caught a glance of a bronze sculpture nearby. It featured a whaling boat with six men harpooning a whale. "I think it's gross how they killed these poor whales." She grasped each of her elbows and cringed.

"Ah, yes, my dear," Janet said. "But at that time, whale oil was needed out of necessity. They also used other parts of the animal, as well. We no longer do that today. But, yes, it's always a shame when we don't respect nature." She turned and pointed to a large, full-sized transom of a whaling ship mounted on a wall. "That's a replica of the stern of the *Essex*. That ship has quite a history." She looked at Armand. "One I know you'll find most intriguing, Mr. Arnolfini. Follow me, everyone, if you please."

As the dignified curator walked toward the large replica, the Arnolfinis trailed close behind. As they did, Armand's eyes were drawn to the scrimshaw display along the way. He stopped, intrigued by the assortment of whales' teeth. He bent over, gazing at all the intricate etchings. His deep appreciation for art was piqued as he scrutinized the exquisite workmanship. His eyes devoured each whale's tooth as he slowly walked toward the transom of the *Essex*. But then he stopped short! His eyes widened as he noticed a large whalebone, featuring etchings of an old ship and its crew. His mind whirled, just like a fisherman's reel amid a deep-sea catch. *Of course! Bones!* he thought, as he recalled how Shirley had also mentioned visions of whalebones. Could this be the clue I need?

He turned and darted over to Janet. "Excuse me," he said. "But I see you have a fine-looking collection of scrimshaw. By chance, did you ever have a whalebone with etchings of Melville's *Moby Dick*? One that was stolen, perhaps?"

Janet's head recoiled. "No. Not that I'm aware of, Mr. Arnolfini."

"Well, what about any other fine pieces of scrimshaw on bones? Have any of them been stolen?"

Janet stifled a chuckle. "No, Mr. Arnolfini. I know you said you're a private investigator, but what exactly are you getting at? There have been no reports of thefts, or any suspicious behavior at our museum, other than your inquiries."

Artemisia and Jack looked at their father, as a slight wave of embarrassment washed over them.

Meanwhile, Armand put on a reassuring smile. "I don't mean to alarm you, Mrs. Harnett. But I have it upon the word of a reputable source that something has been or will be stolen in Nantucket, and I assumed it might be here."

Janet squinted, not sure if she should be appreciative or alarmed. The latter fueled her tongue. "What do you mean by something will be stolen? Do you have verifiable evidence of a imminent theft?"

"No!" Andrea interjected. "He doesn't." She glanced at Armand. "Forget about the bones or whalebones, dear." She turned back toward Janet. "Never mind him, sometimes my husband's hyperactive mind gets the better of him. If you said nothing has been stolen, then I'm sure there's nothing to worry about."

Meanwhile, Andrea's own suspicions were focused more on the famous author than silly bones, as she added, "However, Mrs. Harnett, I believe the kids and I would love to hear more about Herman Melville. If you can offer any insights into his life, that would be fantastic."

Janet took a moment to clear her mind, as she glanced at Armand, suspiciously, shook her head, then said with a slight stutter, "W-well, of c-course. In fact, that is why I escorted you all here." She glanced up at the ornate transom of the old whaling ship. "The *Essex* is the true inspiration and seed of Melville's famous novel."

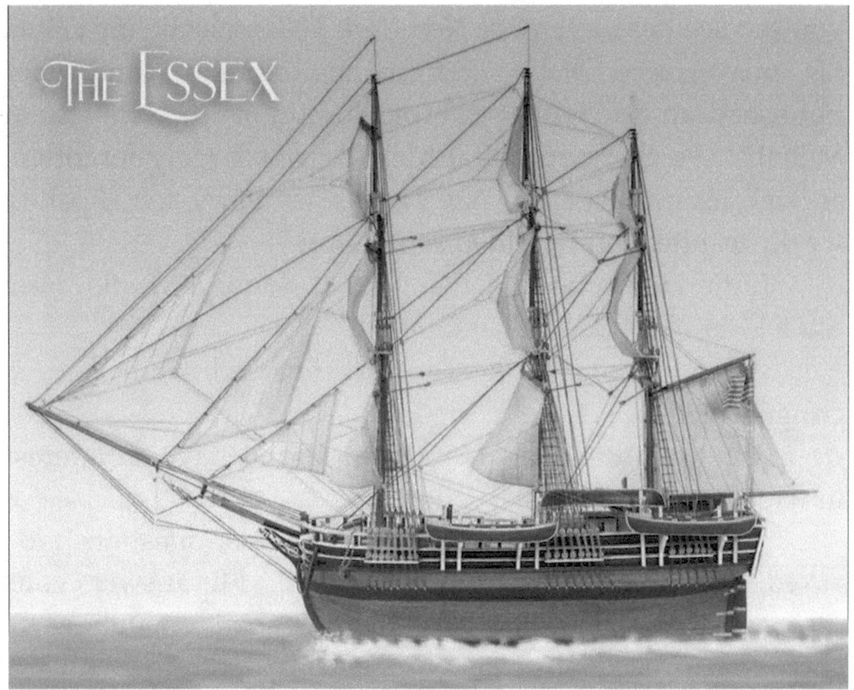

Armand sighed and crossed his arms as he looked at his upstaging wife. Andrea smiled lovingly, then officially quashed his derailed quest with a solid wink.

Meanwhile, the kids gathered around Mrs. Harnett and listened with rapt attention as she began her historical oration. Janet explained that, although illustrious today, Herman Melville's career had sunk, just like the *Pequod,* after the poor reception of *Moby Dick.* Moreover, Melville's subsequent novels met with failure, as well. As such, Herman resorted to writing only poetry for three decades. To pay the bills, however, Herman served as a customs inspector in New York City for almost twenty years. When he retired, it was his wife's family who largely supported the Melvilles.

She turned and pointed to a framed edition of *The New York Times*. "Sadly, Herman died in relative obscurity. As you can see here, even *The New York Times* mistakenly called his masterpiece *Mobie Dick* in his obituary, and later published an article that referred to him as 'the late Hiram Melville'. Further proof that Melville was largely forgotten, as well as proof of *The NY Times's* tendency for slipshod work, despite their heralded reputation."

Little Jack scratched his chin. "I don't get it. So, how did a loser like Melville get famous?"

Armand looked at his son and chuckled, while Andrea cringed.

Artemisia interjected, "Or why did *he* have an interest in whaling? He was just a writer."

Janet was accustomed to the barrage of questions kids asked, and replied with poise, "Well, I'll answer your question first, Jack. You see, Melville had enough early successes to become a notable talent, particularly with the novel *Typee,* among others. However, once he published *Moby Dick,* the reviews and his fortunes plummeted rather quickly. As with many great artistic talents, they sadly don't get the support they need. Many brilliant people have died in poverty and obscurity, only to be appreciated many years or even decades later."

Janet turned her gaze at Artemisia. "As for Melville's interest in whaling, dear. He wasn't an armchair enthusiast; Melville had sailed on whaling ships for many years, which gave authenticity to his novels. He even took part in a mutiny on one ship and spent some time in jail on the island of Tahiti."

Armand's interest was growing with each new sentence that flowed out of Janet's mouth, until her oration was cut short by her associate, Benjamin Jaspers, who approached the group. Benjamin was tall, sported a wiry beard and mustache, and actually looked like a seaman from Melville's novel.

Janet pointed to Benjamin. "Mr. Jaspers will take it from here. He's a specialist on the history of the *Essex*, and its fateful voyage." She turned toward Andrea, leaned in close, and whispered, "You might want to take the kids to another part of the museum, as this tale is frightfully dark and disturbing."

Andrea's head recoiled with surprise. "Is it really that bad?"

Janet nodded discreetly. "Yes indeed. If you wish, I'd be happy to show them around, if you prefer to stay here with your husband."

"That would be most kind," Andrea replied, as she then turned and whispered to Armand the plan.

Janet looked at Artemisia and little Jack and said, "Okay, kiddies, follow me. The next part of the *Essex* story gets rather boring. I'll show you some truly exciting things we have on display here."

Jack and Artemisia glanced at their parents, who acknowledged their consent, and Janet gently grasped both children's hands and escorted them away.

Armand looked at Benjamin. "So, I hear this tale is rather grim."

"Yes, it is," Benjamin said straight-faced, with an uncanny accent like Vincent Price. "Mrs. Harnett has long been against me even telling this tale. Very few people today know of the voyage of the *Essex*. However, in its day, it was a real shocker. That was in 1820, thirty-one years prior to the release of Melville's novel in 1851."

Andrea stepped closer, even more intrigued. "Yes, a real shocker it must be. Mrs. Harnett's warning about your presentation has me even more curious. If Melville's novel is not off limits to youngsters, what makes the tale of the *Essex* so extreme?"

Benjamin Jaspers scratched his thick, wiry beard. "Well, let's not jump ahead of ourselves. Like any good tale, we don't want any spoilers to ruin the adventure. Perhaps you both should take a seat." He pointed to the string of chairs nearby.

As Armand and Andrea complied, Benjamin's face glistened with the anticipation of telling the sordid tale. "As I mentioned, Melville's novel, *The Whale,* better known as *Moby Dick,* was written some thirty years *after* the tragic event of the *Essex*. And get this; Melville never even visited Nantucket before committing pen to paper. He only did so after his book was published. Nevertheless, although Melville based his novel on the true story of the *Essex,* he eliminated the deeply disturbing aspects, of which you shall soon hear."

"Why do you suppose that is?" Armand inquired.

"Oh, I reckon Melville was very much aware of the moral conventions of his time," Benjamin said. "We must realize that the genre of horror stories was something not even invented yet. Edgar Allan Poe was the pioneer who, at that time, was just beginning to explore the dark regions of the macabre. So, by and large, the masses were not yet exposed to or prepared to hear such lurid tales."

Andrea squirmed in her chair and gripped the outer edges of her seat. "You're making me uncomfortable already, Mr. Jaspers."

As Armand placed a comforting hand on her knee, Benjamin cracked a theatrically sinister smile. "Well, perhaps it's a good idea to hold onto your seat, Mrs. Arnolfini, because this *is* a chilling tale alright." He took a deep breath, and commenced, with his Vincent Price voice in full chiller mode: "The tale of the *Essex* begins with Captain George Pollard Jr. Pollard was only twenty-nine years of age when he was granted the commission to sail the *Essex,* along with a crew of twenty seamen on a two-and-half-years-long whaling voyage."

"The captain was only twenty-nine years old!?" Andrea interjected, surprised.

Jaspers struggled to smile, hoping his thrilling oration wouldn't be interrupted every two seconds moving forward, as he nodded. "Yes, Mrs. Arnolfini, that might seem odd by today's standards, but his crew was mostly young men and teenagers." Benjamin grasped the lapels of his jacket like a professor, and continued, "At this time it's important to mention the three other main characters. Pollard's first mate was Owen Chase; he was only twenty-three. Meanwhile, Charles Ramsdell was only a teenager. And not to be confused with Owen the first-mate was Owen Coffin. Coffin happened to be Pollard's younger first cousin."

Benjamin pointed to a large map of the Western hemisphere on the wall. He explained that the *Essex* left port in Nantucket on August 12, 1819. A mere two days later, the 87-foot-long ship encountered a squall, which damaged the topgallant sail. "The ship nearly sank!" he said with emotion.

"Off to a great start, I see," Armand interjected.

"Exactly," Benjamin agreed. "It was a harbinger of things to come." He pointed to the map, his finger on the Atlantic Ocean near the Carolinas. "They managed to make repairs and sailed south. Five weeks later, they reached Cape Horn." His finger traveled down to the tip of South America. "However, they didn't have any luck catching whales or fish. It was at this point that they made the critical decision to leave the safety of the shoreline and venture out, thousands of miles, into the vast South Pacific."

Andrea was already nervous, not thrilled about voyages that lose sight of land. Naturally, that included the deep-sea fishing trips Armand took her on, some venturing out 50 miles into the Atlantic. The eerie feeling of seeing only water all around her and a horizon of only blue always made her queasy. Her appreciation for sailors (especially those during the days of yore in small wooden vessels) was now bolstered to full-blown admiration.

Meanwhile, Armand leaned forward, eyes and ears on full alert, as the tale was just now beginning to dive into the deep, watery mists of a distant past.

At this point, Benjamin's narrative was so immersive and compelling that they could practically taste the salty sea air and smell the bloody-fish-stained decks of the *Essex*.

Captain Pollard shouted to his crew, "Man the sails and point this ship ten degrees northwest! We're heading for Charles Island in the Galapagos. This cursed ocean is void of surface fish and we need to restock our holds."

Owen Chase echoed and amplified the command, then stepped by the Captain's side. He leaned close and whispered, "I can't believe the bad luck that has beset us, Captain. The men are getting wary."

Pollard looked at his first mate. "I'm confident that the Galapagos will offer us plenty of food sources." He placed his hand resolutely on Owen's shoulder. "Hold the line and keep the boys in check. This drought *will* turn around."

Having landed on Charles Island days later, the crew scattered and sought whatever they could capture or kill. As Pollard expected, the crew managed to bring sixty large tortoises aboard. Fully restocked, the ship set sail once again, but not before one of the crew set a fire on the island as a prank, which spread rapidly, killing thousands of wildlife.

Two days later, and many miles away, they could still see the huge plume of black smoke in the distance. Captain Pollard was livid, yet no one came forward to confess or rat out the culprit.

Pollard's concerns, however, evaporated as the *Essex* finally sailed into fertile waters. While the creaking ship rocked and swayed, the ocean undulated with rolling white crests and the distant spray of breathing whales. The vision was glorious to behold.

Young Charles Ramsdell cried out, "There she blows!"

Captain Pollard turned and yelled, "Man the whaleboats!"

The twenty-man crew quickly lowered three whaleboats, each outfitted with six men. Pollard led the charge, as his small boat cut through the waves, propelled by a flurry of oars slicing through the water. As Pollard held onto the rim to steady himself, he could see the glistening, gray backs of several whales breaching the surface. The colossal mammals seemed to swim carefree, unconcerned about the small intruders fluttering on the surface.

As Pollard's men vigorously churned their oars, while their sweat mixed with salty air, he readied his harpoon. Then the moment came. Pollard lunged the massive javelin, which penetrated the whale's enormous back.

Like clockwork, two others had dropped their oars and hauled their harpoons into the bleeding whale. The small boat jolted and was suddenly dragged forward, as the whale took off in a frenzied flight of fear and fury.

In what the crew called a "Nantucket sleigh ride", the small boat was dragged away from the *Essex* and out toward the horizon. After twenty grueling and erratic minutes the frantic whale exhausted itself. With a final whimper, the whale succumbed to the inevitable, the futile mad-dash for life had ended.

As the whale floated listlessly amid a bloody-red sea, Captain Pollard and his crew all cheered and began the process of readying the whale to be properly slaughtered. That is: For its bounty of valuable blubber, which would be melted down into oil for lamps; its large portions of meat for consumption; its ribs for constructing huts; and its bones and teeth for the art of scrimshaw. The day's catch was a huge success, and only the first of several more in the prosperous weeks ahead.

Then, on one still and breathless morning, the *Essex* drifted on a calm sea of liquid glass, its ripples gently caressing the hull with the soft lapping sounds of mermaids making love.

Amid this air of tranquility and contentment, Captain Pollard gazed out over the endless sea, which encompassed the entire horizon.

First mate Owen Chase approached his side. "Captain, being such a beautiful morning, I request permission to stay behind for today's run. There are several planks that need attention, and this calm sea is proving to be quite cooperative."

Pollard nodded. "By all means, Mr. Chase. We shan't be long. These seas are rich with whales and this vessel could use some tender care." He pivoted around, and called out, "Men, ready the whaleboats! It appears we have another day of smooth sailing."

As the men began lowering the boats, Pollard grabbed his cousin's arm as he walked by. "Owen, you will come with me today."

Owen Coffin smiled. "Thank you, Captain!"

With dual splashes, the two boats distorted the calm sea with radiating ripples of concentric rings. As the oarsmen propelled the boats away from the *Essex*, first mate

Owen Chase waved. "Fare thee well, laddies! Happy hunting."

With a flurry of salutes in return, the two boats receded into the blue expanse of sea and sky.

Chase pivoted around, and looked at one of only several mates remaining aboard the mother ship. "Well, let's get to it," he said. "Fetch my tool chest."

"Aye, aye, sir!" came the reply, as they all descended into the belly of the ship.

As the sun moved several degrees across the peaceful cerulean sky, Owen Chase and his mates had made several repairs down below. Chase wiped his sweaty brow and climbed up to the poop deck. He took a deep breath and pivoted toward the starboard side. His eyes scanned the horizon, spotting the two, small whaling boats, several miles away in the distance. He stretched his arms and yawned, when his eyes beheld a white glare, one that marred the glassy-blue skin of the serene sea.

Chase squinted, trying to focus on the shimmering object. He leaned forward and shaded his eyes with one hand. But then his eyes widened! He was taken aback by the strange, ghostly vision. It was a white whale, floating oddly upon the water and facing the ship. Or rather, facing *him!*

Chase could feel his adrenaline tingling his skin, having never seen an albino whale before. That's *if* his eyes weren't deceiving him. Suddenly he recoiled, as the apparition discharged a burst of vapor from its spout, then charged headlong toward the ship!

Chase was dumbfounded as the wild beast barreled toward the ship at great speed. He grabbed the railing, trembling with disbelief, and anticipated the inevitable blow. With a great thwack, the ship jolted as the albino mammoth rammed the hull, creating a huge breach. Chase lost his footing and nearly fell face-first on the deck.

With his heart racing, Chase could hear the whale thrashing under the ship. As the crazed creature smacked the ship's underbelly with its tail, Chase could hear it moving toward the port side of the ship. He and others ran over, only to see the white monstrosity swim away, and then sink into the unknown depths of the ocean.

Chase worriedly shook his head and pivoted toward the crew. "Quickly! Go below and start repairing the breach!" He grabbed one young lad's arm. "And report back to me, *immediately*!"

As the *Essex* continued to sway to the aftershock, Chase closed his eyes, again in disbelief. A moment later, the young lad returned. "Sir, the damage is worse than expected. A great deal of water is rushing in. But we're doing the best we can."

Chase gritted his teeth. He couldn't believe his bad luck. The first time he was left in command, and a bizarre, sea demon had attacked the ship. He was furious, when suddenly, a mate bellowed, "Dear God! He's back! And heading for us again!"

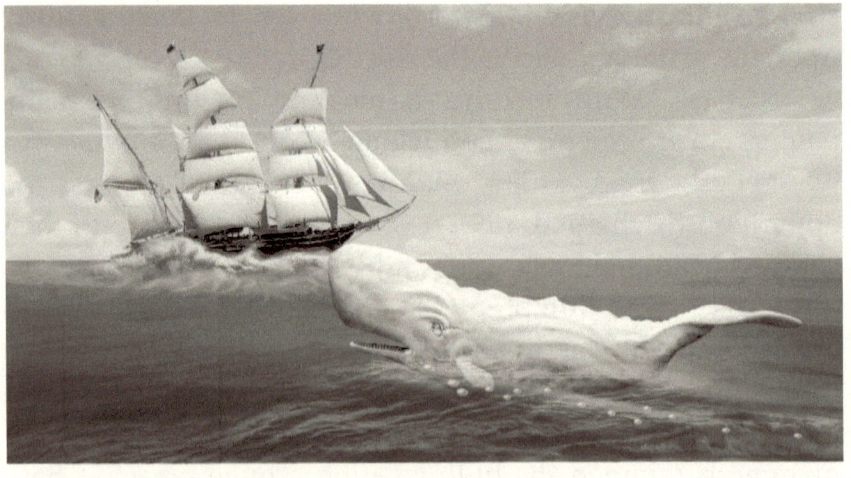

Chase ran toward the bow. There before his eyes was

the white menace, this time bearing down on them with even greater speed. With his large head half out of the water, the enraged sperm whale charged straight into the bow, under the cathead. Inside, the wooden planks cracked like biscuits, as ocean water gushed in with great force.

The crew turned white, like the sea demon itself, knowing repairs were futile. The gaping hole was too large to repair and evacuation was the only recourse. Quickly, they gathered navigational equipment and food, then ran up to the poop deck.

Chase's throat was dry with fear and humiliation. With utter regret, he gave the order to abandon ship. Quickly, the crew manned the remaining whaling boat and, with heavy hearts, pushed themselves off the dying ship.

As the crew drifted off in the small, 20-foot-long boat, tears welled in their eyes as they gazed upon the foundering *Essex*. As the ship listed, its creaks sounded like lugubrious moans of a dying animal. In Chase's trembling hand was a rope, one still attached to their precious mother ship. With dread shredding his gut, he released the rope; it fell like a severed umbilical cord, while the mother ship started to slip, inch-by-inch, into a dark and disturbed sea.

"Dear Lord," Armand said. "That *is* chilling. Especially knowing that it's a true story." He shook his head. "I thought that whole business of a white whale attacking a ship came from Melville's imagination."

Benjamin Jaspers nodded. "Yes, I believe most people never realized it was all from a real disaster. Nor that Melville took that story, white whale and all, directly from the news pages."

Armand nodded thoughtfully. "Indeed, and almost word for word, it seems."

Andrea sat silently, twirling her hair. Sure she was intrigued by the harrowing story, but she was still trying to make the connection to the mystery that brought them to Nantucket, not to mention a bit surprised by the very familiar narration. Finally, she spoke: "Actually, I thought you and Janet said this tale was going to be a horror story. Tragic, yes, but I don't see how this is too gruesome for kids to hear, especially since Melville used those scenes in his novel."

Benjamin smiled. "Ah, yes, but that's because the tale isn't over, Mrs. Arnolfini. Allow me to continue."

Sitting shocked and adrift, Owen Chase and his small crew gazed glumly at their sole means of survival, as the *Essex* continued to sink into a barren sea. With only its ornate transom perched in the air, the mauled vessel teetered amid swirls of bubbling water. Terrified, the crew's hearts dropped, realizing they only had minutes before losing sight of their precious lifeline, the mighty *Essex* would never be seen again, nor would they, so they thought.

Just then, Captain Pollard's small boat arrived along with the other whaleboat. Anxiously, Pollard stood up near the bow. His face was flush, while his eyes were fixed on the *Essex,* like a child watching a dying parent's last breaths. Nervously, he gazed over at Chase. "Owen! Dear God! What happened?"

Chase swallowed hard as he stood up. "Captain, it's hard to fathom myself, but we…" he stuttered, "w-we were rammed by a whale." He shook his head, still trembling with disbelief. "This crazed beast charged us. Not once, but twice, puncturing our starboard side. Then it returned to make a direct blow to the bow, which, well…proved fatal." He glanced back at the terrifying sight of the sinking *Essex*.

All eyes on the three small boats watched as the transom of their beloved mother ship slipped quietly into the depths of its watery grave.

Pollard was speechless, his mind blotted by a dark cloud of death and destitution. The twenty-nine year old was out of his depth, literally. Beneath their three small boats extended unknown legions of dark ocean, harboring unknown thousands of creatures, some, as they just found out, seemingly possessed and hellbent on devastation.

Crestfallen, the crew sat in their boats, devoid of hope. Many hearts sank, just like their precious mother ship, each desiring to be interred along with her. As some prayed, and others conjured up their own eulogies, Captain Pollard's mind clawed away at the shroud of resignation for a solution. Suddenly, he gazed over at Chase's crew, as their boat drifted several feet away. "Chase, you were the last to leave the ship. Did any one of you think to salvage navigational equipment or maps?"

"Yes," one whaler replied, as he reached down and held them up.

"Pass them over to me. I believe the Marquesas Islands and Society Islands are the closest to us. Just north of here."

Pollard's cousin Owen looked up at him and sighed with a modicum of relief. "I knew you'd think of something."

First mate Owen Chase, however, had something to say. "Captain, I've heard that those islands are inhabited with cannibals and savage warriors."

Another sailor yelled out. "It's true, Captain. I heard the same thing. They're treacherous."

"I'd rather take my chances at sea," another cried out, as several others echoed their concerns about the savage natives.

Pollard stood on the cross bench, as the small boat teetered on the waves, his mind dead fixed on their critical crossroad. He pulled a crucifix out of his pocket and gazed down at the cross, one he couldn't fathom why he was now put on one himself. How could he possibly escape this grim fate, he thought. He kissed the crucifix and slipped it back in his pocket.

He looked up and declared, "Very well, then we'll head south. But know this, that journey will be much farther and precarious. It will test our resolve to an extent truly never heard of or experienced before." He grabbed the sextant and, to a round of nervous applause, he plotted their course.

Not long into their journey, their food rations ran dreadfully low. Waves of saltwater had spoiled their bread and the men were suffering from dehydration. The blistering sun beat down on them, further exacerbating their starvation and depression. In time they managed to land on Henderson Island, but the small patch of land only provided enough food for several days. Three men decided to remain on dry land, with hopes of catching fish rather than return to the deadly unknown of the vast Pacific.

Without further ado, the three small boats took off, once again, into the rolling seas. Pollard was examining his maps, when the small boat appeared to hit a rock. Startled, he and the crew searched for the source, only to realize that it was a killer whale! The massive orca was curiously testing the constitution of their sleek hull. With bated breath, the crew nervously watched, waiting for disaster. Yet to their utter relief, the orca realized the wooden fish wasn't edible and swam off. However, over the ensuing weeks, whales routinely menaced the three small boats, adding to the crew's fears and mental torture.

On Owen Chase's boat, one crewman sat dazed, his eyes rolling. Then he stood up, delirious, and cried out, "I want water, damn it! Clean water! And a clean napkin."

The crew looked at Chase, who solemnly shook his head, knowing that the end was near. The poor soul had snapped. With a sigh, Chase said, "Sit down, mate. We'll find something to drink and eat soon enough. You'll be all right."

The sailor's crazed eyes veered toward Chase as his dried lips trembled. Suddenly, he fell to the floor and was overcome by the most frightful convulsions. The crew recoiled as Chase bent over and tried to restrain the deranged boy's flailing arms. It was of no use, as the poor lad gagged, then choked his last breath.

The crew was horrified, well aware that they had just witnessed a harbinger of their own fate. However, another terrifying thought and instinct soon took hold of them. The innate will to survive commandeered their morals as their starving stomachs cried out in utter pain. Without food for days, their mate's body posed the only means of survival.

All the crewmen looked at Chase, as one emaciated soul voiced the opinion of all; "Well, what say you? Is it not the rules of the sea to survive, by any means possible?"

Chase closed his eyes and took a deep breadth. Then he released the most mournful sigh any human could ever utter or hear. If his dehydrated body could have mustered tears, it would have. Without so much as saliva to moisten his tongue, Chase replied, "What an ironic and cruel bit of fate. We had all begged our Captain to avoid the cannibals on those distant islands, yet here it is we've been damned to commit the same ungodly sin."

A long and disturbing silence pervaded the crew, until Chase finally mustered the nerve to speak again. "But we have been put in this grave situation by either our own folly or God's divine punishment. So, yes. If it's a sin we must commit to survive, then sin we must. Take only what we need. Then we shall say our prayers and commit his remains to the sea."

In a grim and solemn exercise, the men removed the limbs from their mate's body and cut all the flesh from his bones. After which, they cut open the torso, took out the heart, then sewed it back up with their makeshift thread and fishing hooks. Somberly, they roasted their mate's organs and meat on a flat stone and, with great trepidation, slowly ate them. After consuming their sustenance, the crew offered prayers and committed their mate's remains to the sea.

Over the grueling weeks ahead, several more men had died, and were duly slaughtered, cooked, and eaten in similar fashion. Between the dark nights, drifting currents, fatigue, and failures at helmsmanship, the three boats had drifted apart and were separated. Without surface fish in such desolate parts of the Pacific, dire starvation besieged each of the three dwindling crews.

It was now February 6, 1821, and over two months since the loss of the mother ship. The four crewmen on Pollard's boat were at the brink of utter delirium, as one pleaded, "Captain, without food we'll all die in a few days hence. What are your plans?"

Pollard had barely enough strength to reply, as he uttered, "Plans I no longer have. We can only await God's righteous hand, to either offer us death or a miracle."

Charles Ramsdell, the scrawny teenager now reduced to a skeleton, had long given up the foolish notion of a loving or righteous God. "Captain, we can't just sit here and wait for one of us to expire. We need food, and we need it *now*. I propose we draw lots to determine who will be sacrificed for our survival."

Pollard's weakened heart convulsed. He knew the rules of the sea condoned cannibalism in dire situations, but eating the remains of a mate who died by God's hand was one thing. For men to play God was another; and the mere thought rippled his dried-out skin. Against his better judgment, and caving to peer pressure and dire hunger, Pollard nodded. "Very well. I'm not in favor of this barbarism; but be that as it may, perhaps barbarism *is* our only option. God have pity on us all."

Ramsdell duly arranged a makeshift set of strings at various lengths and held them out in his bony, clenched hand. "The one who pulls the shortest string will be…" his throat tightened. "Well, let's get on with it."

As each whaler pulled a string out of Ramsdell's hand, they each trembled, and each sighed with relief, one after another, until Owen Coffin drew the last and shortest string.

Pollard's eyes widened, his very soul bludgeoned by horror. He gazed at his young first cousin. "Owen! My dear lad. This can't be! I'll shoot the first man who touches you. On this, I swear!" His enraged eyes veered toward each crewmember. "Do you all hear me!?"

Owen Coffin looked at his older and much admired cousin, his face pale, weathered, and wilted. "Captain, we all made a vow to survive, by any means possible. I like this death sentence as well as any other." His head dropped. "Let it be."

Pollard's weak voice managed to rise up to a dry crackle, "Then I propose that you all take *me* instead!" He glanced at each of the crew, his eyes blazing. "I will *not* have any of this. It's insanity, beastly insanity, I say!" He turned back toward Owen. "You're my dear cousin, for God's sake. I can't. I just can't!"

Owen's shoulders sank into his emaciated torso. "There is no good result here, Captain. We've all been sentenced to sail upon the River Styx. There is no escape from this hell, from what I can see. I'm spent. I've had enough."

Despite Pollard's severity of dehydration, a tear somehow appeared in his eye, as his now-bearded chin fell into his chest.

Ramsdell collected the strings, and uttered somberly, "Well, we need to draw once more."

Pollard looked up. "For God's sake, man. Now what?"

"To see who will perform the execution, Captain."

Pollard gritted his teeth and shook his head. "Dear, Lord! This is utter madness. I refuse to draw. Do what you will."

As the remaining crew drew their strings, the shortest fell, oddly enough, to Ramsdell. He hadn't realized this ugly game of Russian roulette would have so many layers of sinister hexes. If there truly were a Hell on Earth, he'd found it.

Ramsdell looked at Owen. "I'm so sorry, mate," he uttered, as he grasped the pistol. "Take your time, and...well, let me know when you're ready."

Owen Coffin nodded dolefully. "I no longer believe in God, but I reckon at this point, I have nothing left to say but a prayer." He bowed his head. A minute later, Owen crept up and placed his head on the gunwale. Ramsdell placed his left hand gently on Owen's back. "God bless you," he said, as a loud *pop* shattered the silence and Owen's skull.

Another crewman took over the slaughtering detail, while another roasted Owen Coffin's remains on a flat stone. Captain Pollard was overcome with revulsion and self-loathing, yet had no option but to eat his young cousin's remains, all for the hideous business of survival.

Utter depravity and dehumanization, he felt, had finally been reached.

Andrea was in tears, as Armand swallowed hard, trying to accumulate an ounce of saliva. "Dear Lord," Armand managed to mutter. He rubbed his forehead. "I had no idea that..." he lost his train of thought amid the gruesome horror that swirled in his head. "I, I don't even know what to say."

Andrea wiped away her tears. With a sniffle, she said, "Thank God Mrs. Harnett took the kids elsewhere."

"Yes," Benjamin Jaspers replied stoically. "Now you can understand why she warned you. The macabre tale of the *Essex* is not for everyone."

Armand shook his head. "It makes you wonder; why are some people put through such horrific trials and tribulations like that?"

Andrea sighed. "Yes, my heart went out to all of them. I'm still trying to process Owen Coffin's submission to be eaten. I can't imagine being in that position. It's chilling." She shook her head, as the hellish tempest ravaged her mind. "Oh, dear, and poor Captain Pollard. I can't envision having to eat a relative. The moral implications are unfathomable."

Armand nodded solemnly, then looked back up at Benjamin. "So, whatever happened to Captain Pollard?"

"Well, his boat was rescued several days after Owen Chase's," Benjamin said. "In fact, Chase eventually became a captain and enjoyed two more decades of whaling in the Pacific. But as for Captain Pollard, it's said that he and Ramsdell were the only two survivors on their boat, and each were morbidly delirious. They had each resorted to sucking the marrow out of the bones of their fallen mates to survive. Meanwhile, Pollard would not give up his cousin's bone and held onto it with devotional reverence. Some said with deranged rigor."

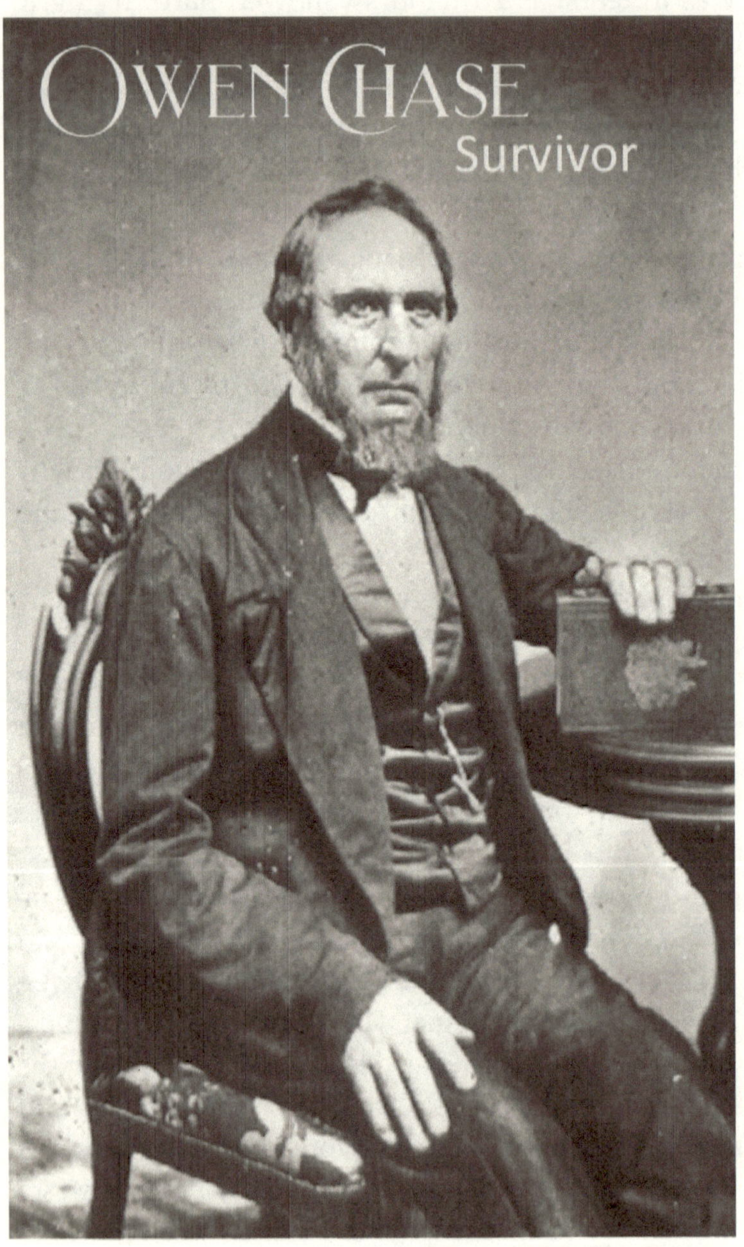

Armand's eyebrows flashed upward. "Of course!" he exclaimed. "It's not a whale bone, it's a *human bone*."

Benjamin squinted. "Of course it was a human bone. Who said anything about a whale bone?"

Andrea got the connection, as Armand replied, "Well, Benjamin, I was actually interested in this story because—"

Just then Janet Harnett returned with the kids, as Jack and Artemisia ran to their parents, babbling about all the fascinating things Janet had shown them.

As Armand and Andrea listened to their kids, Janet turned toward Benjamin. "We have a school tour lined up. It commences in five minutes in the auditorium. Please go and prepare for your presentation."

Benjamin straightened out his jacket, nodded, and took his leave.

Meanwhile Armand turned toward the curator. "Mrs. Harnett, I was about to ask Benjamin about bones, or more precisely, Captain Pollard's bone of his cousin Owen. Has your museum ever had possession of it?"

Janet's eyebrows rose with a bit of surprise as a chill rippled her skin. "Oh, dear. That horrible incident still unnerves me. But, I'm not quite sure if the museum ever acquired it. I only heard tales about it from Walter, one of the old timers who used to work here. But that was some thirty years ago."

"Is Walter still alive?" Armand queried.

"Oh, I doubt it. He'd have to be a hundred or in his nineties, if so."

"Well, could you check, or at least tell me his full name?"

Janet paused a moment, then said, "Very well, his name was Walter Hammersmith. A nice old man. Give me a second, and I'll check my phone book. I might still have his number."

As Janet walked toward her office, Andrea came up behind Armand. "Honey, I just got a call on my cell phone."

Armand spun around, as she continued, "I'm needed at the P.T. Barnum Museum. I can see you've got a lead with this bone thing, so, I think I'll take the kids home with me."

Before Armand could reply, Jack heard the dreadful news and bellowed, "No way! I wanna stay here with Dad."

As Armand and Andrea glanced at Jack, Artemisia chimed in, "As for me, I'll do what ever you both think is best."

Andrea looked at Artemisia. "Thank you, darling." She then turned back toward Jack. "And *you* should follow your older sister's good habits and do as we say."

Jack pouted, as Armand smiled. "Oh, it's fine. If he wants to stay, that's all right with me."

Jack's face beamed, as Andrea looked back at Armand. "You always cave into their whims. Are you sure you won't be distracted?"

"Don't worry," Armand said. "As I said, this is not a full investigation, it's still more of a hunch. I'm not sure where this will lead, but perhaps this sacred, or rather gruesome, bone is the key."

"Yes," Andrea said. "Once again, you were right. It wasn't about Melville but about the bone." With that, she kissed Armand and grasped Artemisia's hand. "I guess I'll catch a train home."

"No, no," Armand insisted. "You take the Lincoln, I'll manage here."

No sooner did they leave, than Janet returned with the number of Walter Hammersmith. Armand thanked her and made the call on his Nokia 5110. To his surprise, Walter was 96 and still alive. Better still, Walter welcomed them to visit him at his house in the village. Armand grasped Jack's hand and they hopped in a taxi.

Fifteen minutes later, they arrived at Walter's quaint, saltbox house, which sat picturesquely near the shoreline. Walter stood by the screen door with his cane and greeted them as they stepped inside. With his gnarled finger, Walter pointed to the worn sofa. "Have yourselves a seat."

"Thank you," Armand said, as he and Jack sat down.

Walter wobbled to his rocking chair, pivoted around awkwardly, then lowered himself into place. With a steady rock, to and fro, Walter said above the creaks of his old chair, "So, what can I do for you fine young fellows?"

"Well, Janet Harnett told me that you worked together many years ago."

Walter's eyes oscillated as he tried his best to parse Armand's words. His tongue fumbled with his dentures, until he finally replied, "Yes, indeed, we did have hornets around here many years ago."

Armand smiled and leaned forward to get within closer earshot of the old man. "No. I said, *Janet Harnett* told me that you worked together many years ago."

"Ah, *Harnett*!" he said. "Yes, indeed, we did. I relished working at the museum." As Walter rocked, his mind drifted into the cobwebs of a distant past, as he uttered, "My, my, that *was* many years ago, all right."

Armand gave Walter a moment to process the happy recollection, then asked, "Well, I'm curious to know about the *Essex*, Walter. Or more specifically, about Captain Pollard."

Walter looked up and squinted. "Who hollered?"

As little Jack giggled, Armand smiled and reiterated, "No, not hollered. I said Captain *Pollard*."

Walter strained to organize every word, then smiled as he pieced it together. "Ah, yes! You mean *Captain Pollard*." His smile inverted to a grieved frown. "That poor soul endured what no man should have."

"Exactly," Armand said. "I'm curious to know, what ever happened to the bone of his cousin, Owen Coffin?"

Again Walter squinted. "Coffin? Well, I'm not sure where Pollard's coffin is, I'm afraid. I imagine its well rotted by now."

As Jack giggled once again, Armand shot his son a stern stare, while stifling a chuckle himself. Sure it was rude, but Armand knew situations like this do give rise to levity. Laughter is one way of dealing with misfortune to avoid the alternative, namely succumbing to melancholy.

Armand got up, grasped a chair, and moved it next to Walter's rocker. Taking a seat, he said again, "No, Walter. I'd like to know about the *bone* of Owen Coffin, Pollard's cousin."

"Oh! The *bone,*" Walter said with a firm nod. "Yes, that was a sad affair. Poor Captain Pollard, he protected that bone as if it were the very bone of Jesus Christ. A sacred affair, it was."

"Yes, I'm aware of that, Walter. But did the Whaling Museum ever have possession of the bone?"

Again Walter squinted. "A confession on the phone? Phone's weren't invented in Pollard's time, son."

Armand glanced back at Jack, who was now holding his hand tightly over his unruly mouth. Armand turned back toward Walter and leaned in, even closer. "No, Walter. The *Museum*. Did the *museum* ever have the *bone*? Owen's bone?"

Walter nodded with a cute cackle. "Ah, yes. Foolish me. You meant the *bone*." He shook his head. "No. Pollard gave the bone to his dear friend, Karl. You see, Karl owned a butcher shop. And well, Pollard felt there was no one better than Karl to properly store the precious relic. It needed to be put on ice, so to speak. You know, in a meat locker."

"Hey Dad," Jack interrupted. "Speaking of meat, when are we gonna eat? I'm hungry?"

Armand turned and nodded. "Yes, don't worry, Jack. We'll eat soon enough. I have no intentions of starving you." Armand's mind drifted back to the gruesome vision of starvation and eating meat on the *Essex, human* meat. Purging the ugly thought, he smiled for Jack's sake and added, "So be patient."

Jack smiled innocently and continued to look at all the old nautical relics on Walter's faded walls and dusty shelves.

Meanwhile Armand turned back toward Walter. "Does that butcher shop still exist?"

Walter nodded. "Sure does. That's where I used to buy all my meats. Nowadays, I can't chew red meat." He tapped his false teeth with his gnarly finger. "You see, these danged dentures don't fit right. So now I only buy fish."

Armand was thrilled; not by the fact that Walter couldn't eat meat anymore, but by the notion that perhaps the bone was still in storage, hidden somewhere in a meat locker. "Can you tell me the name of this place?"

"Most certainly," Walter said. "It's Karl Borg's Butcher Shop. It's just down the road a ways. Family owned for well over a century. A real Nantucket treasure trove."

"That's fantastic!" Armand exclaimed. "And I'll even buy you some fish. How's that?"

"No way, sonny boy! I'm no leech. Never was," Walter said as he shifted in his rocker, aiming to dig out his wallet.

Armand stayed his hand. "No, no! *I'll* buy the fish. It will be my pleasure. You've been most helpful."

Walter paused a moment, then conceded with an adorable old smile. "That's very kind of you, young man." A frown washed over his face. "But I apologize, I forgot your name."

"No worries, Walter. My name is Armand. Just tell me what kind of fish you like?"

Walter mentioned his preferences and Armand and Jack took their leave. They walked several blocks down the street and reached Karl Borg's Butcher Shop. As they entered, Armand went straight to the counter. "Can I speak with the owner?"

"I'm the owner. Herman Borg is the name and meat and fish are the game. In that there is no shame, as making customers' happy is my claim to fame! Yes, it's true. So, how can I help you two?"

Armand smiled. "Well, I like your little jingle. I'm pleased to meet you, Herman. I'll need two heroes." He glanced down at Jack. "My son would like roast beef and lettuce, with mayo. No tomatoes. Right?"

"Yep," came the response, as Armand looked back at Herman. "And I'll have ham and Swiss with mustard. I also have a list of fish that I'm buying for Walter Hammersmith."

"Ah, good ole' Hammersmith!" Herman said. "That's mighty nice of ya."

"It's no problem," Armand said. "He's an awfully nice man. In fact, he told me about the bone of Owen Coffin that your great relative Karl had stored here."

Herman peered left and right, then leaned over the counter and whispered, "Not so loud. That's not the sort of thing we like to advertise. If you get my *creepy* drift."

Armand nodded, half embarrassed and half exhilarated by Herman's verification, as he whispered, "Yes, of course. I apologize. But, you see, I've been searching for that bone. It's a historic relic, one that probably should be in the Whaling Museum."

Herman shrugged. "Well, I'm no history buff, as you might see." He pointed to the large posters of the Red Sox, Celtics, and Bruins on the walls. "Big sports fan."

Armand nodded. "Yes, I've noticed." Armand had also noticed that the store was run-down and empty, save for one old lady. But that had little to do with Armand's mission, as he said, "Do you mind if I take a look at the *item*?"

Herman rolled his eyes. "I don't get all the fuss about a…" He looked at the old lady, and said with a smile, "I'll be with you in a minute, Ma'am."

Just then, Harry Grimes walked in. Herman shook his head. "You're late again, Harry!"

Harry twisted his lips and ran his fingers through his greasy hair like a comb. "Whatever," he muttered. He put on his apron and slipped behind the counter. With a puss, he turned toward the old lady, and said, "Next!"

Herman rolled his eyes and turned back toward Armand. "Follow me."

With that, Armand and little Jack trailed Herman as they walked into the backroom of the shop. Herman opened the large freezer door to the meat locker. "I gotta be honest, I haven't opened the vault for that silly bone in years. I don't even remember why my relatives kept the darn thing. It's weird." He walked to the rear of the chilly meat locker, pushed a cabinet aside, then bent down and opened a trap door.

As Armand and Jack held their breaths in anticipation, Herman stood upright, and said nonchalantly, "Ah, hell. The darn thing is gone."

Armand scurried closer and peered down. "What do you mean, *gone*? Who could have taken it?"

"Beats me," Herman uttered, unconcerned.

"Well, who else knows about or has access to this vault?"

Herman rolled his eyes. With a huff, he moaned, "I don't know, just me and Harry, I suppose. We're the only ones who work here."

Armand's heart sank. "Well, do you mind if I speak with Harry a moment?"

"Knock yourself silly," Herman said as he shut the trap door. "I still don't get all the hoopla about a silly bone, but I'll send Harry back here while I make your sandwiches."

As Armand and Jack waited in the backroom, Armand noticed the empty shelves and the rusted old bicycle parked by the rear door. Just then, Harry walked in, chewing gum and already bored with the canvasser before him, and his little sidekick. "What's up?"

Little Jack blurted, "The sky and the moon."

Harry rolled his eyes and nearly gagged, as he peered down at Jack. "Seriously?" He then looked up at Armand. "Really?"

"No, I'd like to know if you took the bone that was inside the meat locker?" Armand said as he pointed to the rear of the room. "Over there, under that trap door in the floor."

With a stone-faced smirk and a grunt like Lurch, Harry uttered, "Nope."

Armand took a deep breath. "Okay, do you know of anyone who might have taken the bone?"

Again, the disheveled zombie displayed his mastery of one-word answers. "Nope."

Armand huffed. "Were you even aware that a bone was in there?" Before the drone even articulated his one-syllable answer, Armand said, "Never mind, Harry. Thanks for your time."

As Harry turned and shuffled like Frankenstein's monster back toward the front counter, little Jack opined in a whisper, "That guy's creepy *and* guilty!"

Armand smiled. "And why do you say that, Jack?"

"Cause he's not admitting he's guilty. I mean; it's the

way he said it. He didn't even wanna talk. And I don't like his grumpy face!"

Armand laughed. "So, you think just because he's apathetic, he's lying?"

"Yeah, I do. And you're right, he's pathetic, too!"

Armand chuckled. "No, not pathetic. I said *apathetic,* Jack. That means lacking enthusiasm or interest."

Jack scratched his nose. "Uh, well, he's that, too."

"Okay, I see I'll need to spend more time with you about investigative work and vocabulary."

"No!" Jack blurted. "Not vocabulary. I hate English. It don't even make sense a lot a times anyhow."

Armand chuckled. "And I see I'll need to grill you on grammar, too."

Jack crossed his arms and pouted. "Aw, come on, Pop. Forget about the school stuff. What are we gonna do about this bone mystery?" Jack uncrossed his arms. "By the way, whose bone we looking for?"

Armand's mind had been simultaneously figuring out the next step while preaching to his son, as he said, "Never mind that. For now I need to speak with Herman again. Besides, I imagine your hero should be ready by now."

"I don't need no hero. You're already my hero, Pops!" Jack said wittily.

Armand smiled. "Well, at least you don't need any grooming on brown-nosing. You seem to have that mastered."

As they both laughed, Herman returned with two heroes in his hands. "Well, here ya go. Feel free to take a seat." He placed the heroes on the table and pulled out two chairs.

Armand and Jack both took a seat, as Herman added, "There are some sodas behind you in that refrigerator. Feel free to take whatever you please. A buck-fifty each, if you don't mind?"

"Certainly, no problem," Armand said, as he directed Jack to fetch them some drinks.

He turned and looked up at Herman. "If you don't mind, I'd like to know if perhaps you have any family members who might know about the bone?"

Herman's gracious smile withered. He was getting bored with these perpetual questions about a silly old bone. But he figured it would be best to answer the inquiries to finally put this nonsense to rest. He took a seat at the table and said, "Well, I'll give you the lowdown so you can be contented and finally enjoy your lunch."

Armand smiled. "Thank you. I know I can be a persistent little devil, but that's how things get done. I appreciate your time."

Herman nodded wearily. "Sure, sure, no problem. You see, the truth is, my wife died about two years ago. So that obviously rules her out. And I never told my daughter or son about the bone. So this is a dead end. Besides, even if my kids did know, why would they take a silly old bone?"

Armand leaned closer. "Do you recall the story behind that bone?"

"Yeah…well…no. I mean, sort of. My father and grandfather used to go on and on about it, but they died decades ago. Old fish stories, you know. And to be honest, I forget most of it. But basically it's a remnant of some old captain's remains. Bollard, I think it was."

"Well, the captain's name was Pollard, but no, it wasn't his bone. It was the bone of his cousin, Owen Coffin."

Armand turned and asked Jack to get them some mustard from the front counter. Once Jack left the backroom, he then relayed the gruesome tale, at which Herman recoiled with a gasp. "Dear Lord! I plum forgot all about that." He shook his head. "I reckon it was so dang ugly of a tale that I washed it out of my head."

"I can understand that," Armand said, just as Jack returned.

"Here ya go, Pops!" Jack said innocently.

"Thank you, Jack." Armand turned back toward Herman. "So, I would like to speak with your daughter and son, just to make sure. Because, although you have little interest in history, Herman, this bone *is* quite valuable."

Herman sighed, then nodded. "Sure, I guess so. I'll call 'em." He took out his cell phone and made the call. Snapping his flip phone closed, he said, "They'll be here in a jiffy. Well, not a jiffy, but soon enough. Ever since their ma died they seem to have lead in their pants."

Armand and Jack chuckled as they picked up their heroes. They ate their lunch and chatted with Herman, who barraged Jack with trivial stats about his favorite teams, all of which happened to be from Boston.

Twenty minutes later, Dorothy and Philip arrived. After introductions, they took their seats at the table. Herman had sandwiches and drinks ready for them, and they eagerly dived in. Several minutes later, Herman said, "Listen kids, Mr. Arnolfini would like to ask you some questions."

Having taken sips of their sodas, Dorothy and Philip replied accordingly, "Sure," and "Fire away" respectively.

Before Armand said a word, Jack cut in, "Dad, are you sure Harry ain't the one you should be talkin' to?"

As Herman's two children glanced at Jack, confused, Armand said, "Yes, I'm sure, Jack." He then turned back toward Dorothy and Philip. "I'd like to know if either of you know about the trap door..." he pointed to the rear of the room "back there, in the floor of the meat locker?"

Dorothy looked at Philip, who simultaneously looked at Dorothy. Then they looked at their father, and ultimately back at Armand, as Dorothy uttered, "Uh…no." While Philip said quasi-confidently, "No, why would we?"

It was clear to Armand that the kids were afraid to tell the truth, and he looked at Herman, who uncomfortably had gotten the same message. Armand didn't wish to handle the next step and deferred to Herman, who took the cue and asked, "Listen, we're not gonna be mad. We just need to know the truth. Did you know about the trap door?"

Dorothy and Philip glanced at each other once again, and lowered their heads. After a brief moment, they each peered up and uttered, "Yeah."

Armand resumed the inquiry. "Did you take the bone that was in there?"

Dorothy blurted, "I didn't, Phil did!"

"*You* told me to!" Philip retorted.

"Okay, hold on!" Herman said. "I don't care who took it. All this man wants to know is did you take it?"

Philip huffed. "Yeah. I took it. But it's because Dorothy said it was worth a lot of money."

Herman looked at Dorothy. "Who told you that?"

Dorothy's nervous face withered into a solemn stare, as she gazed into the unknown depths of the tabletop.

Her father once again queried, "Dorothy! *Who* told you that?"

Dorothy finally managed to gaze up, as she uttered, "Mommy."

Herman squinted. "Your mother? But she, she died two years ago. Why would you take the bone now."

Armand already knew the answer. It was clear Herman's business was in dire straits. The empty shelves, lack of customers, unkempt workspace, rusted bicycle, they all added up to bad times. But he had to know what they did with the precious artifact, as he cut in, "I imagine you were just trying to help your dad out, Dorothy. The same goes for you, Philip. I can fully understand that. But what did you do with the bone?"

Dorothy uttered, "We sold it."

Meanwhile, Philip turned to his dad, and said enthusiastically, "And we made a killing, Dad! But we wanted it to be a surprise."

Herman shook his head, perturbed. "I don't believe you two little sneaks." Then he grinned. "But that's splendid! How much did you get for it?"

"Four hundred bucks!" Philip exclaimed.

Herman drew his kids in for a hug. "That's fantastic! I'm proud of both of you. We certainly could use the money." He looked at Armand, "I guess I should thank you for the silly questions. I just made four-hundred smackeroos!"

"That *is* pretty cool!" Jack interjected. He looked at his dad. "Ain't it?"

"No," Armand said, to an immediate round of silence and cold stares.

Herman looked at Armand. "*No*? Why?"

"Yeah. Why?" cried Philip, as well as Dorothy and Jack in harmony.

Armand sighed. "Herman, that's the pitfall of not being privy to history or historical artifacts. One man's garbage is another man's goldmine."

Herman's ears sprang up like a dog's awaiting a treat. "Are you saying that silly bone is worth more than four hundred bucks?"

"A lot more," Armand said. "But the important question now is; who did they sell it to? If it's someone from the underworld, we might never find him, and you've just been cheated out of a windfall." He turned toward Dorothy and Philip. "Do you have the person's name or contact information?"

Dorothy said, "Yeah, well, at least his first name. But no phone number."

Armand and Herman sighed, as Armand said, "Well, that's as good as saying good bye to a ton of money. We can't do much with just a first name. Do you recall what he looked like?"

"Yeah. He was tall with a fluffy beard," Dorothy said, while Philip moaned, "Jeez, I knew we shouldn't have trusted Benjamin, he even looked like a pirate."

Armand and Jack glanced at each other, as Armand said, "Benjamin!? With a fluffy mustache and beard, who looks like an old sailor?"

"Yeah," Philip said. "Why, do ya know him?"

"I believe I do," Armand said. "It makes sense."

"Okay, what makes sense?" Herman asked. "Who is this crumb?"

"I'll tell you about it on the way," Armand said.

Twenty minutes later, Armand, Herman, and Jack arrived at the Whaling Museum. Armand marched up to the front counter and asked for Benjamin Jaspers. Several minutes later, Benjamin strut towards them, but stopped short. He hesitated as he looked at Herman Borg. He was about to make a detour, but Armand called out, "Benjamin! Hold on, we need to talk."

Benjamin grumbled under his breath, as the trio walked his way. As they approached, Armand said, "I believe you just made an acquisition, yes?"

Benjamin rolled his eyes. "And what about it? It was paid for in cash. No receipt was necessary, if that's what you're here for?"

Armand snickered. "Oh, no, we're not here to give you a receipt, Benjamin. I believe my clients are wondering when the final payment will be made?"

"What do you mean, final payment? It was paid for in-full."

"Well, you obviously don't have a receipt or a contract to prove that, now do you?"

"What is it you're looking for, Mr. Arnolfini?"

"For a fair deal, Mr. Jaspers. That's all we're looking for. You know darn well that that historic artifact can draw in millions of dollars of revenue in ticket sales, yet you bamboozled two innocent kids out of an equitable price. A price that could seriously help Mr. Borg with his business."

Just then Janet Harnett overheard their rousing conversation and walked over. "What seems to be the trouble?"

Armand reiterated his plea, to which Mrs. Harnett shot Benjamin a nasty stare, then looked back at Armand. "I wasn't aware of how he acquired it, Mr. Arnolfini. But Mr. Jaspers just approached me moments ago, saying that we should display Owen Coffin's bone. He believes audiences today are enthralled with horror, zombies, and all that sort of rot. I never bought into such things, but he wore me down with pure business logic. So, yes, I do believe that people would flock to see Owen Coffin's bone, just as millions stop to gape at accidents or watch the most horrific and wretched movies. So, what price do you have in mind, Mr. Arnolfini?"

"Well, considering the long-term windfall you'll have over the ensuing years, I could easily see you buying this historical artifact for around twenty-five thousand dollars."

As Herman, Jack, and Benjamin gasped, Armand added, "And that's a steal. I'm sure other nautical museums would love to have it, but it really belongs here. And you know that. The price is fair."

Janet, however, wasn't ruffled by the figure, and just stood motionless and mute for an odd moment. Finally, she sighed and said, "Very well, I think that's a reasonable price. I'll need to run it past the board, of course, but I'm sure this new attraction will pay off in spades. I suppose the haunting tale about Owen Coffin *is* one to be finally heard."

Little Jack was awed, as he blurted, "Well, that puts the last nail in Coffin's coffin!"

As Armand shook his head, and Herman chuckled, Janet and Benjamin just sighed. Janet said her good-byes, then walked to her office to draw up the proposal for the board. Meanwhile, Benjamin's lips twisted heatedly under his fluffy mustache and beard. He pivoted and left without a word.

Herman shook Armand's hand vigorously. "You're fantastic, Mr. Arnolfini, truly fantastic! How much do I owe you for that stellar performance?"

"Never mind," Armand said. "It's on me."

Herman was caught off guard as his eyes teared up with gratitude. He swallowed hard and said, "Thank you! Thank you from the bottom of my heart. My family and I are deeply grateful. If it weren't for you I never would have known that silly bone could fetch such a huge price. You have no idea how much that will help my business."

"Actually, I do," Armand said. "That was an additional impetus to get you what you deserve, Herman. My only advice is this, either train Harry better or replace him. He doesn't make a good impression, and he represents your family's good name. Walter Hammersmith spoke very highly of your shop, yet it was clear that he hasn't visited your store for well over a year. I think he'd also be very disappointed."

Herman's shoulders lowered. "Yes, you're right. The business has been steadily declining over the past two years. You see, my wife handled the books, advertising, and all that PR stuff. It's time I did that and hired a butcher and someone to handle the front counter."

"That sounds like a good plan. And who knows, perhaps one of your kids would like to chip in one day."

"Yeah," Jack interjected. "Like I'd like to chip in with my Pa one day!"

Herman smiled, as Armand hugged Jack, then shook Herman's hand. "I wish you the best of luck."

"Much appreciated," Herman said. "And best wishes to you."

Exiting the museum, Armand and Jack walked toward a taxi. Armand pulled out his cell phone and rang Andrea. Once she answered, he said, "Well, everything went rather well here, honey. I need to call Shirley to let her know things panned out. I found the bone of Owen Coffin and secured a hefty selling price for the owner."

"That's marvelous, darling," Andrea's voice rang out. "So his bone really did exist. I guess it wasn't an old wives' tale."

"No, darling. I suppose you could say it was an old whale's tale."

Andrea giggled, as Armand added, "Well, those old whaling adventures surely aroused a lot of thoughts. It makes you wonder: Did Captains Ahab and Pollard bring about their own destruction? And was it due to their obsession of hunting majestic fellow mammals of the sea? Was it bad karma, God's harrowing lesson, or simply the randomness of nature?"

"Sweetheart," Andrea said, "You're getting way too deep for me right now. I have dinner cooking and Artemisia is asking me a million questions at the same time. When do you plan on coming home?"

"Oh, I might stay a day or two more, so Jack and I can enjoy the peace and beauty of Nantucket." He blew a kiss into the cell phone. "I love you. And give my love to Artemisia. Now go and enjoy your meal. As I said, everything went well here. Shirley Taylor will be pleased to know this cryptic case has been solved. Have a good night!"

POLLACK'S PAINT

Sitting in fourth-row seats at Lincoln Center, Armand and Andrea clapped wildly as the thunderous coda of Franz Liszt's *Totentanz* (Death Dance) ended with an ominous death punch.

"Dear Lord," Armand said. "Liszt was truly light years ahead of his time, wasn't he?"

Andrea nodded. "He certainly was. I thought he only wrote solo piano pieces. I never knew he composed orchestral works, as well."

"Unfortunately, most people don't, either," Armand said as he gazed down at the *Playbill*. He rolled his eyes.

Andrea caught his dour expression. "What?"

"I didn't realize, the next piece is *4′33″* by John Cage."

"And? You don't like it?"

Armand scoffed. "Like it? I guess you forgot or you're simply not aware of this piece."

Andrea shrugged. "You know I was never into Classical music, honey, at least until I met you, that is." She pulled a Lifesaver candy out from her purse and offered one to Armand.

He took the candy and popped it in his mouth. "Thank you," he said. "With this titanic disaster about to sink my spirits, I needed a Lifesaver."

Andrea couldn't help but giggle at Armand's melodramatic wit as she gazed at the stage, which was now cleared of the orchestra players. A pianist walked on stage and took his place at the Steinway grand piano.

A narrator then announced over the loudspeaker; "Please, we ask for silence. The next piece is *4′33″* by John Cage. We hope you'll give it the attention it deserves."

The concert hall simmered to an eerie silence, as the pianist sat majestically at the shiny black Steinway and adjusted his bench. He then reached over, straightened the sheet music perched on the piano, then picked up a small alarm clock. He closed the cover to the piano keys, then clicked the alarm clock on and placed it on the piano.

While some knew of Cage's iconic piece, most heads in the auditorium gazed quizzically at one another, wondering what was going on, as the pianist just sat there, regal, mute, and seemingly frozen like a manikin.

After two minutes of this peculiar scene, amid total silence, Andrea looked at Armand. He rolled his eyes and pointed to the Playbill. Andrea's eyes cascaded down to read the synopsis.

It explained that John Cage's piece, *4'33"*, instructed the performer to sit idle for exactly four minutes and thirty-three seconds, hence forcing people to reexamine the very essence of what constitutes music.

Nearby, an old man covered his mouth in a poor attempt to muffle a cough, only to be quietly shushed by an angry Cage fan.

Armand and Andrea stifled chuckles as they turned to resume watching the droll performance on stage. However, after two more minutes, of what Armand felt was absurd torture, he couldn't restrain himself any longer. He covered his mouth with both palms and blew, *hard*! The result being a boisterous *faux-fart*!

Andrea turned, appalled and shocked, as others looked on, aghast! One Cage fan bellowed, "How rude!" Then quite unexpectedly, the audience burst out into laughter, as one laugh launched another and another, engulfing the auditorium.

Even the pianist had to turn and laugh as he clicked the alarm clock off, and stood up. Once the hall simmered to near silence, the pianist said, "I apologize for not being able to complete this historic piece of music. But it's obvious you all had a *gas*!"

With another round of laughter, the lights grew brighter and people began to applaud. The pianist then pointed to Armand in the audience and said, "I cannot take full credit for this performance. Whoever you are, please stand up to receive our congratulations. I can honestly say that this has never happened before. You even upstaged John Cage."

Armand chuckled, stood up, took a bow, and said, "Thank you, it took many years of hard practice to master my instrument. But I'm honored you approve of our impromptu duet." With a combination of applause, much laughter, and a few irritated huffs, the crowd readied themselves to leave the hall.

Armand and Andrea walked through the lobby and toward the exit, when Andrea frowned and said, "Well, I'm sure that was the most unique Classical concert anyone has ever attended, one that I'm sure will be burnt into their memories." She stopped Armand in his tracks. "What the heck were you thinking? You're the smartest man I know, yet that was the dumbest and most juvenile thing I ever experienced."

Armand laughed. "You mean dumber and more juvenile than Cage's four-and-a-half minutes of idiotic silence?"

Andrea paused but a second, then chuckled. "When you put it that way, perhaps not."

"Listen, I only expressed my opinion. That's truly how I felt about it. It stinks."

Andrea shook her head, smiling. "You never cease to amaze me. I suppose it *was* funny, but you truly baffle me. Lately you've been acting a tad bit sillier than usual. What gives?"

Armand shrugged. "Who knows? Perhaps it's because we now have kids. You know, they do bring out the child in adults. And that can be a good thing, at least sometimes. We get old too fast, and too serious, and forget how to enjoy life and be happy."

"Hmm," Andrea said with a thoughtful nod. "Very true. You always manage to clarify chaos with logic. Or in this case, immaturity with insight."

As they resumed walking towards Broadway, she added, "But happy is one thing. Giddy and childish is another. So, no more fake farting in public. Is that clear?"

Armand giggled. "Sure, sweetheart. As long as we never have to sit in Cage's absurd *cage of silence* ever again."

"Agreed," Andrea said with a chuckle, then added, "Oh, yes, let's head downtown to Brixton's Art Gallery."

Armand squinted. "Brixton's? That gallery is for contemporary and modern art. You know I'm not an advocate. I mean, yes, I do like *some* modernist works, but my love and expertise is..."

"Yes, I know, dear," Andrea said. "For Renaissance masters, right up to a select few in the twentieth century. But Nancy Simmons is my new assistant at the P.T. Barnum Museum and she stressed that I must go see the new sensation, Pol Jackson. His works are a combination of Jackson Pollack and other modern artists. It sounds interesting."

Armand rolled his eyes. "Dear Lord. And it appears this Pol Jackson even stole Jackson Pollack's name. Very original."

"Oh, come on, don't be a brooding child," Andrea said with an endearing smile and a wink.

Armand huffed. "I'll go under one condition. If I'm bored or annoyed by what I see there, the no-farting deal is off!"

Andrea laughed, grabbed his arm, and walked toward the parking garage.

Hopping into Armand's new collectible, a 1957 blue Corvette, the couple drove down to Brixton's Art Gallery.

As they entered, Armand's eyes scanned the large canvases hanging on the white walls and partitions. No sooner had they stepped in, than a tall woman, with blonde hair tied in braids and wrapped around her head, approached them. "Greetings, and thank you for visiting us. I am Gerd Olsen, Pol Jackson's manager."

They each shook hands, as Gerd escorted them toward the first display. Gerd elegantly pointed at the four large canvases before them in a sweeping fashion. "These are some of Pol's most recent and famous works." She gazed at them proudly, almost lovingly, then turned back toward Armand and Andrea. "So, is this your first time?"

Andrea nodded. "Yes, I'm the curator of the P.T. Barnum Museum in Connecticut, and my assistant, Nancy Simmons, suggested that we come down to visit."

As Gerd's eyes widened with glee, Andrea turned toward Armand and added, "And this is my husband, Armand Arnolfini, he's an art expert and private eye of art crimes."

Gerd's smile grew into a giddy grin as she said, "Oh my! I've read about you many times, Mr. Arnolfini. It's an honor to meet you."

Armand nodded politely. "Thank you," he said, as his discerning eyes veered back at the four canvases.

One was a lackluster imitation of a De Kooning with Pollack-like splatters of paint obliterating most of it. Another was a geometric imitation of a Mondrian, with splatters of Pollack-like paint despoiling it. The third appeared to be an arrangement of Hans Hoffman-like blocks of color, also splattered with paint. And the fourth was a Warhol-like print of Elvis Presley, again, bulleted with splatters of paint.

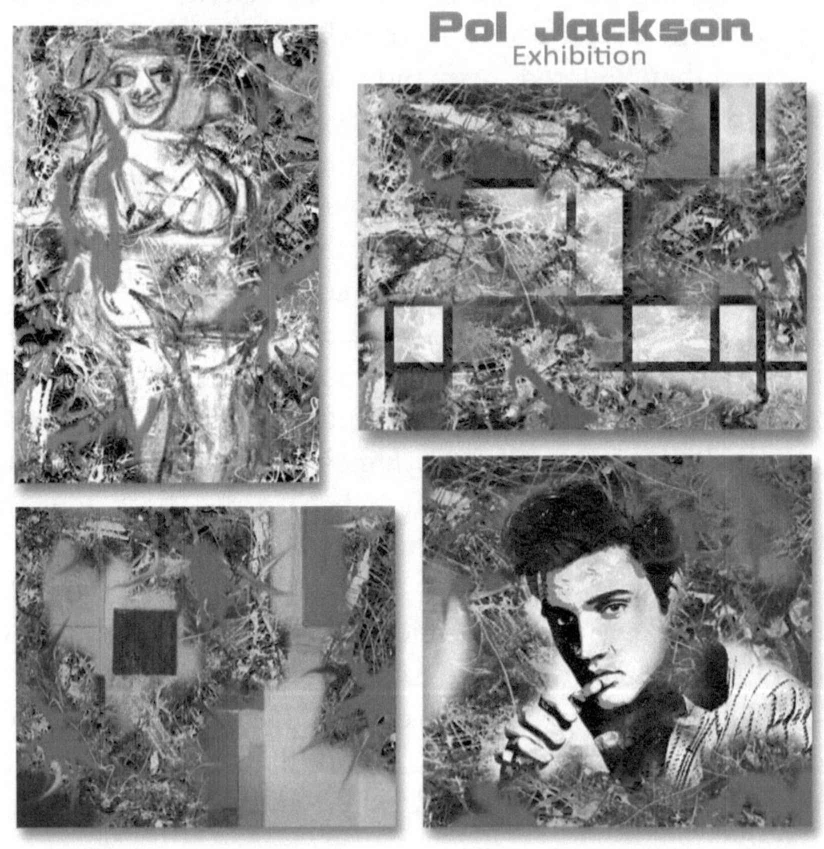

Gerd waited impatiently, sensing Armand's keen eye as it scrutinized each panel. Like an eagle sizing up its prey, or more like an electron microscope analyzing microbes, Armand methodically examined each canvas, up close, then from a-far. Finally, he turned back toward her, as she asked impatiently, "So, what do you think?"

Armand glanced at Andrea, whose piercing eyes preemptively pleaded with him not to be rude, then he gazed back at Gerd, as he said diplomatically, "Well, I can say that they are quite…well, how do I say…familiar."

Gerd squinted. "Familiar?" Her eyebrows rose. "Oh! Yes, I suppose you're referring to Pol's inspirations, his idols." She turned toward the paintings. "Yes, Pol loves to honor his idols. You can really feel the depth of his love." She looked back at Armand. "Can't you?"

Once again, Armand wrestled with his mind to conjure up words, words that wouldn't upset Gerd or Andrea, as he said, "Well, I'm not sure if *love* is what I'm feeling or, more importantly, *seeing*."

Gerd shook her head tersely. "Not love? What exactly are you *seeing*?"

Armand stepped closer to the canvas before him, which appeared to be Hans Hoffman's blocks of color annihilated with wanton splatters of paint. He leaned toward the canvas, almost penetrating the dried oils with his nose, and then sniffed. He leaned back, paused, and said, "Well, I'm intrigued."

Gerd smiled. "Yes! Of course! That's splendid. Intrigued by what?"

Andrea discreetly grabbed Armand's hand and squeezed it, fearing the worst, as Armand said, "I'm intrigued by the fact that all of Pol's paintings are splattered with red blotches of paint."

Gerd blinked, confused at first, then looked back at the four paintings. Like a spark amid night, Gerd's eyes widened. "Oh, yes! They all do have quite a bit of red in them, don't they? I never noticed." She rubbed her chin. "Perhaps red is symbolic for love, love from the heart. Yes, yes, that must be it!" She turned back toward Armand, proud of her impromptu analysis. "The mysteries of abstract art are what make this all so fascinating. Don't you agree?"

Just then, her cell phone rang. "Oh! Excuse me," Gerd said. "I'll only be a minute."

Armand leaned toward Andrea and whispered, "You see, abstract art is so abstract even Pol's manager can't see, or understand, what's before her eyes."

Andrea squeezed his hand again. "Yes, but be polite. I know you mean well by giving others constructive criticism, but sometimes you come off a bit strong. Let's just try to enjoy this."

"Well, that's my main gripe," Armand whispered. "Abstraction doesn't communicate anything substantial, except shapes on a canvas and colors." He gazed back at the canvas, then at Gerd. "Scratch that last item, evidently even color sometimes evades communicating to the viewer. Even if it's to the artist's manager."

Andrea couldn't help but giggle, as Gerd clicked off her cell phone. She stepped back, closer to the couple, and said, "That was Pol. He's running a little late, but I'd love to have you meet him. You *will* stay a while. Won't you?"

"Certainly, no problem," Andrea said, as Armand muffled a sigh.

"I've been meaning to ask," Andrea said. "What is Pol's real name? Surely it's not Pol Jackson?"

"No," Gerd said. "He indeed took on Jackson Pollack's name, but in reverse. His real name is Sven Larsen. He's Norwegian." Her eyes glanced at the door. "Oh, please excuse me," she said. "I need to greet some other guests. But we'll rejoin once Pol arrives. I promise."

With that, Gerd graciously approached the newcomers, as Armand turned toward Andrea. "So his real name is *Larsen*, huh?" Armand snickered. "It makes sense. Larsen's art is the epitome of larceny. He steals other people's work and claims it as his own. He's a sham."

"Behave!" Andrea scolded. "You've managed to be good so far. Be polite for just a little bit longer."

Armand twisted his lips and grasped her hand. "Okay, *mommy*. So, let's see what else Pol Jackson has to offer."

Forty minutes later, after viewing a variety of Pol's repetitious canvases, and testing Armand's patience to the limit, Pol Jackson finally arrived. Dressed in ripped denim jeans and a 60's tie-die shirt with a peace sign emblazoned on the front, Pol staggered into the gallery.

Gerd immediately ran over to Armand, and whispered, "You must excuse him. Pol get's a bit tipsy sometimes. But please, don't let that sway your opinion of him. He's really a nice person underneath the fog."

Armand nodded with a pseudo smile. "Sure, no problem. We all have gotten tipsy at one time or another."

"Thank you," Gerd said, as she swiftly grabbed Pol by the hand and dragged his lanky body over. "I'd like you to meet Andrea. She's the curator of the P.T. Barnum Museum."

Pol's glazed red eyes, which matched his newest paintings, scanned Andrea from head to foot, like a chef sizing up his prize-winning plate, and said, "Gorgeous, and simply delectable. Pleased to eat you."

Gerd chuckled nervously through gritted teeth, while Andrea's smile withered.

Meanwhile, Armand said firmly, "I'm sure you said '*meet* you,' Mr. Jackson, Isn't *that* correct?"

Pol's glassy eyes turned toward the masculine voice, as Gerd said quickly, "And this is Armand Arnolfini, Andrea's *husband*."

"Yikes," Pol mumbled with a silly grin, as he gazed at

Armand's muscular build and stoic face. "Yeah, *meet* is what I said, Arny. No offense."

"His name is Armand *Arnolfini,*" Gerd corrected promptly, trying to avoid further disaster. "He's a famous art expert and private investigator." She looked into Pol's oscillating eyes. "Surely you've heard about him? Right, *Pol*?"

"Yeah, s-sure I did," he replied. "*Twice*...by *you*! So, give it a rest, Hurdy Gerdy."

Gerd looked at Armand, embarrassed. "Excuse him, he—"

"Stop it!" Pol snapped. "Stop acting like my father!"

"Okay!" Armand cut in. "Calm down! Let's just take a look at your art. Shall we, Pol?" With that, Armand grabbed Pol's arm firmly and walked him away toward another display.

Meanwhile, Andrea and Gerd both exhaled, and opted to stay behind to chat among themselves.

Armand led Pol to another large canvas; this one being a crude imitation of a Rothko, again with Pollack-like splatters of paint smothering it. For well over twenty minutes, the two men talked about various aspects of art and their disparate backgrounds, united only by their love of art.

Pol Jackson, or rather Sven Larsen, had the gift of gab, and rattled on about how he grew up in North Dakota. Born into a poor Norwegian family and living in the desolate outback of rural America, life was hard, he said. But it was at age thirteen when he saw his chance to escape the provincial nightmare, especially the philistine mediocrity of his overbearing father.

Before Pol could catch his breath, Armand took that split-second to cut in. He explained his long and winding path in life, from professional *fútbol* player for AC Milan to art student under his father (who was curator of the Uffizi Gallery), and finally how he moved to America to become an FBI agent, then private investigator.

However, Pol's nebulous mind often could only focus on one thing—himself. As such, his cocaine-infused-blood powered his tongue like nitro-methane, as he rattled on and on, sometimes coherent, other times off into the celestial ether of cosmic absurdity.

Armand did his best to appear to be listening, but Pol's abstract flights of fancy, which mirrored his artwork, were making less sense as the night progressed.

Distracted, Armand turned toward one of Pol's newest paintings and, once again, became fixated with Jackson's red paint. There was something very different or even off about it. Armand had examined thousands of famous paintings up close for well over two decades, and he never saw a red hue like Pol's. At this point, it was the only thing that intrigued Armand, and he had to ask, as he cut Pol off midstream. "So, tell me, Pol. How do you get that unique red color?"

Pol didn't even grasp the termination of his cosmic rant, as he turned toward his painting, stared at it for a moment, then giggled. "Yeah, that's my big secret." He looked back at Armand. "I guess it would take a keen art expert or a private eye to discover that."

"Yes, I've developed a keen eye and sense, all right," Armand said. "In fact, I even think I know how you developed it."

Pol's eyebrows rose. "R-really? Go ahead? T-tell me?"

Armand looked at the red paint intently, then turned slowly back toward Pol. "Its blood."

Pol glanced around, ensuring their privacy, and clapped tepidly. "Bravo! I'm i-impressed, Mr. Arny."

"Arnolfini," Armand corrected. "So, where do you get all that blood?" He glanced back up at the huge canvases. "You obviously use many gallons of it."

"Right again, Columbo," Pol said with a touch of sarcasm. "Since you're s-so s-super smart, I'll let you know. But it m-must remain our secret." Pol's cocaine-infused body was so jacked up he didn't even wait for a response. "You see, a guy I know w-works at a s-slaughterhouse, and he gives me b-buckets of cows' blood. Pretty cool, huh?" He turned and peered proudly up at his vibrant paintings. "Surely even m-my idol, Jackson P-Pollack, can never compete with *me*! Can he?"

Armand stifled a yawn. "Surely not. He's dead."

Pol squinted, then laughed.

Thirty minutes later, Armand and Andrea were cruising along the New York Thruway in their blue '57 Corvette, heading home to Westport, Connecticut. Blaring on the newly installed CD player was the latest song by Blue Öyster Cult, *See You In Black*.

Andrea turned down the volume. "You've been unusually quiet. Is anything wrong?"

Armand's head was still rocking to the head-banger riffs as he glanced at her. "Actually, between Liszt's *Totentanz* earlier and BÖC's song, it seems there *is* a dark spell hovering in the air tonight."

"What do you mean?"

"Well, Liszt's *Death Dance* is self explanatory. Meanwhile, BÖC's song is about a woman who is being routinely beaten by her husband. And this man, who loves her, would love to see her wearing black. In other words, bump off the creep husband so she can attend his funeral, wearing black. Then they can run off to Greece."

Andrea chuckled. "I try to tune out the heavy music, but I like those lyrics. However, that doesn't answer my question. What's wrong? Or more importantly; what dark spell is hovering above us?"

Armand glanced at her, his face stricken with concern. "You remember how fixated I was about Pol Jackson's use of red paint, right?"

"Yes. So what? He likes to use red in his paintings. Picasso had his blue period."

Armand glanced at the full moon in the starlit sky, then over at Andrea. "It's not the over-use of red that I'm concerned about. You see, upon closer examination, I had the eerie feeling that his unique, crimson hue was not created with standard pigments and oils. And when I spoke to him directly later on, he *did* admit how he formulated that color."

"Okay, so what's the big deal about how it was made?"

"Pol's red colors, my dear, are made from *blood*. Cows' blood."

Andrea cringed as a ripple of goose bumps ran across her body. "Ew! Dear Lord. That *is* creepy. Why would he do that?"

Armand sighed. "I don't know. His explanation was that he got the blood from a buddy who works at a slaughterhouse. Evidently, it enthralls him that his unique color makes him superior to his idol, Jackson Pollack."

"How does that make any sense?"

"To us, none at all. But to a warped mind, and one obviously high on drugs, I guess it makes a lot of sense *and* money. I don't know how people buy into that nonsense, especially since his work is far from unique, other than the cows' blood."

Andrea snickered. "Yes, although I'm open to modern art a lot more than you are, in this case I can fully agree. Pol Jackson's art is a rip-off, just like his name."

Armand's face withered to a solemn stare as the headlights of cars in the on-coming lanes reflected off his pensive eyes. Amid the dark interior of their '57 Corvette, Armand uttered. "Yes, a rip-off, and a bloody mess. There's death in all of his works."

Eight days later Armand was sitting in his home office, staring at the monitor of his new blue and white Power Mac G3. As little Jack and Artemisia played in the den down the hall, Armand scrolled through the news pages online.

Andrea walked in with a cup of coffee and a bowl of yogurt with fresh fruit. She placed them down on his desk. He glanced up at her. "Thanks, sweetheart." He grasped his cup of coffee, and sighed with humiliation. "This darn dial-up Internet can be so slow sometimes, it's aggravating."

"Yes, we should think about up-grading."

Before Armand could respond, his eye's caught a headline. "Wow! Look at this. President Clinton finally admitted that he had an improper, physical relationship with Monica Lewinsky. And that he lied and misled the American people."

Andrea just smirked. "No kidding. As if we all were stupid enough to think otherwise." She bent over and picked up the wastebasket. "Do you have anything else that needs to be thrown out?"

Armand didn't respond as his eyes caught another headline. He leaned closer and scanned the article, as Andrea huffed, waiting. "Well? Did you hear me? Do you have any other garbage?"

Armand shook his head and finally looked up. "I need to go to North Dakota."

Andrea recoiled. "What? What are you talking about? What for?"

"It says here that another young girl is missing in Minot, North Dakota. The third disappearance in two years."

Andrea now shook *her* head. "Sometimes you can be so cryptic, Armand. You're a private investigator of fine art. What do missing girls in North Dakota have to do with you?"

Armand sighed, disturbed. "These missing girls have me thinking. Well, actually in a dark place. I think Pol Jackson is somehow connected to this. Perhaps he's even a serial killer."

"Dear God! You're not serious? Are you?"

"Yes, I am," he said as he looked up at her. "Let's face it, Pol is certainly unstable. And it has to be more than a coincidence that these missing girls happen to be where Pol grew up, and where he gets his blood."

"Christ, he sounds like Dracula," Andrea said impulsively. She shook her head. "I'm sorry, I didn't mean to be funny. So, you think it's human blood on Pol's canvases?"

Armand glanced back at the monitor, his heart dropping as he looked at the photo of the cute, innocent face of the young, missing girl. "I hate to say it, and I hope I'm wrong, but it *is* possible."

"So, why go to North Dakota? Shouldn't you call Gerd or Pol and speak to them first, directly?"

Armand turned off the computer. "No, I don't want to alert them. Best I go alone, incognito. I'll be gone for a few days, or…well, as long as it takes." He glanced at the wastebasket in Andrea's hands. "And perhaps I can get rid of some human waste in the process."

Two days later, Armand landed in Bismarck, North Dakota, rented a car, and drove two hours north to Minot. The quaint township consisted of a mere 36,000 people. Armand, as usual, made it a point to include some culture on his trip. As such, he drove through the town and eventually came upon the Gol Stave Church museum. The unique edifice had just recently been built and was a replica of the original church in Norway, which was built in 1250 AD.

Heritage Park, of which the church stands as its centerpiece, was dedicated to five Scandinavian nations, namely Norway, Sweden, Finland, Denmark, and Iceland. Armand walked through the grounds, taking in the unique culture, a culture that found its way to the United States, primarily in the colder, northern regions, akin to their native homelands. As he visited each site and explored the church museum, he encountered numerous Scandinavians, each gracious and informative, bolstering his appreciation of their heritage. Along his travels he also encountered many German-American visitors, as they too had settled in North Dakota in large numbers.

Two hours later, Armand hopped in his rented car. He turned on the ignition and exhaled with a sigh. He was now ready to clear his mind of the enjoyable part of his trip. It was time to focus on the grim reality of a missing young girl, and Pol's obsession with blood.

Armand drove to the Minot Police Station and entered the building. He approached the officer at the front desk. "Hello. My name is Armand Arnolfini. I'm a private investigator."

The officer was drawing doodles, and looked up, nonchalantly. "Yeah, and how can I help you?"

"I read about the missing girl, Brit Johansen."

The police chief overheard Armand's remark and walked over. "Did the Johansen family hire you? And if so, why?"

Armand peered up at the tall man, well over six-feet-four and sporting a thick mustache and beard, as he said, "No. I read about this online. I'm from Connecticut."

"Connecticut?" Chief Sørensen said with a snicker. "Well, I don't know why you'd waste your time coming all the way out here. But as you can see, this is the Minot Police force, and we've got this covered."

"I'm sure you do," Armand said. "But I have some information that might aid in your investigation."

Sørensen crossed his muscular arms. "And just what might that be?"

"Are you aware that Pol Jackson, or rather Sven Larsen, uses blood in his paintings?"

Several officers nearby laughed, as Sørensen shook his head and snorted. He looked at Armand with discerning eyes, scanning his dark wavy hair, slightly olive complexion, and said, "Arnolfini, you said?"

"Yes, Armand Arnolfini."

"Is that I-talian?" he said, to a round of hyena-like giggles.

Armand face remained rock solid and unaffected. "Yes, I'm sure we Italians are a novelty here, and can be quite funny at times, but now can we get back to the issue at hand? I'm sure with a town this small you know Pol Jackson, the artist. But are you aware that he uses blood in his paintings?"

Sørensen rolled his eyes. "Personally, I don't give a rat's ass what Pol uses on his canvases. He could use cow shit, for all I care. Them crazy artists are always up to something stupid."

As the officers all chuckled, Armand took a deep breath, and said, "Well, Pol might certainly be crazy, but to ignore that he uses blood, when three young girls are missing in your town, is also *crazy*!"

Amid the instant silence, Sørensen leapt forward, right in Armand's face. "Listen, Petrocelli, you have some nerve walking in here and making *crazy* comments. Okay, so Pol uses blood. If you think it's the blood of young girls, *you're* crazy! Cause if it's blood, it most surely is from his dad's cattle ranch, which slaughters thousands of cows and can supply scrawny little Pol with as much blood as he needs."

Armand's eyebrows rose. "Pol's *dad* owns the cattle ranch?"

"Yeah. I guess you didn't do your homework, Petrocelli," Sørensen gloated. "Its The Larsen Cattle Ranch. It's out in Granville, about a half-hour from here. Maybe you should hop on your pony and take a ride out there."

"I think I will," Armand said, as he looked at all the officers eating funnel cakes or Danish kringles at their desks. "Because it certainly doesn't look like much is being done around here."

Sørensen snapped, "You have a sharp tongue!"

"And mind," Armand quipped swiftly, as he walked toward the door. "And I intend to get to the bottom of this."

"I doubt you'll find anything," Sørensen said. "These girls were all in their teens. And one of the sad facts around here is that we know many go off to become Mormons. And once that happens, they'll never be seen again, living in a world of polygamy and sin."

Armand opened the door, and said, "Well, it's nice that you idly sit here and speculate rather than actively go out and investigate. To paraphrase an I-talian named Leonardo da Vinci: 'One must examine nature for the answers. Experience in the field never errs, it's only idle conjecture that errs.'"

As Armand stepped through the threshold, he turned back and added, "And by the way, Petrocelli was a defense attorney, not a private eye. Good day, boys, enjoy your just desserts."

With that, Armand walked to his rented car and hopped in. After meeting numerous warm and pleasant townsfolk at the park he didn't expect the reception he received at the police station. With a sigh, he started the car and drove twenty-five miles out to Granville.

Along the way Armand gazed out at the endless panorama, with miles and miles of barren flatlands. His mind wandered as his heart dropped, wondering if those three lost girls were either locked up or dead and buried somewhere, out there in the endless expanse of nothingness. The sheer torture and endless torment that all the families were forced to endure weighed heavily on his mind. The horrifying thought of either Jack or Artemisia being abducted, and God forbid killed, crushed his heart and brought a tear to his eye.

As he pulled up to the Larsen Cattle Ranch, Armand swallowed a lump of dread. He looked at the sprawling fields filled with cattle. Their destinies and those of their calves faced a similar dark fate, and the grim aura of death fell upon him like a guillotine. He sat for an odd moment, pensive and solemn, then exited the car, somewhat relieved. The fact that millions of people didn't have to deal with the ugly business of slaughter and death was an enormous gift, all due to the largely neglected and grueling work of ranchers.

Armand walked toward the wooden fencing, which corralled thousands of cattle, and came upon a rancher, who turned, tipped his hat, and said, "Howdy. How can I help you?"

Armand glanced at the huge building nearby. "Well, I'm looking to speak with whoever is in charge of your slaughterhouse."

The rancher pointed to a hefty man several yards away. "He's right over there. Hans Schulmann is his name."

"Much obliged," Armand said, as he turned and walked over to Hans.

Hans was the size of an ox and dressed in overalls and rubber boots. Blood decorated every aspect of his clothing, as Armand said, "Hello. I see you're a hands-on manager."

Hans smiled. "Indeed I am. Nothing gets done right otherwise. Employees need to have some respect for their bosses. And a guy wearing a nice pair of jeans and a cleaned and pressed shirt like yours just wouldn't cut it here."

Armand smiled. "I'm sure it wouldn't. And no offense, but I'd never want your job. I give you all a lot of credit."

"Well, thanks for the credit, but what brings you here, Mr?"

"Arnolfini. Armand Arnolfini. I'm a private investigator."

Hans sighed with relief. "Oh, thank goodness. I thought you were from the Health Department or one of those Environ-*mentals*."

Armand chuckled. "No. Have no fear. I'm just here to ask a few questions." He glanced at the huge building with the placard "Slaughter House" above the door. "Actually, I'm interested in Sven Larsen, or Pol Jackson as he calls himself now."

Hans chuckled. "Ah, yes, puny little Pol. The art-*teest*."

"Yes, exactly," Armand said. "Are you, by chance, aware that Pol uses cows' blood in his paintings?"

Hans's amiable face withered to one of bewilderment, then outright disbelief. "That's ludicrous, Mr. Arnolfini. Besides, Papa Larsen would never condone or tolerate such nonsense. He's a stern SOB and runs this ranch like my father ran his regiment in the *Wehrmacht*."

Although Hans's father being a deadly Nazi raised a red flag, Armand's thoughts immediately switched over to Papa Larsen. "So, what is Papa Larsen's first name?"

"Magnus," Hans said. "If you plan on going to see him, be prepared. That's all I can say."

"Thank you," Armand said, as he turned and walked toward the large estate, situated several hundred yards away. Enshrouded by manicured gardens, the cedar-sided mansion, with four chimneys billowing smoke, was enormous. Armand knocked on the door and was greeted by a servant. Without much fuss, he escorted Armand to Magnus's office down the hall.

Armand stepped in and was immediately overcome by the huge room with a cathedral ceiling. It was decorated with animal heads mounted on every square inch of wall, while bronze sculptures of cowboys and Indians by Frederic Remington sat on Magnus' massive desk.

Magnus was on the phone and raised a finger, signaling to wait. Armand nodded and continued to scan the room, noticing the photos of cattle, certificates, and awards in gold frames, and the box of Cuban cigars on the desk.

Magnus hung up, and said, "Howdy do. And you are?"

"Armand Arnolfini, a private investigator."

With a snort, Magnus continued jotting invoices with his gold pen, and said, without looking up, "What brings you here?"

"Well, in one regard, I guess you could say your son."

With another snort, and still not looking up, Larsen said, "Yeah, what about that loser?"

Armand flinched, not expecting such harsh candor. "Well, I'm curious to know if you, or someone here, supplies Pol with cows' blood."

Magnus's head snapped up, his face stern and gnarled with disgust. "What the hell do you mean by that? Why the hell would I, or anyone, supply that demented twit with anything, let alone cows' blood!?"

Armand took a seat, took a breath, and replied, "Because I found out that Pol uses cows' blood in his paintings. He even told me so himself."

Magnus slammed his pen down on the desk. "Why the hell would you, or anyone, be interested in nonsense like this? Sven is a lost soul, a frail, weak-minded wannabe who walked away from my good graces and massive fortune to dilly-dally with splattering paint on canvases. He's an embarrassment to my good name, a name that I forged in blood to make into the most successful cattle ranch in the state. And to add insult to injury, and to spit in my face, the messed-up waste of life even trashed my good name to take on that silly pseudonym or whatever the hell it is!"

Heaving out a breath of hot, foul air, Magnus added, now exasperated, "Actually, I'm glad Pol Jackson discarded my good name. Perhaps that's the one and only joy that drugged-out flake ever gave me."

Armand was done listening and stood up. "Well, I'm sorry to have bothered you. I'll take my leave." Before turning, however, he added, "I see you only have two photos on your desk, each of young girls." He glanced around the huge office. "In fact, they're the only photos of people you have here. Who are they?"

Magnus glanced at the photos, his harsh, rocky face morphing briefly with a touch of warm affection. "Ah, yes, those are my two gems. Oydis and Thyra, my beautiful nieces. Oydis is indeed my goddess of good luck and, well, Thyra *is* like thunder."

Armand looked around once more. "No wife or children?"

"My wife died twenty years ago. And no. No children. Well, no children, at least, that I care to call my own."

"That's a shame," Armand said. "I'll see myself out."

Armand drove back to his motel in Minot. He unpacked his luggage, then went out to the local tavern. He ordered a 16 oz. rib-eye steak with asparagus and garlic, mashed potatoes. As he cut into the juicy steak, red blood oozed out onto the plate. Armand placed his knife and fork down.

Thoughts of how Leonardo da Vinci was a vegetarian filled Armand's mind. Leonardo would even go to the market to buy birds, only to set them free. Armand knew he would never give up meat, not only for the benefits of a balanced diet, but for the savory taste, as well. However, tonight he couldn't bring himself to eat the animal or its blood.

He sat for a moment as thoughts of Andrea came back into his mind, specifically her comment about Dracula. Armand shook his head. *Aren't we all a bit like Dracula,* he thought, as he pushed the dish of bloody meat away.

Armand went back to his motel and laid down on the bed, his mind filled with disturbing thoughts, thoughts of Pol Jackson and his obsession with blood, and then thoughts of Pol's father Magnus, who only had photos of his two young nieces on his desk. Could either of these men be the monster who abducted these young girls, or God forbid killed them? An hour later, Armand called home, spoke to Andrea and the kids, and bid them good night with loving words of affection.

The next morning, Armand showered, got dressed, and hopped in his rented car. He stopped to have breakfast, then drove back to the Larsen Cattle Ranch. This time, he parked down the road a bit and crept discreetly toward the slaughterhouse.

The fact that no one admitted being the supplier of blood to Pol Jackson had weighed on his mind, especially since Magnus clearly disowned his son. Without access to the ranch, Pol had to have someone act as his supplier, as Pol even admitted himself. Therefore, Armand had to find Jackson's so-called "buddy."

As Armand tiptoed toward the door of the slaughterhouse he saw Hans Schulmann in the distance, speaking to a group of cowhands. Discreetly, Armand entered the building. Immediately, he pinched his nose, overwhelmed by the gruesome stench of dead carcasses, entrails, and the hundreds of gallons of blood, which ran like rivers into a Red Sea of waste.

Off to the side, Armand spotted a young man, standing by himself, taking a break. Amid the din of horrors, Armand walked over and introduced himself. Jake Koenig was thin and a bit awkward and, as Armand immediately deduced, a bit slow.

Jake wiped the blood off his face and replied with a slight stutter, "Nice to m-meet you, Mr. Ar-feeni."

"Tell me, Jake," Armand said. "Are you aware of anyone who is friends with Sven Larsen, known as Pol Jackson?"

Jake's jittery eyes widened as he sheepishly looked around, then uttered, "Well, I—"

"Shut up!" Hans bellowed as he walked up from behind Armand. "Break is over, get back to work!"

Jake cowered at the reprimand, nodded at Armand, and dutifully returned to the slaughter line.

Hans looked at Armand, his face red, this time not with cows' blood, but with his own blood that rushed through his bulging veins. "Mr. Arnolfini, I was nice enough to speak with you yesterday when you came directly to me. But to sneak into my slaughterhouse and take my workers away from their jobs is unacceptable. And I won't tolerate it. I have strict protocols and deadlines to maintain."

"Mr. Schulmann," Armand said, "I was—"

"Never mind the excuses," Hans snapped as he pointed to the exit. "Please go!"

Armand walked back to his car, got in, and closed the door. He sat there, his mind reeling: first, how Jake was just about to reveal the accomplice, who might be himself, and second, how Hans Schulmann morphed from an amiable soul yesterday to a grumpy blowhard. Was that because Magnus somehow got wind of him talking with Armand and slammed the hammer down on him? Or perhaps, did Hans fear that Jake was about to reveal that he was Pol Jackson's accomplice?

Then again, having noticed the security cameras on the premises, Armand wondered if Magnus was spying on all of them, possibly to ensure his own safety from child abduction or murder. Armand knew that gossip travels fast in small towns, and if by chance one of his workers found out about any wrongdoings, Magnus could nip it in the bud, if need be.

Armand shook his head and looked into the rearview mirror at himself. *Am I getting too paranoid?* He thought. *Magnus could just be a hard-ass businessman who's a micromanager and loves his nieces.* He exhaled and gazed down. *Where do I go from here?* He thought. *Christ, the police have no interest, these suspects have not provided enough information, and*—he looked back up into the mirror. *Of course!*

Armand slammed the car into gear and turned around. He sped down the dusty road toward The Taube Museum of Art in Minot. He had read about the local museum in the brochure at his motel. As such, Armand was sure they had to know their local hero, or hack, Pol Jackson.

Twenty-five minutes later Armand walked into the Taube Museum and eventually tracked down the curator, Mrs. Freda Heinemann. Freda was a tall, slim, and dignified woman in her fifties, and she greeted Armand warmly. "Nice to meet you, Mr. Arnolfini. I have indeed read about you in the news. Your work in the art world has been most impressive." Her pleasant face morphed into one of concern. "But, dare I ask, has one of our pieces raised a red flag? A forgery perhaps?"

Armand smiled. "No, Mrs. Heinemann. No forgeries or red flag. But rather red blood."

Heinemann squinted, startled. "Dear Lord, red blood? What ever do you mean?"

Armand had quickly perused the gallery before her arrival and spotted three of Pol Jackson paintings, as he now clarified his cryptic remark. "I'm referring to Pol Jackson, Mrs. Heinemann, specifically his use of red in his paintings. Are you aware that his red hues are created with blood?"

Heinemann cringed with a shiver. "Dear Lord! I do hope you're joking?"

"No, I wish I were," Armand said. "But it's true. More to the point, I suspect there might be a chance that along with the cows' blood, which Pol obtains from his father's ranch, there might also be the blood of the missing girls in your community."

Freda's face went pale. With a trembling hand, she rubbed her temple, dazed, and sickened. She looked back at Armand. "That's a horrible thought, Mr. Arnolfini."

"Indeed it is," Armand said. "I have a daughter of my own, and can't even imagine the horror and loss those poor families are going through. That's why I jumped on this case. I took it personally, so to speak."

Freda managed to crack a subtle smile. "That's very commendable, Mr. Arnolfini. As it happens, I know the family of the latest missing girl personally. I knew Brit Johansen quite well. She was a smart and talented teenager, with so much promise." A tear welled in her eye, as she turned toward one of Pol Jackson's paintings, then back at Armand. "The thought that that painting might contain Brit's blood shakes me to the core, Mr. Arnolfini. How can I help you? Just ask, and I swear, it *will* be done."

"Well, I know this is very unconventional," Armand said as he glanced at the painting. "But I would like to take a few samples of the red paint, or rather blood, on his paintings to get them tested for a potential forensic match."

"By all means!" Freda said impulsively. "That's a splendid idea."

"It would also help if you provide me with the most recent painting of Pol's."

Freda turned and pointed. "You're in luck. That one is called *Moans in Spring*. It's his latest work, which he sold to us about two weeks ago, just before leaving for New York."

Armand swallowed hard. "The title alone gives me shivers." He paused a moment to collect himself, then continued, "That will do perfectly. I just need to scrape a few chips off, then I'll overnight them to my forensics specialist in New York. But I'll also need the DNA of Brit Johansen to add to the package. Do you think you could help in that regard?"

"No problem," Freda said confidently. "I'll call the Johansens right now and get some clothing, hairbrushes, or whatever is needed to get some samples for you."

Armand nodded solemnly. "Thank you."

"And to expedite the process," she added, "I could even get you the address of the local forensics lab that our police use, if that would help?"

Armand smiled. "Well, yes, that would indeed save time. But, you see, I had gone to the police first upon my arrival yesterday, and they weren't very cooperative. In fact, they were curiously uninterested."

"Well, Magnus Larsen owns this whole town," Freda said with humiliation in her voice. "And many of us suspect that he's the reason why the police have never looked into these cases, which includes the two missing girls previously."

"Yes, I know political implications can incite police corruption, but I thought their complacency was rather odd, especially in a small town like this. I imagine everyone knows everyone else to some extent."

"We do," Freda said. "But human nature is a strange thing. Not everyone manages to be friends with their neighbors. History proves as much. Just like the Hatfields and McCoys, rivalries always seem to rise up, somehow."

"Yes, it's a sad state of affairs," Armand said. "Imagine how productive and peaceful life would be if everyone at least shared a sense of moral decency."

"I suppose that's what dreams are for, Mr. Arnolfini."

"Very true, Mrs. Heinemann."

"Please, call me Freda. And I'll have those DNA samples to you A-SAP. What's your cell phone number and where are you staying?"

Armand supplied his contact information, thanked her again, and took his leave.

Two days later the forensic lab in New York called Armand. The samples of red paint revealed large quantities of cows' blood, but also a miniscule amount of human blood. Specifically that of Brit Johansen's, which matched the DNA samples from her hair, taken by her mother from her hairbrush.

Armand ended the call on his cell phone and stood momentarily in a bittersweet zone of excitement and profound sadness. This was certainly a big step toward solving the case, but it also meant Brit Johansen was very likely dead. His throat tightened with dread at the thought of losing a child and at the horrible job that was now imminent, telling the Johansen's that a deranged psychopath very likely killed their beautiful daughter. He took a deep breath, grasped his car keys and walked out the motel door.

Minutes later, Armand arrived at the police station and summoned Chief Sørensen. Sørensen exited his office and walked up to Armand. "Back again?"

"Yes, and this time with solid evidence."

Sørensen nodded unenthusiastically. "And what's that?"

"The red paint in Pol Jackson's artworks are indeed cows' blood. But one sample also contained a DNA match to Brit Johansen's."

Sørensen, along with five officers, drew their attention to Armand, wide-eyed and stunned. Sørensen gazed aimlessly at the floor, then back up at Armand. "I reckon I owe you an apology. That's fine detective work, Mr. Arnolfini. Truly impressive. Who would have thought to check a painting for evidence? Blood no less. It's morbid." He glanced behind him at his fellow officers, then back at Armand. "Again, *we* sincerely apologize for the poor reception we gave you last time."

Armand nodded solemnly. "Thank you, but there's still much to be done if we intend to find the killer. I know

Magnus Larsen is a powerful man in this town, but my visit to him posed no threat. However, if I arrive with the police, I'm sure he'll think twice, and perhaps we can get closer to solving this case."

Sørensen's face suddenly took on a look of doubt. "Mr. Arnolfini, how does this DNA breakthrough connect with Magnus? I don't wish to approach him unless there's substantial evidence to tie him to these murders. That's even *if* the previous two girls were in fact killed."

"Well, it seems quite clear that these three missing girls met the same fate. And I'm confident that once we take samples of red paint from Pol Jackson's older paintings, we'll get the evidence we need for the two other girls, who by this time most likely are dead. The four main suspects in my mind are Sven Larsen, Magnus Larsen, Hans Schulmann, and Jake Koenig."

Sørensen shook his head. "Jeez, Magnus watches over his brood like a Gestapo chief, yet you managed to round up the Larsen gang in a few days. Except, of course, for his son. I imagine you've found out that Pol was banished."

"Yes, that was made quite clear," Armand said. "But you can't cower to Magnus any longer. These killings *are* connected to his bloody ranch. And even if he's not the culprit, he surely is part of this grim circle. So, it's very possible that he knows something about who's supplying Pol with the cows' blood. Once we discover the supplier, it's possible that person is killing these girls and mixing their blood into the cows' blood, with or without Pol's knowledge. Or perhaps, Pol Jackson is the murderer, and mixing their blood with the cows', with or without anyone else's knowledge."

Sørensen shook his head, trying to comprehend Armand's logic. After a brief moment, the scenarios jelled.

"Okay. I think I see where you're going with this, and it makes sense." He turned toward his team. "Lars and Aiden, gear up and come with me. We're paying Magnus Larsen a visit."

With that, the foursome rode out to the Larsen Cattle Ranch and marched straight toward Magnus Larsen's office. As they stepped through the door, Magnus looked up from his desk. At first startled, his alpha grit resumed control, as he sprang up and barked, "What the hell is this!? How dare you storm into my office! Get out!"

Sørensen led the pack toward his desk, and said, "Listen, Magnus, we just have some questions to ask, serious questions to help our investigation. That's all."

"You know the drill, Sørensen!" Magnus blustered. "You should have called first and made an appointment." His eyes finally spotted Armand. He huffed like a wild boar and looked back at Sørensen. "And what's *he* doing here? I imagine this was all *his* doing, right?"

"Calm down, Magnus," Sørensen pleaded. "He brought to light some damning evidence. Hard evidence."

"And what might *that* be?" Magnus snapped.

"He found out that the red paint in Pol's paintings not only contain cows' blood, but also the blood of the missing girl, Brit Johansen. So, this *is* very serious, Magnus."

Magnus looked at Armand like a wild bull about to charge. "So are you trying to pin this on *me*, you mangy mutt?"

Before Armand could respond, Sørensen replied, "No, Magnus. But we need to know who is supplying your son with the cows' blood. One step at a time."

Magnus snorted and gritted his teeth. He wasn't used to being forced to speak about anything. *He* made the demands. He shook his head. "I have nothing to say."

Sørensen sighed. "Nothing to say, as in, you refuse to speak? Or nothing, as in, you know nothing about the stolen blood activities?"

Magnus sat back down with the bearing of a pissed-off gorilla. "Look, this whole thing is messed up, bizarre, just like my son. I wouldn't put it past that degenerate to steal blood from my ranch. So, you can put this on the record, I want nothing to do with this bloody mess. Is that understood? Now get the hell out of my office! *Pronto*!"

Sørensen looked at Armand and his men and whipped his head toward the door. "Let's go."

As the foursome walked outside, Sørensen looked at Armand and smirked. "That went well, just as I expected. Now what?"

Armand looked over at the slaughterhouse. "I say we speak to Jake Koenig."

"Who is he?"

"A slaughterer," Armand said. "He was about to tell me something when his supervisor cut him off. I'd like to know what or who that was."

Sørensen looked at his officers and pointed toward the slaughterhouse. "Let's go." He turned back toward Armand. "But this will be the last interrogation. We need to take baby steps with Magnus. He has this entire place on camera, and to be quite frank, he's the largest donator, or should I say, puppet master, of the mayor and our department."

Armand nodded. "I get it. I know how the system works. That's why I decided many years ago to leave the FBI and go it alone."

With that, the foursome entered the slaughterhouse and Armand pointed out Jake. As they approached the lanky youth, Jake's face turned as pale and bloodless as the dead carcasses he butchered.

Again, Sørensen took the lead, and queried, "Jake Koenig, we need to ask you a few questions."

Jake stood frozen, trembling with jittery eyes, as Sørensen continued, "Who supplies Pol Jackson with cows' blood?"

Jake scanned the faces of the four men before him as adrenaline surged through his veins. With a crack in his feeble voice, he uttered, "I…I do."

Armand stepped forward. "Jake, do you supply Pol with anything else?"

Jake nervously looked at Armand. "Ugh, like w-what?"

"Anything else at all?" Armand said. "Or is it just the cows' blood?"

"Ugh, yeah, just c-cows' blood," Jake muttered.

"Why?" Sørensen cut in.

Jake nervously looked back at Sørensen. "Cause I f-follow orders."

"*Whose* orders?" Sørensen growled.

Jake cowered. "Mr. Schul—"

"What's going on here!?" Hans Schulmann barked, as he heatedly approached.

Sørensen looked at him. "Just asking some questions. And you are?"

"Hans Schulmann, the supervisor. What questions?" He suddenly noticed Armand. "Oh! I see. I guess this is about the cows' blood in Pol's paintings."

Armand stepped forward. "Yes. Last I was here you said it was ludicrous. But Jake just informed us that it's *you* who instructs him to supply Pol with cows' blood. So, why did you lie, and why are you supplying Pol with blood?"

Hans glanced up at the camera, then back down. "I reckon Magnus has been informed about this already?"

"Yes, he has," Armand said. "So, there's no need to walk outside or hide somewhere. Just tell us. Why?"

Hans sighed. "Listen, we all have someone to answer to, and Pol Jackson is still Magnus's son, no matter what." He paused, swallowed hard, and continued, "This all began two years ago. Pol was living here and, at that point, he still had clout. Naturally, that was before his dad kicked his ass out and disowned him. So, Pol asked me to supply him with the blood for his paintings." Hans took a deep breath, and went on, "Yeah, sure, I knew it was weird, but so too is Pol. And Pol threatened to tell his dad and get me fired if I didn't comply. So, there you have it. I complied, and then lied, to you."

As the two officers and Sørensen looked at Hans with growing interest, Armand said, "Okay, that explains why you give the blood to Pol. But we just learned that the blood in Pol's recent painting also contains the blood of the missing girl, Brit Johansen. So, how did *that* get in there?"

Hans looked at Sørensen, then back at Armand. "Ah, come on! I know nothing about that. That's insane! Look, I don't know what goes on in that crazy kid's head, but I just supplied Pol with the cows' blood. That's it!"

Sørensen breathed a sigh of relief. To take down one of Magnus' men as the murderer would be bad news for the Larsen ranch, the mayor, and the police department. A sense of decorum needed to be maintained, and since all of Minot knew that Pol Jackson was no longer a part of the Larsen machine that would make his conviction a separate matter. Sørensen sighed again, as his job was now safe from repercussions.

Sørensen glanced at his men then back at Hans. "Thank you, Hans. I think we're done here." He looked at Armand. "Nice work! We owe this all to you. I reckon we need to have a good hard chat with Pol Jackson, once he returns from New York."

Armand nodded. "Yes, we do. And you're quite welcome."

Sørensen patted his officers on their backs. "Okay, boys. Let's go."

As the three officers left, Armand trailed behind. Armand slowed his pace and watched all the officers get into their vehicles and leave. He opened the trunk of his rented car and pulled out a long-range listening device with a built-in recorder. Discreetly, he crept back to the slaughterhouse and walked around the side of the building.

Tactfully, he rose on his tiptoes and peered through a window. He saw Hans issuing orders to his workers, then he made a beeline to the exit. Armand scurried back toward the entrance, where he saw Hans slip out, then scurry toward a vacant barn. Furtively, Hans peered around, then entered.

Armand followed and placed the listening device against the barn's dirty window. As he tuned it in he saw Hans look around to ensure his privacy. Then he pulled out his cell phone and dialed.

"Listen, just a heads up, Po," Hans's voice resonated in Armand's earpiece. "Expect the police and this guy named Armand Arnolfini to call you about the blood in your paintings."

"No problem, Hans," Pol's faint voice resonated. "But I might as well tell you. I already told Arnolfini that I use blood."

"Yeah, cows' blood," Hans said. "But not about the human blood."

"Human blood!?" Pol exclaimed. "What the hell are you talking about?"

"Yeah, they found the missing girl's blood in your painting, Pol. A forensic test confirmed it. What the hell did you do, Pol!?"

"Me!? You son of a bitch! It must have been *you*! You freakin' pedophile!"

"Don't call me a pedophile! You rat bastard!"

"How could I not!?" Pol yelled through the receiver. "What's this? Now you have dementia, Hans? You can't remember how you abused me? You're lucky I never squealed on you, you deviant reject!"

"Don't give me that nonsense, it was consensual."

"Consensual, my ass! I was fourteen and on drugs, drugs *you* gave me! You raped me, you sick bastard, and got me hooked on drugs, you soulless pusher. And the only reason you're not in jail is because I need you to feed my addiction and supply the blood, lucrative blood that's now finally compensating me for all the bullshit in my life, namely your abuse and my father's oppressive iron hand, which collectively caused my addiction to drugs. You're both responsible for screwing up my life!"

"Fine, so I had a one-off dalliance against your will, but I'm not going down for this girl's blood. You're already branded in the news as a weirdo, Pol, and they'll never connect me to the missing girls. At least not once I kill them."

"What do you mean, you wretch? You kept them alive all this time?"

"Yeah, I kept them locked up, out in the boonies, where no one will ever find them. And once I kill them and get rid of their bodies—with a bit of *your* blood, which I swiped from your syringe as insurance—*you'll* be implicated as the killer!"

"I think not!" Armand bellowed as he stormed into the barn.

Hans spun around, eyes wide, as he quickly shoved the cell phone in his pocket. "What the hell are *you* still doing here?"

"Never mind that, Hans. I heard your entire conversation and confession. It's over, you're going down!"

"Ha!" Hans blustered. "Won't happen," he growled, as he rolled up his sleeves. An unnerving madness filled Hans's eyes, like the stare of a rabid grizzly, as he waddled toward Armand, slowly, methodically, with deadly intent. "I don't know how much you could have possibly heard, Mr. P.I." He peered left and right. "But there's no one around." He grabbed a pitchfork and started to walk faster toward his prey.

Armand pulled out his 38 special. "Okay, big guy. Stop right there!"

Hans's eyes widened as he froze in place. He gritted his teeth, annoyed by the impasse.

Armand raised the long-range listening device in his other hand. "This apparatus not only is capable of listening in on extremely low-volume conversations, but it can also record them. I have it all on tape. So, I know you have the girls locked up in a cabin somewhere. You just need to tell me where that is."

Hans snickered as he rocked the pitchfork to and fro. "And why would I do a stupid thing like that?"

"Well, since you like doing stupid things, Hans, like raping and drugging boys, abducting young girls, and God knows what else, I think you better tell me, and *fast*, before I put a bullet in your head! I have no patience for child molesters!"

"Now wouldn't that be *stupid*, to kill me?" Hans said cockily. "Then you'll never know where they are."

Armand pulled the trigger, as the 38-caliber bullet tore through Hans's thigh. Hans fell to the ground, squealing in agony as he tried to stop the bleeding. He gazed up at Armand, shocked and trembling. "You crazy bastard! You shot me!"

"You're very observant, Hans. Yes, I did. But that was just in your leg." He walked and stood above Hans, pistol pointed at his meaty head. "I know you're stupid, Hans, but can you guess where my next shot will be?" Armand cocked the pistol. "I'll give you a hint, it's like the bullets you fire into the heads of your clueless cattle."

Hans's eyes bulged as he blurted, "Okay! Okay! You crazy bastard! They're in a cabin, near Stink Lake."

"Don't toy with me," Armand blasted. "The only thing that stinks around here is *you*! Now tell me the truth?"

Hans blinked hard. "That *is* the truth. It's called Stink Lake."

Just then, police arrived, having been called ten minutes earlier by Armand. They were on their way back to Minot when they got the call and turned around. Sørensen and his men rushed into the barn and the two officers attended Hans' leg, while Sørensen called an ambulance.

Once Sørensen hung up, Armand explained the chain of events: namely, how Hans threatened to kill him with a pitchfork, which prompted him to shoot Hans in self-defense.

Armand added with immediacy, "The three girls are alive! Hans locked them up in a cabin near Stink Lake. We have to leave immediately."

Sørensen ordered his men to stay with Hans until the ambulance arrived, and he and Armand ran to their cars. Some thirty minutes later, Armand finally spotted the hidden cabin, some 300 yards from the lake. The dilapidated shack sat amid a large overgrowth, its windows boarded up, with a shroud of ivy engulfing it.

Armand ran to the door, followed by Sørensen, and banged on the door. "Girls! Are you all right?"

With the most wretched of voices, wracked with fear, the cacophony of squeals sent chills down Armand and Sørensen's spines.

"Stand back!" Armand yelled, as he pulled out his pistol. "I'm going to shoot the lock off the door."

With that, he cocked the gun and shot the lock clear off. He kicked open the door, only to see a heart-wrenching, yet beautiful, sight, as the three young girls staggered out into the sunlight. Pale and frail, they squinted and covered their eyes from the light, which two girls hadn't seen in two years. Finally, they broke down, weeping inconsolably, as they clutched onto their saviors. Armand and Sørensen tenderly wrapped their arms around them, and gently escorted them back to their cars.

The reunion of the girls with their families was a bittersweet moment, as tears of joy bathed the faces of all. The gratitude heaped on Armand was so profound that the Scandinavian Heritage Association decided to fund a new addition to the Heritage Park. Along with future plans to erect a bronze statue of Hans Christian Andersen, they would also have one made of Armand Arnolfini. He would be the only non-Scandinavian to be honored there, but one surely worthy of the tribute.

Two days later, Armand returned home satiated and content, knowing that the lives of the three girls were slowly getting back to normal. Much therapy and support would be needed, but the dark days of horror were behind them as the glorious light of salvation now shone upon them. Armand smiled with a deep sense of gratitude, as he walked into his house and hugged his beautiful wife and two precious children.

Animal Delight

Several days after returning home from North Dakota, Armand sat at the dining room table with his wife and kids eating filet mignon, mashed potatoes, and vegetables.

After seeing the bloody slaughter house in North Dakota Armand had abstained from eating meat for several days, but the succulent flavor was too hard to resist.

"Hey, Pop," little Jack said. "Can I have another filet?"

Andrea looked at Jack and shook her head. "No. That will be enough, Jack. You already had two pieces."

Artemisia's eyes widened. "Then can I have it? I only had one."

Armand interjected, "Why not eat more broccoli or carrots. It's important to have a balanced diet."

Andrea gazed back at Jack. "Do you hear that, Jack?"

Jack pouted, then quickly turned on the melodrama. "Well, I'm just tryin' to help out, Mom. I hate to see good meat go to waste."

Andrea stifled a chuckle and started collecting dirty dishes, as she replied, "Nice try, darling, but I'll cut it up and put it in a nice healthy salad for tomorrow. Nothing goes to waste around here, kiddo. So, if you're done, hand me your plate."

Just then the phone rang. Artemisia jumped up and sprinted into the den to answer it. As Andrea and Armand started clearing the table, Artemisia called out from the den. "Ah heck. Dad, it's for *you*!"

Armand handed the dirty plate to his wife and strolled into the den. Artemisia handed him the phone with a sad yet adorable pout on her face. As he grasped the phone, he said, "I guess you thought it was Johnny?"

Artemisia sighed as she blushed. "No! I thought it was Cindy."

"Okay, sweetheart," he said as he grasped the phone, knowing she truly wished it were Johnny. He recalled the secrecy and embarrassment of youth when it came to such matters of the heart, and dropped the subject. "Thank you, honey" he said simply, as Artemisia lumbered back into the dining room.

Armand placed the phone to his ear. "Hello?"

"Good evening, Mr. Arnolfini. This is Stan Logan of Stan Logan's Supermarkets."

"Oh! Hello. I frequent your stores quite often. What can I do for you?"

"Well, you see, Mr. Arnolfini, I have a great interest in livestock, as you can imagine, but I also happen to be an avid collector of animal art. I have many exquisite paintings and illustrations, including works by Robert Bateman and even some rare originals by John Audubon."

"Ah, yes," Armand replied. "I'm very familiar with their work. Bateman is a modern master and Audubon was a true pioneer and ornithologist."

"Well, yes, however they're just two of many in my growing collection. You see, I recently purchased three new paintings by a lesser-known artist. In fact, it's a nineteenth century woman named Rosa Bonheur. Are you familiar with her work?"

Armand smiled at the odd coincidence, knowing that Rosa loved to paint cattle, the main course he and his family just had for dinner. "In fact, I am," Armand replied with enthusiasm. "Especially with her painting in the Met, *The Horse Fair*. It's a massive canvas, about sixteen-feet-wide. Its truly a masterpiece of technical skill and dramatic composition."

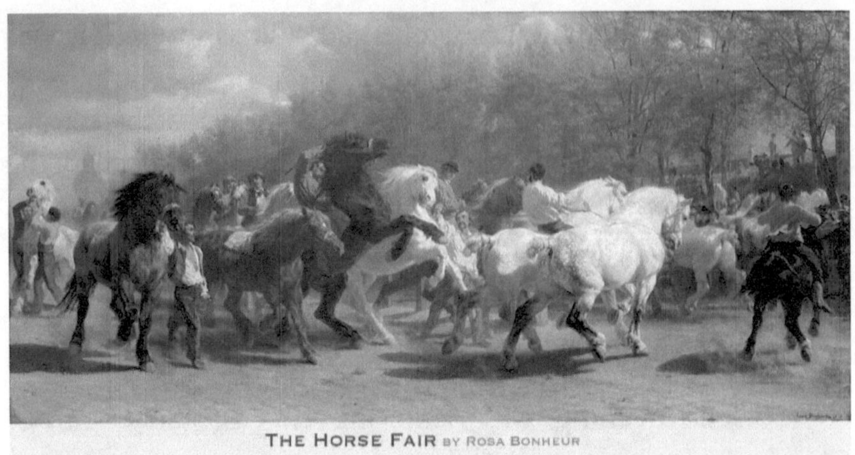

THE HORSE FAIR BY ROSA BONHEUR

"Well, I'm delighted to hear that," Logan said. "Not that I'm surprised, mind you. You're reputation was highly lauded by Harold Rittenhouse at the Metropolitan."

"Ah, yes, Harold and I are good friends," Armand replied. "So what's this in reference to?"

"Well, Harold had also recently purchased a work by Rosa Bonheur, and, not too surprisingly, from the same art dealer."

"So does Harold believe there's a problem with his acquisition's authenticity?" Armand inquired.

"Yes, Mr. Arnolfini. He believes his painting is either a forgery or misattributed to Bonheur, which might very well be by another artist. However, since we both purchased our acquisitions from the same man, he suspects some or all of mine might be fakes or misattributed. Hence, that's the reason for my call, Mr. Arnolfini. I would like to hire you. Are you available to come to my office?"

"Certainly. Would tomorrow morning around nine o'clock work?"

"That's perfect," Logan replied. He issued Armand his corporate address, and then wrapped up the conversation with a cordial "Until tomorrow, good-bye."

Nine o'clock the next morning, Armand pulled up to Stan Logan's office in Danbury, Connecticut, in his '57 Corvette. He strolled into the lobby and was directed to Logan's office at the end of the corridor. With a knock, and a response to come in, Armand entered.

The large room was decorated with rough-sawed pine planking on the walls, a large bronze statue of a cow, and a variety of paintings featuring animals in nature or on farms. The two men shook hands as Stan said, "Well, it's a pleasure to meet you in person. You cut out one helluva reputation for yourself, Mr. Arnolfini."

"Well, it's been one heck of a rodeo," Armand said, as he glanced at Logan's Western-styled office. "I've come across all kinds in this business. The good, the bad, and the ugly." As Logan chuckled, appreciating his cowboy and spaghetti western references, Armand glanced at his broad collection, once again. "And you cut out one hell-of-an art collection."

"Thank you," Stan said. "It didn't happen over night. I'll tell you that much."

"I can certainly believe that," Armand replied.

Meanwhile, Stan escorted him to the three new paintings. "Well, let's get right down to it," he said. He pointed to the first painting. "This one is a preliminary study that Rosa Bonheur had painted for *Weaning the Calves,* which I was told was created sometime in 1879."

"Ah, yes," Armand said with delight. "I'm familiar with the final work, which also resides at the Met." Armand leaned closer, scrutinizing the finesse of Rosa's brushwork and exquisite detail. He leaned back. "No need to show Harold Rittenhouse this one. Its authentic all right."

"Dear me, you can verify it that quickly?" Logan said, surprised.

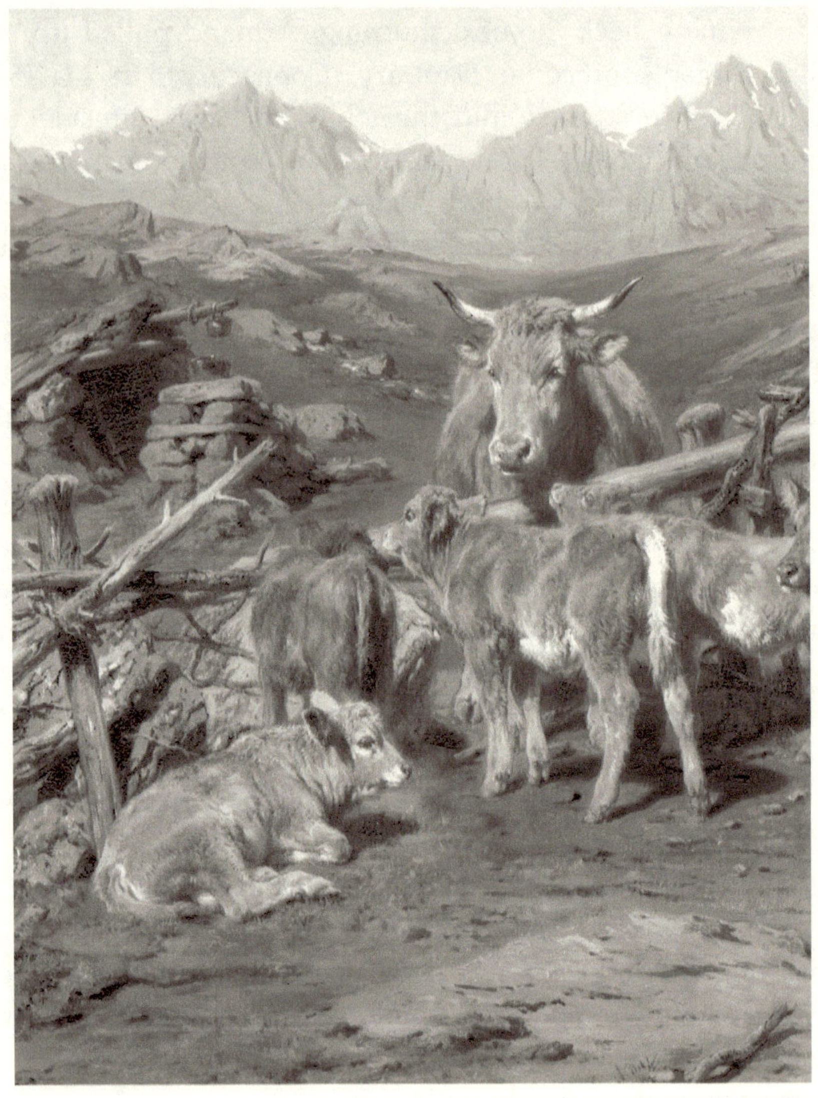

"Rosa had a very unique touch in the way she handled her brushstrokes, Mr. Logan. In fact, Edouard Dubufe had painted a portrait of her but didn't have the expertise of painting animals. So he let Rosa add a bull to his painting. The signature style of each artist is as clear as day, with Rosa's being far superior. Rosa had the rare ability to create animals that looked alive, not stiff or like plastic."

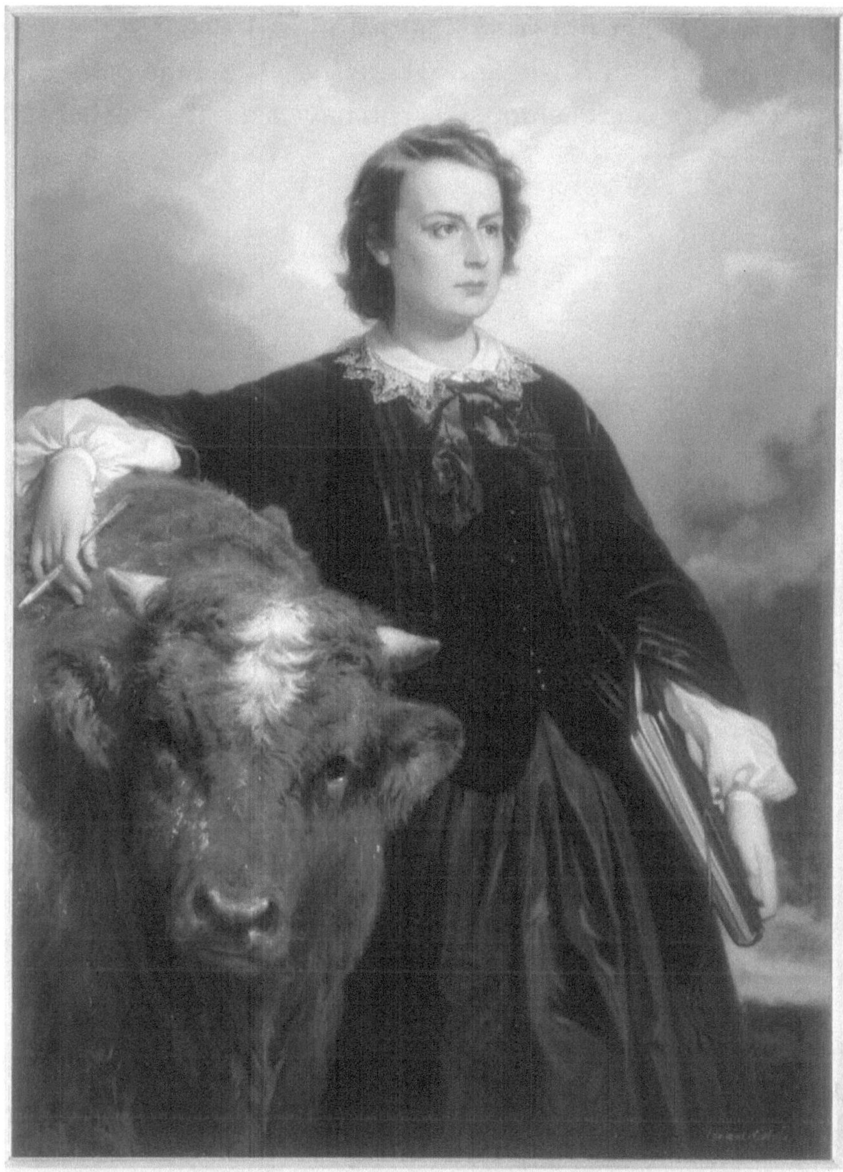

ROSA BONHEUR BY EDOUARD DUBUFE BULL BY ROSA

Glancing back at the painting of calves, Armand added, "And this is unquestionably Rosa's handiwork. I noticed she utilized a better color palette on this one as compared to her full-scale final painting. I also like the way she cropped it in closer and where she placed the baby calf. It's very nice compositionally. You have a great piece here."

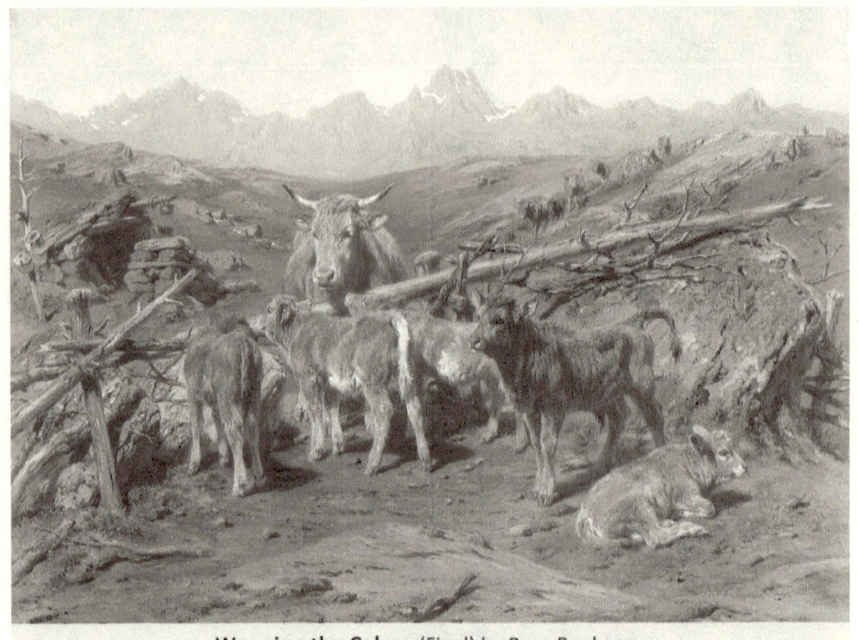

Weaning the Calves (Final) by Rosa Bonheur

Stan wiped his forehead and sighed. "Thank heavens. I thought so myself. But having that confirmed by an expert is a great relief." Stan pointed to the second acquisition. "This one is entitled *Blue Jay in Winter*. I simply fell in love with this one. Unlike my Audubon works, which are illustrations that focus primarily on the bird, this one has such a unique composition and looks quite real and peaceful in its natural environment."

Armand leaned closer, eyeing up the work for several minutes, then leaned back to take in the overall arrangement. "It is quite beautiful, Mr. Logan. As you say, the composition and technique are very compelling. The bird, rotted tree stumps and snow are all very well rendered. But two red flags spring up in my mind."

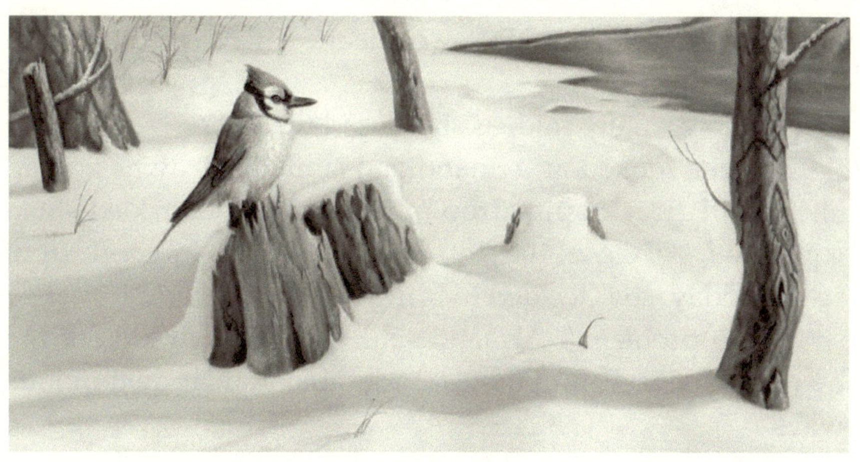

Logan's proud grin withered. "Oh dear. What are they?"

Armand looked at Stan. "First, Rosa Bonheur, to my knowledge, didn't paint birds. Her forte was large animals: horses, cows, oxen, sheep, goats and the like. Second, the brushstrokes are not the same. Rosa used heavier layers of paint. Now, I could be wrong, since I have not seen the full catalog of her works in person, as well as the fact that there's never been a solo exhibition of her works in recent memory."

Armand paused a moment, then continued, "You see, sadly Rosa's works went out of favor after she died. Realism waned as Impressionism became in vogue. And we can't ignore the fact that Rosa was a woman, which also contributed to her being unfairly marginalized and not readily promoted."

"Well, that's another reason for these acquisitions, Mr. Arnolfini. You see, I have three daughters, and I would never want their lives or achievements to be diminished or ignored."

Just then, Logan's ten-year old daughter, Sally, popped her head in from the side door. "I heard you say *daughters,* Pa. Do you need us?"

Stan chuckled. "No, sweetheart. I'll have lunch with you later. Okay?"

"Okay," Sally said, as she closed the door.

Logan looked at Armand and smiled. "Sally has radar. She could hear a pin drop." As Armand chuckled, Stan continued, "Excuse the intrusion, my girls are off from school today, so I decided to bring them to work."

"No problem," Armand said. "I have two kids of my own. One of each, and they *are* adorable in their own unique ways."

"Yes," Stan said, his face now pensive. "Those girls changed my life," he said with deep reflection. "I must confess, I was a bit of a male chauvinist before I had them. Now I would defend them with my life, and fight for women's equality. That's why my intentions are to present a Rosa Bonheur Exhibition. And that's also why I contacted Harold Rittenhouse." He glanced nervously at his new acquisitions. "But if these works prove to be fakes or misattributed, then I fear the Metropolitan will shelve the idea."

"Well, let's not lose hope," Armand said. "I happen to have some pull at the Met, and together we can pull some strings."

"But I fear if these paintings are not authentic works by Bonheur, we're doomed." Logan turned anxiously and pointed to the last painting. "This one is entitled *Heronry*. Please tell me this is by Rosa?"

Once again, Armand leaned in and scrutinized the painting. It featured a mother heron, while its two chicks sat in a nest on a branch, amid marshes. Armand leaned back. "I wish I could be more supportive, Mr. Logan. But although this painting is quite endearing, it also raises the same two red flags."

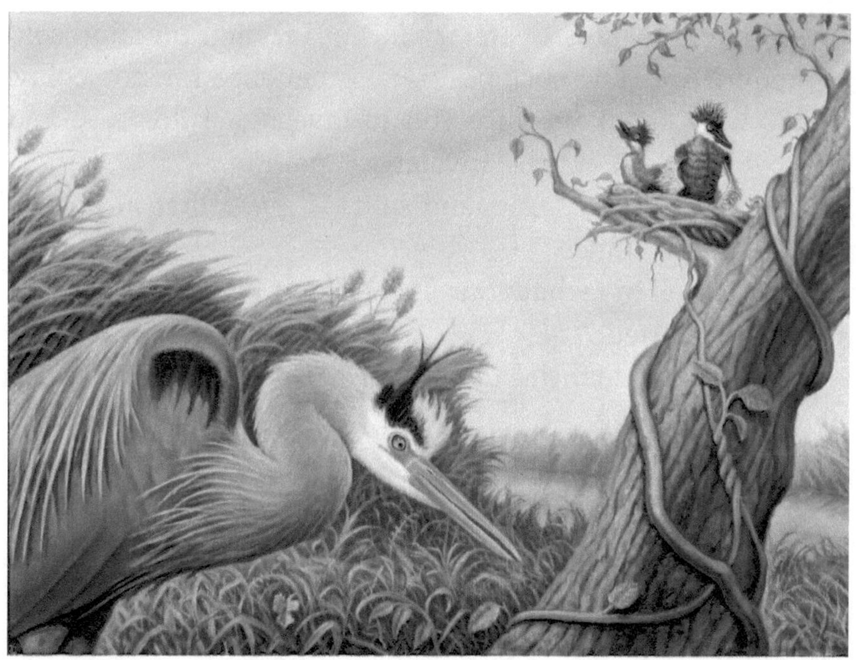

"Oh dear Lord," Logan sighed as he shook his head dejectedly. "I hate being taken. Somehow I strongly doubt that the seller knew, he must have been duped himself."

"Who was it?" Armand inquired. "I might know him."

"I believe many people know him, at least in France. It was Alain de Boissieu, noted French military hero and son-in-law of Charles de Gaulle."

Armand's eyes widened. "Yes, of course. Well, I don't know him personally, but I've read about him. I wasn't aware he dabbled in art."

"Well, that's why I don't believe he's aware that these two works are not authentic, including the piece he sold to Harold Rittenhouse, entitled *Night Owl*."

"So," Armand said as he pensively rubbed his chin. "We have three mysterious bird paintings."

"Yes, and worse yet, I have tried to call Alain de Boissieu several times, yet with no response. I know he's a busy man, but his secretary keeps giving me the cold shoulder. And I'm not one to have patience for horseplay. That's why I'd like to hire you to investigate this case and get to the bottom of these mysterious paintings."

"I'm all yours," Armand said. "I guess that means I'll be heading to France."

"Just tell me what your fees are and I'll cut you a check to get you started."

With the financial details set, Armand bid Stan *adieu* and took his leave.

Two days later Armand landed at Charles de Gaulle Airport. He rented a car and drove into the heart of Paris. Being one of Armand's favorite cities, he took his time to tour and admire its distinct architecture before finally arriving at Alain de Boissieu's office.

The secretary asked him to wait and, forty-three minutes later, she said, "You can go in now."

Armand sighed, heavily, got up and walked headlong into Boissieu's office. Boissieu looked up from his majestic mahogany desk with ornate gold hardware, and said, "*Bonjour, Monsieur* Arnolfini. Have a seat."

Armand took a seat as his eyes scanned the office, from the flamboyant furniture to the original oil paintings on the walls by Gerome, David, and Bouguereau. Suppressing his displeasure about the delay, he said cordially, "Excellent taste in art, I see."

"Indeed, and all French," Alain said with a proud air.

"Well, I suppose your war record for defending France justifies that. But I'm here on Stan Logan's behalf, and to a lesser extent Harold Rittenhouse's. They each bought paintings from you, paintings that they were led to believe were by Rosa Bonheur."

Alain's distinguished face turned militantly stern. "Are you insinuating that *I* sold them fakes?"

"I'm merely saying that they are *not* by Rosa Bonheur. I don't suspect that you were aware of that," Armand assured him. "But after examining the works myself, and conferring with Harold Rittenhouse, we're confident that they are either forgeries or most likely misattributed, especially since none of them were signed. May I ask, how did you come by them?"

Alain's stiff face mellowed, gaining relief that the accusation wasn't personal, as he replied, "I purchased them from Philippe Boidelle. I must admit, I might not have vetted him as well as I should have, but the paintings he offered struck me with their sheer beauty. After all, you must know, most high-end purchases are made under similar conditions, as we don't throw masterpieces under an X-ray machine before purchasing them. Art is collected either for its intrinsic beauty or financial investment, and often predicated on hype."

"That's true," Armand conceded. "So, do you have Philippe Boidelle's contact information? I'd like to speak with him."

"Certainly," Alain said as he opened his desk drawer and pulled out his phone book. As he strummed through the pages, he said, "I knew Philippe during the war years. Not intimately, mind you, more so by name. So when he approached me about the works, I simply, or perhaps foolishly, let my guard down." Alain's hand stopped on a page. "Ah! Here it is."

As Alain rattled off the number, Armand jotted it down in his pad, then slipped it in his jacket pocket. "*Merci, Monsieur* de Boissieu. I appreciate your time and assistance."

"Happy hunting, *Monsieur* Arnolfini. I do hope you get

to the bottom of this. And when you do, please make sure to contact me. I don't wish to have my good name besmirched by a tainted transaction, one I was not privy to."

"I'll do my best," Armand replied, then took his leave.

Armand walked to his rented car and slid in behind the wheel. He pulled out his cell phone and dialed Philippe Boidelle's number, who answered. After introductions, Armand asked, "I'm calling about the paintings you recently sold to Stan Logan and Harold Rittenhouse. Specifically, the three bird paintings."

"*Oui*, what about them, *Monsieur?*"

"It has been revealed that they are either forgeries or have been mistakenly attributed to Rosa Bonheur. Since they are not signed leads us to believe that they were misattributed. That being the case, they are not worth the price you asked for and received."

Philippe's voice rose with agitation. "How dare you accuse me of trickery, *Monsieur* Arnolfini! I have a sterling reputation and prominent standing among my peers. I'll have you know that I served under the Head of Government Pierre Laval during the war as his Minister of Art & Culture and have legitimate contacts and dealings within the art world."

Upon hearing the name Pierre Laval, Armand's ears perked up. He knew Laval was in the Vichy government, which parlayed with the Nazis. Now even more curious, Armand inquired, "So, tell me, which contacts do you have in the art business, Philippe?"

"Plenty, that's all you need to know!"

"Actually, it's not. I've been hired to investigate this matter and I *will* get answers, from you or someone else. And I'm very persistent, Philippe. So you can try to waste my time, but eventually I *will* get to the bottom of this."

Philippe's huff was enough to rattle Armand's ear through the phone, as he irritably complied. "Very well, *Monsieur* Arnolfini. I've been in this business for over half a century. I am seventy-nine years old and I've dealt with men like Paolo Savini, Camille Boucere, Rene Gimpel, Ira Burnbaum, and many others. Feel free to snoop around and ask any dealers alive in Paris today, and they'll know my good name."

At this point, Armand was now focusing not on Philippe's name but on the name Rene Gimpel, which Philippe just mentioned. Armand was well aware that Gimpel had been a Jewish art collector in Paris during the Second World War. During the Nazi occupation, Rene's business and home were confiscated and his art collection looted, by either Nazis or Vichy henchmen. Gimpel had fled Paris but was captured in the French Riviera. Thrown on a train, Rene was sent to a concentration camp, where he met his fate, along with six million other poor souls.

Armand's mind was reeling faster with each word that was flowing out of Philippe's rotten mouth. "I will indeed investigate your good name, Philippe. Be assured of that. But I'd like to know the provenance of those three bird paintings. How did you acquire them and what's their history?"

It was clear Philippe was becoming aggravated with the interrogation, as his grunts grew louder. "This is the last question I will answer, *Monsieur* Arnolfini. I bought them from Samuel Hartford from his Hartford Gallery in London. He, too, has a reputable name. So feel free to badger him to your heart's content. But I'm too old and tired for this petty nonsense. Our conversation is over. *Au revoir, Monsieur* Arnolfini!"

Hearing an abrupt click, Armand likewise clicked off his cell phone. Perturbed, he stared out the car window in total silence, except for the busy conversation going on inside his head. Armand's cerebral conference was posing a series of questions and possible answers, trying to piece the puzzle together. Moments later, Armand picked up his cell phone and called information, asking for the number of the Hartford Gallery in London.

Armand dialed the number, and Samuel Hartford answered. "Greetings! Samuel Hartford here. How may I help you?"

"Hello, Samuel. My name is Armand Arnolfini. I'm a private eye working on behalf of clients in America who bought the three bird paintings you sold to Philippe Boidelle."

The cell phone was dead silent, until Samuel finally responded, "Oh, yes, yes of course, ol' boy. I gather you're referring to those three lovely paintings by Rosa Bonheur."

"Yes, I'm trying track down their provenance, and like Paul McCartney says, it's been a 'long and winding road.' Can you tell me how you acquired them?"

"Certainly, ol' boy," Samuel replied with a British bounce in his voice. "And I like the bloody Beatles reference, ol' boy. Anyhow, as you might know, my good fellow, Rosa Bonheur had lived in the United Kingdom for several years, producing a splendid assortment of works. Let me tell you, Rosa was a dandy piece of work herself. In those days women weren't believed to be artistic, you know, and were stymied by bigoted blokes in high places. Yet good ol' Rosa smashed the taboos, she did. She not only painted as good or better than most men, but dear ol' Rosa also smoked cigars, wore trousers, and wasn't afraid to hide her lesbian lifestyle. She was a bloody dynamo, I tell you. A real rebel rouser."

Armand wasn't looking for her biography, as he was privy to many aspects of Rosa's volatile life, yet Samuel couldn't bridle his passion, as he galloped onward. In his British accent, he said that in order to wear trousers, Rosa had to obtain permission from the police. With a chuckle and a snort, he continued on, stating that her plea was rather simple, namely that in order to study livestock she had to go into the muddy marketplace. Hence, the necessity to wear trousers and boots.

With a hefty guffaw, he then added, "I say, ol' boy, isn't that a kicker?"

Before Armand could respond, Samuel droned on, "And here's another bloomin' knee slapper: When our dear ol' lesbian was asked 'What are your feelings about men?' Good ol' Rosa said, 'I only like the bulls I paint!'"

Samuel's bluster blared through the receiver, forcing Armand to pull the phone away from his ear, only to return it to hear: "How devilishly divine is that, ol' boy? Could you bloody well blame her?" Without a lull, Samuel went on, "As I see it, the attempt to prohibit Rosa from the marketplace was by men who were bigger horses' asses than the studs they sold."

To that Armand couldn't resist chuckling, while Samuel couldn't be silenced. He wished that Rosa had stayed in England, yet she had packed up and moved to France. She lived out the remainder of her life there with her first lover, Natalie Micas, then with the American painter Anna Elizabeth Klumpke. "All three lasses are buried together in Paris," he said. "In fact, you can—"

"Excuse me! Samuel!" Armand finally cut in. "Thank you for the history lesson, but I'm quite familiar with Rosa's unconventional and impressive life. What I had asked you, and need an answer to, is the provenance of the three bird paintings you sold to Philippe? So please, can you answer that?"

After a brief moment of silence, Samuel uttered, "Oh, blimey. Yes, of course, ol' boy. I have a bloody bad habit of wandering off the farm, don't I? My apologies. But to answer your question, I acquired those exceptionally fine paintings from a distinguished family here in London. Their lineage, I'll have you know, extends back to the actual time of Rosa's stay here. So I assure you, they are authentic Rosa Bonheur originals."

Armand shook his head, still disturbed by one of the red flags that had initially arisen upon inspection. "But Mr. Hartford, in all my searches of Rosa's works I don't recall seeing paintings of birds. She loved large animals: cattle, oxen, goats and the like. I don't claim to know every piece by her, as I'm sure many were lost or misplaced, especially due to her being a woman. But I find it odd that you unearthed not one but three paintings of various birds."

"Mr. Arnolfini, ol' boy. From what you say, *you,* and dare I say, most of us, are indeed not privy to her entire oeuvre. As such, none of us can say unequivocally that birds didn't enamor Rosa. Can we?"

"Well, yes, there *is* a void in her catalog. But these birds still strike me as a little odd. Not to mention that the brushstrokes of these three paintings differ significantly from her known works."

"My good man. As an art expert, you bloody well know, many artists go through periods of experimentation until they master their voice, or more pointedly, their unique style of expression. Therefore, my good fellow, these bloody works might simply be from one of those transitional periods."

Armand nodded, knowing that to be true, yet shook his head to himself. "Point taken, Mr. Hartford. Artists do go through periods of development. I'll leave it at that, for now. I thank you for your time."

"It's been bloody good speaking with you, ol' boy. And if you're ever in London, do stop by," Samuel replied, ending with a final, "Cheers!"

Armand clicked off his cell phone and remained sitting in his car, the wheels of his mind turning while the car's wheels remained idle. The long trail he had followed to discover the location of the paintings' origins had finally arrived, yet he still was no closer to solving the initial and most important quandary: Who created these bird paintings?

Armand felt sure they were not by Rosa's hand, despite the valid assumption of being from a transitional period of experimentation. He also knew that his gut instincts were often the best compass, and he now knew what direction to take next.

He lifted the cell phone and dialed for information. Receiving the phone number of *Le Figaro,* Armand called the newspaper and placed an ad, namely:

If anyone has information about three bird paintings, entitled *Blue Jay in Winter, Heronry,* and *Night Owl,* please call this number….

Shifting the car into gear, Armand sighed, then smiled as he headed to the Louvre. It was time to clear his mind of the case and enjoy some culture while waiting for calls to his ad.

Armand's first stop was to view Leonardo's, nay, the world's, most famous painting—the *Mona Lisa*. Despite having visited the original numerous times, its beauty never failed to amaze Armand. Yet, he was also quite aware of what many others failed to see. That, he knew, was for three main reasons:

First, the famous painting had been encased in a bullet-proof display due to potential theft or vandalism, hence limiting close inspections; second, few realized it was such a small painting, expecting its size to mirror its enormous fame; and lastly, and perhaps most importantly, was the unique and pioneering process Leonardo used to create this small wonder.

And this is what Armand sought to gaze upon once again. Being granted close proximity, due to his illustrious credentials, Armand stepped right up to the display case as his eyes filled with wonder. Leonardo's new technique (of building up layers of glazes) gave the painting a special luminosity and 3-D realism that no other painter in his day ever thought possible, or could ever rival. Moreover, his unique three-quarter view pose would become a template for numerous portraits henceforth.

With his eyes and heart illuminated, Armand then strolled over to view Leonardo's *Saint Anne*, and then on to one of Armand's favorites, Leonardo's *Virgin of the Rocks*.

Strolling through the majestic corridors of the Louvre, Armand's eyes devoured the random statues and string of paintings that decorated the walls. Stopping to admire the *Astronomer* by Jan Vermeer, then *The Bolt* by Fragonard, and a series of works by Rubens, Delacroix, David, Rembrandt, and others, Armand unexpectedly came across *Young Christian Martyr* by Paul Delaroche.

Taken in by the work's eerie yet shimmering beauty, Armand couldn't help but think about the many great artists who never gained the attention or fame they deserved. It was a perpetual irritant that routinely incited his frustration, as well as remorse over the folly of humankind.

After that pensive foray, Armand moved along and located Elisabeth Vigee-Lebrun's *Self-Portrait with Her Daughter, Julie*.

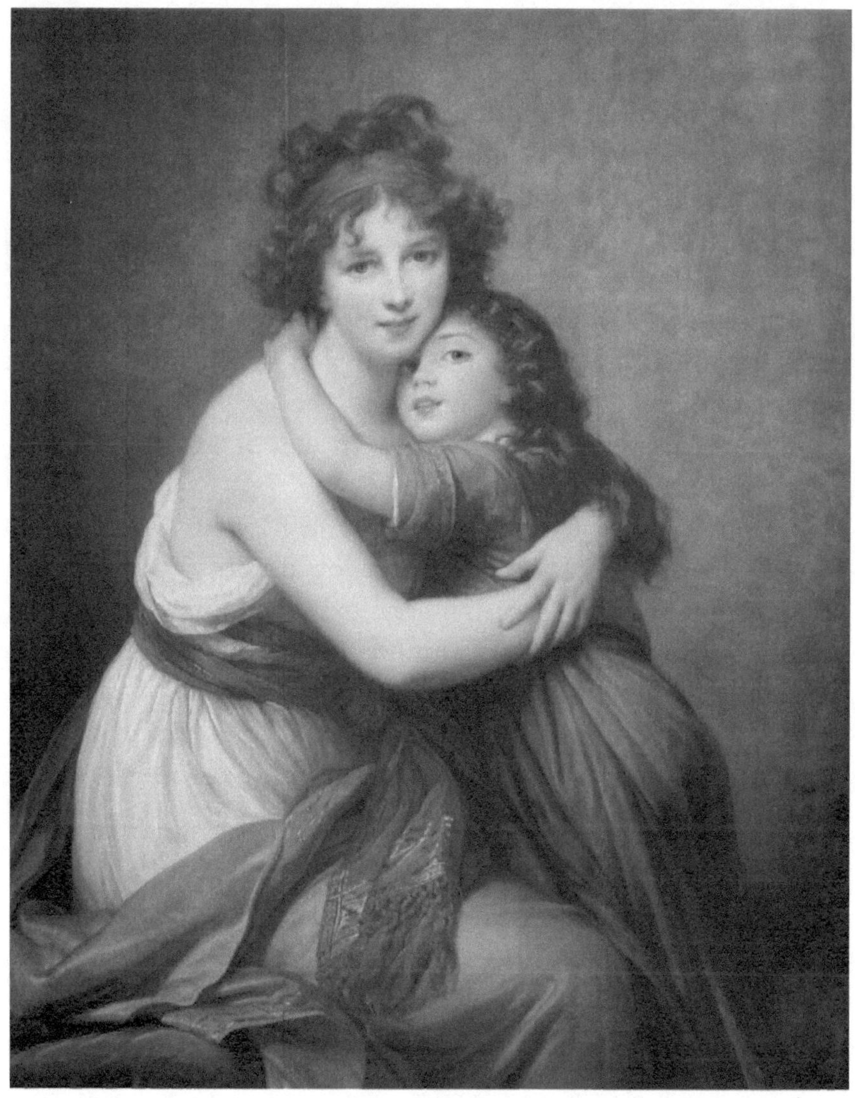

Once again, Armand reflected on how women's voices and visions had been silenced for centuries, wondering what their views on life would have added to our knowledge of the past.

While gazing at Vigee-Lebrun's delicate and intimate self-portrait with her daughter Armand was struck by the polar difference in Rosa Bonheur's paintings of wild animals in nature. No sooner had that thought entered his mind, than his cell phone rang. With a jolt, he reached into his pocket, slipped out the phone, and whispered, "Hello?"

The voice said, "Hello, Armand, Stan Logan here. I'm just calling to see how things are moving along in France?"

Armand walked toward the exit, and replied, "Well, it took some time to track down the various sellers of the bird paintings, Mr. Logan. Evidently they went through several other people's hands before landing in Alain de Boissieu's possession."

"So, I imagine Alain has no knowledge of them being forgeries or misattributed, correct?"

"I'm inclined to say yes," Armand replied. "Alain is the least likely suspect thus far. However, nothing can be ruled out at this point." As Armand exited the museum and descended the stairs, he continued, "I have been told that the paintings originated in England, during Rosa's stay there, but I'm still skeptical. I have things in motion that will hopefully settle that score soon enough. I'll keep you posted on my progress or setbacks in the days ahead."

"Very well, Armand. Thank you, and when you can, try to enjoy the beauties that Paris has to offer."

"Oh, I already have. I just left the Louvre."

Logan laughed. "If I would have bet on that I could've been a heck of a lot richer!"

"Well, I never let a chance to expand my artistic horizons pass, Mr. Logan. Until we speak again, be well."

"Will do, and same to you."

Armand reached his rented car, then drove to *Le Bizet*, one of his favorite restaurants, one name after the famous composer of *Carmen*. He greeted Marcel, his friend and *garçon*, and placed his order. Taking a sip of his Chardonnay, he then enjoyed an assortment of fine French cuisine, from *escargot* and *aubergines* to the main course, *veal duxelles*.

Armand leaned back and rubbed his stomach. He gazed out the window, gaining a splendid view of the Arc de Triomphe. He recollected how the arch was commissioned by Napoleon for his victories at war, then gazed down at his Napoleon pastry. He smiled as he lifted his fork, and thought, *well, you're losing this battle, Napoleon.* Finishing his dessert with a cup of cappuccino, Armand wiped his mouth, satiated and relishing the additional perk of working in Paris.

Before retiring to his hotel, Armand stopped at a crepe vendor along Rue Saint-Saëns to have a raspberry-and-cream-filled crepe, another vice he couldn't resist.

Over the next three days Armand was pleasantly surprised at the number of phone calls he received from his ad. However, out of sixteen calls, not one panned out as genuine or productive. From hair-brained claims that they themselves had painted the works but could not describe them, to clowns making bird-brained jokes about the bird paintings, Armand was losing hope, when his cell phone rang again.

With a sigh, Armand rolled his eyes and said, *"Salut,"* as he sat down.

"Bojour, is this Mr. Arnolfini?"

"Oui. And you are?" Armand asked, as he wearily sank into the couch, his eyelids heavy.

"I am Sarah Burnbaum. I'm calling in response to your ad in *Le Figaro*."

With a yawn, he inquired, "And? What do you know about these paintings?"

"I know that they are all mine. Or rather property of my family's estate."

Lethargically, Armand rested his elbow on the arm of the couch, with his hand and phone propping up his drowsy head. "And how do you know that?"

"Because they were looted by the Vichy regime during the Second World War."

Armand's eyes widened as he sat up straight and grasped the cell phone tighter. "Do you have proof, Ms. Burnbaum?"

"I most certainly do. And you may call me Sarah."

"Well, Sarah, to start, do you mind if I ask a basic question, namely can you describe the three paintings?"

"By all means. The *Night Owl* features an owl perched on a branch amid a foggy landscape with a river. There is a full moon in the night sky, peering through the clouds."

Armand smiled. "Correct! And how about *Heronry*?"

Sarah's voice resounded with affection as she said, "Oh, that one was my favorite as a young girl. I used to admire it every time I walked past it in our living room. It features a mother heron with its two chicks perched in a nest. And those chicks were simply adorable."

A grin swiped across Armand's face, as he stood up and asked, "And the last painting, *Blue Jay in Winter*?"

"That one was equally beautiful, yet serene. It was actually a rather unique snow scene. I recall the day my father bought it. It features a blue jay perched on a rotted tree stump, surrounded by snow. There were a few barren trees, and a lake in the background. I'll always remember it for its elongated horizontal dimension. Does that satisfy your curiosity?"

"For the most part, yes."

"What do you mean *for the most part*?

"Well, although I do believe you, Sarah, you could be someone who saw these works at an exhibition or gallery somewhere, or perhaps in a rare art book."

A hum came through Armand's receiver. "I suppose that could be true. However, I have my father's invoices for each work, as well as old black and white photos of those paintings hanging in our living room. My father, Ira, was a well-known art dealer along with his friend, Rene Gimpel."

Armand twitched upon hearing the name Gimpel, as Sarah's voice suddenly deepened with emotion. "Well, you see, that was before the Vichy government stormed in to our house. They took possession of our home and all of our valuables. Then the monsters forced my parents, brother, and me onto a train and shipped us to Dachau." Her voice buckled. "That was when…well…it was hell on earth. I was the only one to survive."

Armand's throat tightened with a grievous lump, as he said, "That's very disturbing to hear, Sarah, and a compelling story." Armand paused a moment, then continued, "I'm so sorry. My heart goes out to you and all those who suffered. It was one of the darkest periods in human history. I had read about Rene Gimpel's plight, but not about your family's. I would like to meet you, right away, if that's possible?"

"By all means," Sarah replied.

She offered Armand her address, and thirty minutes later, Armand arrived at Sarah's home on the distant outskirts of Paris.

The estate was impressive from the outside, but Armand was even more taken aback by the treasures within. As he gazed at Sarah's art collection, he found it quite exquisite and diverse. It included unknown works by great masters along with intriguing works by unknown masters. His eyes eventually landed on a painting of a bright yellow tanager perched on a branch amid muted greenery and a vivid blue sky.

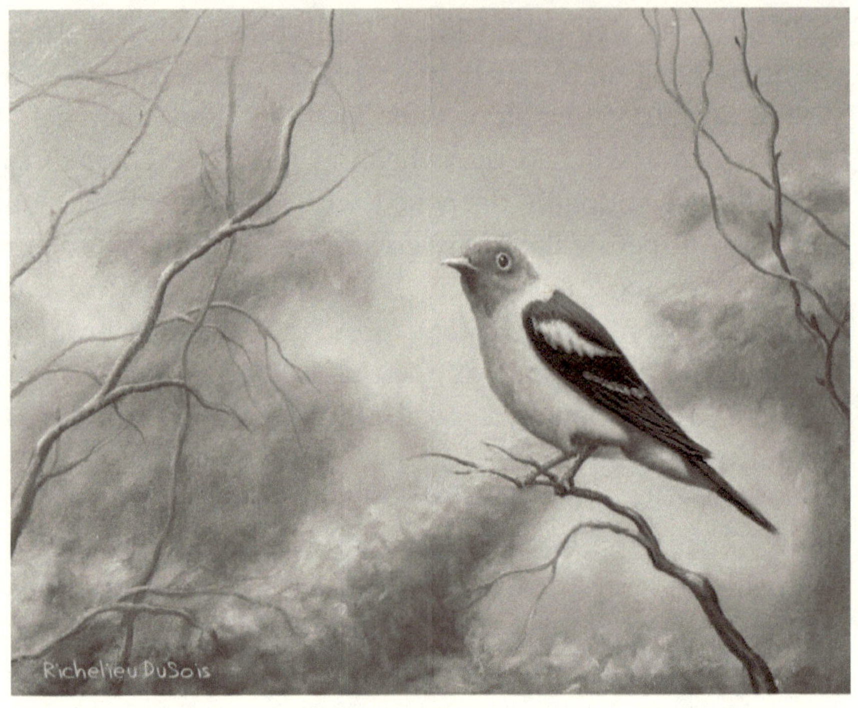

Sarah approached Armand's side. "I'm curious, of all the large and beautiful works I have here, you've stopped to admire this small painting. Why?"

Armand glanced at Sarah, then back at the painting. "It's not that it's better than the others, it's just that, well—"

"Does it look familiar to you?"

"Yes, it does," Armand said.

"That's because this one, entitled *Tanager,* is by the same artist as the three bird paintings you mentioned in your ad," Sarah said.

"Yes, of course!" Armand exclaimed with a sense of *déjà vu*. "I've become better acquainted with this artist's technique and brushstrokes." Glancing at the signature on the painting, then back at Sarah, he said, "The other paintings weren't signed, but this one is." He smiled. "So they were all painted by Richelieu DuSois, not Rosa Bonheur."

Sarah smiled. "Yes, they were *not* by Rosa Bonheur. Richelieu was a contemporary of hers. Unfortunately, he was overlooked or ignored and remains relatively unknown today."

Armand nodded as he stroked his chin. "I knew it had to be someone else's work." His smile withered to a frown as his recurring pet peeve took hold. "Yet, it's sad so many great artists never got the limelight or appreciation they deserved."

"Life in general is not fair," Sarah said dolefully.

Armand's fingers dropped from his chin as his shoulders wilted, embarrassed. "Of course, you and your family know that better than most. I can't imagine the horror you lived through as a young girl, and the never-ending pain you've been forced to live with every day since." An uneasy moment of silence pervaded the opulent room, with its gold chandeliers, Corinthian columns, and array of priceless artwork on the walls.

Finally Sarah said, "Yes, it has *not* been easy. But allow me to show you what you came for." She grasped a manila folder from an end table and slid out several old, black-and-white photos from 1938. Each featured the bird paintings when they hung in her parents' living room in Paris.

As Armand's eyes scanned the cracked and faded photos, Sarah slipped the invoices before his eyes, and said, "Beyond these documents, my grandfather knew Richelieu DuSois personally. So there's no question as to who the real artist is."

Armand looked up into her sincere and solemn eyes. "Thank you for taking the time to show me all these documents and photos. I never got the chance to even tell you; your three bird paintings have surfaced in America. My client, Mr. Stan Logan, along with Harold Rittenhouse at the

Metropolitan Museum of Art, had purchased them from Alain de Boissieu."

Sarah's eyes widened with excitement, as he went on, "And Alain had purchased them from Philippe Boidelle, who in turn said he purchased them from Samuel Hartford in London."

Sarah shook her head and said wittily, "Dear Lord, those birds surely took flight, didn't they?"

Armand laughed. "Indeed they have. But have no fear, Mr. Logan has every intention of returning them to you, and I suspect Harold Rittenhouse at the Met will do the same."

"That's fantastic!" Sarah exclaimed, as she spontaneously embraced Armand with deep emotion. "What a joy it will be to see my childhood memories brought back to life again."

Armand smiled. "And that brings *me* great joy to bring you this good news, Sarah." As they separated, he said, "However, this case, for me, involves a mystery that is still unsolved."

Sarah's smile withered. "And what is that?"

"The paintings have been misattributed to Rosa Bonheur, and Misters Logan and Rittenhouse both bought them at substantially higher prices than what they should be appraised for."

A frown etched itself across Sarah's face. "Ah, yes, the inequitable world of art appraisals. Let me tell you, the joy those paintings brought to my family and me far exceed whatever price tag they would pin on them." She paused, then continued, "But, yes, I can see how your investors would be eager to find the culprit who sold them as Bonheur originals. That's *if* they even knew they were wrongly labeled themselves. Correct?"

"That's a distinct possibility," Armand conceded. "But I suspect wrongdoing by one of these art dealers. Your painting of the tanager was signed; yet the three in America weren't. I believe the signatures were intentionally erased. And knowing that you confirmed these works as authentic paintings by Richelieu DuSois, I need to call Samuel Hartford, once again."

Spending an additional hour with Sarah, viewing her lovely art collection and engaging in conversations about her turbulent past, Armand then drove back to his hotel and called Samuel Hartford. Their conversation yielded nothing new however, since Hartford stuck to his story of the paintings being Bonheur originals, while also debunking Sarah's claims.

Armand knew Samuel Hartford was lying and also knew he'd have to physically visit him to extract the truth. However he would first take advantage of being in Paris, where he could meet face-to-face with Philippe Boidelle. Making the call to Philippe, Armand was told to meet him at the Créateurs Café on Rue Lamarck at ten o'clock that very evening.

Armand ate dinner, then at the prescribed time, he walked up Rue Lamarck. The sun had set hours ago, while the glow of street lamps dotted the mountainous terrain. As he stepped closer and closer to his destination, Armand gazed up at the illuminated dome of the *Sacré-Cœur* as it glistened in the night sky. The beautiful basilica sat atop Montmartre, just across the street from the Créateurs Café.

Armand stopped and pivoted to take a final glance at the panoramic view of Paris down below, then swung around and entered the café.

As he entered, there was no mistaking who Philippe Boidelle was, as the café was vacant, except for two men.

Philippe was a distinguished old man with gray hair and dressed in an expensive Italian suit. His body was lanky and looked almost too frail to touch, while his young muscular sidekick was built like a rock, with a granite face to match.

"*Bonne soirée*," the old man said. "Mr. Arnolfini, I presume?"

"Yes. And you must be Philippe Boidelle."

"*Oui*, please have a seat," he said while pointing to a table. It was nicely decorated with a gold silk tablecloth and a small vase in the center with red roses and white baby's breaths.

As the two men took their seats, Armand peered around and said, "Where is everybody? Bad food?"

Philippe laughed. "No, Mr. Arnolfini. I own this establishment. But I made sure that tonight would be set aside exclusively for our meeting, for privacy."

Armand looked up at the muscular ox, still standing with his arms crossed. "And why is *he* here?"

Again Philippe laughed. "Have no fear, Baldor may look like a bull but he's tame as a lamb. He will take good care of us." Glancing at his minion, he ordered, "Baldor, fetch us a round of espresso."

Looking back at Armand, he inquired, "Would you like a shot of Anisette or Sambuca with that? I mean, with you being Italian and all, I aim to please."

Armand smiled. "Very well, I'll have a shot of Anisette on the side. *Grazie*."

"*Prego*," Philippe said. He glanced over at Baldor. "Bring our guest a shot of Anisette, as well." Gazing back at Armand, he continued, "I always strive to be a cordial host, Mr. Arnolfini." Pulling himself closer to the table, he added, "So, how may I help you?"

"Well, as I had mentioned, my client is very concerned about the acquisitions he made. And it has come to my attention that those paintings were not by Rosa Bonheur, but rather by Richelieu DuSois."

As Baldor placed their cups of espresso before them, along with Armand's shot of Anisette, Philippe's cordial expression took a downturn, as he said, "Well, what has that got to do with *me*? I believe Alain is the one who sold your client those pieces, correct?"

"Yes, but I spoke to Alain. He informed me that he bought them from you under the impression that they were works by Rosa Bonheur. So the question is, who mislabeled these works?"

Philippe's wrinkled old smile reappeared, as he adjusted his dentures with his tongue, then pointed to the espresso. "Drink. Would you care for some biscotti with that?"

Armand sighed. "No, thank you. I appreciate the offer, Philippe, but I would really like to—"

"I reserved my café for the entire night," Philippe said. "So, please, I know you Americans are all business, but reflect upon your Italian roots, and enjoy the beauty of relaxation, conversation, as well as good food and drink. Is there anything I can get you to eat?"

Armand stifled his impatience and said, "Well, thank you Philippe for the hospitality. You are a fine host." With that, Armand took a sip of his espresso then downed the shot of Anisette in one gulp."

Philippe squinted. "I thought Italians put Anisette *in* the coffee?"

"Well, I prefer to savor their distinct flavors, keeping them pure and *authentic,* Philippe. You know, unsullied by human hands. If you get my drift?"

"Oh, I got your drift, all right," Philippe said with a

beguiling smile. "But are you starting to feel *my* drift?"

Armand squinted, confused, when suddenly Philippe's face morphed into a distorted haze. Armand blinked hard to regain clarity, yet felt himself drifting off into a dark and nebulous void. Then, all went black.

Awaking from his slumber, Armand's glassy eyes struggled to focus, while feeling that his wrists were tied behind his back. Quasi lucid, Armand realized that he was indeed tied to a chair, entrapped in a dark cellar.

Armand shook his foggy head, then peered around, only to see that he was in a storage room, filled with various foods and beverages along with menus, each imprinted with the Créateurs Café logo.

Just then, Philippe and Baldor came down the rickety set of stairs and turned up the light. As Armand squinted, Philippe said, "You've been out for an hour, a bit longer than expected."

"Nice trick, Philippe. What exactly do you plan on doing with me?"

As Baldor the bull crossed his muscular arms, looking like the Minotaur, Philippe said, "Just cooperate with us, Armand. Drop this case. That's all I ask."

Armand glanced at Baldor, then back at Philippe. "And if I can't do that, Philippe, does that mean you'll have your pit-bull tear me to shreds or possibly bury me in the backyard with his other bones?"

Philippe laughed as he ran his hand through his wispy gray hair. "Oh, Armand, you have a marvelous sense of humor. We are not the Mafia. We don't kill people."

Baldor added, "*If* we don't have to," with his gravelly voice.

Armand looked up at the goon. "Well, I knew an ox-headed thug *like you* wouldn't be a lover of fine art, Baldor."

"Aren't *you* brilliant," Baldor grunted. "No, I'm a lover of the art of pain...and making wise-guys, like *you,* rest in peace."

Philippe interjected, "Now, now, let's not get riled or ahead of ourselves, Baldor. Mr. Arnolfini is a world-renowned art connoisseur and private investigator. I'm sure he can be reasoned with, unlike the dregs who tried to expose our operation in the past." He looked back at Armand. "Isn't that right, Mr. Arnolfini?"

"Well, since you know I'm a man of reason, Philippe, untie me so we can discuss this like gentlemen and reach an equitable arrangement."

"So," Philippe said happily, "a monetary agreement will end this inquiry?"

"I can't see why not?" Armand replied. "The newspapers never knew of my secret dealings, and that's why my public reputation is pristine. I know how to keep a secret, Philippe."

Philippe looked at Baldor. "You see, not everything requires brute force or lethal solutions, Baldor. Take note of that."

"I still don't trust him, boss," Baldor growled. "I say let me work him over a bit first. I'll get the truth out of him."

"*Silencieux*!" Philippe fired back. "Enough of that!" He turned toward Armand. "I guess I've gotten too old for this line of work. But you *are* an honorable man of your word, Armand, yes?"

"Of course."

"And you *will* keep a secret, correct?"

"Most certainly."

Philippe looked at Baldor. "Untie him."

Baldor rolled his eyes with a snort, then bent over to undo the rope. Once untied, Armand sprang up, smashing

Baldor in the chin with his head! Baldor fell backward to the floor, clutching his broken jaw, as Armand lunged over and pulled the gun out of Baldor's holster.

Pointing the gun at Baldor's head, he growled, "Stay put, Baldor, or I'll make sure *you* rest in peace!" He turned toward Philippe. "And don't *you* move, either!"

Philippe, still in shock, grinded his dentures and spat, "You lying dog! You said you were a man of honor, and could keep a secret?"

"Yes, I am, and the secret is…I am a *true* man of honor, Philippe, not a loyal liar who covers for his gangster friends."

With the gun now pointed at Philippe's head, Armand said, "I know you sell art that you looted from Jewish collectors, Philippe. So I need to know, did you steal the three bird paintings or buy them from Samuel Hartford? And I warn you, I *will* use this if you lie!"

Meanwhile, Baldor had stealthily maneuvered on the floor and clutched a pipe. Springing to his feet, he attempted to hit Armand, but met with a solid kick to the gut, sending him backward. Baldor pulled a switchblade out of his pocket and charged again, but was crippled by a bullet to the thigh. Falling to the floor in agony, he spat, "You bastard!" as saliva spurted with each syllable.

Pointing the gun back at Philippe's face, Armand demanded, "I told you I'd use this, old man. Now tell me, were the bird paintings acquired from Samuel or stolen from Ira Burnbaum's collection?"

Philippe squinted with animus. "You're smarter than I assumed, Mr. Arnolfini. So you know of Ira Burnbaum?"

"Indeed I do. Ira's plight mirrored your other poor Jewish victim, Rene Gimpel. His name struck me the moment you mentioned it on our first phone conversation."

"You're well informed, Mr. Arnolfini. But there's no need to use that gun again. As you can see, I'm an old man, and a smart businessman, one who knows when he's lost a battle. So, yes, I paid Samuel to lie if he was ever contacted about the paintings."

Armand glanced at Baldor, who was still applying pressure to his bullet wound, then turned back toward Philippe. "That covers why Samuel lied to me, but what about the paintings themselves? Knowing that you worked for Laval, I assume you or he stole them from Ira Burnbaum, correct?"

Philippe sighed, almost at peace to get his dirty past off his rotten chest. "Well, yes, under direct orders by Laval, I had taken them from Ira Burnbaum's collection and we stockpiled them in a vault. However, after the war, Laval was captured by de Gaulle's regime and put on trial. He was executed. That's when I inherited the entire art collection."

"You mean *stole*!" Armand said. "A minor correction in your warped mind, I'm sure, but I guess that's the first and only time you ever told the truth, Philippe." As Philippe gritted his dentures, Armand added, "Well, thanks for the confession. But you'll need to repeat it to the police."

Armand pulled out his cell phone and made the call. Within minutes, French police arrived on the scene. They listened to Philippe's confession, then duly took him into custody, and rushed Baldor off to a hospital. Armand finalized the situation with the police, then watched as they drove off into the serene vista of night.

Standing in front of the café, Armand gazed up at the *Sacré-Cœur*. Still bathed in spotlights and glowing amid the night sky, the basilica's white luminance beautifully exemplified its heavenly aura. Exhaling a sigh of relief, Armand crossed his arms and smiled, overcome by a profound feeling of satisfaction. Not only had the mystery of the paintings' true creator been solved, but the divine justice of restoring precious works of art to Sarah had righted at least one wrong of her tragic youth. It was a moving denouement.

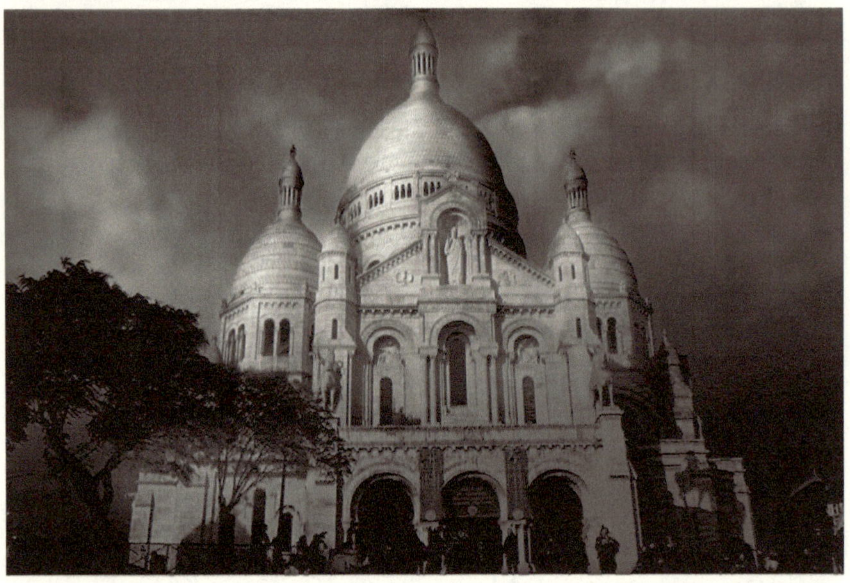

Two days later, Armand was sitting with Stan Logan in his Connecticut office.

"Well, Mr. Logan, so that's the twisted tale of woe. I'm sorry you bought two stolen works of art. But I suggest you and Harold at the Met speak with Sarah Burnbaum and make arrangements to sort out ownership."

"Indeed we will," Logan said as he scribbled out a check and handed it to Armand.

Armand glanced at the check. "Thank you, but you've made a mistake. This is five thousand dollars more than my fee."

"I know," Logan said with a warm smile. "You deserve much more, Armand. I admire men who dig through the muck to expose dirty snakes and reveal the truth. It still amazes me how so many works of art were stolen by the Nazis and their French minions during the war."

"Yes, it keeps me quite busy," Armand said solemnly. "In fact, the French government is still chided for being lax about those crimes." Armand paused, then continued, "I suppose exposing all their corrupt political and military leaders would open a can of worms. Bad enough they sent thousands of Jews to Nazi concentration camps, but stealing their homes and valuables just adds another layer of disgust upon the whole sordid affair."

"Well, I hope to focus on the brighter side of things now, Armand," Logan said as he stood up from his desk chair. "I plan on giving Sarah back her long-lost bird paintings. I only hope that she'll agree to lend them to us, so Harold Rittenhouse can present a Rosa Bonheur Exhibition at the Met, one that would also feature these bird paintings as works mistakenly attributed to Rosa. It would allow the public to assess these works for themselves."

"That's a wise and noble proposition," Armand replied as he reached over, shook his hand, and added, "I'd look forward to attending such an exhibition. Rosa's works are gaining more attention these days, and perhaps so will those of Richelieu DuSois. Thank you again for the bonus. It's greatly appreciated."

"My pleasure," Logan replied. "I'm glad to have made your acquaintance. And before you leave, I prepared a package of prime meats and steak sauces for you. You can collect it downstairs. Just ask for William Peterson, he's our supervisor."

With a smile, Armand said, "Thank you very much," then gazed at Logan's prized painting, *Preliminary Study for Weaning the Calves* by Bonheur. "We know Rosa loved to study and paint cattle, but I wonder if she loved eating steak?"

Logan nodded. "I imagine a tough, cigar-smoking gal in pants and boots like Rosa would relish a good, thick steak."

Armand chuckled. "Perhaps she would. But I'm glad her work will be getting more attention, attention long overdue and well deserved. Thanks again." With that, Armand exited Logan's office, collected his package, and headed toward home in his '57 Corvette.

An American in Paris

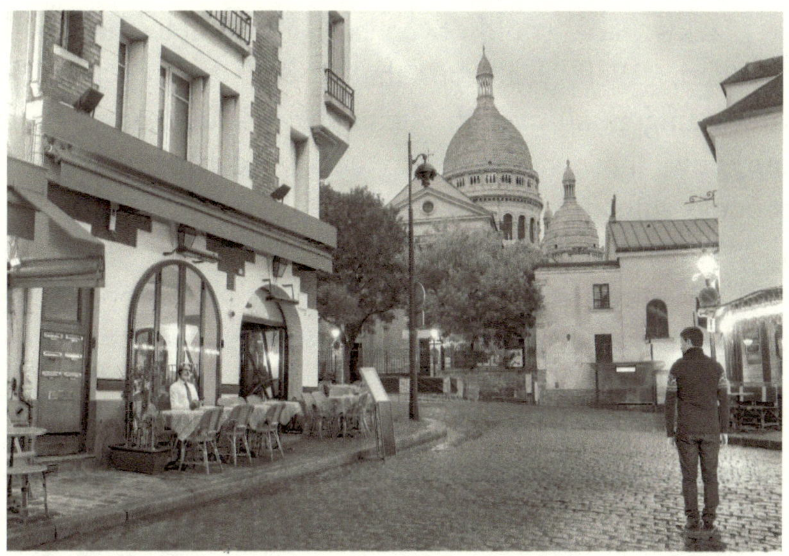

Armand was sitting in the den listening to Saint-Saëns 5th piano concerto, when little Jack ran into the room with Artemisia hot on his heels.

"Dad!" Jack bellowed. "Tell, Arty Farty to stop taking my books!"

Before Armand could respond, Artemisia barked, "I don't think he even knows how to read, Dad! He only looks at the pictures."

Armand glanced at the book clutched in Jack's hands. It was an art book on Salvador Dali. He lowered the music with the remote, and looked up at Artemisia. "Listen, honey, if its Jack's book, let him do as he pleases. *Did* you swipe it out of his hands?"

"Yeah!" Jack cut in. "She's a pain in the butt, Dad!"

"I am not!" she snapped, gazing back at her father. "He looked at it for two seconds then put it down. That's when I took it."

Armand looked at Jack, sternly. "Did you put the book down?"

Jack's face couldn't conceal the white lie, as he conceded, "Well, yeah, but that doesn't mean I want her grubby fingers all over it. She always bends corners down, you know, those stupid doggy ears. And I hate having my art books ruined."

Armand now gazed sternly back at her. "Artemisia, you have to respect Jack's wishes. Those are *his* books. And quite frankly, I also frown upon damaging pages in an art book like that."

Artemisia smirked. "I don't see what the big deal is with this book. It's Dali. He bent watches and even people into weird shapes, so why get bent out of shape over a bent page?"

Armand laughed. "Clever point. Dali *did* like bending things. But again, its Jack's book. Have respect for other people's possessions. Is that understood?"

As Jack shot his sister a gloating smile, Artemisia smirked and nodded begrudgingly. "Fine!" she belched. "But I bet pee-wee doesn't even know how old Dali was when his mother died."

Jack frowned. "Who cares anyhow?"

Artemisia turned, and as she walked away, said, "Sixteen. And Dali was devastated." As she reached the doorway, she turned and added, "Then his father married his wife's sister! So *there*! Dummy!"

Before Armand could scold her for the last remark, Artemisia was gone. He turned back toward little Jack. "Well, despite the dummy remark, she *is* right. If you really like something you should try to learn as much as possible about it."

Jack pouted. "But Dali was an artist, and I like his kooky art. Who cares about his personal life."

"Well, personal experiences are part of an artist's mindset, Jack. Often times their artwork are reflections of their life, whether it be blatant, subtle or subliminal."

As Jack squinted, perplexed by his father's last word, Andrea popped her head in the doorway. "Honey, the babysitter is here. Time for us to go."

Armand grasped the remote and turned off the stereo receiver. Little Jack looked at his father. "I don't get why you like that sappy old music. Your new stuff *rocks*! It's so much better."

Armand stood up and patted Jack on the head. "Well, it's good to expand one's horizons, Jack. Variety is the spice of life." As he walked toward the door, Jack asked, "Who was that old fart anyhow?"

Armand laughed. "Camille Saint-Saëns, a Frenchman."

"Camille? Camille was a *man*!?" Jack burst out laughing. "I know a girl at school named Camille."

Armand smiled and glanced back. "You see, you're expanding your horizons, Jack. Now you know Camille can be either a boy or a girl."

With that, Armand and Andrea walked into the garage, hopped in their classic '57 Thunderbird, and headed to the train station. From there they took the train into Penn Station, then walked up 7th Avenue to Carnegie Hall. Taking their seats in the second row of the orchestra section, Andrea opened the Playbill and scanned the works on the playlist.

Meanwhile, the dignified gentleman seated next to Armand struck up a conversation. "Excuse me, my name is George Herbert. You look rather familiar."

"That's probably because we have season tickets. Do you come to Carnegie often?"

George smiled as he glanced at his wife then back at Armand. "Hell No! This stuff isn't my cup of tea. But my wife badgers me about that quite often. Therefore, it certainly wasn't *here* that I've seen you."

"Then perhaps you saw my photo in the *Times* or *Daily News*."

George squinted in thought, then his eyes widened. "Ah! Yes. That's it. You're that famous art detective, Mr. Arnold or something like that. Right?"

"Arnolfini, Armand Arnolfini," Armand corrected.

"Yes, yes, that's it, Arnolfini. I knew I was close. Well, this is quite a serendipitous encounter then, Armand."

"And why is that?"

"Because I recently bought a painting for my wife by William Bouguereau. I imagine you're familiar with his work?"

"Of course. He was the nineteenth century's premiere academic painter. My wife and I both admire his work."

"Well, as I've made clear, I'm not much of a culture vulture." He leaned over and whispered in Armand's ear, "So I have no idea if I made a good investment." He glanced at his wife, then back at Armand. "She only cares about the beauty of the painting," he whispered, "but I'm a Wall Street financial analyst. So I bought it for investment purposes. I'd love to have you look at it to assure me that my money was well spent. Naturally, I'll gladly pay you for the appraisal."

"I'd be happy to, Mr. Herbert."

"Call me George," He said as he sat upright. He pulled his business card out of his wallet and wrote his home address on the back. "Here you go, Armand. When can you come over?"

"Well, since you don't like Classical music, we can go right now."

George looked like a deer in headlights, as Armand chuckled. "I was kidding. I can stop by tomorrow."

George shook his head free of the jest, then shook Armand's hand heartily with a grin. "You had me there! Then tomorrow it is."

Just then the lights dimmed and the concert began. Armand and Andrea listened intently to the evening's performances of Sibelius' *5th Symphony* and Tchaikovsky's *Tempest*.

After intermission, the concert continued with Liszt's popular *Les Preludes* and ended with his obscure and philosophical *From the Cradle to the Grave*. While George had struggled to avoid slipping *into a grave* from boredom, Armand stood up and applauded vigorously.

The two men glanced at each other, smiled at the disparity, then bid each other good night, as the two couples exited the Hall.

The next day Armand hopped in his '57 Corvette and cranked up *Sound Chaser* by Yes. With his adrenaline pumping to the band's lightning-fast virtuosity and his mind analyzing their stunning innovation, he headed out on the highway. Then a smile came across his face as he recalled little Jack's comment about music that *really rocks!*

An hour later he arrived at George Herbert's mansion. It was beautifully nestled in the woods in Lloyd's Neck on Long Island. The expansive edifice sat on a bluff overlooking Long Island Sound and featured a west wing with a six-car garage.

George came out and showed Armand his 1936 Mercedes-Benz 500K, his 1998 Ferrari Testarossa, a 1935 Auburn Speedster, and a 1936 Bugatti 57SC. After an enthusiastic and lengthy exchange about collector cars, George escorted Armand inside his sprawling mansion.

"Follow me," Herbert said. "I'll now show you my wife's hallowed gallery."

Walking down a long, marble-floored corridor, they reached a handsome set of double doors and entered. Decked out with wainscoted walls, Corinthian columns, crystal chandeliers, and an array of paintings and sculptures, the room was simply magnificent.

Armand was impressed as he scanned Herbert's fine collection, featuring works by Jean-Léon Gérôme, Lawrence Alma-Tadema, and John William Godward.

George pointed. "And there is our first work by Willy Bugger-Row."

Armand chuckled. "Well, I never heard William Bouguereau's name butchered like that, but let's have a look at it."

As they both approached the painting, George said, "Its entitled *La Confidence*."

Armand looked at the two pretty young women, with one leaning close to whisper in the other's ear while holding a letter. He leaned in closer to inspect the brushstrokes. After several intense moments, he leaned back to inspect the overall composition. His eyes then observed the natural palette of colors, which included the blue skirt, magenta shawl, and subtle skin tones, each with slightly muted colors to capture realism, and avoid overblown chromatic intensity. It all seemed right to some extent, but something still tugged at his gut. He analyzed the faces of both young women and shook his head with a sigh.

Having noticed Armand's reaction, George stepped closer, concerned. "What? What is it? Please tell me this is indeed a Bouguereau."

Armand glanced at George. "Yes, I think you have a Bouguereau, George, but not the Bouguereau you thought you purchased."

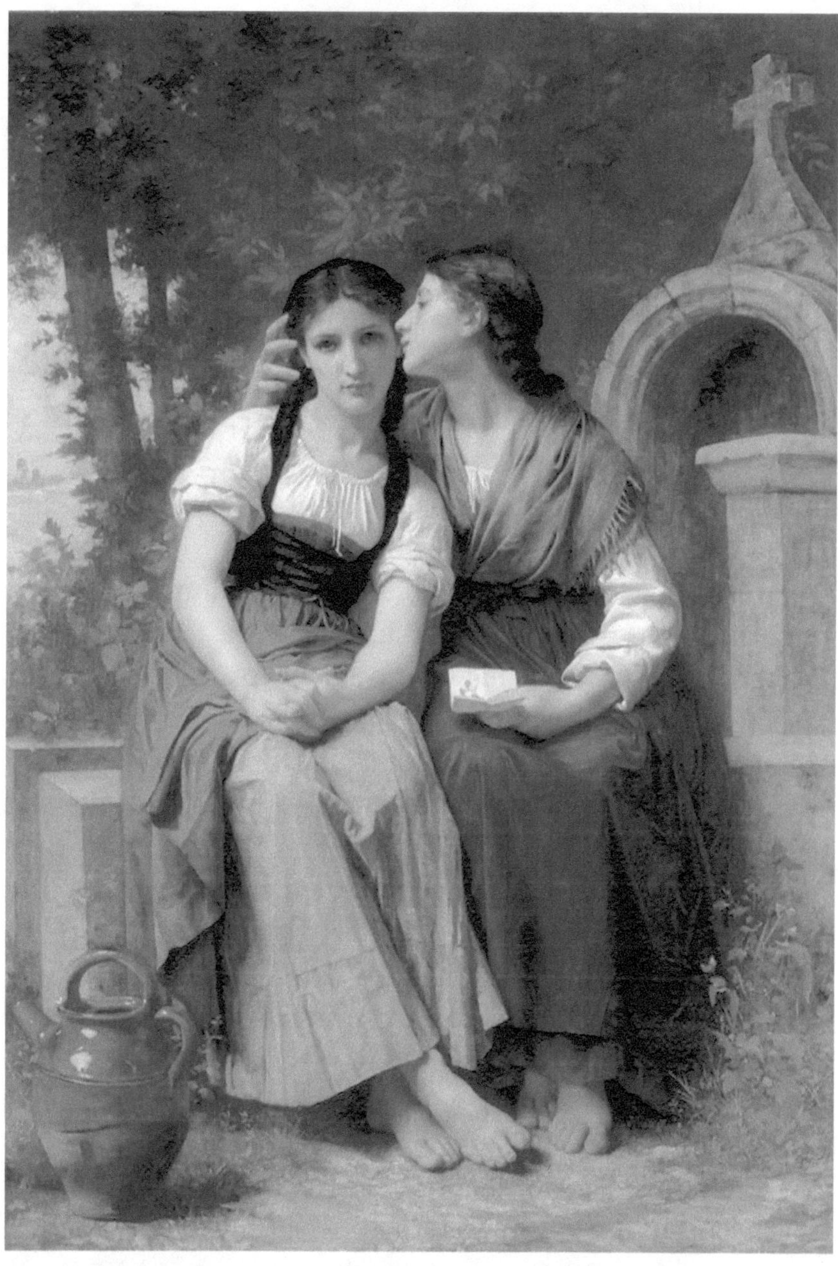

George squinted, even more confused. "What are you saying? I told you I'm no aficionado, so I have no clue as to what the heck I'm looking at, or what you see."

Armand pointed to the woman's face. "She's leaning toward her friend to whisper in her ear, but the perspective is off. Her head is actually in front of her friend's head. Therefore, she's whispering not *in* her ear, but in front of her face, into thin air."

George peered back at the painting, his eyes zeroing in on Armand's point of contention. "Jesus! I never noticed that." He looked at Armand. "Does that really matter?"

Armand stepped back. "It matters to a seasoned pro. Although I can't be a hundred percent sure, that doesn't seem like a mistake William would have made. Moreover, the paint and brushstrokes, although very much like William's, also seems slightly different."

"Wait a minute!" George said, recalling Armand's initial response. "You said this is *not* the Bouguereau I thought I purchased. What did you mean by that?"

Armand gazed at him. "Well, I think this might be by William's second wife, Elizabeth Jane Gardner."

George blinked hard. "What!? You mean, his wife was a painter, too?"

Armand nodded as he explained how Elizabeth was initially William's student. Yet after Bouguereau's first wife Nelly died, William and Elizabeth wished to marry. However, William's mother had previously forced him to make a pact, whereby he would never remarry after Nelly's death. Therefore, it was only after William's mother had passed, and after a nineteen-year engagement, that he and Elizabeth Gardner married in Paris, on June of 1896.

George shook his head. "Jeez, that's a long time to wait to get married. But you didn't tell me, why did Elizabeth paint in the same exact style as her husband?"

"I can't answer that," Armand said. "She obviously had talent and technical expertise, but not much in the way of originality. However, she was somewhat popular during her life time, but history has cast her aside."

"I imagine it's pretty darn easy to copy someone else's work if you're right there in their studio studying their technique," Herbert complained.

"Well, to some extent that's true," Armand said. "However, Henri Matisse was also a student of William's, yet his early paintings show that he never could paint realism like his mentor very well. That's why his works became even more simplified and very primitive, even childlike."

George shook his head and sniggered. "That's why I never got into this art nonsense. I just don't get Picasso, Matisse, or any of those baby paintings. Financial markets and numbers are far easier for me to understand." He scratched his chin. "Getting back to Elizabeth. If she had some talent but was forgotten, was that because she was a knockoff artist or because she was a woman?"

"Perhaps to some extent because she was a woman, but more so because she was a copyist. She was very talented but not very original. In fact, I recently worked on a case about Rosa Bonheur's work. Rosa was technically skilled but also very original."

He turned back toward the painting *La Confidence.* "Don't get me wrong, Elizabeth Gardner created some very beautiful paintings, and I'm sure your wife loves this work for its charm. But since your concern was financial, I have to say, I think you were either intentionally duped or the seller didn't even realize the error himself."

George wearily rubbed his temple. "Dear Lord. I spent a good arm and a leg for this fake. Who could have ever guessed William's student-turned-wife was a darn plagiarist." He rolled his eyes. "Excuse me, I meant painter."

He shook his head angrily. "No! I meant what I said. She was a damn plagiarist! I'm pissed! I can't condone that. She copied her husband's style so intently that there's nothing else to say, but *deceitful*! Especially being that I'm an unsuspecting investor."

Armand rubbed his chin, recollecting his earlier talk with his son Jack; namely, how it was wise to read up on things you like or love. And in George Herbert's case, to avoid buying something with a high price tag that you knew little about, especially if purchased as an investment.

"Well, George. As I said, there *is* a very slim margin of error, but I am confident that this is *not* William's work. I'm quite familiar with his brushstrokes, coloring, and that special spark of life he gives to his characters."

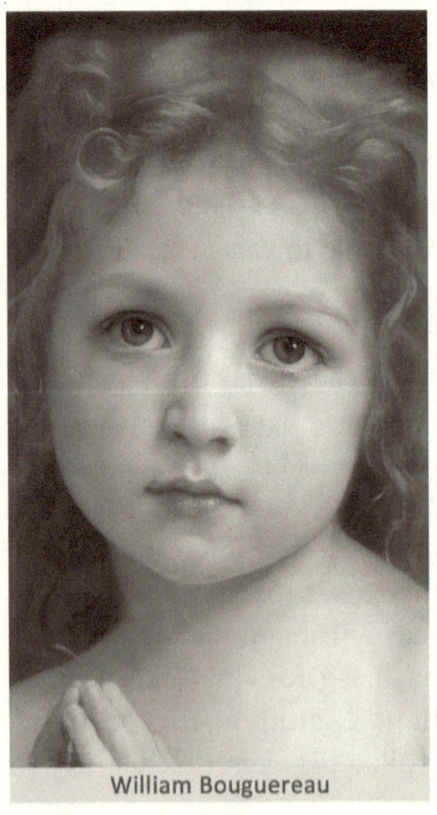

William Bouguereau

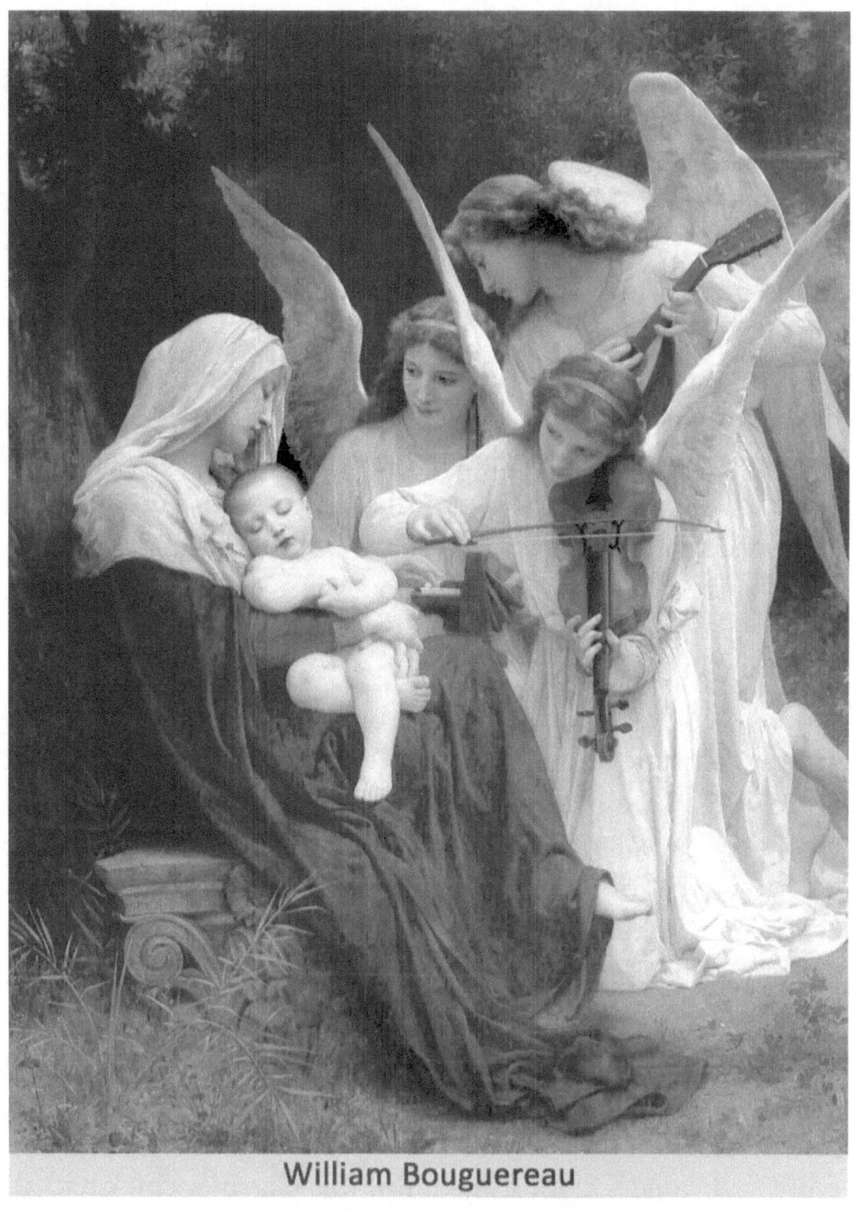

William Bouguereau

As George listened intently, Armand continued, "In fact, just last night, in preparation, I had searched through a catalog of William Bouguereau's works to see if I could find *La Confidence*. But no such luck. There is a slight possibility that this is an unknown work of his that recently surfaced somehow, but that's speculation. So, I'm curious, from whom did you buy this painting?"

George continued to gaze half-dazed into space, still peeved about the bad investment, as he uttered, "Some French fag named Camille La Charme." He finally broke free of his gaze and looked at Armand. "I'd like to break that flimsy rodent's neck!"

Armand paused at the coincidence of having discussed the name Camille with his son recently, then regained his bearings, as he responded, "Now hold on!" he advised. "Don't lose your wits over this, George. If you like, I'll contact Camille and try to get to the bottom of this."

Herbert nodded. "Yeah, I guess it's best if you handle this. I have little patience for con men."

"Well, as I said, there *is* a slim chance that Camille didn't even know himself, since Elizabeth's works are in the same exact style and very competent. After all, she was right there in his studio, able to study the master's technique and even use his exact oil paints and canvases. There is no better way to create forgeries, or legitimate imitations." He paused a moment, then added, "I must admit, however, that although Elizabeth painted in the same style as her husband, her subjects and viewpoints *were* slightly different."

George Herbert huffed. "Well, that's still fraudulent in my book. From what I gathered from what you said, a modern day forger would have a hard time trying to get the paint and canvas to look aged. But this Gardner chick had all the ammunition sitting right at her fingertips. And here it is a century later and I'm stuck with her flimsy fake."

"Well, let me call Camille first before you jump to the worst case scenario. As I said, there is a slight chance that I'm wrong. Even geniuses like Bouguereau had off moments, and perhaps this small error of perspective and variance of brush stokes were a natural oddity."

George pointed to the telephone. "It's all yours. Good luck!"

Armand walked over and made the call. However, the call was exceedingly brief, lasting less than a minute, as Armand hung up, firmly. He turned toward George. "Well, this Camille fellow is pretty darn rude all right. He wouldn't answer my questions and hung up on me."

"I could have told you that," George said, now even angrier. "I knew I shouldn't have trusted that snobby weasel. Those damn French have such an odious air about them. Don't they?"

"Well, some of them do, but certainly not all," Armand said. "I have many friends there."

"Well, that's a topic for debate at another time, but the question now is, will you take on this case?"

"Certainly. I'd be glad to." Armand smiled, knowing he'd be heading back to France once again, just like his previous case.

The two men discussed fees and Mr. Herbert cut Armand his first check. They shook hands and Armand headed back to Westport, Connecticut.

Two days later Armand arrived in Paris and made his way to Camille La Charme's gallery. The female receptionist told him that Camille was in his studio with a client and to wait five minutes. However, five minutes turned into forty-five minutes.

Having lost his patience, Armand stood up, marched up to the receptionist's desk, and demanded, "I've waited long enough! Where is Camille?"

The woman cowered just as Camille La Charme

entered the gallery from the front entrance. "Here I am," he said. "And who might *you* be?"

Armand turned toward Camille, then heatedly back at the receptionist. "You told me he was in the studio. Yet he wasn't even on the premises!"

Camille stepped in front of Armand with a pseudo grin and extended his hand. "Don't mind her. She's paid to do my bidding. How may I help you, *Monsieur*...?"

Armand looked back at Camille, and the exotic figure before him, with his designer jeans with rhinestones, silk shirt with flowers, and bright red sneakers. Armand grumbled. "You would have gotten my name over the phone two days ago, but you rudely hung up on me."

Camille's smile deflated into a scowl. "Oh! So you're the interloper who thinks I sold Mr. Herbert a fake." Waving his hand dismissively, he walked toward the filing cabinet next to the receptionist. Without looking back at Armand, he opened the drawer and said, "Just sit tight. I'll prove you're wrong..." he looked back, "*Monsieur?*"

"Arnolfini. Armand Arnolfini."

"Oh! Like Jan van Eyck's *Arnolfini Portrait*."

Camille scanned Armand from head to toe, then snickered like a hyena. "You *must* be related. You even look like that sickly man."

Armand almost laughed at the absurd insult and said, "Well, Camille, for a La Charme, you certainly have no charm. And although I am related to that Arnolfini, please, do me a favor, just produce the proof and spare me your dull wit."

Camille gritted his sparkling white teeth as he pulled out the folder with a huff and then walked toward Armand. He slid out the first document and showed it to him. "*Here!* This is the bill of sale I received from Pierre Voulveau, the owner."

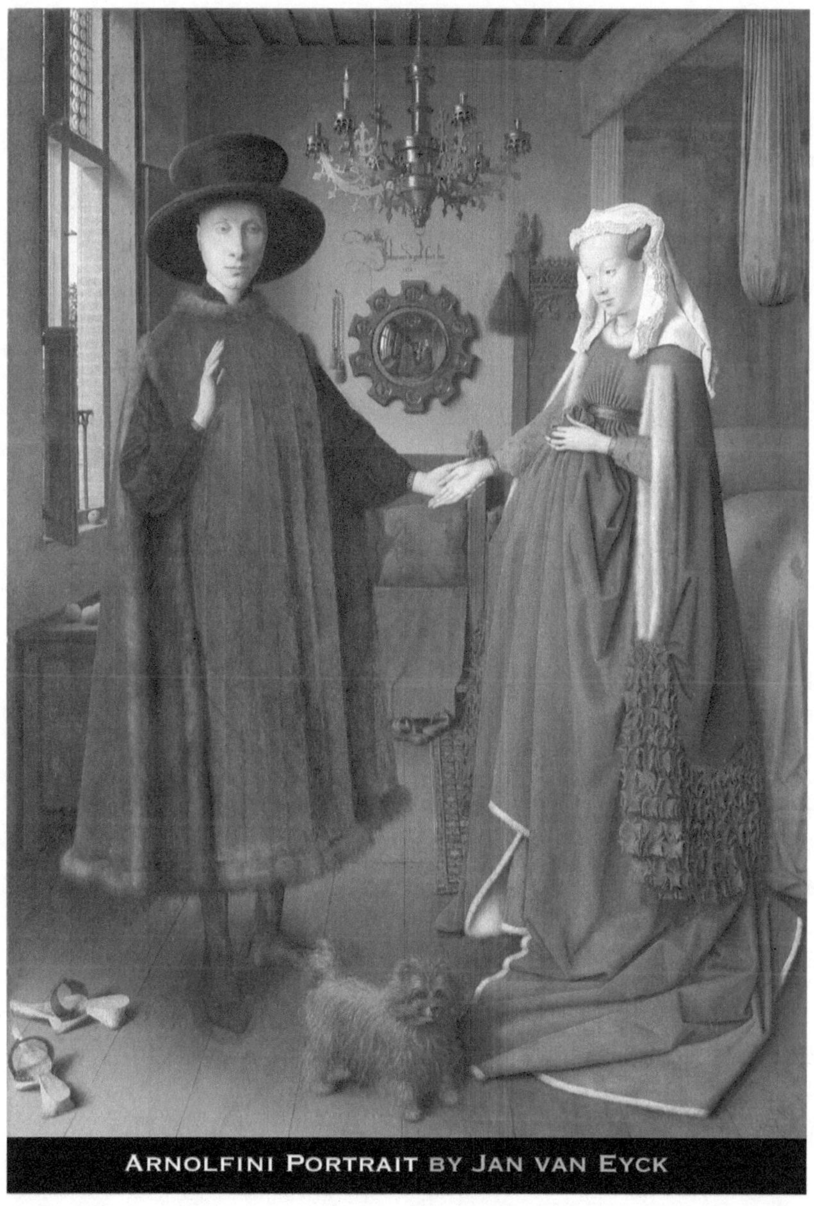

ARNOLFINI PORTRAIT BY JAN VAN EYCK

He then pulled out another document, which was old and yellowed. "And here's the very first sale of the piece, made in 1878. As you can see, the master himself issued this to Pierre's ancestor, Claude. Therefore, *La Confidence* has been in the Voulveau family's possession since it was created."

Armand scanned the documents, which seemed legitimate, while Camille unexpectedly swiped them out of his hands and growled, "Now get out of my gallery! You foreigners are all alike, *morons*!" He shoved the papers back in the cabinet and slammed the drawer shut. Irritated, he continued, "The work is an original by William-Adolphe Bouguereau, just as I stated, and now proved beyond a shadow of a doubt. *Au revoir, Monsieur* Arnolfini!"

"Since I obviously can't have those documents verified by my friends here at the Art Academy, I'll say *ciao, for now*."

"No! Not *for now, Monsieur*," Camille growled as Armand strode toward the door. "For good!"

Armand walked to his rented car and pulled out a pen and pad. He immediately wrote down the name and address of Pierre Voulveau that he had seen on the document. He typed in the address into the Magellan GPS, then slammed the car into gear.

An hour and ten minutes later, he arrived at Voulveau's lavish chateau. The expansive edifice, with its decorative mansard roof, was beyond impressive, as a ten-car garage sat several yards away, with several acres of lawn, manicured gardens, and fountains beyond that. To Armand it looked like a mini Versailles.

Armand knocked on the front door. Several moments later, the door finally opened. Standing before him was a thin, frail man with a well-manicured goatee, and sporting a white silk shirt with a gray vest and matching slacks. "*Salut. Comment puis-je vous aider?*" he said, as he wiped his dirty hands with a washrag.

"I'm sorry," Armand said. "I don't speak French."

"I said, hello. How can I help you?"

"Oh, I'm looking for the master of the house, Pierre Voulveau."

"I am he," Pierre said with a genial smile.

Armand had expected the man before him to be the servant with that smelly rag in his dirty hands, but replied, "Oh, I see. It's a pleasure to meet you, Pierre. My name is Armand Arnolfini. I'm a private investigator specializing in art crimes. I'd like to ask you a few questions. Specifically about your sale of *La Confidence* to Camille La Charme."

Pierre's pleasant smile withered into a solemn stare. "Ah, yes, it was such a beautiful work. Parting is such sweet sorrow, as they say. Please, come in."

Pierre finished cleaning his hands and placed the rag on a console table. Then he escorted Armand through the opulent foyer and into an enormous room filled with antique furniture and fine artwork.

Armand gazed at the exquisite collection. "Very impressive, Pierre. You have excellent taste."

"*Merci, Monsieur* Arnolfini. Most of these paintings have been in my family for well over a hundred years. Yet, sadly, quite a few had to be sold. I loathe having to part with some of them, especially with *La Confidence*. It held such a special meaning for me and my dear Camille."

Armand squinted. "Are you...well, are you and Camille—"

"Partners? Lovers?" Pierre said with a wistful smile. "Yes. Does that shock or offend you?"

"Of course not," Armand said, "I pride myself on being an enlightened soul, Pierre. Furthermore, any lover of art and culture certainly knows the void our world would have suffered without the likes of Michelangelo or Tchaikovsky."

As Pierre smiled, Armand continued, "But I must ask, if *La Confidence* was so special, why did you sell it to Camille? Especially if, well, if you're partners."

Pierre glanced solemnly at the floor, swallowed a lump of hurt, then looked slowly back up. "Well, we had a bit of a falling out. I trust, well I hope, it's only temporary. But..." Pierre paused to regain his composure, then continued, "You see, Camille needed money, and said he had an American who was interested in a work by Bouguereau. He assured me that he'd secure a very good price for it. So I conceded, because, well, I think...well, I *hope* it will rekindle our relationship."

Armand looked at the distraught man before him, paused a moment, then said, "Well, no pun intended, Pierre, but do you have confidence that *La Confidence* is an original work by William Bouguereau?"

Pierre waved his hand dismissively. "Oh, of course it is. If you've seen it, you'd know. It truly is sublime, Mr. Arnolfini." A wave of melancholy swept over him once again, as his shoulders wilted. "As I said, it wounded my very soul to part with it. It had profound meaning for Camille and I. The two girls in that painting seemed to be very close, perhaps even lovers." He paused a moment as his imaginative love dream refueled his tongue. "And who knows, perhaps the note in her hand might be a love letter. One that finally reveals their mutual and everlasting love, like Camille's and mine."

Pierre's love dream faded, as he said, "That painting has been in my family for many years. And is even more special since it was sold to my great grandfather, Claude, by William Bouguereau himself."

"Yes, I saw the original bill of sale," Armand said. "Camille showed it to me."

Pierre smiled. "Well, don't tell him, but I have the original. I made that copy for him on authentic paper."

Armand's eyes lit up, curious and eager. "Can I see the original?"

Pierre shrugged his slim shoulders. "*Oui*, of course."

He walked to a vault, discreetly blocked Armand's view, and entered the combination. He pulled out the document and handed it to Armand.

Armand grasped the frail, old document, as his eyes scanned it closely. His head recoiled. "I see here that the sale was made in 1881."

"*Oui*. So?"

"Camille's document stated 1878," Armand said, as he looked deep into Pierre's eyes.

Pierre snorted and grabbed the document out of Armand's hand. "What difference does it make!?" he scoffed. "So it's a few years off. As we French would say, '*C'est la vie!*'" Irritably, he placed the document back in the vault, and said, "Furthermore, who cares about a silly date or reading about a picture's history? I just loved looking at that piece."

"You sound like my son," Armand said.

"Excuse me?"

"Never mind," Armand said. "But dates *do* matter."

Pierre sighed heavily which morphed into a doleful whimper. "Oh, why does that matter now? Some man in America has my beloved painting, my precious Bouguereau. I'm heartbroken. I don't care to hear about silly dates, Mr. Arnolfini. You're upsetting me."

Armand could see that Pierre was on the verge of tears, and said, "Very well, never mind, Pierre. I apologize for upsetting you. I thank you for your time. I'll see my way out."

"*Au revoir,*" Pierre uttered somberly, as Armand exited the mansion and Pierre closed the door.

Armand drove back to Paris and headed straight to the Art Academy. He walked downstairs to the archives department and saw Ivan Petrov, his friend and archival manager, who was sitting behind his desk reading a magazine.

He walked over and patted Ivan on the shoulder. "So, my dear old comrade, I need a favor."

"Most certainly," Ivan said in his thick Russian accent with an odd French twang. He placed the art magazine down. "What can I do for you?"

Armand took a seat. "Back home, I had tried to locate a painting in our American catalog, called *La Confidence* by William-Adolphe Bouguereau. But I came up empty. Moreover, our archives have little to no information on his wife, Elizabeth Gardner. I suspect the work might be hers or a forgery. And being that they lived here in Paris, I'm hoping your catalog is definitive and more complete. Can you help me?"

"Of course," Petrov said. "If it was documented at all, we should have it on file. Follow me."

With that Ivan stood up and walked over to the main terminal. He typed in 'Elizabeth Jane Gardner' and pulled up her catalog. As Armand stood by his side, Ivan scrolled through, then stopped on the listing. "Here it is!" he said with a smile. "*La Confidence,* by good ol' Elizabeth Jane Gardner."

Armand leaned over and looked at the computer screen. He smiled. "I knew it. I could tell by the slight differences in brushstrokes and her color palette that it wasn't William's work."

Ivan looked up at Armand. "You never cease to amaze me. You have eagle eyes, Hephaestus."

Armand chuckled. "Well, a Greek god of Art, I'm not. But I *thank you* just the same."

Armand glanced back at the screen, noticing the date of

the painting's creation. It read 1880. He thanked Ivan and drove back to Camille's gallery.

As he arrived, Camille was near the front door and tried to block Armand, but Armand pushed his way through. "Nice try, Camille. But if you want your pearly white teeth knocked down your throat, try it again."

Camille knew he was no match, and stepped back. With a grunt, he said, "What do you want, Arnolfini?"

"I just went to the archives and learned that *La Confidence* was painted not in 1878, like your document states, but two years later, in 1880."

Camille rolled his eyes. "Who cares? It's a minor error. That's not unusual."

"What *is* unusual, Camille, is that *La Confidence* was painted by *Elizabeth* Bouguereau, *not* William."

Camille squinted and shook his head adamantly. "Impossible! As I showed you, this painting was in the Voulveau collection ever since it was first purchased from William Bouguereau himself. Its provenance is impeccable and unassailable!"

"Well, that brings me to Pierre Voulveau," Armand said. "He revealed to me that you two are, or were, intimate partners. So one of you is lying. I suspect that since Pierre admitted that he printed up your duplicate bill of sale that he might be the culprit. Yet, if you don't want me to summon the police to investigate your gallery, I think you should talk. And quickly!"

Camille gritted his teeth and shook his head. "Listen, Arnolfini, I don't know what Pierre is up to, but I bought that painting for a good reason. Pierre is a sweet and sentimental soul with a flighty imagination. He read into that painting meanings that weren't there. But for his well-being I pressured him to sell it to me, since I had Mr. Herbert already lined up, eager to buy it." Camille paused, his eyes growing solemn. "You see, Pierre is on the verge of losing his estate. As the sole heir to his family's immense wealth, he squandered it all away on frivolous things; lavish parties, posh clothing, a Lear jet, and expensive cars."

Armand nodded. "Yes, I saw the ten-car garage."

"Yes, but what you *didn't* see was that all of those garages are empty. He had to sell all of his priceless show-cars off. Or rather, I had to. He's an incompetent child and deep in debt, *Monsieur* Arnolfini. I may be a grumpy bastard, but that's because I had to put up with his juvenile blunders for many years. He's a frail little boy in a man's body. But I've grown sick and tired of always trying to bail him out and selling off his belongings. It's a damn shame. His parents must be turning in their graves at how he's destroying their once noble and glorious legacy."

Armand nodded thoughtfully, then said, "So, as far as you're concerned, you had no idea that *La Confidence* was by Elizabeth Gardner Bouguereau?"

"Absolutely not," Camille said. "I imagine he concealed that from me to get more money out of me, or should I say, from Mr. Herbert." Camille gritted his sparkling teeth. "That bastard! And after all I've done for that namby-pamby. I could strangle him!"

"Never mind that," Armand said. "Perhaps I might do it for you." As Camille looked at Armand quizzically, Armand added, "I just hope I don't have to come back here if I find out anything different."

"You won't," Camille said. "I've finally washed my hands of the mess. He's the dirty dog."

"We'll soon see. But in the interim, I suggest you call Mr. Herbert and arrange either a partial refund or a return. Settle your affairs, Camille!"

With that, Armand exited the gallery and drove back to Pierre's chateau. As he pulled up he saw a figure on the second floor, who then drew the curtain closed. Armand marched up to the door and banged hard. After a minute or two, the door creaked open, only slightly, as Pierre peeked meekly outward. "Ah! *Monsieur* Arnolfini, what brings you back?"

"*You,* Pierre. Or rather, your lovely painting that you adored so much. You know, the one by *Bouguereau.*"

Pierre smiled awkwardly and was somewhat perplexed by Armand's tantalizing tone. Still well concealed behind the door, he said through the crack, "Well, why did you come *here*? You know its in America, *Monsieur* Arnolfini."

"Yes, it *is* in America, Pierre. But although it *is* by Bouguereau, it's not by William, as you told me, but rather by his wife, Elizabeth. Why did you lie?"

Pierre bit his lips as a bead of sweat formed along his receding hairline. "I don't know what you mean. Did Camille tell you that lie?"

Armand pushed the door open, and Pierre firmly backward. As they stood in the foyer, Armand stared deep into Pierre's jittery eyes. He grabbed Pierre by the collar, tightly, and drew him in close. "I've had enough of running back and forth between you two love birds. Camille said you're in the red. And he had to sell off all of your expensive cars. Is *that* true?"

Pierre struggled to speak, his throat pinched by Armand's knuckles. "You're h-hurting m-me!"

"I'll do more than that if you don't start talking!"

As Armand loosened his grip slightly, Pierre coughed and replied meekly, "Well, yes. I'm in a bit of a...bind, financially. But what does that have to do with the painting?"

"Are you serious?" Armand said, giving him a good, solid shake. "You're desperate, Pierre. You're so desperate that you even lied to your lover and sold him a painting by Elizabeth as if by William. There's a huge financial difference between the two. And my client also got ripped off. So, it's time to talk and come clean, Pierre!"

A tear welled in Pierre's eye. "I never wanted to lie to Camille, but life isn't fair. I need the money."

"You're a desperate soul, all right, Pierre. I can understand now why Camille is such an ornery bird." Suddenly Armand's nose wriggled. "What's that I smell?" He looked Pierre over, head to toe. "That's turpentine." He edged Pierre backward, still holding him tight, and noticed paint on his hands. "Dear Lord, don't tell me *you're* an artist, Pierre?"

"Then I won't," he uttered nervously.

"Yes, just like you didn't tell me a lot of things, Pierre. What are you painting up there on the second floor? Is that your studio?"

"Very well, so I'm an artist. But only a novice. What's that got to do with anything?"

"Maybe nothing, but maybe a hell-of-a-lot more." Armand glanced at all the paintings hanging on the walls. "How many of these are fakes?"

Pierre struggled to free himself from Armand's tight grip, yet couldn't. "Let me go!" he demanded with a pathetic whimper. "Or I'll call the police. You are in *my* house, against my will. I could have you shot!"

"Yes, you could, but you can't, Pierre. Or at least I dare you to try. I'll rip your rotten little head off your frail neck if you do."

"Okay, okay!" Pierre pleaded. "Let me go! I'll confess."

Armand loosened his grip again, slightly. "I won't let you go until you spill the beans. Now talk!"

Pierre closed his jittery eyes for an odd long moment, then opened them, hoping the image of Armand would have been gone. But his dream was shattered, as he reluctantly complied. "Very well. But know this, I only created forgeries of four paintings. Only four, I swear! And *La Confidence* was one of them." His voice went up an octave, "But *pleeease,* don't bring this to the attention of the police. You and I can settle this. I promise. I'll even gladly reimburse Camille for those paintings I lied to him about."

Armand just stared at him, annoyed and breathing heavily.

Again Pierre pleaded, "Do you promise, *Monsieur* Arnolfini?"

Armand sighed. "Fine. I promise. I will *not* call the police about this. But you better come clean and rectify this mess with Camille and anyone else you sold fakes to or misled. Is that clear?"

"Yes, but Camille is the only one I deal with, *Monsieur* Arnolfini. You can even ask him yourself. He handled all the transactions of everything I needed to sell to pay the bills." His head spun around. "As you can see, I no longer even have staff here. I had to let them go six months ago." He choked up. "And the thought of losing Camille is the latest dagger in my heart."

"And what about all the daggers of lies you stuck into *him*? Is that any way to treat a loving partner?"

Pierre wiped his runny nose as a tear streamed down his face. "I know I've gone off the rails, but I vow to change that, here and now. That's why I'll show you my studio and my works."

With that, Armand released Pierre, who swallowed hard and straightened out his vest. "Thank you," he said, in a raspy voice. "Follow me."

With that, Pierre led Armand upstairs to the second floor. They walked over to a door with a combination lock, which Pierre discreetly unlocked. He glanced back at Armand. "Naturally, I had to make sure Camille never knew about my artistic activities."

Armand was about to scold Pierre once again about yet another secret he kept from his lover, but just shook his head, disgusted.

Pierre opened the door and they both stepped inside the studio.

There, before Armand's eyes, were four easels: Two featured works that looked like Bouguereau originals, while two were in the process of creation, or rather fraudulent imitation.

As Armand approached the first easel, he heard footsteps behind him. He pivoted, only to see Pierre charging toward him with a palette knife. Armand swiftly grabbed Pierre's lethal hand and kicked his leg out from under him, thereby sending Pierre to the floor.

A brief scuffle ensued, but Armand easily wrestled the palette knife out of his hand and subdued Pierre, firmly with his knee in his chest and hand on his throat.

"My patience is exhausted, Pierre. Are you going to comply, or do I need to crush your larynx?"

With a choke and a grunt, Pierre muttered, "*Oui*, you b-barbarian! Yes, yes, I'll c-comply. I c-can't breathe!"

Armand released him and Pierre wobbled up to his feet, massaging his bruised neck, while Armand glanced back at the paintings. "So, tell me. It's obvious you're cranking out fake Bouguereaus, but I'm not familiar with these two particular works."

"Of course you're not. They're not works by William, but rather by his wife, Elizabeth."

"I don't get it," Armand said. "You have to know that people will eventually realize they're not by William."

"No, they won't," Pierre said. "Allow me to educate you," he said with a superb air of French condescension. "Elizabeth had several things going against her: First, she was a woman. As such, her works were not afforded the care and attention of her male peers, as unfair as that might be. Therefore, knowledge of her works remains obscure. That's a splendid bonus for me, as I possess several of her works."

As Armand listened intently, Pierre continued, "Second, Elizabeth's obscure works allowed me to create so-called 'previously undiscovered works' by her husband William, as they are near imitations of her master's style."

As Armand nodded, Pierre continued, "That makes it quite easy for me to merely project these paintings onto a blank canvas." He pointed to a rack nearby. "As you can see, I have many rolls of canvas in stock, all leftovers fabricated in the nineteenth century, and simply trace her lines on to them. Then comes the extremely difficult task of painting them accordingly. It took me many years to master how to create oils that appear dated, not to mention mastering the styles and nuances of their paintings. But you must concede, *Monsieur* Arnolfini, that my sterling talents unquestionably rival both Bouguereaus."

"Yes, but you and Elizabeth lacked one thing, Pierre."

"What's that?"

"Originality."

As Pierre's haughty air deflated, Armand went on, "So after you copied and sold them, what did you do with Elizabeth's originals?"

Pierre revealed a devious smile. Then he walked over to another easel, draped in a red velvet cloth, and pulled it off, revealing *La Confidence*. "*Voila*!" he said with a grin. "The one and only...*original*."

Armand sighed. "So you turned on all that melodrama earlier about losing this painting, and it's been right here all the time, for your everlasting pleasure."

"Yes, *Monsieur* Arnolfini. There are certain things I can *never* part with. Surely you have things that are so precious that you'd never part with?" Pierre's face withered to a solemn picture of remorse. "I've had to part with many treasured items over the past few years, things that would have driven my parents into the grave had they been alive. I carry this burden every day, *Monsieur* Arnolfini. That's why you must not bring the police into this matter. I have enough woes in my life, and…" he clutched his heart, "God knows what I'll do if, if, well—"

"You can stop the play acting, Pierre!" Armand snapped. "You're as skillful an actor as you are a forger. But this is the final curtain. So, take your bow, because this is the grand finale. It's over." Armand pulled out his cell phone and punched in three numbers."

What are you doing!" Pierre bellowed. "That's not the police, is it?"

"I'm afraid so, Pierre."

"But you promised! Y-you lied to me!"

"Your act of lying to me and trying to kill me with a palette knife terminated that agreement, Pierre. Actually, I had every intention of having Camille call the police in order to keep my promise, of not *personally* calling them, but this charade has to end, and *now*!"

"You're a devious man, *Monsieur* Arnolfini."

"Well, I don't always agree with Machiavelli, Pierre, but in this case, the end *does* justify the means."

Two days later Armand arrived back home in Westport, Connecticut. The following day he went to George Herbert's house. Armand relayed the bad news about his fake Bouguereau, as well as the good news that Camille will fully refund the price. He explained how the French police raided Pierre's estate and put an end to his so-called forgery factory.

George decided to keep the forged version of *La Confidence,* with his wife's approval, yet purchased the original from Pierre's collection and donated it to the Georgia Museum of Art, where it remains today.

Herbert and his wife both thanked Armand, and not only squared away the final payment, but added a respectable bonus.

The Mystery of Authorship

Armand cut off the engines of his Owens cabin cruiser and glided up to his backyard bulkhead. Meanwhile, little Jack and Artemisia dutifully hopped off, set the bumpers in place, and secured the ropes to the cleats.

Andrea took off her sunglasses and stepped onto the dock carrying a small cooler with their catch of the day. "Okay, kids, make sure to bring your dirty clothes and towels into the house." She turned back toward Armand. "Is there anything else you need us to do?"

"No, all good here, sweetheart," he said, while grasping the hose. "I'll just give the *Mona Lisa* a quick washing and tidy up."

"Ok, honey, I'll start dinner."

An hour or so later the foursome sat at the dining room table eating a meal of freshly caught bluefish, marinated in Armand's special sauce, along with peppers, mushrooms and zucchini with oil and garlic, and salad. No sooner did they start dessert, than the phone rang.

Artemisia jumped up and ran to the phone. But as was often the case, it wasn't for her. With a pout, she turned and said, "Pop, it's for *you*."

Armand likewise pouted as he glanced down at his tiramisu and cappuccino. "Honey, can they call back in fifteen minutes?"

Artemisia relayed the request, then looked back at her father. "Well, it's James Langford from the Met. He said no problem, the amazing new find in Italy can wait."

Armand's eyes lit up like a child meeting Santa. "New find!? Hold on! I'll be right there." He dashed to the phone and practically ripped the receiver out of Artemisia's hand. "James, old boy. What new find?"

"Well, Armand, it appears an exquisite statue has been discovered in Prato, Italy. We're not sure if it dates to the Renaissance or Baroque periods. But I don't wish to disturb your meal. I know how important fine cuisine is to you. We can talk about it tomorrow."

"Well, I'll certainly come in tomorrow, James. And no worries, dinner tonight is fairly simple, but you can't keep me in suspense. What is it?"

"Well, it appears to be a statue of *Apollo and Daphne.* Well, not *appears to be,* the girl is turning into a tree, for Pete's sake. So we know it definitely *is* a rendition of *Apollo and Daphne.* What we don't know is the author."

Armand's curiosity blossomed like a laurel tree. "Well, I can't wait to come in, James. I'll be in the city by nine o'clock tomorrow morning. Does that work?"

"Excellent. Till then, go and enjoy your meal."

"Oh, I will, James, I will. Good-bye."

As the morning sun cast its luminous rays across the façade of the Metropolitan Museum of Art, Armand arrived at 9AM, on the dot. Excitedly he quick-paced up the stairs and into James Langford's office.

"Good morning, Armand," Langford said, sitting at his desk. "Come here. Take a look at the photo they emailed me. The statue is absolutely gorgeous."

Armand scurried over to Langford's side and peered down at the computer screen. He leaned in closer. "My, my, it *is* stunning, all right. What a marvelous find." His eyes ravished the photo. "Where exactly was it found?"

Langford leaned back in his swivel chair. "At the Villa di Poggio a Cabano in Prato, Italy."

Armand stood erect. "That's one of the Medici's villas."

James nodded. "Yes it is, or rather *was*, it's a museum now. But the Met is eager to get first dibs on this find. The experts there have just dated the piece to be around 1558, but they're still not fully certain who created it. They're leaning toward Baccio Bandinelli, which makes sense. After all, Baccio was one of the Medici's premiere sculptors."

Armand squinted, then looked back at the screen. "Well, I'm not sure about that, James. I mean, it's certainly possible."

Langford peered at the photo. "However, I tend to agree with you. I'm inclined to believe that it just might be by Michelangelo. As you know, he and Bandinelli were intense rivals, and Michelangelo might have done this in response to losing the commission to sculpt a copy of the *Laocoön*."

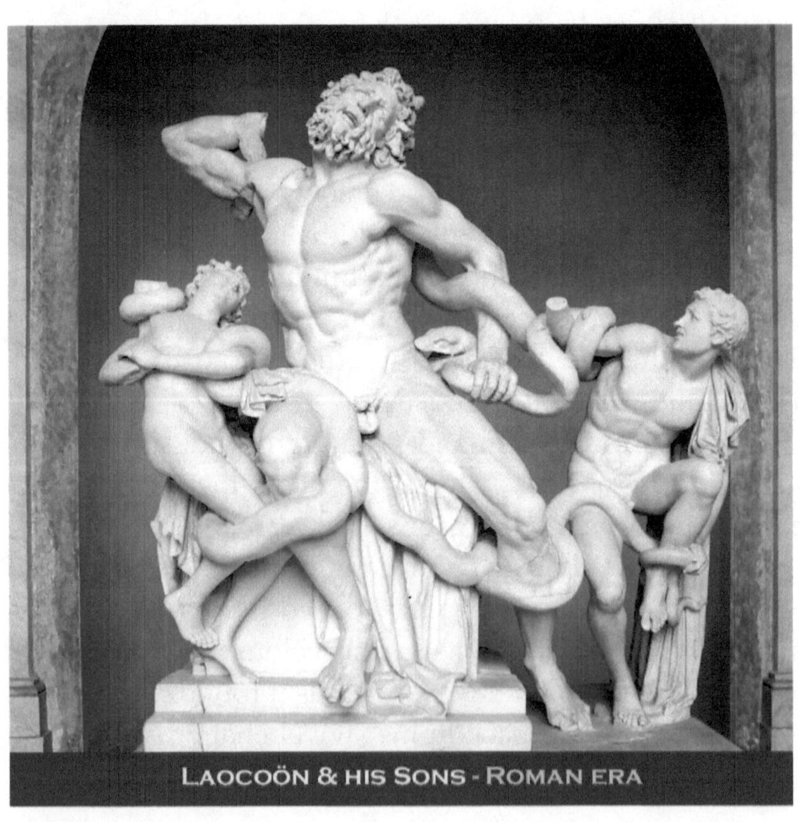

LAOCOÖN & HIS SONS - ROMAN ERA

Naturally, Armand was well aware that the *Laocoön* sculpture was a prized discovery in 1510; moreover, that Michelangelo had witnessed the unearthing firsthand. A masterpiece of ancient Roman sculpture, Pliny the Elder described the *Laocoön* in 77AD as "A work better than any other art of painting and sculpture ever made. And sculpted from one block of stone."

Although later found to be constructed of five blocks of marble, not one, the *Laocoön* group (featuring three figures entwined with a huge snake) proved to be the ultimate sculpture of virtuosity and complexity. And that referred not only to all of antiquity, as it even surpassed anything created by Renaissance masters, which at that moment astonished and challenged them. As such, Baccio Bandinelli won instant fame for his exquisite copy of the *Laocoön* in 1525. And Baccio's triumph stuck a needle in Michelangelo's jealous gut.

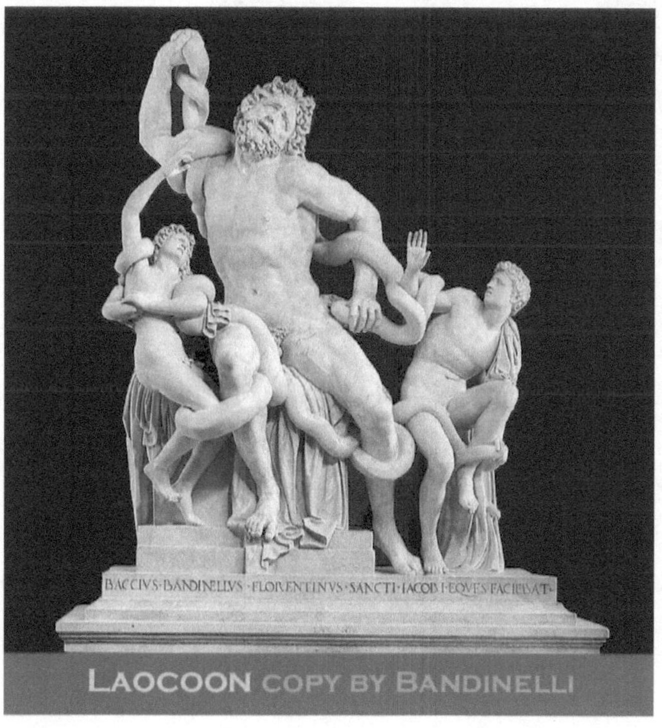

LAOCOON COPY BY BANDINELLI

Armand looked at the screen photo then back at Langford. "I'm sorry, James, we both may have doubts about Bandinelli being the author, but I'll have to disagree with you. These figures are too detailed to be by Michelangelo at this stage of his career. You said 1558, which means Michelangelo was 83 years old. At this point he had abandoned the refinement of his earliest works, like his *Pieta* or *David,* while his later years were marked with herculean figures or they were unfinished and roughly carved slaves."

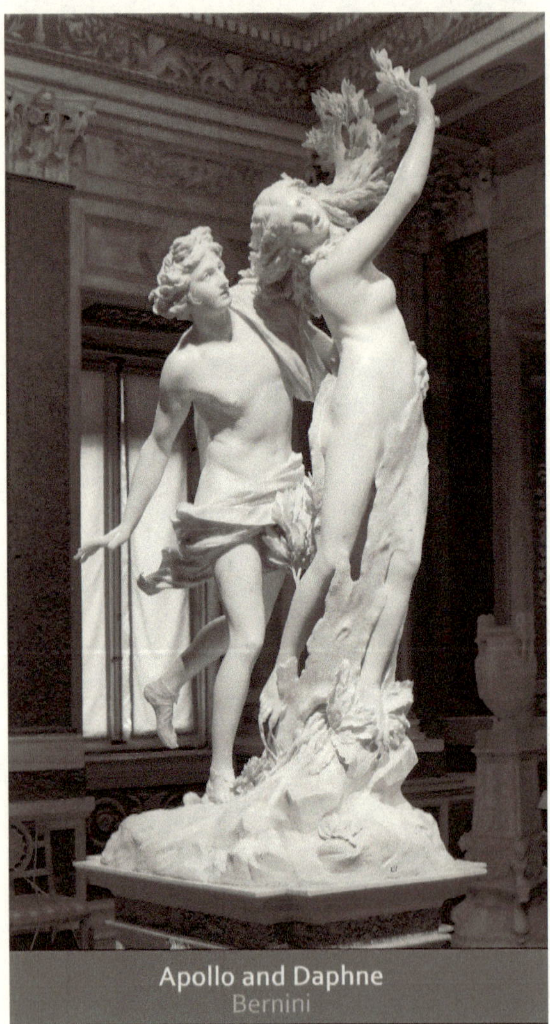

Apollo and Daphne
Bernini

He glanced back at the photo on the computer screen. "And those intertwined figures are quite supple and natural with refined detail. In fact, if it were dated to be sixty years later I would have even believed Bernini to be the author. After all, he sculpted his own *Apollo and Daphne,* and this simply could have been another version."

Langford nodded. "Indeed, Bernini's rendition is a masterpiece of virtuosity, but, yes, the date is too far off. However, I'm still inclined to believe Michelangelo is the author. His later works may have been more muscular or unrefined, Armand, but perhaps his jealously and rivalry with Bandinelli drove him to return to his former style."

"There is little to no evidence to support that," Armand said. "Most of his slaves and pietas in old age were roughly hewn and raw. Some have speculated he left those works unfinished as an attempt to invent a bold new style. But I'm inclined to believe it had more to do with his melancholy. Old age and younger rivals winning commissions all played a role, not to mention how the fame, adulation, and respect that he craved had evaporated. All those slaves he carved, each imprisoned and struggling to free themselves from the stone, seemed to echo the frustration, resignation, and melancholy he was prone to at the end of his life."

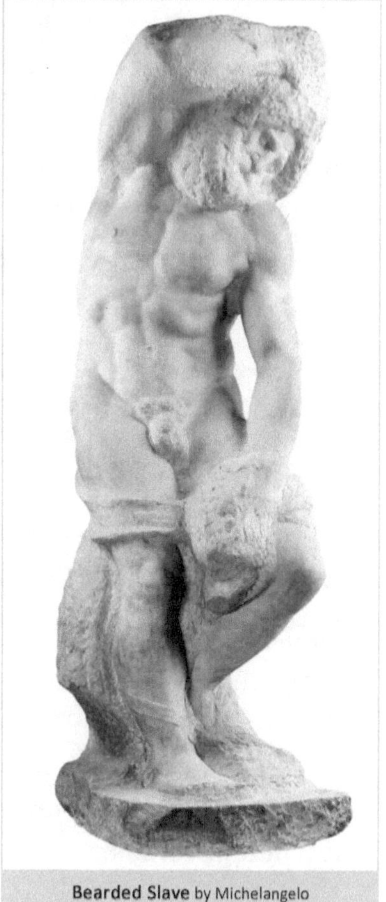

Bearded Slave by Michelangelo

Armand looked at the photo, once again. "Meanwhile this newly found statue of *Apollo and Daphne* is highly polished with very intricate details, things not common to Michelangelo's latest works. As you know, Michelangelo was a master of the old Classical style, which lauded elegance rather than dynamism, and was generally static with limited movement. He never exhibited the dynamic virtuosity of action that others mastered, nor did he create freestanding sculptures with entwined figures, expect for one unfinished and preliminary mold of two fighters. Michelangelo's *David* and Bernini's *Abduction of Proserpina* come to mind."

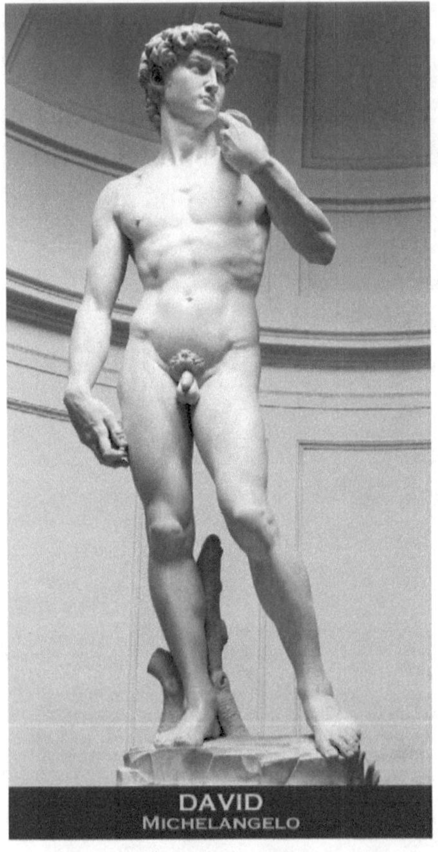
DAVID
MICHELANGELO

Armand looked at Langford. "I know *you*, like many, have a soft spot for Michelangelo, James. I get it; he was a dynamo. But you can't let adoration cloud your judgment. It's akin to how Bach, Mozart, and Beethoven are hailed as gods by the elite, yet there are countless others who rival and even surpass them. Yet those poor souls remain on a second or third tier or even obscured in the shadows."

He looked back at the photo, trying to gain a better assessment.

"Anyhow, it's difficult to tell from this low-resolution image." He looked back at Langford. "So, when do you plan on flying there to inspect it?"

"That's the thing, Armand. I have a new Hellenistic Sculpture exhibit opening in two days. So I can't go anywhere. Besides…" he leaned close and whispered, "Your expertise is legendary. That's why I trust your judgment more than my own." His eyes darted furtively left and right. "Just make sure you never repeat that!"

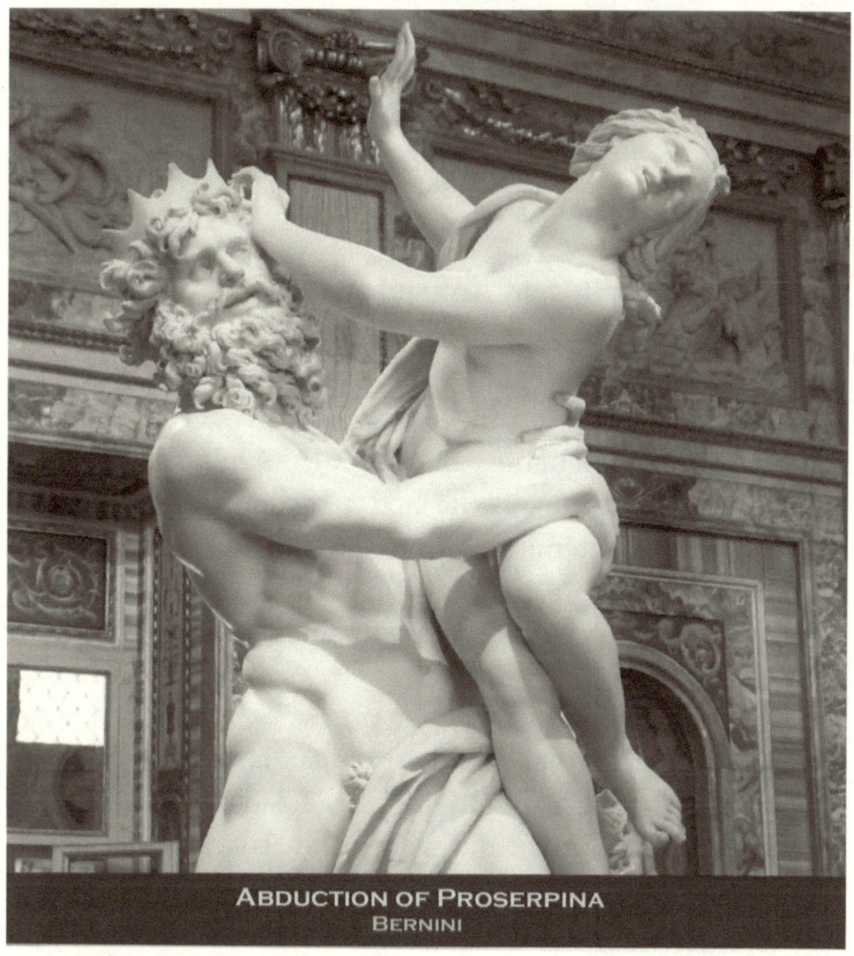

ABDUCTION OF PROSERPINA
BERNINI

As Armand chuckled, James leaned back and added, "You certainly would make the best curator of several of our departments here, Armand. Why haven't you done so?"

"Simple, because I enjoy the freedom and the hunt, James." He glanced at the screen. "Unraveling mysteries, uncovering forgeries and crime rings are the things that motivate me. It's a great feeling to rescue works that were stolen or lost, as well as see criminals go behind bars. And in this case, I'm eager to try and find the true author behind a beautiful piece of work like this."

"That's why I wish to hire you to fly to Italy to inspect this work firsthand."

Armand smiled. "I'd be delighted to, James."

The two discussed finances and James cut Armand a check.

An hour and a half later, Armand arrived home in Westport, Connecticut.

Greeted by Andrea and the kids, Armand then walked into the den followed by his inquisitive clan. As they assailed him with a battery of questions, Armand responded excitedly, especially since he had a secondary surprise. He decided to take Artemisia with him to Italy, being that is was summer vacation. And of course he knew the cultural aspects of the trip would be a valuable learning experience for her, as well.

Two days later, Armand and Artemisia landed in Florence, Italy. He rented a car and they traveled twenty minutes through the lush hills and valleys of Tuscany. Artemisia devoured the picturesque countryside as they passed towering rows of cypress trees and robust vineyards. At one point, they stopped to allow a farmer and his goats to cross the street, which amused Artemisia. Resuming their journey, Armand regaled Artemisia with tales of his youth when he lived in Italy.

Eventually they arrived in Prato at the Medici's villa/turned museum. As they drove up the pebbled driveway they looked over at the double set of spiral stairs that led up to the main entrance. Above that, on top of the roof, stood a clock tower with a bell.

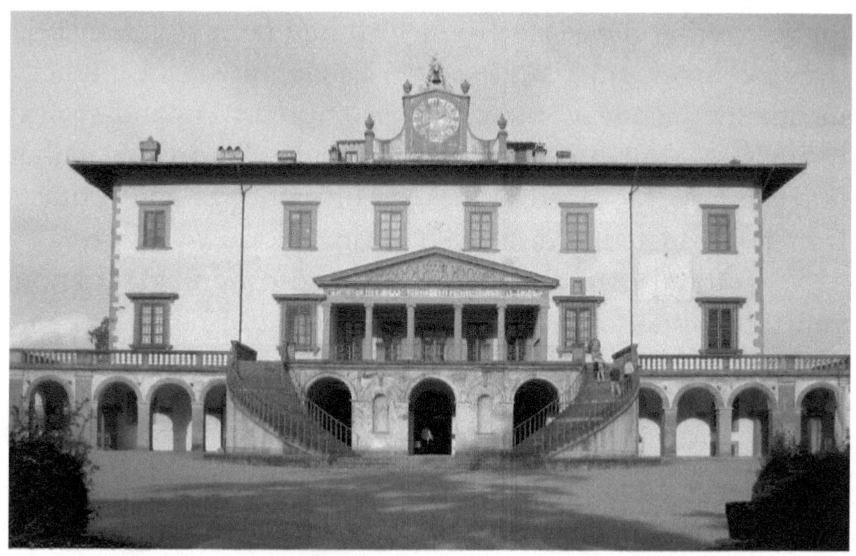

As Armand started walking up one set of spiral stairs, Artemisia took off and dashed up the other set, eventually beating her father to the top. Armand chuckled as he arrived. "You're a spitfire, all right!" He looked around at the sprawling grounds, then up at the palace. "It sure is a nice little spare mansion, isn't it?"

"It sure is!" Artemisia said with a giggle, as she gazed up at the large façade of the villa. "Boy! Were *they* loaded!"

"Well, I'm sure there's a lot more to see inside, darling, so let's go."

As they walked toward the main entrance a distinguished-looking gentleman with a mustache and wavy hair greeted them. "Welcome to the Medici Museum, my name is Mario Poggi." He extended his hand.

Armand shook his hand, provided both of their names, and inquired, "Poggi? Are you by chance related to Giovanni Poggi?"

Mario nodded. "Indeed, I am, *Signore* Arnolfini. He was my great-uncle."

Armand knew that Giovanni Poggi had been lionized for recovering the *Mona Lisa,* which had been stolen in 1911 by Vincenzo Peruggia. However, Giovanni was also crucial in another endeavor, which prompted Armand's next response: "Your great-uncle was a hero, Mario. My father told me how he saved thousands of paintings and artifacts from being looted or destroyed during World War Two."

As they entered the villa, Armand continued, "I know valuable works of art were stored here during that time." Armand's discerning eyes scanned the walls, as he added, "So, was this newly found statue part of your great-uncle's operation?"

Mario nodded warmly. "Yes, it was. I'm impressed, *Signore* Arnolfini." He paused, then said, "Actually, I'm not. I should have expected as much. Your reputation, and that of your eminent father, preceded you."

Armand nodded with appreciation and grasped Artemisia's hand, as Mario continued, "But, yes, my great-uncle indeed stored precious works of art here during the war, among several other locations. Sadly, some works were lost in the chaos as well as ledgers documenting those works. That's why we had no knowledge of this particular statue of *Apollo and Daphne*."

Mario shook his head as he thought of his great-uncle's humiliation during those dark years. "My uncle Giovanni took great pride in protecting those works, but was duped. Unfortunately, the Nazis weren't as honest as they led him to believe, and some works were smuggled to Germany."

Armand nodded with a smirk as he glanced at the decorated walls of the villa-turned-museum. "Yes, I know he worked with Alexander Langsdorff, who looted works from the Uffizi, where my father was the curator."

"Correct," Mario said, as the threesome continued to walk through the museum-villa. "Against his wishes, my great-uncle was saddled with the Nazis, and even Mussolini, who knew as much about art as a blind dog."

As Artemisia chuckled, Mario glanced down at her with a smile, then continued, "But yes, the Nazis pretended to cooperate with us to protect famous artwork and historical buildings from air raids. However, Hitler and Goering were the two biggest looters of art the world has ever known."

"Indeed, they were," Armand said. "Hitler made sure his henchmen grabbed Lucas Cranach's painting of *Adam and Eve*. He had seen it at the Uffizi earlier in 1938 during his visit with Mussolini."

"You know your history and art very well, Armand." Mario gazed down at Artemisia. "And I imagine you'd like to see some of our art in the museum before we get down to business, yes?"

Artemisia nodded eagerly. "Yes! I sure would," she said, as her youthful eyes devoured the building's opulent interior.

Yet as the threesome entered a large gallery, her eyes gazed upward. The large, barrel-vaulted ceiling with intricate designs captured her attention first. But then her eyes landed on all the frescoes on the walls below, one more beautiful than the next.

Mario smiled and said, "This villa was commissioned by Lorenzo de Medici, also known as Lorenzo the Magnificent. He was not only a vital member of the mighty Medici family of bankers, but he was also a great patron of the arts." He paused and bowed his head reverently. "Unfortunately, Lorenzo didn't live to see his summer residence completed." He raised his head, then pointed at all the walls. "But his son Giovanni did so on his behalf, hiring various artists to paint all these frescoes."

Artemisia's head rotated and oscillated; trying to take it all in. "It *is* magnificent." She laughed. "Like Lorenzo's nickname."

Mario chuckled. "Yes, indeed. And this Leo X Salon is just one of many magnificent things the Medicis bequeathed to us."

Artemisia's enchantment halted as she turned toward Mario. "If this was the Medicis' villa, why is this gallery called the Leo X Salon?"

"A very good question, young lady," Mario said. "That's because Giovanni eventually became Pope Leo X."

Artemisia squinted. "A banker became a pope?"

"Yes, my dear," Mario replied. "But Giovanni was only the first Medici to become a pope. His cousin Giulio later became Pope Clement VII. The Medici family even spawned Catherine, Queen of France. They were a very ambitious family. Some say ruthless. It all depends on what side of the Medici fence one stands." Mario chuckled, but then spun around as his finger pointed at all the works of art and architecture around them. "Yet in their turbulent wake the Medicis left behind a truly magnificent legacy."

Artemisia smiled and nodded, as Mario glanced at Armand, and said, "Now, if you please, follow me, so I may show you a piece of art never seen before by *modern* eyes!"

With that, he turned and walked out the rear of the villa and onto the veranda. With Armand and Artemisia trailing behind, the threesome then walked over the well-manicured grounds and toward an old stable. Construction workers and equipment surrounded the structure as the noise of hammers and chisels filled the air.

As the threesome approached the building, Mario waved for the workers to stop work. Still gazing forward, he stepped inside the stable and said to his guests behind him, "Now for the moment you've both been waiting for."

"Yes, indeed!" Armand said eagerly, as he strained his neck to look around Mario's back. However, the statue remained partially blocked.

Oblivious to his obstruction, Mario continued, "You see, while renovating, our construction crew unearthed this incredible find. It was hidden in an underground crate." His head spun around to gain Armand's attention, yet Armand merely glanced at him as he squinted to focus on the statue. But alas, Mario's body still blocked it.

Still unconscious of his obstruction, Mario continued, "It was quite fortuitous that the backhoe didn't destroy the work." He looked back at the statue and stepped closer. "However, a few small pieces did chip off." He glanced back at Armand. "So please, tell Mr. Langford that we *will* mend them and restore Bandinelli's lost masterpiece to its original splendor."

Armand grasped Artemisia's hand and eagerly escorted her around Mario and up to the statue.

Despite the lower parts being laden with dirt, the exquisite detail and charm of Apollo chasing Daphne was enchanting. The beauty of Daphne's body captivated Artemisia, not to mention the surreal nature of it turning into a tree. However, the reason for such a fanciful transformation eluded her, as she looked back at her father. "It *is* beautiful, but also kind of weird. Why is she turning into a tree?"

Armand smiled and relayed the ancient Greek tale: namely, how Apollo, the god of light, chided Eros, the god of love, for using a weapon (bow and arrows). Eros was incensed and vengefully crafted two arrows, one of gold and one of lead. He shot Apollo with the gold arrow, which infused him with a burning love and desire for Daphne, a water nymph. Eros then shot Daphne with the lead arrow, instilling in her a hatred for Apollo, thus denying Apollo of his passion.

As Apollo pursued Daphne with intense desire, Daphne called out to her father Peneus, the river god, pleading, "Help me, father! Change my form, which caused this danger. Free me of Apollo *forever*."

Peneus complied and cast his spell, turning Daphne into a laurel tree: her torso turning into the trunk, her limbs into branches, and her hands and hair into leaves. Meanwhile, Apollo (still madly in love and heartbroken) vowed to honor Daphne forever by making the laurel tree an evergreen.

"And that symbol of longevity," Armand continued, "is another reason why Roman emperors wore a laurel branch around their head in lieu of a gold crown."

Artemisia's lips twisted. "I can get the longevity bit about evergreens, but that whole fairytale is weird." She glanced back at the statue. "For such a pretty work of art, the story is really sad, and creepy."

Armand chuckled. "Well, Greek tales about the gods *are* bizarre, sweetie, at least by today's standards. However, the ancient world was filled with a myriad of gods, like Mithras, Isis, Sol Invictus, and others. Oddly enough, some weird aspects of those pagan tales found their way into Christianity."

Artemisia smirked. "No way! We're not pagans, Dad."

Armand gazed down at his daughter with a professorial stare. "Well, did you ever stop to realize that Saturday, which is the Sabbath, had long been the holy day in Jesus' time, and still is in the core Jewish faith? Yet, Christians, while under Roman rule, decided to worship on Sunday, the day of the pagan Sun god."

As Artemisia's smile withered, Armand continued, "Or how Christ's birthday, of which there are no public records, was nicely paired to coincide with almost every pagan god before him, which is during the winter solstice. The solstice was a universally symbolic time of year for the ancients of all cultures, and breaking that tradition would have been extremely unsettling to the masses."

Artemisia's doubtful smirk morphed into one of utter bewilderment, then eerie revelation.

Armand directed her eyes back to the statue. "But I'd like you to take a closer look, specifically at the anatomy of both figures: the intricate detail of the leaves and branches, the surface of the stone, how it is finely honed and polished, and the texture of the rough bark. You should familiarize yourself with such details."

"Why?" Artemisia inquired, now even more baffled, as the subjects of art and religion ping-ponged in her head.

Armand smiled, realizing he was testing her cognitive and creative abilities to the max. "Because now I'll be taking you to Florence to show you works by Bandinelli and others. That's the only way to make sound judgments, by comparing each work firsthand."

As Artemisia sighed, Armand looked back at Mario Poggi. "Will you join us?"

Mario nodded. "It would be my pleasure. But I assure you, this work *is* by Bandinelli."

Armand smiled. "Well, we'll see about that."

The threesome traveled 10 miles southeast of Prato, journeying over the lush hills of Tuscany with its spotted array of cypress trees and random medieval villages in the distance, and finally arrived in the glorious city of Florence, the jewel of the Renaissance.

Armand parked the rented car, and they walked through the narrow streets until they came upon the wide-open Piazza della Signoria. At the far end stood the famous landmark, the Palazzo Vecchio, with its tall and distinctive crenellated tower. Standing before the entrance stood a copy of Michelangelo's *David,* and to the right, Bandinelli's *Hercules and Cacus.*

Armand made a beeline to Bandinelli's colossus, trailed by Mario, while Artemisia lagged behind. Armand and Mario gazed up at Hercules, the muscular demigod, as he clutched the hair of the beaten, fire-breathing Cacus at his feet. The pure white marble glistened in the sunlight, giving the figures the aura of brawny albinos frozen in time.

Exhilarated, Armand turned to share the moment with Artemisia, but she was gone! Adrenaline surged through his veins when he spotted her several yards away, standing at the Loggia, with its series of three huge arches. He turned back toward Mario. "Excuse me, but I need a moment with my daughter."

Mario nodded in agreement, as Armand dashed toward his daughter. Meanwhile, Artemisia stood staring up at a colossal statue in one of the archways of the Loggia, captivated. Frozen, like a statue herself, Artemisia gazed in amazement at the dramatic configuration, featuring two men, one of which was sweeping a woman away against her will, while all three bodies intertwined like a biological pretzel.

Armand reached her side, and said, "Honey, you shouldn't wander off like that! Always let me know where you're going."

Startled, she turned, then smiled. "Sorry, Dad. But my eyes caught this statue. I just had to check it out." She gazed back up at the twisted arrangement. "I don't get it. How come everyone knows about Michelangelo's *David* and other works, yet something this awesome is not known?"

"Well, life isn't always just, honey," Armand said as he turned to look up at the masterpiece. "And this..." Armand's eyes widened as only air oozed out of his mouth.

"And this, *what*?" Artemisia inquired, now even more curious.

Armand blinked; glanced at Artemisia, then back up at the sculpted group. The astonishing virtuosity of the work was like an autograph in itself. "Uh, w-well, honey," he stammered. "This masterpiece was carved by Giambologna. It is called the *Abduction of a Sabine Woman*. I think this is the answer to the riddle.

"What riddle?" Artemisia asked, until she finally connected her father's dots. "Oh! You mean...you think this Giam-whatever guy carved the *Apollo and Daphne* that was found?"

Armand looked down at her, a grin across his face, then instantaneously picked her up with a loving hug and kissed her. "Yes! Giambologna. His name is Giambologna!"

Artemisia tried to squirm out of her father's arms, embarrassed. "Dad! Come on! Put me down. You're acting weird. Not in public."

Armand put her down and released her. "I'm sorry, dear. I forget you're a big girl now."

Artemisia smiled as she looked up at the statue. "I mean, come on, Dad, you made me look like *her*."

As the two chuckled, Armand glanced up at the statue. "Well, this is a good education for you, honey. Look at this statue closely. Then compare it to the *Apollo and Daphne* that you saw at the Medici museum."

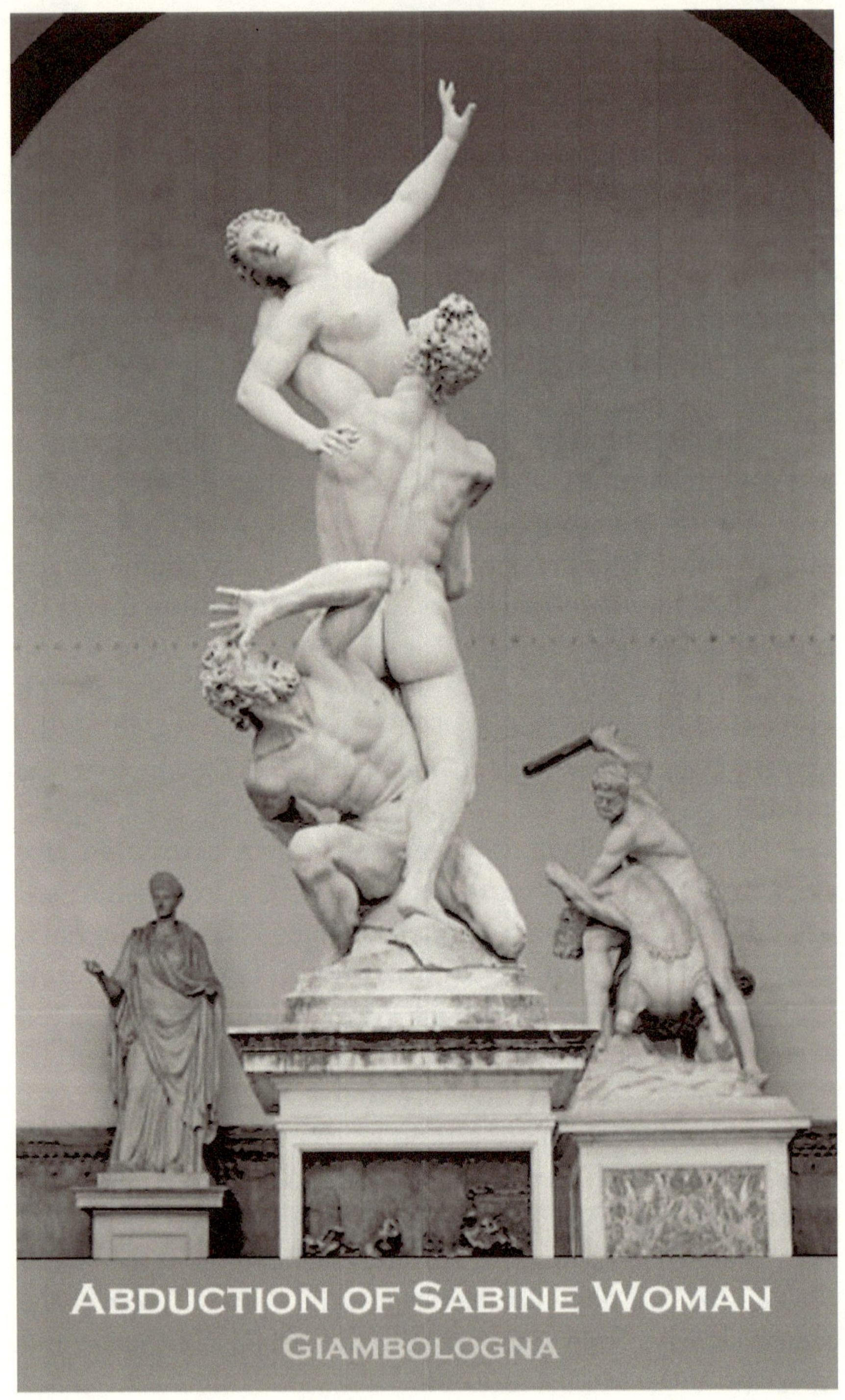

ABDUCTION OF SABINE WOMAN
GIAMBOLOGNA

Artemisia rolled her eyes. "Dad, I'm not an expert, like you."

"Honey, experts come in all shapes and sizes. In fact, children often have very perceptive eyes, because they haven't been filled with decades of ill-informed opinions and half-truths, which can dull their senses and jade their opinions. So, look closely."

Artemisia's youthful eyes peered up at the entwined group of three figures. "Well, I can see how both statues have more than one figure and are twisted around each other."

"Yes, now look closer at the anatomy," her father instructed, "and at the precision of how real and natural the muscles, limbs, and skin look. Cold hard marble seems to vanish as a warm life-like vision of reality takes hold. I can almost see the blood in those veins. Can you?"

Artemisia giggled as she looked at her father. "Well, you certainly have better vision than me, Dad. Or maybe it's a better imagination, because I can't see any blood." She gazed back up. "But, I do sort of understand what you're saying. This Giam...bolo...dude really made these people look alive."

Armand chuckled. "Yes, *Giambologna,* dear. This Flemish-Italian dude really did."

"*Flemish*-Italian?" she inquired.

"Yes, his name actually means Giovanni from Bologna."

Armand then explained how Giovanni was born in Douai, Flanders. However, in his early twenties, Giovanni moved to Bologna, Italy, and later settled in Florence, where he was given his nickname and did most of his work.

Armand then brought her attention to the statue several feet behind the colossus standing before them. "And that one is also by Giambologna. It is called *Hercules Beating the Centaur Nessus.*"

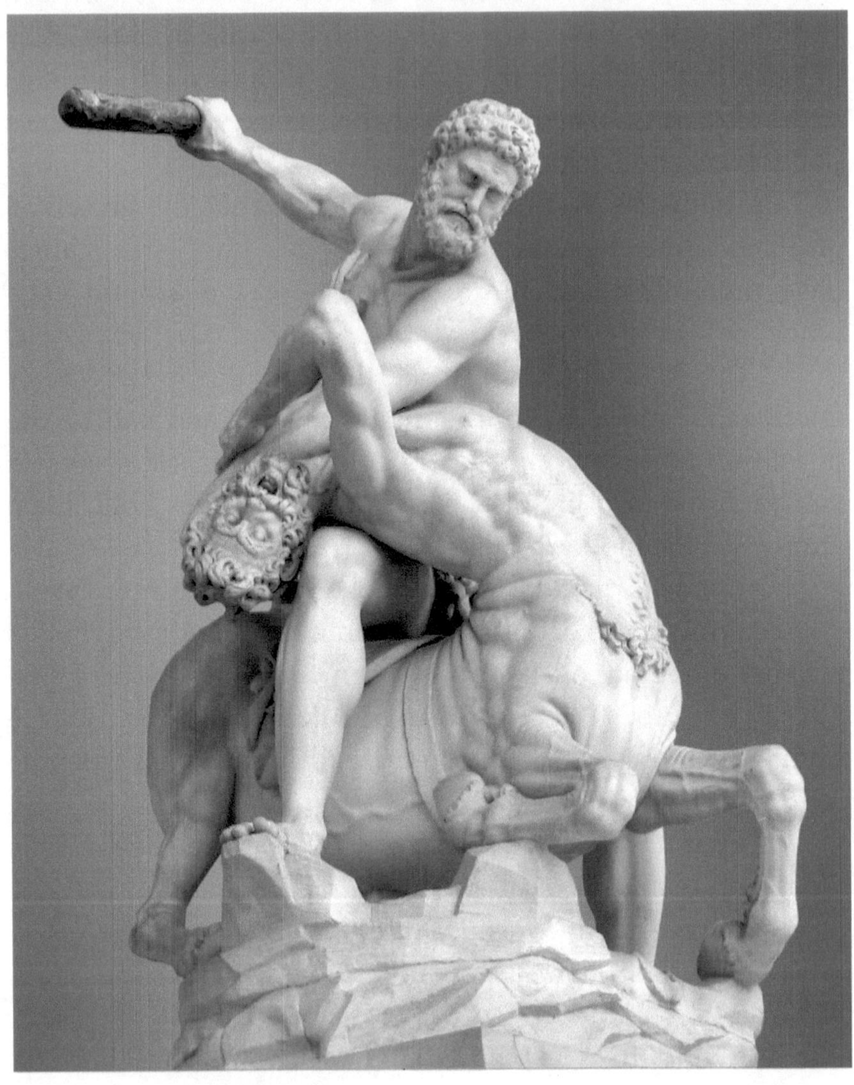

They both stepped up into the Loggia and walked over to the statue. Artemisia's face cringed at the savagery of the piece; featuring Hercules pulling the centaur's head back with one hand, while raising a club in the other, ready to bludgeon the creature. However, after acclimating to the brutality, she soon was enthralled by the dynamic figures, as well as by the miraculous feat achieved by this amazing sculptor with a difficult name to pronounce.

Armand stepped beside her. "So, what do you think of this one?"

Artemisia glanced back at her father with excitement in her eyes. "Even though it is nasty, I love it!" However, her effervescence fizzled as a frown etched itself on her adorable face. "I still don't get it. Once again, I find this more amazing than Michelangelo's *David*, yet this guy is unheard of. That's not fair!"

Armand nodded thoughtfully. "Yes, my dear. Life is often not fair. Many great artists have been washed away by the tidal wave of adulation showered upon the chosen ones. But Giambologna *was* famous in his day. It's just that his name didn't make it into as many books or classrooms as Michelangelo's. So, lack of exposure begets lack of fame. The same neglect can be said of Bandinelli."

Armand explained that Michelangelo had achieved a tremendous outpouring of admiration for his *David* in Florence that cemented his reputation as the leading sculptor, at least in his youth and middle age. Yet he explained that, in reality, when the younger Bandinelli came on the scene, he was lauded for his dazzling copy of the *Laocoön* in 1520.

By this time, Michelangelo was 45. He was deeply angered and jealous that Bandinelli was given the commission, as the *Laocoön* broke the tradition that Michelangelo and others followed, since single-figure statues that aimed for elegance were thought to be the pinnacle of perfection, not twisted groups of dynamic action.

As such, the recreation of this ancient Roman masterpiece (with its dynamic and complex configuration) proved to be the new wave of the future, and the ultimate endeavor in sculpture, one Michelangelo yearned for, but never demonstrated the ability to achieve. Nevertheless, the art of copying has never outshone original creation, hence perhaps explaining why Bandinelli's *Laocoön* eventually faded from memory.

They both glanced back up at the complicated arrangement of Giambologna's *Hercules Beating the Centaur Nessus*. Armand then glanced over his left shoulder. "Now let me show you *Hercules and Cacus* by Bandinelli. It is right over there near the entrance of the Palazzo Vecchio."

As they strolled up to the colossal statue, Artemisia's youthful eyes scanned the protruding, rocklike muscles of Hercules' abdomen. "This is very nice, too." She glanced back at Giambologna's *Hercules* in the distance, then at her father. "But this Hercules doesn't have much action, and well…" she hesitated to criticize, knowing she could never craft something this magnificent. Yet, she had to giggle as she added, "Well, I hate to say it, but his chest and muscles looks hard and stiff, like one of those iron breast plates I saw at the Met. You know, the kind ancient soldiers used to wear."

Armand nodded. "Yes, it's not easy to criticize a beautiful work like this, sweetheart. It obviously took a great deal of time and talent. But I'm elated that you're developing a discerning eye." He glanced back up at the statue. "But yes, Bandinelli's *Hercules* has muscles that are a bit rigid and unnatural compared to Giambologna's version.

Just then, Mario Poggi approached them, accompanied by Carlo Signorelli. Poggi shook his head at Armand, having only heard his last statement. "Tisk-tisk," he scolded with a paternal smile. "You should not disparage Bandinelli's great work of art like that, *Signore* Arnolfini. Especially in front of a young and impressionable mind."

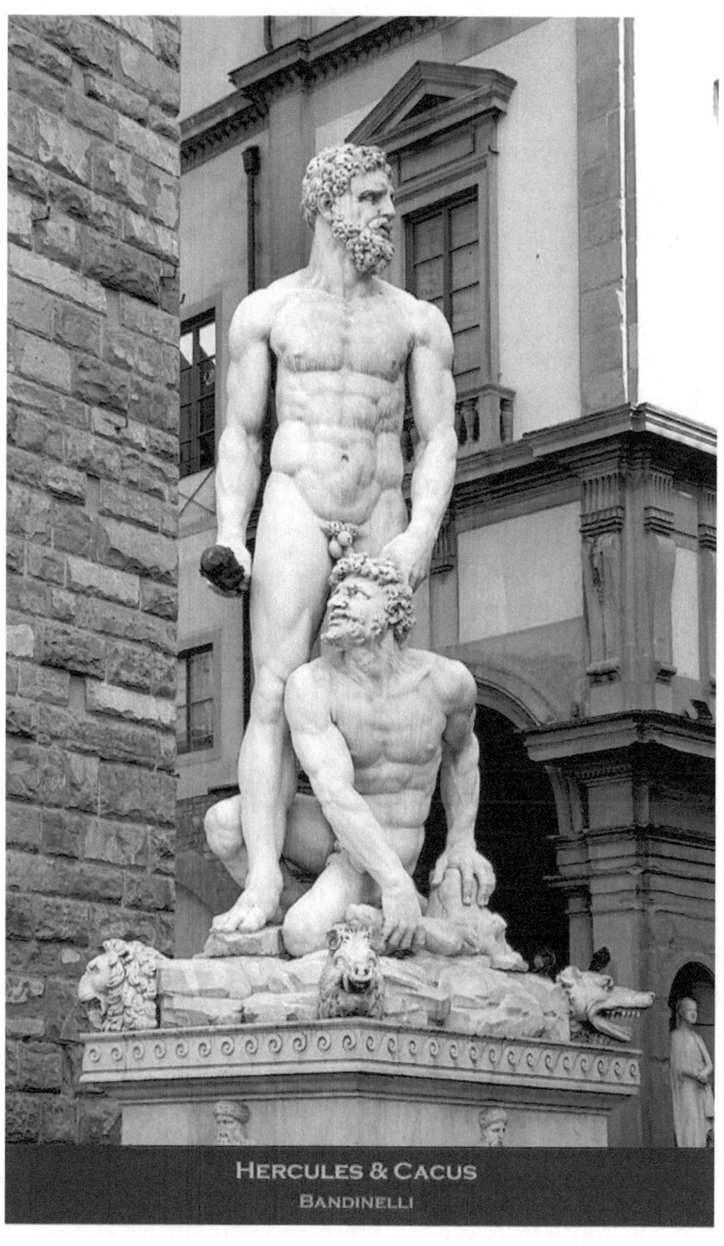

HERCULES & CACUS
BANDINELLI

"Well, Mario, I merely presented the statues to her. She made the critical analysis herself. As any great teacher knows, you don't imprint your own perceptions on students. You merely present the world to them, ask for their interpretations, then answer their questions with viable explanations."

As Mario nodded in agreement, Armand continued, "And have no worries, we all know that Bandinelli was a very important and talented artist, Mario. He rejuvenated the lost tradition of dynamic group sculptures, which eventually led to Giambologna and Bernini. However, it's imperative that I guide my daughter to decipher the differences between artists. And thanks to her bringing my attention to the works of Giambologna in the Loggia, I now feel quite certain that our new *Apollo and Daphne* is by Giambologna, not Bandinelli."

Poggi turned toward his associate. "Well, on that note, allow me to introduce Carlo Signorelli. He's a highly regarded expert of antiquities."

Armand shook Carlo's hand. "Hello, I've read about you. I'm pleased to finally meet you."

Carlo nodded. "*Grazie*. And I have read about you, *Signore* Arnolfini. I knew your father. I spoke with him on several occasions when he curated at the Uffizi. Sergio was a good man, a brilliant man."

"Thank you," Armand said. "I've learned a great deal from my father, rest his soul. But, I'm curious to know *your* assessment of the *Apollo and Daphne*."

Carlo smiled. "Well, I'm quite certain that it's by Bandinelli." He glanced up at Bandinelli's *Hercules*. "I'll grant you, this statue might not be Bandinelli's best specimen to make a comparison with the dynamism of the *Apollo and Daphne*. But if you were to view his magnificent *Laocoön*, perhaps you would change your mind."

"Well, yes, I'm quite familiar with Bandinelli's *Laocoön,* Carlo, which *is* magnificent. However, there's a certain freeness of motion in Giambologna's works that Bandinelli didn't always achieve."

"Perhaps," Signorelli conceded. "But at this point," he glanced at Mario, and continued, "We here have made the final decision. The new *Apollo and Daphne* has been attributed to Baccio Bandinelli. So, feel free to convey that to Mr. Langford at the Metropolitan. Our pricing will be finalized over the next day or so and sent to him in due course."

"Very well," Armand said. "I will indeed relay your assessment along with mine."

Poggi and Signorelli glanced at each other with raised eyebrows, then back at Armand, as Carlo said, "You're a man of strong conviction, *Signore* Arnolfini."

Armand smiled. "Indeed I am. But I do hope you and the Met can come to an agreement on price. It's a beautiful find and I'm sure they'd love to acquire it."

Carlo peered down the Uffizi corridor to his right. "Well, we do have others who are very interested, as well."

"I'm sure you do," Armand said. "That's the nature of the game." He looked at Poggi. "Well, I thank you for your time, Mario, for showing us the work." He glanced at Carlo. "And we look forward to hearing the price."

They all shook hands and the two men left, as Armand peered at Artemisia. "Well, that concludes our business here. Now let's get a bite to eat."

Armand took Artemisia to one of his favorite restaurants, where they ate a splendid meal of pasta, eggplant, and veal, then finished it off with Florence's world-class gelato.

Afterward, they walked to the Uffizi Gallery. He introduced his daughter to several of his friends on the staff, then to the many great works of art in the collection. Those included Leonardo's *Adoration of the Magi,* as well as Botticelli's *Birth of Venus* and *La Primavera.* Naturally, he didn't fail to show her less popular masterworks by Caravaggio, Raphael, Titian, Bellini and others, as some of those indeed scored higher on Artemisia's personal chart of favorites.

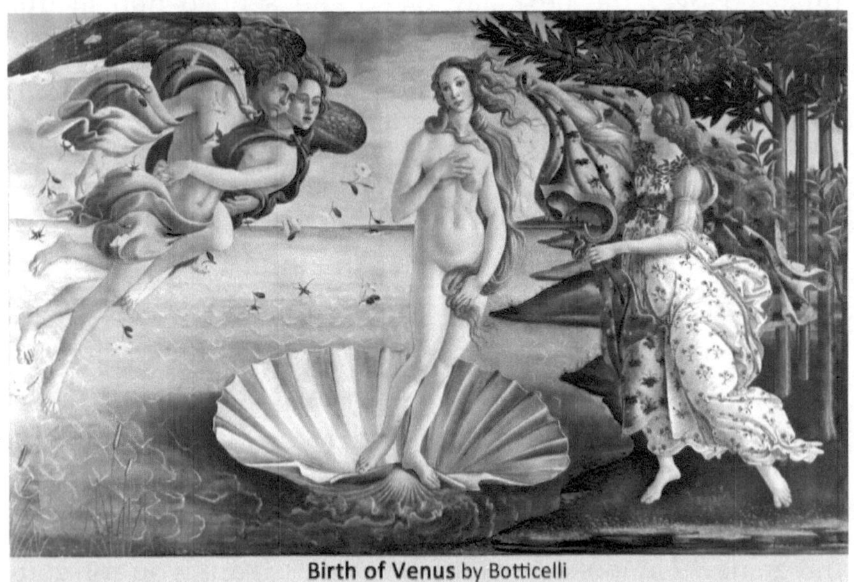

Birth of Venus by Botticelli

Armand then explained how his father had been the curator there for many years and later an Art History professor, inspiring him to embrace the art world. He then escorted her through the Vasari corridor, over the Ponte Vecchio, and to his father's house, where Armand had grown up.

He knocked on the door and was greeted by the new owners, who were delighted to show Armand and Artemisia around the house. Meanwhile, Armand regaled them with

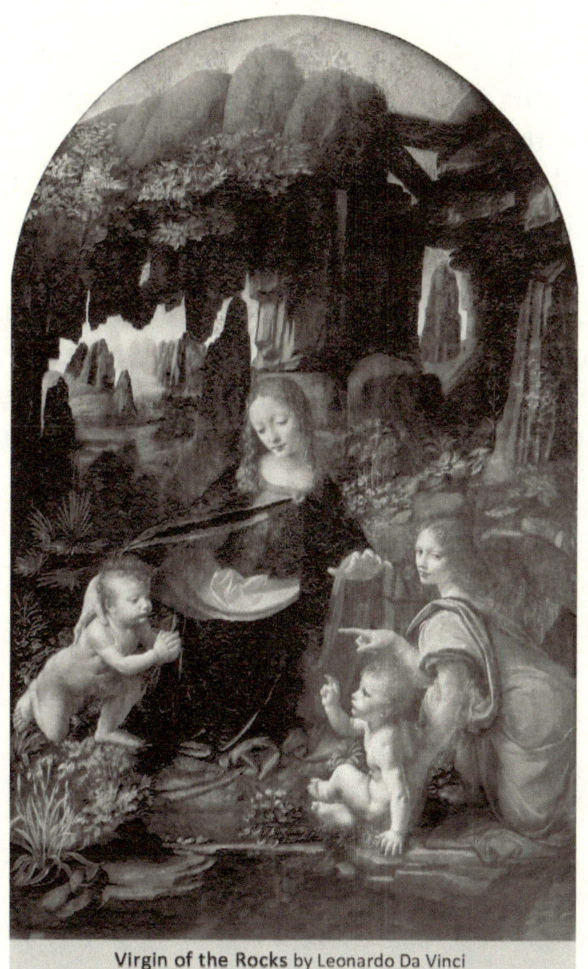

Virgin of the Rocks by Leonardo Da Vinci

memories of his childhood, including how he loved to play *fútbol* as a kid and eventually played pro-ball for AC Milan. He recalled his diversion from sports into investigation and how he focused on art crimes specifically. That, he explained, was primarily due to his father's great intellect and influence; a debt he owes to his beloved father.

A tear welled in Armand's eye as he noticed a reproduction of Leonardo's *Virgin of the Rocks* on the wall. It was a gift his father had left behind for the new owners.

Afterward, Armand and Artemisia enjoyed the owners' hospitality by drinking Amaretto and Pellegrino respectively, then took their leave.

Over the next few days they toured the city, stopping at the Academia, to see Michelangelo's *David*, then on to the Dante and Galileo museums, to gain insights about the iconic bard, hailed as the Father of the Italian language, and the rebellious scientist, hailed as the Father of Science.

The next day they scaled Brunelleschi's famous dome, which crowns Florence's cathedral and dominates the city's skyline. The view of the city, as the sun appeared to touch the distant hills, was breathtaking.

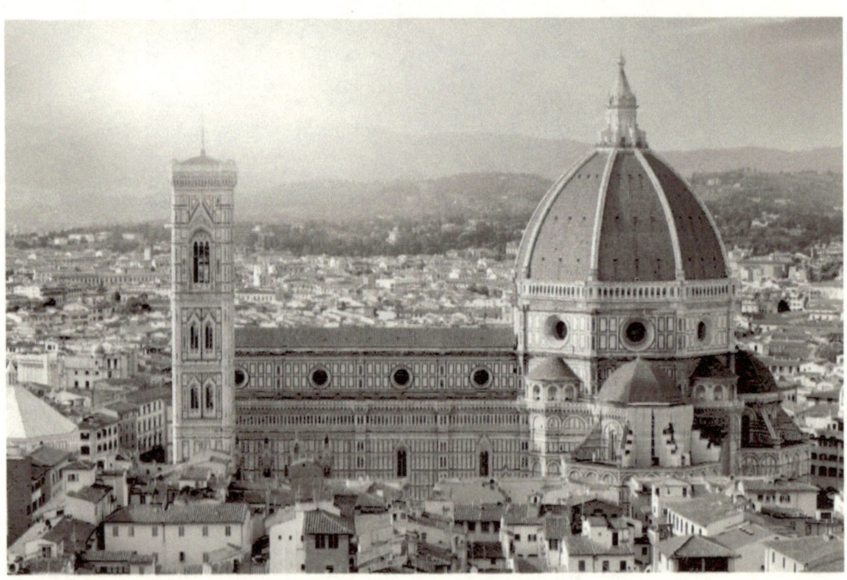

Then they descended to the street and walked to the Baptistery nearby. There, they viewed its famous bronze doors of *Paradise* by Lorenzo Ghiberti.

Saving a special treat for last, Armand grasped Artemisia's hand and escorted her through the narrow streets to Casa Buonarroti. It was a small museum off the tourist trail, but which happened to be a house owned by Michelangelo. Artemisia squinted as she scrutinized several early works by the master, but was truly taken aback when her father revealed the real surprise, as he pointed to a painting entitled *Allegory of Inclination*.

Artemisia looked up at her father, overwhelmed with joy and affection, as she gazed back at the painting, a work created by her namesake...Artemisia Gentileschi!

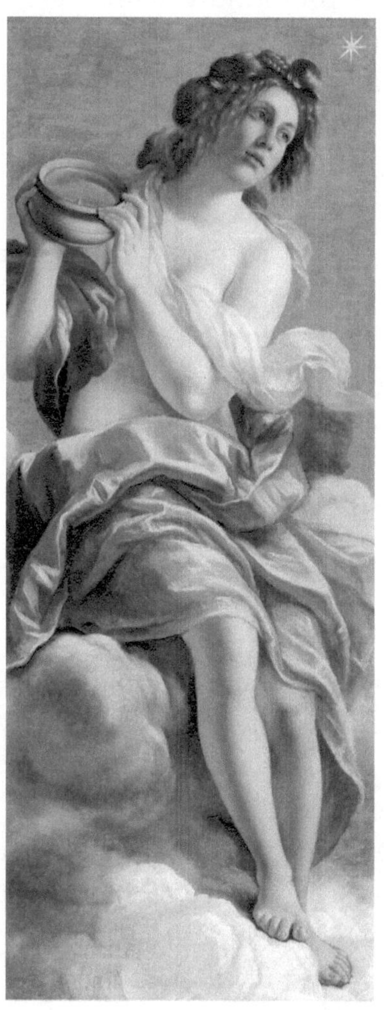

Tears welled in Artemisia's eyes. She knew this painting wasn't executed as well as some others she had seen, nor was it particularly unique in any way, generally speaking. But the fact that her father named her after this woman artist (who boldly triumphed over fierce opposition and sexual abuse) meant the world to Artemisia. As such, this pretty, unassuming painting struck a profound chord on her tender heartstrings. For as she had learned, art *is* subjective, and if it resonates profoundly with one's mind, heart and / or soul, then it is indeed *great*.

Artemisia turned, hugged her father tightly and kissed him.

Armand smiled, elated, but jested, "Honey, come on! Please! Not in public."

Artemisia laughed, and the two gazed back up at the painting.

After fully ingesting the cultural extravaganza, one Artemisia would never forget, it was time for the Arnolfinis to head home.

Arriving in Westport, Connecticut, Artemisia was taken aback by an immediate impression, namely the vast differences between American and Italian architecture. The plain and simple wooden structures in America were in stark contrast to the decorative stone and marble edifices she had seen on every corner in Italy. Where cost, simplicity, and practicality reigned in America, she realized that creativity, grandeur, and exuberance reigned in Italy.

Meanwhile, Andrea and little Jack were happy to see them return. Although in Jack's case it was more so to see his father to receive the souvenir he bought him rather than see his annoying sister. Yet, despite their occasional tiffs, their love for each other ran deeper than they even knew themselves.

Two days later, Armand was in the den listening to *Tarkus*, by Emerson, Lake and Palmer, when James Langford called. Armand turned off the trailblazing title track, as James said, "Armand, I'm glad you're back. I just wanted to thank you again for your outstanding insights."

"Well, I do hope my assessment helped, James. So, tell me, do you own the Bandinelli?"

James paused, then said, "Well, *no*, Armand. We don't."

"Ah, shucks! That's too bad, James. Its truly a beautiful sculpture."

"Yes, it most certainly is, Armand, just like you told us. But we didn't *really* purchase a Bandinelli, even though that's what's stated on the contract. Because, as of today, it turned out to be a Giambologna. *You were right!*"

Armand squinted. "Wait. What are you saying? They reassessed its authorship?"

"Yes, Armand, just moments ago, *after* we bought it yesterday." As Armand's eyes widened, James continued, "Actually, they had no option but to do so. You see, this morning they found an inscription at the excavation site, several centimeters below the statue's crate. In fact, the inscription was buried there by Mario's great-uncle when they hid the statue from the Nazis."

Armand smiled, amazed, yet somehow not too surprised, as Langford continued, "So, we now have unequivocal proof that the *Apollo and Daphne* was by Giambologna. It's an amazing find, and it's thanks to your glowing assessment that we bought the piece, even as a Bandinelli. And here it is, it already accrued twelve thousand dollars as a Giambologna. So, I'm splitting the profit and sending you an additional check for six thousand dollars."

"That's not necessary," Armand said. "But I'm elated that you bought the piece, and at a great price. It will make a splendid addition to your collection."

"It will indeed, Armand. It will indeed!"

The American Stonehenge

Andrea strolled into the den, only to see Armand transfixed as he listened to *"Das Wunder."*

Armand was immersed in Franz Liszt's sacred portrayal of *The Miracle,* which evoked the moment when Christ calmed the stormy seas that terrified his disciples. After which, the music is transcendent and ethereal, being one of the most sublime evocations of spirituality ever penned.

Andrea knew to remain silent until it ended, knowing full well how such works consumed and groomed Armand's mind and soul. As the last fading strains of music reached utter silence, she cleared her throat, "Uh, hum," then said, "Do you have a moment?"

Armand appeared to awaken from a heavenly coma, as he turned off the stereo and glanced up at her from the couch. "Uh…c-certainly," he said, a bit disoriented at first as he rejoined the Earthly realm of mortals.

Andrea sat down beside him. "Well, I just read an article, which was buried in the back of the newspaper. It was about the Georgia Guidestones."

Armand squinted as his head lowered pensively to switch gears. He looked back up. "Oh, yes, that's a granite monument of sorts. Wasn't it dubbed the *American Stonehenge*?"

"Yes," she said. "I know not many people know about it, but since my aunt Clara lives in Elbert County, she made me aware of its odd beginning, as well as the conspiracies that surround it; including Satanic worship and alleged ties to a New World Order."

Armand snickered, especially after listening to Liszt's sacred piece about Christ. "And?"

"And there was also a small tablet placed a few feet away. Its a ledger, which states the monument's structural dimensions and lists the monument's various capabilities to track astronomical events."

Armand sat upright, as astronomical features of ancient structures (such as those found in Aztec or Egyptian pyramids or England's Stonehenge) always piqued his interest. "What kind of capabilities?"

Andrea smiled, having snagged his full attention. "Well, supposedly, one attribute is how it indicates the celestial pole through a channel in the stone. Another is how a horizontal slot indicates the annual travels of the sun. Meanwhile the sunbeam that goes through the capstone marks noontime throughout the year."

Armand nodded thoughtfully. "Interesting, very interesting. But why all the religious fervor and conspiracy theories?"

"Well, that's just it. Besides those controversies, the ledger also contained a mystery."

Now even more intrigued, Armand placed his *Christus* CD down and inquired, "And what's that?"

"The ledger mentions that a time capsule was allegedly buried, and many religious groups and secularists are curious as to what it might say."

Armand rolled his eyes. "Well, come on, time capsules are often mysterious, Andrea. At least until the day they're opened."

"Maybe so, but the group that funded this monument, which was to remain anonymous, was put forth by frontman R.C. Christian, a name that also raises suspicion. But this Mr. Christian can't be located."

"Granted, that's not very helpful."

"Exactly," Andrea replied. "However, a Mr. Paul Monroe just called for you, but…" she giggled, "I didn't want to disturb your musical séance with Liszt or Christ or wherever your mind and soul travels during those cosmic sessions."

As Armand chuckled, she went on, "Anyhow, it's a rather exciting coincidence that Mr. Monroe would like to know where this time capsule is, if it exists, and perhaps more importantly, what it has to say. And he's willing to offer you an unlimited budget to do so."

Armand was now even more skeptical. "Unlimited budget?" He rubbed his chin. "And why *me*?"

"Well, he's read about you in the news, Armand. And let's be serious, your cases have expanded over the years, from art and architecture to literary and musical mysteries. And this American Stonehenge *is* a monument." She handed him a piece of paper with Paul Monroe's phone number. "I'm going to fix dinner. Give him a call, if you're interested." She started to rise off the sofa, and added, "Who knows, it might prove to be a religious revelation of sorts. And don't forget the unlimited budget!"

Armand smiled. "Very well. But if I do decide to take it on, you'll accompany me on this one."

Andrea squinted as she halted and sat back down. "And why is that?"

"Because you know more about this satanic, secular, or religious monument than I, and…" to add a touch of guilt, he added, "You can visit your Aunt Clara, who you said many times you've been remiss in visiting."

Andrea smirked demurely. "You're a sly one, Mr. Arnolfini. But very well." She stood up. "Hopefully you can uncover all the mysteries in this case with the same guile you just used on me." With a smile, she turned and strode toward the kitchen, calling out through the walls and ceiling, "Artemisia! Jack! Down stairs, *now*, in the kitchen!"

Three days later, Armand and Andrea were on a Delta flight heading to Georgia. Having landed and rented a Mercedes, they first visited Aunt Clara for several hours, then drove several miles to their hotel.

As they unpacked, Andrea said, "I think Mr. Monroe's refusal to speak about details over the phone was rather suspicious. Don't you?"

While Armand took off his shirt and jeans and slipped into a suit, he said, "Well, honey, plenty of millionaires don't wish to speak on the phone these days. Let's face it, after Watergate they're more prudent, and a bit paranoid, about wiretapping."

Andrea looked in the mirror as she brushed her hair. "Well, that only gives us more reasons to question this man. What's he afraid of?"

Armand shrugged. "Who knows, but we'll meet him face-to-face soon enough." Straightening out his tie, he added, "Let's grab a bite to eat first, then we'll head over to his estate."

Two hours later, the satiated couple headed to their destination. Eventually, they drove up the long driveway lined with tall trees and pulled up to Monroe's Georgian Revival mansion.

They walked up the front stairs, past the towering white columns, and came before a set of double-doors, which swung open. Standing erect, and in a dashing white suit, Mr. Paul Monroe extended his hand. "Welcome to my humble abode, Mr. and Mrs. Arnolfini."

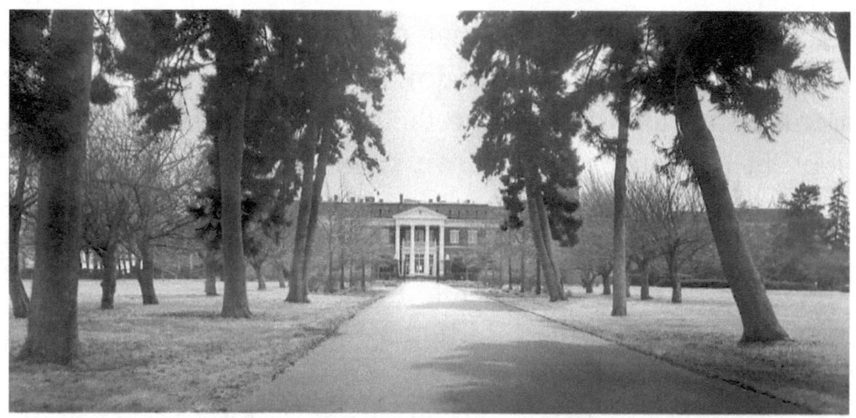

They each shook hands, as Armand gazed at the opulent marble foyer then up at the exquisite spiral staircase. "Humble? Really? I reckon our meanings of the word differ."

Monroe chuckled. "Well, yes, I must confess. I was born into wealth, Mr. Arnolfini." He glanced at the oil-painted portrait on the wall. "My great grandfather, Reginald, was an ambitious soul. Against great odds and religious persecution, he founded this plantation. So I've only known this place to be my humble home. I reckon it's all about one's perspective."

Armand glanced at the portrait, then back at Monroe. "I assume you're a Christian then?"

Monroe's head nodded, but quickly came to a halt. "Well, I was born and raised a Christian, Mr. Arnolfini, but one with profound concerns. Why do you ask?"

"You stated your great grandfather endured religious persecution," Armand said. "So I can't imagine that being an issue, especially here in the South, unless he was not a Protestant or a Baptist."

Monroe smirked. "Exactly, Mr. Arnolfini. The Christian religion experienced many years of intense strife among its various denominations. Puritans brutally burned and killed

Catholics, while Catholics hated Protestants and vice-versa. Christians today may look down upon other religions that demean or kill others within their own faith, but they fail to look in the mirror of our own past. We had our problems, for sure. However, Christians have gotten past those years of brutality and stand united in the faith, even if separated by dogma. We're a special lot. Meanwhile, other religions, especially those in the Middle East and Asia, are trapped in a dark and archaic past."

Andrea jumped in. "Well, if you're referring to Sunni and Shiite sects, I think many Christians view Muslims as barbaric for one main reason. That's because the handful of radical leaders at the top have complete control over the masses and silence the majority who disagree. But I pray the suppressed moderate Muslims will find salvation one day."

Monroe gazed at Andrea with a tepid smirk and a shrug. "I suppose their radical leaders *are* a major reason for their archaic ways, but I have little faith that things will change. Their religion not only suppresses women but also mutilates young girls who stray from their scriptures. Not to mention how they train and inculcate young men to focus on killing infidels."

Again, Monroe shrugged. "Well, enough of that. Allow me to escort you to my terrace out back. It's a pleasant day outside and I had my servant make a refreshing pitcher of lemonade. I hope that will suffice, as I have no alcohol on the premises. I'm not a drinker, but rather a thinker." He chuckled at his own witticism and winked.

Armand and Andrea cordially smiled and followed Monroe out to the rear terrace. It was beautifully paved with red brick, with a white trellis overhead, covered in wisteria that draped down in soft, colorful veils of white and purple flowers. Several yards back stood an empty stable, its double doors wide open with old rusted pipes and construction debris scattered about.

Monroe caught Armand's line of sight, and called out to his servant, "James! I told you to tidy-up. Close those doors. We have visitors."

"Yes, Sir!" came the reply, as Monroe looked back at his guests. "Please excuse that eye-sore. As you can see, this estate is very old, built in the eighteenth century. So repairs are a perpetual occurrence. Anyhow, please grab yourselves a glass and have a seat."

Grasping their glasses of freshly squeezed lemonade, the couple took their seats on white, rattan chairs with beige cushions.

Meanwhile, Monroe remained standing. He took a sip, then started to pace, back and forth, yet only within a few steps. He then stopped. "I'll get right down to it. As I mentioned over the phone, I would like to hire you to locate the time capsule that was buried under the Georgia Guidestones, or *American Stonehenge,* as it is often called."

Andrea placed her lemonade down on the end table. "Mr. Monroe, I have read several articles about this monument, and it's been said that the time capsule was only speculation. Do you have proof that it was in fact crafted and buried?"

Monroe smiled. "Andrea," he hesitated. "May I call you *Andrea*?"

As she nodded, he continued, "Being a Christian, Andrea, as I assume you and your husband also are, I have *faith* that the capsule is a reality and was indeed buried. However, *where* it is buried *is* the mystery." He turned his gaze toward Armand. "So, the question is: Do *you* have faith, Mr. Arnolfini?"

Armand chuckled. "Well, I'm not sure if you're referring to faith in religion or to the existence of the capsule, Mr. Monroe. But I suppose each are shrouded in mystery." He placed his lemonade down. "But since you wish to hire me to find the capsule, I'll say simply this, I'll take on the challenge."

Monroe grinned and stepped closer to shake Armand's hand.

Armand stood up, but refrained from shaking. "To clarify, I said *challenge*, Mr. Monroe. Which means, we can't be sure there ever was a capsule. So don't be disappointed if I turn up with nothing but dirt."

Monroe smiled and nodded affirmatively. "By all means, I can sense that you're a bright and *faithful* man, Armand." He flinched. "Oh! Excuse me, may I call you *Armand*?"

Armand smiled as he shook his hand. "Well, I wouldn't want you calling me Judas."

Monroe squinted, then laughed heartily, as Armand added, "But, as I said, there is a good deal of mystery as to where this capsule might be. My wife read that it was allegedly buried either under the monument or somewhere near it. *Under it* poses a significant problem, as I'm not sure we can get permission to disturb the structure. So, that eliminates a very viable location from my search. Are you prepared to accept that?"

Monroe opened his white suit jacket and pulled out his checkbook. Taking a seat by the table, he said, "You just use that miraculous intuition and intelligence I have read about, Armand, and I'm sure you'll be successful." As he began writing out the check, he said, "And if by some odd occurrence you fail in your preliminary endeavors, I will eliminate all roadblocks. I'll get tractors and cranes to move the darn monument so you can fulfill your duties uninterrupted."

Having finished filling out the check, he looked up at Armand. "Failure of trying, Armand, will *never* be an option." He stood up and extended the check to Armand. "Here's your first payment of five thousand dollars. Now don't be shy. Ask me for whatever you need, as there's no limit to what I'll pay to find this capsule."

Armand gazed at Monroe pensively as he accepted the check. He turned and handed it to Andrea, then turned back toward Monroe. "I must ask why? Why is this capsule so important to you?"

"Good question, Armand," Monroe replied, as he grasped Armand's elbow and ushered them both toward the front door. "I believe that this mysterious monument, and any time capsule related to it, has much to offer the world. And since no one else has the ambition, sense, or money to do this, I stepped up to the plate. Or should I say, up to *the granite stones*."

As they all approached the front door, Monroe stopped and looked deeply into Armand's eyes. "Truly contemplate the magnitude of this, Armand. Six large stones, each inscribed in various languages, speak of multi-nationalism, population control, eugenics, and other topics, and yet the author, or authors, remain completely anonymous. Unknown!"

He grabbed Armand's shoulder firmly, and shook it. "So tell me, *who* would do such a thing? Other than the devil or some enlightened group of religious disciples." He paused as his eyes gazed erratically upward, then added, "But if disciples, then disciples of what religion?" He shook his head, agitated, then looked back at Armand. Again, he jiggled Armand's shoulder firmly. "I hate secrets, Armand!"

He opened the front door, and practically shoved Armand out, as he added, "So, *go*! Go and do what you do so brilliantly, Mr. Arnolfini, and find me that capsule!"

As Armand and Andrea hopped in the car and headed back toward the hotel, he said, "Well, Millionaire Monroe is a bit obsessed all right."

"Yes," Andrea replied with a chuckle. "And a bit rude!"

They looked at each other, then giggled.

Back at the hotel, Andrea sat at the edge of the bed slipping on a pair of sneakers, while Armand took off his suit and tossed on a pair of old jeans and a black polo shirt. "It's nice to get out of that suit," he said as he grasped the car keys. "Now it's time to get down and dirty." He glanced at her. "Are you ready?"

Andrea nodded as she took off her jewelry and whipped her bag over her shoulder. "Let the Easter egg hunt begin!" As they both chuckled and walked to the car, she squinted. "Actually, what the heck is the Easter egg hunt all about anyhow? I mean, why and how would such a silly tradition start?"

As Armand put tools and shovels in the trunk of the rented Mercedes, he said, "From what I've learned, it all started with Martin Luther. The egg was symbolic of a tomb, from which the chick, aka Jesus, emerged on Easter Sunday. So hiding the eggs was a way to make children search for God, with hopes of finding Him and receiving a reward. And kids always found the reward."

Andrea nodded. "Hmm, very interesting. But what about the candy that Americans put in plastic eggs?"

Armand smiled as he closed the trunk. "Things have a way of morphing over time and by different cultures. So I suppose candy became the reward. And if candy were given up for lent it would make a splendid reward on Easter Sunday. Right?"

Andrea smiled. "It would indeed. But I paid the price as a kid. The dentist seemed to gain all the rewards."

Armand chuckled. "Well, lets dig some cavities in the ground so we can find this capsule."

"Roger that!" Andrea said, as the couple hopped in the car and drove off. Twenty minutes later, they arrived in town and parked at Town Hall.

Andrea volunteered. "I'll go see about getting permission to dig around the monument."

"Go to it, darling."

Fifteen minutes later, Andrea returned with a slip in her hand. Standing by the driver's door, she peered down at Armand. "I've got it. This slip only allows us to dig in the grassy areas around the monument, as long as we don't disturb the monument, ledger, or any walkways or bushes around it."

"Okay, well, that's a start," Armand said.

Andrea placed the slip in her bag. "Oh, yes. They also mentioned how that mysterious person with an alias, R.C. Christian, donated the land and monument to the Town. So it appears the Town Board now makes all the calls, unless this R.C. Christian made some other secret arrangements."

As she walked around and got into the car, she looked at Armand. "You have to admit, this whole thing *is* rather mysterious. I can see how this gave birth to conspiracy theories and satanic rumors."

Armand nodded. "Exactly. That's one of the reasons why we're here. While Paul Monroe is eager to find the capsule, my objective includes finding out just what this monument is all about."

Several minutes later they arrived at the curious site, as the monument stood on a barren mound surrounded by grass and bushes. Four large slabs of granite stood on-end in a starburst configuration, with a fifth one in the very middle, and a smaller one lying flat on top. As they both gazed at the enigmatic structure, an unsettling sense of primitive, pagan rituals or extra-terrestrial monoliths filled their minds and very souls.

A shiver rankled Andrea's bones as she gazed at Armand. "Are you feeling what I am?"

Armand nodded. "If I'm right, *yes*. It has an otherworldly appearance, all right. Whether its from *One Million Years B.C.* or *2001 A Space Odyssey*, I don't know. But let's read the inscriptions."

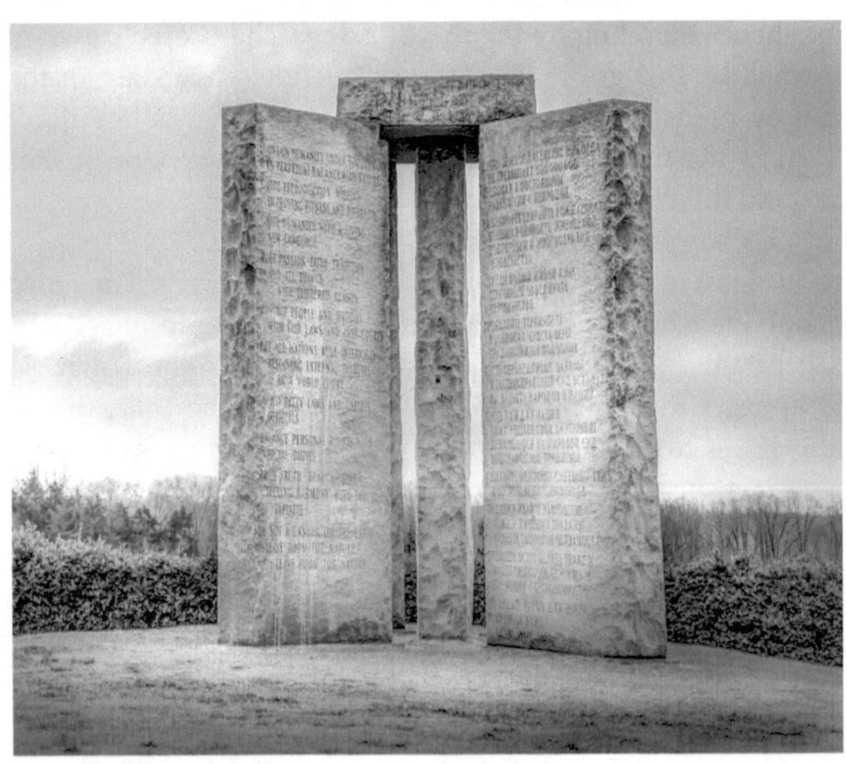

With that, the duo walked headlong toward the structure and merely glanced at the ledger nearby. The inscription stated: LET THESE BE GUIDESTONES TO AN AGE OF REASON.

As Armand and Andrea approached the huge granite monoliths, their eyes gazed upward. They read the inscriptions in English, while recognizing six other languages, namely Spanish, Russian, Hebrew, Swahili, Hindi, Arabic, and Chinese. Essentially, the monument stood erect and rigid, proclaiming ten guidelines or Ten Commandments.

(1) Maintain humanity under 500,000,000 in perpetual balance with nature.

(2) Guide reproduction wisely — improving fitness and diversity.

(3) Unite humanity with a living new language.

(4) Rule passion — faith — tradition — and all things with tempered reason.

(5) Protect people and nations with fair laws and just courts.

(6) Let all nations rule internally resolving external disputes in a world court.

(7) Avoid petty laws and useless officials.

(8) Balance personal rights with social duties.

(9) Prize truth — beauty — love — seeking harmony with the infinite.

(10) Be not a cancer on the Earth — Leave room for nature — Leave room for nature.

Armand looked at Andrea. "Well, I don't see these guidelines being too extreme or inflammatory. Most, so far, do posit a valid sense of reason." However, as he kept reading, he said, "Hold on a minute. A few lines *can* be a bit troubling. Like, how exactly do we keep the world population down to five hundred million?" He looked at Andrea. "Are they advocating sensible contraception? Abortion? Or perhaps eugenics, to kill off the weak in order to create a super race?"

Andrea nodded. "Yes, that does pose serious problems. It sounds a bit familiar, like the Aryan super race." Her eyes scanned other inscriptions. "But quite surprisingly, I find myself agreeing with the other guidelines. It would be wonderful if we all could get along, speak one language, and live in harmony."

Armand reflected. "Well, that reminds me of my dearly departed friend, John Lennon. *Imagine*."

"*Imagine*, indeed!" A man said, as he stepped closer to the couple. "Excuse me, but I couldn't help overhearing you mention Lennon's *Ode To Reason*, as I call it." He extended his hand. "Please allow me to introduce myself, I'm a man of wealth and taste," he said with a giggle.

As Armand shook his hand, the man added, "If you hadn't noticed, my introduction was a lyric sung by Mick Jagger."

"Oh, I noticed, all right," Armand said straight-faced. "And Mick sung that as the *Devil*." Armand stared deep into the man's eyes, as the man now squinted, a bit unnerved, while Armand added sternly, "And I have *no* Sympathy For The Devil."

The man twitched, as he stood mute and unsettled, when Armand suddenly laughed. "Pleased to meet you. Hope you guess my name."

The man chuckled with relief. "Ha! Good one! You know that song all right. You had me there." With a sigh, he added, "You're a clever one, I see, and a jolly good jokester. My name is Jonathan Orwell."

"I'm Armand Arnolfini, and this is my wife Andrea." As Andrea nodded with a grin, Jonathan said, "It's a pleasure to meet you both." He reached over and quickly shook their hands, and continued, "But as I was saying, Lennon's song *was* brilliant. It was a clear declaration of how stupid mankind has been." He glanced at the engraved granite stones. "And this glorious monument, to an Age of Reason, echoes and enshrines Lennon's mantra."

Jonathan paused, then seemed to drift into a trance as he began to utter softly, yearningly, "Imagine there's no heaven. It's easy if you try. No hell below us. Above us, only sky—"

Andrea cleared her throat. "Excuse me, Mr. Orwell. But I happen to believe in God, as well as Heaven and Hell." She glanced at the gargantuan granite tablets. "And these guidelines make no reference about not believing in God. In fact, all it states is that we should rule over our *faith,* and all things, with tempered reason. And that we should be seeking harmony with the infinite, hence with God."

Jonathan sniggered as he shook his head, agitated. "Oh boy, here we go!" he huffed. "Andrea, people of *blind faith* can never understand the truth, even when it's placed right before their eyes, whether that be in black ink or chiseled in stone. Religion, or godly faith, can *never* be believed if one has reason. They are diametrically opposed. Religious faith is based on fairytales. Reason is based on facts. And the twain shall never meet."

Armand interjected, "Well, there *is* something else that's a *fact*. And that's that humankind, since the beginning of time, has always interpreted the same fact from diametrically opposed viewpoints. It's just like how one person can view a glass as half-full while another sees it as half-empty. That's another reason why I have little faith that humankind will ever live in total harmony, or speak one language."

Armand looked at Andrea. "As for one language, sweetheart, while that would indeed be fabulous for bringing the world closer together, it would simultaneously destroy and vaporize countless cultural identities and rich traditions. So, even one language has diametrically opposed ramifications."

Andrea and Jonathan glanced at each other and shrugged with a nod, while Armand added, "Excuse us, Jonathan, but it's time for my wife and I to look for the time capsule."

Jonathan looked at Armand. "Well, as the inscription states, the capsule is buried six feet below the monument."

"We missed that," Andrea said.

"Yes, we didn't get to read every tablet," Armand said. "Exactly where is that inscription?"

"Follow me," Jonathan said as he walked away from the structure and pointed at the small ledger nearby, the same one they had passed on their way in. "Right there."

Armand looked at Andrea. "Our grand and intriguing monument certainly lured us away from this little gem here, didn't it?"

"Indeed it did," she replied. "I guess we failed Detective Class 101 today."

"We're all entitled to a day off, even if cognitively," Armand said with a chuckle.

Yet as Armand and Andrea read the inscription, their hearts dropped. Andrea shook her head. "Oh dear. A dead end." She looked at Armand. "I guess we'll need to call our millionaire client. He needs to ask the Town for permission to move the entire monument."

"Hold on," Armand said as he stared at the inscription. "The dates for the capsule's burial or when it should be opened are left blank." He smiled.

Andrea followed his line of sight and flinched. Then she looked at Armand. "Why are you smiling? Doesn't that mean the capsule was never made *or* buried?"

Armand shook his head. "Not necessarily. Once again, it appears diametrically opposed viewpoints are gleaned from the same inscription."

Andrea playfully smirked as she placed her hand on her hip. "So, what did *you* glean, Sherlock?"

Armand chuckled. "Well, the fact that they didn't inscribe dates for the capsule simply means they didn't have it at the time of construction. Therefore, it very well could have been buried *after* the monument was erected. So it must be somewhere else, *if* it exists at all."

Jonathan had grown intrigued, as he interjected, "It's about time someone else tried to find that capsule."

Armand and Andrea looked at Jonathan, again with diametric reactions: Andrea disheartened that someone before them was unsuccessful, while Armand hoped to learn from those mistakes to achieve success.

Armand inquired, "Who else looked for it? And where did they search?"

Jonathan's frown and slumped shoulders telegraphed the first answer, while he now expounded on the second. "I looked for it over *there*." Pointing at several patches of grass, he added, "I dug up the entire perimeter of this monument at night so the Town wouldn't catch me. But it was all in vain. Not only did they catch and fine me, but I came up empty handed. So, if you know somebody who can have these granite slabs moved, perhaps the capsule *is* under it. After all, the blank dates on that inscription might have been intentional, to protect the capsule from thieves."

Andrea's inquisitive lips twisted, as she looked at Armand and said, "Perhaps *you*, my dear Sherlock, were wrong, as well. We have a third interpretation." Glancing at Jonathan, she added, "And that sounds quite plausible, especially considering how this monument was made and donated anonymously." She gazed up at the intriguing slabs of inscribed granite. "Everything about this monument is mysterious."

Armand nodded. "Yes, my dear, foiling potential thieves with blank dates *is* another possibility." He looked at Jonathan. "So, what did *you* expect to find in the capsule?"

"Obviously something entirely opposite to what you and your wife hope to find."

"As I said," Armand replied, "most things in life are interpreted differently. So my expectations are quite possibly different than what you or even my wife might speculate."

"Perhaps," Jonathan said. "But I believe the capsule's message is not some evil conspiracy or juvenile curse by a fictitious Devil or vengeful God. Rather, it's a view of hope, hope built on logic to eventually eliminate all the false faiths on this planet. Let's face it, countless religions and gods were conjured up and worshipped since the beginning of time by fanatics without the use of reason or hard evidence. Instead, they fabricated gods based on their fear of death and misfortunes with a fanciful imagination borne of ignorance. And let's not forget the power they wielded over their naïve sheep."

Andrea snorted with a huff. "I've heard enough, thank you." She turned and started walking toward the car. Glancing over her shoulder, she said, "Are you coming, Armand?"

Armand smiled and looked at Jonathan. "In some instances my wife's reactions are diametrically opposed to mine, so I'll have to say, please excuse us. Thank you for the insights about your digging quest. It's been quite helpful."

"No problem," Jonathan said with a shrug, as he shook his head and gazed wearily up at the provocative monument.

As Armand approached the car, he said, "Was it necessary to rudely walk away from him?"

Andrea sighed, heavily. "Armand, I have little patience for atheists. I'm sorry, I know it's not the Christian way, but the older I get the less I wish to be around negative people, people who are too haughty to believe this miraculous world and life we have was made by a higher being."

"He wasn't negative, Andrea. He simply has another viewpoint, one with solid logic to stand on. From Ra and Horus to Zeus and Apollo, or from Mithras to a plethora of others, mankind *has* fabricated numerous false gods. And I emphasize *man*kind, since it's telling that ancient men predominantly invented or worshipped male gods, including your own."

"Let's not go there, Armand."

"That's *exactly* why religion has some profound flaws, Andrea. Not going there, not listening to others, or not delving deep into religious history leaves many ignorant and only breeds ignorance and intolerance. Religion has caused countless wars and billions of tragic deaths, despite its many obvious good points."

"Okay, catechism is over for today, Armand. Let's go!"

Armand smirked. "Catechism would never entertain open debate, Andrea, it's based on autocratic indoctrination. But yes, it's best we leave."

Slipping into the Mercedes, Armand started to drive back toward the hotel. Several long and uneasy minutes of silence passed, until Armand finally said, "Okay, so do you really think the capsule is buried under the monument?"

Andrea rolled her eyes without even looking at him. "So I guess *my viewpoint* is wrong, just like my thoughts about religion?"

Armand sighed. "Darling, I'm not looking to lure you back into a heated debate, I merely want to know if you really think I should talk to Monroe? I'm not fully convinced we should have cranes and tractors disturb that monument at this juncture."

"And what juncture is this?" she said, now turning to look at him. "Jonathan said he dug up the entire perimeter. So what's left?"

"I just think it needs more thought. Moving the monument seems drastic at this moment," Armand opined. "It's best if we kept that as a last resort."

"*We*?" Andrea sniggered, as she turned to look out the window once again. "Why don't you just do what you want? You always do."

Armand pulled the car over and shifted into park. "Andrea, that's *not* true! And let's not get derailed over this. You're allowing frustration to fuel your anger rather than rallying reason to simmer your passion. Are you really going down this *negative* path?"

Andrea's smile broke through her anger as she turned and looked back at her husband. "You had to put *negative* in there, huh?"

"Well, you said so yourself, sweetheart, you don't like being around negative people. And neither do I. So let's just talk about this."

"I guess that's another reason why I love you," Andrea said warmly with deep affection. "You're so damn understanding and level-headed." She reached over and kissed him. "I'm sorry. I guess I was acting like a petulant fool."

"No, not a fool. Religion and politics are volatile subjects. I get it. But I've learned to break through the religious walls we were programmed to uphold as children and question things. *Seek and ye shall find* has been my motto ever since."

A warm and loving smile emanated from Andrea's beautiful face. "Okay, so if moving the monument is the last resort, then what do you propose we do now?"

"Get lunch."

Andrea laughed. "*Eating*. Of course, one of your other fortes."

"Well, feeding the stomach feeds the brain, dear." With that, Armand swung the car around and headed to a restaurant.

Eating appetizers at a small Southern café, the couple enjoyed the spicy flavors of home-cooked dishes along with glasses of white wine.

As Armand took a spoonful of his lobster bisque, Andrea asked, once again, "So, what do we do after this?"

"I can think of several things," Armand said romantically, eyeing up his wife as if the main course.

Andrea smiled and rolled her eyes. "No, seriously. What's our next step?"

"That little ledger that we overlooked has been circling in my head," Armand said as he swirled his glass of wine. Taking a sniff of the Pinot Grigio's bouquet, he then placed the glass down, as well as his spoon. He slid the empty bowl of soup away, and continued, "I'm thinking that if the capsule was made after the monument was erected, they very likely buried it under the ledger."

"Of course," Andrea said, as she finished sipping her wine. "That makes sense, all right." As the waiter placed their entrées in front of them, Andrea picked up her fork and said, "Let's finish this up and get digging, literally."

Armand chuckled as he waved his hand cautiously. "Slow down, sweetheart. Take your time. The capsule, if its even there, has been sitting there for many years. It doesn't have legs." He gazed down at his entrée. "But this does!" With that, Armand picked up the Alaskan king crab leg and cracked it open.

An hour later, Armand and Andrea returned to the monument, just as the evening sun's rays sliced their way over the treetops and pierced through the gaps of the granite slabs. The laser-like spectacle was an enigmatic sight to see as Armand stood for a moment, analyzing them. He then turned and pulled two shovels and a lantern out of the car trunk. He handed a shovel and the lantern to his wife, then they walked toward the dimly lit monument.

As Andrea surveyed the dark and vacant grounds, she said, "Shouldn't we have requested permission from the Town about this?"

"Don't worry," Armand said. "We'll have this dug up and put back to normal in no time."

As they both pushed the ledger a few feet back, he added, "The fact is, I did contact them. They said there were several forms that had to be filled out, and that an approval, if accepted, would take several weeks to clear by the Town Board. We simply don't have that much time, nor can we wait for a possible rejection. So let's get on with it."

For almost an hour Andrea and Armand gouged the earth as the dim glow of the lantern shone at the ditch's edge. A light breeze rustled the distant trees while the last hues of dusk shimmered on the darkening horizon.

With the sound of footsteps, a young woman approached. Curious, she gazed down at the couple. "What are you doing?"

Armand glanced up at the woman but kept digging as Andrea crawled out of the four-foot-deep hole. She brushed the dirt off her jeans and said, "We're looking for the time capsule that goes with this monument."

The woman smiled. "I figured as much. This place gets a lot of curious folks doing strange things. Even I'm a bit curious to know if a capsule exists. Do you mind if I help?"

"Well, that's very nice," Andrea replied. "But we only have two shovels."

The young woman's eyes furtively peered left and right, as she said, "I'll stand guard and divert anyone who attempts to stroll by," she said. "We do get a few nighttime strollers or joggers through here, and even a few vandals."

Armand lifted his head. "That's a good idea. We don't need any attention or problems."

The woman gazed down at Armand. "It would be my pleasure. My name is Susan, by the way."

The Arnolfinis offered their names, then continued digging for twenty more minutes, until Andrea's shovel made a metallic sound. Armand looked over, their eyes connecting. "Sounds promising!" he said, as they both smiled and continued to dig deeper. Within minutes they unearthed a 3-inch wide rusted pipe, 18 inches long, and with two rusted end caps screwed on.

Armand lifted it out of the dirt. "It's rather crude. It's just an old plumbing pipe."

"Well! Open it!" Andrea exclaimed.

Susan heard Andrea's excited plea and returned to the excavation site. "Your voice carries, Andrea," Susan said, as she gazed down the six-foot ditch at the couple.

Armand's head was barely at ground level as he looked up. He raised the rusted capsule in his hand. "We found it!"

"That's fantastic," Susan said, as Jonathan Orwell walked up beside her.

"Excellent work!" Jonathan said, not to Armand, but to Susan. "Thanks for calling me, honey bunch. I knew they'd return here *sooner* rather than later."

As Armand and Andrea glanced at each other, perplexed, Jonathan looked down the ditch at Armand. "Hand it over! Now!" he demanded with a menacing growl.

"Not on your life," Armand said, as he handed the capsule to Andrea. He brushed the dirt off his shirt, then started to climb out of the ditch.

Jonathan lunged over and kicked Armand back into the hole. "Not on my life, huh? Well, I'll *end your life* if you don't, Armand." As Jonathan's crazed eyes pierced deep into Armand's enraged ones, he revealed the shovel behind his back. "Quite conveniently, you and your wife are in a six-foot grave, Armand. So, if you don't want me to bury you alive, I strongly suggest you hand it over. Now!"

"As I said," Armand retorted. "Not on your life!"

"Then you're a damned fool!" Jonathan blustered. Angrily, he shoveled dirt at Armand's face, then started filling up the hole in a frenzy.

Meanwhile, Susan nearly choked, stunned by her lover's actions, and grabbed his arm. "Jonathan, *stop*! What are you doing? This wasn't the plan."

Jonathan turned, eyes blazing. "You stupid fool! As I told you, the Town threatened to imprison me if they found me digging here again. I had to let these two do my dirty work. But they're interfering. Now leave me alone! I know what I'm doing!"

"No you don't!" she cried.

Unexpectedly, Jonathan pushed Susan to the ground. Standing over her, he growled, "Stay put! I just—"

Jonathan fell to the ground as Armand clocked him from behind. Having quickly scaled the ditch, Armand was now huffing, his face twisted with venom. "You moron!" he barked. "You would murder two people just for a time capsule? Get up! Now!"

As Jonathan wobbled to his feet, holding his swollen cheek, Susan rose by his side.

Meanwhile Armand demanded, "Tell me? Why?"

Jonathan cowered at Armand's commanding stature and physical prowess, realizing he was no match. In a quasi-whimper, he uttered, "I only wanted to scare you. I had no intentions of burying you both. I swear."

Meanwhile, Andrea had finally managed to climb out of the ditch and approached Armand's side. She looked at Susan, angrily. "So you played us for fools!" Glancing at Jonathan, she added, "*Both* of you!"

"Once again, I'll ask you," Armand demanded. "Why? What do you expect to find in this capsule?"

Jonathan quivered. "Evidently you both are not from around here." Rubbing his bruised cheek, he continued, "Because a local paper accused millionaire Paul Monroe of burying a false capsule." His demeanor deepened with animus. "Monroe happens to be a fanatical Christian, and I'm sure the message in that capsule, if it's the one he buried, has a hostile message about atheists. I imagine it will state some nonsense about how this monument was built by godless infidels, prompting Christians to unite and destroy it."

Armand and Andrea glanced at each other, shocked by the mention of their patron, especially if Monroe had paid them to find his false capsule just to incite a hostile religious agenda.

Armand squinted. "We were actually hired by Paul

Monroe to find this capsule. So, you're telling me he was accused of burying a time capsule? With his own message?"

"Exactly!" Jonathan spat, infuriated. "He's an agitator of hate and intolerance. He's a religious zealot. And if you make this discovery public, that will only play into his evil scheme."

Andrea looked at Armand, not convinced, then back at Jonathan. "Well, coming from someone who tried to bury us alive and doesn't believe in God, I'm inclined not to believe a word you say."

Jonathan rolled his eyes. "There you religious zealots go again! You're always the only ones who know the truth, yet in reality are simply pigheaded as hell, the same phony Hell you foolishly believe in."

As Andrea's ire surged through her veins, Armand sensed the impending eruption, and intervened. "Both of you; *calm down*!"

Grasping the capsule from Andrea, Armand said, "We'll see soon enough just what this message has to say." With that, he unscrewed one of the caps on the rusted pipe. He peered in, then extracted a piece of thick, archival paper hermetically sealed.

As all four gazed at the enigmatic document, Armand began to read it aloud:

On this 24th day of March, 1980, this time capsule has been buried with a sacred message for all humanity.

This enigmatic monument, purported to be erected by atheists…

"There you go!" Jonathan interrupted. "I told you Monroe has it out for us!"

Andrea stifled a smile, as Armand glanced at Jonathan.

"Hold on! Allow me to finish."

Armand continued reading:

...is no such abomination. As clear evidence, these sacred tablets were donated under the pseudonym R.C. Christian. Heed the name: R.C. *Christian*. Not *Jew*, nor *Muslim*, nor *Hindu*, nor *Buddhist*, nor any other denomination.

It is imperative that Christians unite to save not only our religion, but the entire human race, as infidels of all stripes have no place in a New World Order.

Thus our message is clear and simple: One God, One Religion, One Language, One United New World Order, all under the name of our One and only Lord.

MAY JESUS' MESSAGE REIGN SUPREME!

Jonathan sighed, as revulsion curdled his blood. "So, Monroe duped me and cleverly changed the message. Atheists didn't create this monument for evil purposes, but rather holier-than-thou Christians did to save the world from us devils. There you have it. Religious fanaticism at its worst."

Andrea took a deep breath and subdued the rumblings in her heart and soul, as she said calmly, "Listen, Jonathan, while I'll refrain from criticizing you for your beliefs, you should do the same about ours, which happens to be far larger than the atheist community."

"Oh, that's fine for *you* to say," Jonathan retorted, "since this draconian message fits right into your indoctrinated belief *prison*. But for those of us who are free to think for ourselves, we prefer to analyze life and the cosmos with logic. As such, we find this capsule's message to be archaic and a death knell to progress and true enlightenment. With all the knowledge mankind has accrued since the dark and crude ages of false gods and fake miracles, it's disheartening to hear such ignorant and hateful proclamations like this."

Armand interjected, "Well, it *is* disheartening to see humankind still divided by many religions and secular belief systems, but my task was to simply find this capsule and deliver it to Mr. Monroe. So, that's what I intend to do."

As Jonathan gritted his teeth, Armand said, "And if you don't wish for me to file a complaint about your attempt to kill me and my wife, I suggest you fill up this ditch. Pronto! Then go home, *quietly*."

"Oh, yeah?" Jonathan retorted. "And what about you digging at this site without a permit? I can report you, too!"

Armand sighed. "Jonathan, you profess to be a man of logic and reason. Can you truly compare attempted murder to failure to file a permit?"

Susan nudged her boyfriend. "Jonathan, *shut up*! He's right. Let's fill this hole, then try to repair the hole you made in our relationship. I'm not sure I even know you anymore."

"I told the truth, Susan!" He blustered. "I had no intentions of murder. I just wanted to scare them into handing over the capsule."

"But why?" she demanded. "Armand opened it and read it. So why did only *you* need to read the message?"

"You all still don't get it," Jonathan said, infuriated as he glanced at the threesome before him. "Like I said, this message was by Paul Monroe. And this whole fiasco is part of his plan. It had to be stopped. What he's accomplishing here is distorting the message of this monument, which was built to praise the coming Age of Reason. The guidelines are *not* purely Christian, as anyone can see if they read them honestly. So, with his millions, Monroe will change the message to his own warped and hostile beliefs and get them published while remaining anonymous. And anyone who knows how millionaires operate knows they operate in the shadows. You're all fools! Pawns of a radical king. And you don't even realize it."

Armand glanced at Andrea, then back at Jonathan. "This game of chess is *not* over yet. But for now, I'm punching the time clock. It's your move, Jonathan. Start filling the hole!"

Jonathan huffed as he grabbed a shovel, while Susan did the same. Grudgingly, they both began filling in the hole, as Armand and Andrea headed back to the car.

Sitting in their rented Mercedes, Andrea looked at Armand. "So, what are you going to do about this capsule, and its radical Christian message?"

"I'm still calculating my next move, darling. But, yes, the message *is* quite provocative. Not to mention dangerous. Christians are taught to be tolerant and forgiving of others, even of thy enemies, and not to judge them. Yet at the same time commanding them to bring all others into the faith. Meanwhile the Old Testament advocates an eye for an eye. As with most scriptures, they're plagued with contradictory guidelines, as if radicals first committed their directives to papyrus, while moderate-minded scribes added lines to soften the blow. And sometimes vice-versa. Nothing about religion is unified or easy."

"Yes, hence the mystery of the faith," Andrea said.

Armand turned on the interior light and looked at the document, closely. His eyes scanned the typed letters, trying to analyze any clues or telltale signs of what model of typewriter was used. He handed it to Andrea. "You have a better acquaintance with typewriters. I'm not sure if we can link anything back to Monroe that way. But give it a look."

Andrea scrutinized the letters, then said, "Yes, I would need to research this at home, where I have sample sheets of various typewriters." She looked at Armand. "So for now, this is futile. Besides, I'm sure a millionaire like Monroe has many different typewriters at his disposal, so linking this document back to him is a dead end."

"True," Armand said, as he brushed the dirt off his pants and started the car. "Well, it's time to call it a day."

Three days later the couple drove up the long driveway to Paul Monroe's Georgian estate. Once again, they were greeted, this time with a luminous grin, as Monroe gushed, "I'm so glad to see you! I knew you could do it!"

Armand and Andrea walked side-by-side up to Monroe, as Armand handed him the capsule.

Eagerly, Paul unscrewed the top and pulled out the document. "I'm curious to see what this has to say."

"You know *exactly* what it has to say," Armand retorted.

Monroe's head jerked backward, perplexed. "And what *exactly* do you mean?"

"Those are *your* words, Paul," Armand said sternly.

"That's quite an accusation, Mr. Arnolfini!" Monroe snapped. "I'm insulted! How dare you come here to my humble abode and make such an outrageous claim. Do you know who you're speaking to?"

"Yes," Armand said. "I do. A religious fanatic who is looking to stir up hatred and conflict by altering a monument's meaning."

Monroe's piercing gaze could cut rawhide as he said, "For a famous private eye, hailed as a brilliant investigator, you certainly have proven to me only one thing, Mr. Arnolfini. And that's that you're an incompetent fool!"

Monroe gritted his teeth, and with a huff, continued, "I dare you to prove your wild-eyed claim with hard evidence."

"Oh, the evidence is hard, all right," Armand said. "Because its right in your hands."

Monroe looked down at the document. He scrutinized it to see if any telltale signs were evident, yet nothing raised a red flag. He gazed irritably back at Armand, now impatient. "I don't know what you're getting at, Armand! *Nothing* here is hard evidence. The document is typed, for Christ's sake! And I own many different brands of typewriters. So, there's no way to prove I wrote this."

"That's true," Armand said. "But that's not the hard evidence I'm referring to. Take a good *hard* look at the *hard* rusted pipe in your other hand. You can't get much harder than that."

Monroe glanced at the pipe, then back at Armand. He laughed. "And what about it? Its merely a standard plumbing pipe. Anyone could have put this together."

"No, not anyone," Armand said. "Because it is not standard plumbing pipe. It happens to be very old *lead* pipe, Mr. Monroe. Just like the lead pipes I saw in your stable last week, when we first met."

Monroe gazed down at the rusted pipe and bit his lip. He looked back up at Armand, now more annoyed at himself than the brilliant investigator. But he still wasn't willing to cave in, as he replied, "You are obviously very observant, Mr. Arnolfini. However, I am not the only one in Georgia who has old lead pipes in his home. This pipe could have come from anywhere."

"But it didn't," came a voice from behind Monroe.

Monroe pivoted quickly. He couldn't believe his eyes, as James, his servant, stood there. In his hand was a piece of rusted lead pipe, identical to the one in Paul's hand, being that it was cut in half to fabricate the time capsule.

James lowered his head. "I'm sorry, Mr. Monroe. But when Mr. Arnolfini returned here yesterday, inquiring about the lead pipes, I just had to tell him the truth."

Monroe sighed. "As a fellow Christian, James, I'm appalled you would betray me like this. Like Judas, you made a terrible mistake and must pay the price. You're fired!"

James raised his head, resolutely. "I expected that, Mr. Monroe. But integrity is far more important to me than money."

Monroe shook his head. "You're a fool, James. As I told you when drafting that document, my cause, or rather, *our cause* is the greatest and most sacred any Christian could undertake. This wasn't about my white little lie, but rather about the salvation of mankind. And that can only happen under the complete unity of religious belief, all under one faith, the one and only *true* faith…Christianity!"

Andrea finally spoke. "Mr. Monroe. I pride myself as a devout Christian. But your plan to alter the message of an apparently secular or quasi-religious monument to your own militant world view is troubling, to say the least."

Monroe looked at Andrea with a professorial look on his stoic face. With a pedantic tone that accentuated every syllable, he lectured, "Mrs. Arnolfini, if Christians continue to focus only on the pacifistic Words in the Bible, they will indeed remain the meek sheep that they are. Meanwhile the wolves of other religions will devour us. More and more Christians are being attacked and ridiculed with slanderous insults. Yet when we state the brutal facts about Muslims, Hindus or Scientologists, for example, we get censored and labeled as hate mongers or racists. There is a brewing double standard in this country, and we of stout Christian blood and religious fidelity must be strong and proactive. Do you think my namesake, Paul, was a complacent and meek apostle, content to let others go their own misguided ways? Never! Paul was the most crucial conversionist to follow in Christ's footsteps. Footsteps that inevitably led to *me*!"

"Well, Paul," Armand cut in. "Unlike your namesake, you certainly won't be beheaded, but your sacred mission of propaganda *is* officially terminated. It's over."

Paul snickered. "Ha!" he blustered. "My mission is *not* over, Armand. You may file small claims against me for this initial attempt, but I'm far too wealthy and wise to be deterred by you or any court." Heatedly, he glanced at James, then back at the Arnolfinis, and demanded, "Now get off my sacred estate! This minute!"

Armand snickered. "I thought it was your *humble abode*?"

"Get out!" Monroe shouted, as saliva foamed at the edge of his mouth like a rabid wolf's.

As the threesome sighed and took their leave, Paul Monroe snorted and threw the rusted lead pipe to the ground.

CASPAR'S GHOST

Armand was listening to *The Gates of Delirium* by Yes, loosely based on Tolstoy's *War and Peace,* when Andrea stepped into the den. Once again, she stopped short, knowing not to disturb his sonic séance, especially since it was the sublime finale where the music and vocals evoke one of the most transcending pieces of art ever penned.

As the music came to an end, with Jon Anderson's uplifting lyrics *Soon oh soon the light...The Sun will lead us, our reason to be here,* Andrea stepped fully into the den. "I'm surprised to hear such a beautiful ending to such a volatile piece of music."

Armand turned off the stereo remotely. "Well, sweetheart, it was the chaos of war that preceded it, which was quite a tour-de-force of virtuosity. But, yes, that ending is...well, its...beyond words."

"Well, a Mr. Brendenberg is on the phone and he'd like *a word* with you. So, try to conjure up some coherent words as best as you can," she said with a smile.

Armand chuckled as he stood up. "Yes, darling, I'll try my best to get my brain firing on all cylinders." As he walked toward the phone, he looked back at her. "But sometimes things of such utter magnificence and beauty defy words, like *you*!"

Andrea shook her head with a smile. "I knew that keen wit would kick back into gear."

Armand smiled and picked up the phone. "Hello?"

"*Guten Morgen,* Mr. Arnolfini. My name is Karl Brendenberg. I'm the new curator at the Hamburger Kunsthalle. As you must know, our museum is one of the largest in Germany."

"Yes," Armand replied. "I'm quite aware of your museum. I was a good friend of your previous curator. Caspar Hein's death last week came as a shock. In fact, I just returned from Hamburg two days ago from his funeral."

"*Jawohl,* I mean *yes*. My apologies. My native tongue is hard to suppress sometimes. But, yes, I heard you were good friends. I was also told that your reputation is widely known in our industry. Excuse my naivety, I'm only twenty-seven and have much to learn. But I'm grateful to have just received this honorable appointment today."

"Well, congratulations, Karl. How can I help you?"

"Actually, it has something to do with Caspar, or as some here at the museum say 'Caspar's Ghost.'"

Armand squinted, not a believer in spirits of the dead. "Just what exactly is the issue, Karl?"

"Well, I suppose you can say it has to do with the ghosts of two Caspars."

Armand rolled his eyes, now even more suspicious and losing interest.

Karl continued, "As you must know, Mr. Arnolfini, Caspar Hein was an avid admirer of Caspar David Friedrich."

"Yes," Armand said, "As am I."

"And that's why you're the best person to handle this mystery."

Armand looked at Andrea and rolled his eyes, then sat down on the sofa. "I'm all ears, Karl."

"Well, you see, Caspar Hein had placed our prized painting *Wanderer Above a Sea of Fog* in a very unsecure location in our museum the day before his passing. And it mysteriously disappeared yesterday. A mere six days later."

Armand's head recoiled. "I'm shocked about the theft, Karl, and the timing of it *is* a coincidence. But obviously

Caspar didn't steal it; he's dead. So, I'm missing the point of this strange timing?"

"Of course I'm not suggesting that Caspar stole it," Karl said. "But the fact that he has several heirs, namely two sons and a daughter, perhaps this was a setup to secure their futures. I've been told that all three children are in their late twenties or early thirties and none of them are financially well off."

Armand nodded solemnly. "Yes, that unfortunately is true," he uttered. "Caspar's one and only successful son, Helmut, had passed away two years ago in a tragic car accident. It broke Caspar's heart. I believe that loss was the last straw after losing his wife only a month before that accident, and that led to his own sickly state. He deteriorated after that."

Armand sighed, having known Caspar's wife and son to be admirable souls. His mind then jumped tracks, which led him to the dead end of Caspar's remaining three deadbeat children. Armand shook his head, and said, "Well, it's true; Robert, Hans and Hilary never lived up to Caspar's expectations. They each were perpetually in debt and constantly begged him for money. But after years of seeing no progress, and then experiencing the loss of his wife and eldest son, Caspar shut down. He was a shell of a man, depressed and had no will to live. They all killed him in one way or another. It's tragic."

"Yes," Karl said, "That's pretty much what I was told. So for two years, since Helmut's death, it appears his three remaining children have been in extreme debt. That's why I suspect that Caspar must have known his end was near and placed this valuable painting by Caspar David Friedrich near the rear exit. Our security cameras don't really cover that area, as there's a blind spot there. So, if one or all of his children took it, they'd be set for life. It's worth a hundred and forty million dollars."

Armand blinked and swallowed hard. "Yes, that's enough to keep them all living on easy street for the rest of their lives and even their kids' lives."

"Exactly," Karl said. "That's why I believe it appears Caspar's ghost, so to speak, is behind the theft of this valuable Caspar David Friedrich masterpiece. I think Caspar orchestrated it while his kids physically carried it out."

"However," Armand said. "That's all speculation. Granted, Caspar's relocating of the painting, the timing of his death, and this recent theft all add up to a viable indictment, but we mustn't be reckless. I've seen stranger coincidences."

"That's true," Karl agreed. "But being that you know the family, you wouldn't be suspected as investigating them if you simply spoke to them. Perhaps they'll even drop their guard and incriminate themselves or the true thieves."

"Yes, that's true," Armand said. "And under the odd circumstances, questioning them does seem like the first course of action."

"So, does that mean you'll take on this case, Mr. Arnolfini?"

Armand nodded as he put the phone in his other hand and pulled out his planner from his breast pocket. "Most assuredly. I can hop on a flight in a day or two and we can meet to discuss this further."

"That's fantastic," Karl said. "I look forward to meeting you. *Auf Wiedersehen.*"

With that Armand hung up the phone and looked over at Andrea. She had been reading a magazine and placed it down. "So, I hear you're going back to Germany."

"Yes," Armand said solemnly as he penned in his

itinerary. "It seems Caspar Hein's children might have stolen a valuable painting."

"Oh dear!" she said. "Which one?"

"*Wanderer Above a Sea of Fog.*"

Andrea squealed as she clasped her hand around her mouth, then let go. "That's my favorite one!"

"Yes, mine, too," Armand said glumly.

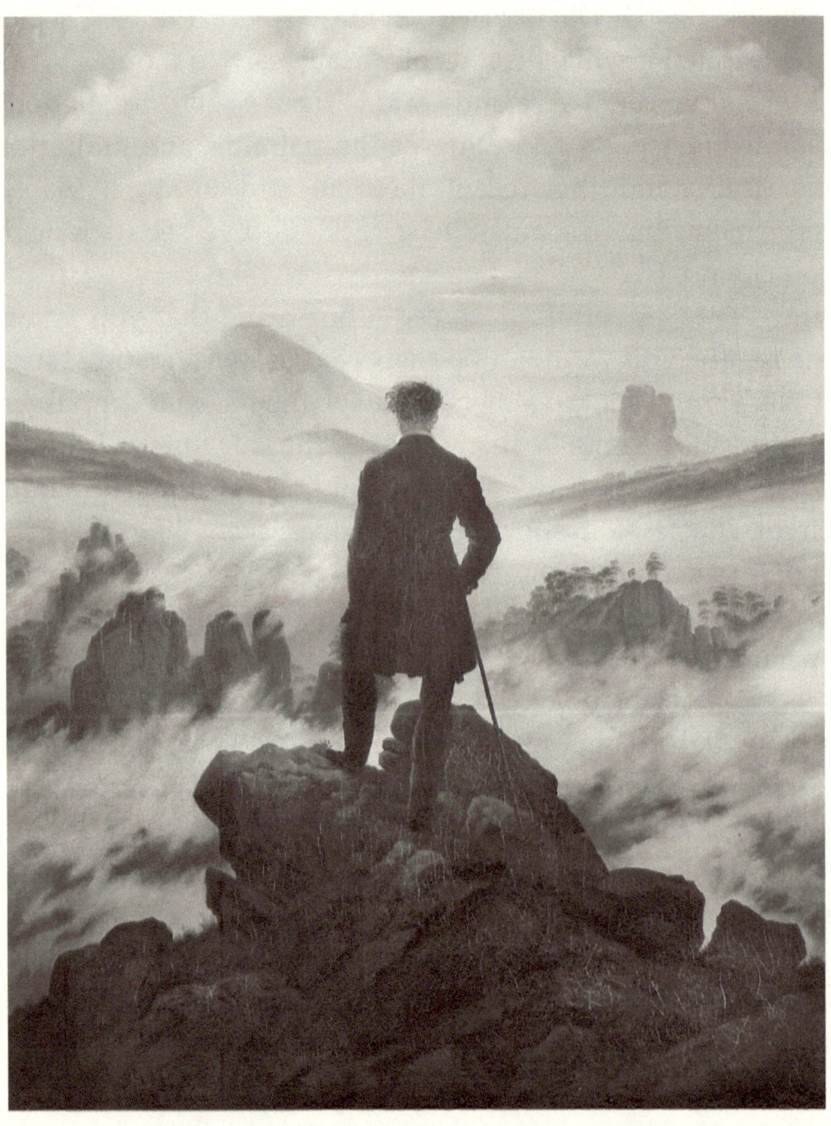

Two days later Armand landed in Hamburg, Germany, and drove to the Hamburger Kunsthalle. He met with Karl, established the scope and financial details of the investigation, then immediately set out to Robert Hein's apartment, Caspar's eldest surviving son.

Arriving at the small apartment complex on *Böckelweg*, Armand rang the doorbell.

A moment later, Robert Hein answered the door. "Ah! Armand. What brings you back to Germany?"

"Well, to be honest, I truly miss your father and wanted to spend some time in Hamburg." He turned and looked around at the horizon. "We spent some good times in this city." He looked back at Robert. "So I figured I'd just drop by to say hello and see how you're doing."

Robert opened the door wider. "Please, come in. Have a drink."

"Thank you," Armand said, as he stepped into the small and unkempt living room.

Meanwhile, Robert went to the portable bar and opened the cabinet door. He spun around. "What will it be? Vodka? Bourbon? Schnapps?"

Armand smiled. "Just a shot of Schnapps would be fine." A melancholy look washed over his face as bittersweet thoughts entered his mind. "That's what your father and I used to drink when we got together."

After the two clinked glasses and took a sip, Armand said, "So, how have things been since your father's passing?"

Robert sat on the decrepit couch and sighed. "Well, not easy. My wife left me and took our three kids. It gets very lonely around here." He took another swig of his Vodka on the rocks, and added, "But I did receive a call from her this morning. It seems there's a good chance we'll be reunited again at some point."

"Well, that's good to hear," Armand said consolingly.

Robert uttered, "Yeah, even if it's for the sake of seeing my kids. Truth be told, I'd prefer being a stay-at-home dad." He stared down at his glass of Vodka almost mesmerized as he swooshed the ice around the glass in a circle.

Armand just nodded and took a sip of his Schnapps. He waited a minute, then cleared his throat to gain Robert's attention. He looked deep into Robert's eyes as he posed the next question. "I happened to stop in the Hamburg Art Museum. They told me Caspar Friedrich's *Wanderer Above a Sea of Fog* was stolen."

Robert's eyes veered slightly and just gazed blankly into space, when Armand noticed a very small twitch. Robert looked back at Armand, and uttered, "Is that so?"

"Yes," Armand replied. "It happens to be one of Friedrich's most prominent masterpieces. It's worth a fortune."

Robert just nodded mechanically and said, "I was never into art, like my father. But I hope they get it back."

Armand paused in thought; Robert's responses could have been innocent aloofness or well-rehearsed acting to mask his guilt. He wasn't sure.

They talked for about an hour, then Armand stood up, shook Robert's hand, and departed. He then drove to Hilary Hein's apartment, several miles away.

After a warm greeting, Armand was welcomed into Hilary's small apartment. It, too, was in dire need of tender loving care. However, Hilary herself was decked out in expensive designer clothes, while on the end table, Armand saw a Gucci bag and fine jewelry scattered about. He figured this could simply be her one vice, however when he mentioned the stolen painting, she appeared to be somewhat nervous. Then again, their conversation just prior had been about her father, whom she seemed to show great affection for; hence her nerves were on edge to begin with.

Some twenty minutes later, Hilary finally looked at Armand with a solemn smile. "It's been great to see you again. Mr. Arnolfini. You brought back fond memories of my father. As a kid I enjoyed listening to you both talk and laugh for hours. I learned to love art because of those talks."

Armand nodded. "Well, thank you, Hilary. That's nice to hear." As Armand walked toward the door, he stopped and looked back at her. "That's why it's very disturbing to learn about the stolen Friedrich painting. It really pains me to know that it might never be seen again."

Hilary's lips pinched, then she nodded. "I agree. It *is* sad. Are you going to investigate the matter?"

Armand nodded. "Yes, I feel obligated. It's a tremendously valuable piece of Western art and worth hundreds of millions. It *must* be found *and* returned."

Hilary glanced aimlessly at the floor. "Yes. It must." She looked back up and tried to crack a smile, but the result was an odd mixture of sadness, nervousness, and fondness. "Well, again, it's been swell to see you again."

"Same here," Armand said, as he kissed her on the cheek and took his leave.

As Armand hopped in his car he couldn't nail down what Hilary's emotions amounted to. Could it have been nervousness to cover her guilt, or perhaps a touch of remorse for stealing the prized painting, or was it simply a matter of conflicting emotions of a young woman who just lost her father?

Armand rubbed his forehead, then he slammed the car into gear and took off toward Hans's apartment, several blocks away. Hans had a brand new Mercedes parked out front and, as he entered Hans's apartment, he was surprised to see that it was immaculate. Again, Armand made small talk and then popped the question regarding the stolen masterpiece. However, Hans showed no signs whatsoever of flinching or nervousness as he responded with great poise and confidence.

Hans looked at Armand and said, "Well, it's sad to hear about the theft, Armand, but, to be honest, I personally don't give a crap about art." Nonchalantly he glanced at his watch and said, "Unfortunately I do have an appointment, so perhaps we can meet up another time? That's *if* you'll still be in Hamburg?"

Oh, I'll be in Hamburg," Armand said. "I started an investigation into the stolen artwork."

Hans just nodded unaffectedly and shook Armand's hand. "Well, good luck with that." Hans escorted Armand out, locked the front door, then hopped in his Mercedes and sped off.

Armand stood for several moments contemplating the responses of Caspar's three children. Each showed some signs of possible guilt, yet he wasn't wholly convinced or satisfied. He hopped in his rented car and drove to the museum.

He walked into Karl's office and was greeted by a hyper-anxious curator with a burning question on his mind. "So, what did you find out!?"

Armand took a seat, as Karl sat on top of his desk, waiting impatiently for the response.

Armand sat silent, as thoughts swirled inside his head for an odd moment, while Karl leaned forward and prodded, "Well!? Come on! Do you think one or all of them are in on it?"

Armand finally looked up at Karl. "It's too soon to say for sure. But yes, I feel each of them exhibited some sense of uneasiness."

Karl leaned back and nodded with relief. "Yes, I'm sure they're all uneasy. I'm convinced they're guilty, and they'll slip up somehow." He rocked to and fro in thought, then stopped. "Actually, it's sad. If they did steal the painting I imagine they're in a quandary as to how they'll ever fence it on the black market. To my knowledge, their father wouldn't have had those types of connections. But you'd know better than I would."

Armand nodded. "Yes, Caspar was clean all right. Clean as Clorox. And bright as Clorox. He used to have a sunny disposition and was quite brilliant, at least up until two years ago. But no, Karl, underworld dregs were something he never would have associated with."

Just then Hilda Behrens walked into Karl's office. Her eyes widened as she came to a halt. "Armand!? I didn't know you were back in town?"

Armand looked over. "Oh, hello, Hilda. I'm just taking in a bit of Hamburg and conjuring up memories of our dear Caspar."

Hilda's head dropped, along with her once perky shoulders. "Yes, it was a hard blow. As his assistant I worked side by side with him for thirty-three years. He was an outstanding boss, and a wonderful man."

"Indeed he was," Armand said.

She glanced at her watch. "Well, I've got to run, but if you're around town for a few days perhaps we can do lunch sometime?"

"Certainly, if I can squeeze it in, by all means."

Hilda looked at Karl. "Now, you make sure you have the new Friedrich painting hung for the premier. I don't want to ruin this campaign." With that, Hilda dashed off.

Armand looked back at Karl. "She's your *assistant*, right?"

Karl laughed. "Yes. Hilda is a demanding woman. I imagine because of my age and being the new kid around here, she mothers me."

Armand smiled. "Well, truth be told, she was also pretty assertive with Caspar. So don't feel too threatened. But as the new curator, it might be wise to nip it in the bud, that's *if* running this place under your own direction is what you want."

Karl nodded thoughtfully. "Yes, I know. Even my own mother tells me to man up."

Armand now had to get to the burning question on his mind. "So, what's this new Friedrich painting she's talking about? I wasn't aware of a new find."

Karl hopped off the top of his desk. "Actually, Hilda just presented it to me earlier today. We plan on debuting it in a few days. I have quite a bit to do, you know, getting the advertising in place and marketing materials printed and all that fun stuff."

"Well, I don't want to hold you up," Armand said as he stood up.

"Oh, not at all," Karl said. "You're a very special guest and I imagine you're dying to see this new acquisition."

"I am indeed!" Armand exclaimed. "Caspar David Friedrich was a fascinating artist. After all, who wouldn't admire his mysterious landscapes?"

"Certainly not I," Karl said enthusiastically.

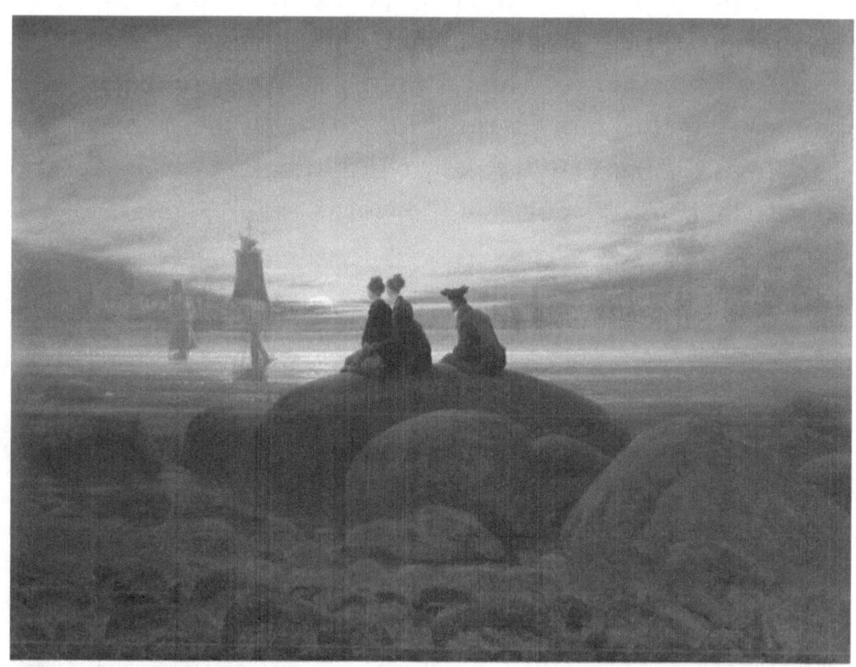

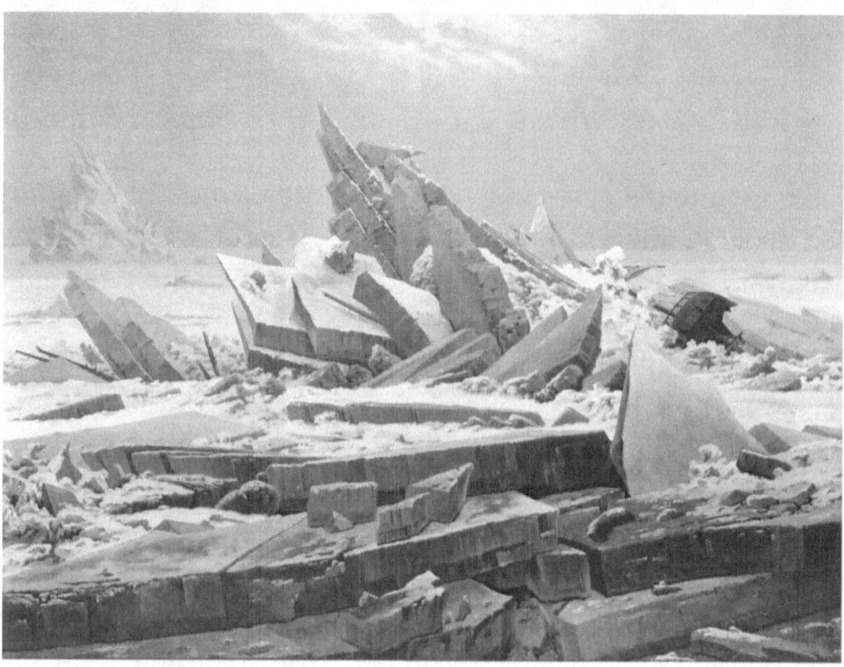

"Follow me," Karl said, as he took off down the decorative corridors with Armand close behind.

Karl escorted Armand into the storage room and pointed at the new acquisition. "Well, there it is! An unknown Caspar David Friedrich right before our eyes. And soon to be before the eyes of the world."

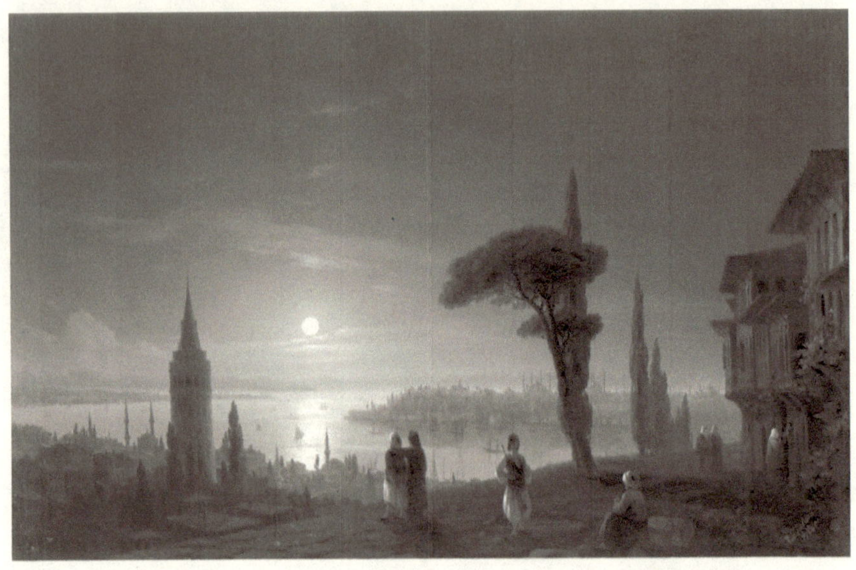

Armand's eyes widened. "It *is* rather nice," he said as he took in the entire composition. After a critical overall analysis, he then stepped closer to scrutinize the paint and brush strokes.

Karl looked on like a protégé watching his master in action. "I've heard a lot about your amazing ability to decipher originals from fakes. So what do you think?"

Armand was silent for a long moment, making Karl very uncomfortable. Finally Karl added, in a nervous utter, "It *is* an original Friedrich, isn't it?"

Armand was still lost in the mists of artistic analysis, as his eyes methodically examined the painting like an electronic scanner. He focused on the brushstrokes, the lighting, perspective, as well as the architecture and people in the scene. After another moment or so, he slowly emerged out of his analytical trance as he backed away from the painting and nodded. "Yes, I believe so," he seemed to say to himself.

Karl sighed with relief. "Thank God! We have our hearts set on this world premiere. We expect to reap great returns."

"Well, speaking of returns," Armand said, now looking at Karl. "Perhaps you should return this beautiful imitation to the dealer."

Karl almost collapsed as the blood fled from his face. "Imitation!? Dear Lord! No!" He shook his numb head. "But you said *you believe so,* that its an original by Friedrich."

"Oh, I'm sorry, I was speaking to myself. I didn't hear you," Armand said. "I was merely saying yes, I believe so, that its an excellent imitation of a Friedrich."

Karl rubbed his forehead. "Are you sure? After all, Hilda confirmed its authenticity with the dealer."

Armand squinted. "Well, I'd like to know who this dealer is?"

Karl nervously searched through the chaotic thoughts flying around inside his head, but his state of panic obliterated any sense of clarity.

Here it was, Karl was the new and youngest curator of one of Germany's preeminent art museums and on his first day he had a fraudulent acquisition on his hands.

"Uh, well…I think…I uh," he turned and looked in the direction of his office. "I think I need to check the acquisition papers on my desk." He looked back at Armand. "Oh, dear God, this can't be happening." He blinked hard, almost hoping to blink the nightmare away. But a world of pain remained, as he uttered, "Would you care to follow me?"

"Certainly," Armand said calmly. "We'll figure this out, Karl. Take a breath and let's go."

Moments later, Karl had extracted the documents out of the folder and Armand looked them over.

Armand looked at Karl. "I happen to know most dealers of fine art, Karl, and I can say that I never heard of Dmitri Beldakov."

As Karl struggled hard to calm his quivering nerves, Armand said, "But that doesn't mean a person can't discover a lost work of art and sell it. In fact, many rare finds come to light this way. So try to relax."

Karl took a deep breath. "Well, I thank you for trying to calm my nerves, Mr. Arnolfini, but that still doesn't turn my fake into a Friedrich."

Armand nodded solemnly. "True. I'm just trying to say that this happens to the best of them. Many museums have forgeries hanging on their walls or works that have been misattributed. In fact, you'd be surprised at how many."

Karl actually managed to crack some semblance of a smile, or possibly a quasi frown. Either way, he thanked Armand, then asked, "So, what do we do now?"

"We get Hilda in here to—"

"To what?" Hilda cut in, as she breezed into Karl's office.

Armand and Karl turned, somewhat startled, as Armand said, "To ask you this: How did you manage to meet Dmitri Beldakov?"

Hilda continued walking to Karl's filing cabinet, opened the drawer and sifted through folders, as she said, "He contacted me." Her head spun around, looking at Armand, as her hands still sifted, and said, "Is there a problem?"

"Actually, there is," Armand said, while Karl jumped in like a rabid dog. "You had me buy a fake, Hilda!"

Hilda's sifting halted as she closed the drawer slowly, like a robot with a dying battery. "A fake?" Her head turned toward Karl. "Did you say a fake?" Before he could answer, her head snapped toward Armand. "I assume *you're* the one who instigated this nonsense. Am I right?"

"I didn't instigate anything, Hilda. You mentioned the new Friedrich, which Karl kindly showed me, knowing my affection for Caspar's work."

Hilda squinted with one eye. "How can you be so sure it's a fake?"

"It's what I do, Hilda. You know that," Armand said. "The fact is, I know it to be the work of Ivan Aivazovsky. He was a Russian artist who was a contemporary of Friedrich. Several of his paintings do have similarities to Friedrich, however, what you all failed to notice was that this painting featured a scene of Turkish people in Istanbul. And Friedrich never painted scenes of the Middle East."

Hilda rolled her eyes. "And why should we believe you?" Heatedly, she looked at Karl. "Don't let his assumptions ruin this chance to premiere a new Friedrich, Karl! You're young and impressionable. Stand your ground."

Armand gazed at Karl, who at first appeared to flinch, but suddenly rose in stature as his chest inflated. "Listen, Hilda, I trust his expertise and judgment. What I'm having a hard time trusting is *your* judgment to buy this work. Especially from an unknown source."

Hilda's lips furled. "Don't you dare blame *me*! I didn't buy it, Karl. *You* did! You're the curator here."

"Yes, I am!" Karl snapped. "And it's high time that you remember that! You've been running roughshod around here ever since I came on board. I know I'm new and young, but I'm not incompetent or stupid. Nor do I like being bossed around by my assistant. Is that clear!?"

Again, Hilda rolled her eyes and huffed. Restraining herself, she said in a quasi-calm voice, "I don't mean to be bossy, Karl, it's just my nature. I'm a perfectionist and I like to make sure things get done."

"And they will get done," Karl said. "Just don't bulldoze me or anyone else here. Work *with* people. Don't trample over them." Taking a breath, Karl shook his head, then said, "Now listen, Armand believes we bought a fake Friedrich, or rather a Russian piece of artwork. So we need to call Dmitri. I don't see his contact info on the papers in my folder."

Hilda glanced down at the floor, then meekly up. "I have his contact info in my desk drawer."

Karl gritted his teeth. "Important information like that should *not* be in *your* drawer, Hilda. Please get it," Karl ordered. "Now!"

As Hilda obediently left the office, Karl looked at Armand. "I guess I'm finally nipping it in the bud."

Armand tilted his head, acknowledging Karl's new stance.

Moments later, Hilda returned with the contact info and Karl made the phone call. Simultaneously, Hilda received a call on her cell phone. She took two steps away, and answered, "Hello. Oh, Mr. Valdoff. I can't speak right now. I'm in a meeting. Yes, Boris, don't worry, I'll call you back later."

Meanwhile, Karl hung up the phone. "I told Dmitri to come here to my office." He looked at Armand. "He'll be here in twenty minutes. Can you wait?"

As Armand nodded, Hilda attempted to leave, when Karl demanded, "And I want you here, too, Hilda."

Hilda spun around. "Sure, fine. But is that really necessary?"

"Yes it is," Armand interjected, to the surprise of Hilda and Karl.

Hilda squinted and scoffed, "I thought we were friends, Armand? Now what? You suspect I had something to do with this?"

Armand sat down on a nearby chair and said, "We're acquaintances, Hilda. I know you vaguely and only because you were the assistant to my friend Caspar. And know this, in a criminal case, I don't exempt anyone, friend or foe, if I suspect they might be involved. And I did say *might be*. So take that with a grain of salt."

"Well, you already rubbed salt in my wound, Armand, so be that as it may, I'm not happy with any of this," she grumbled.

Twenty minutes later, Dmitri Beldakov walked through the door. His eyes scanned Karl and Armand, then landed on Hilda. "So, what is this all about?"

Hilda's eyes veered over toward Armand. "That's Armand Arnolfini. He's a private investigator of art crimes."

Dmitri's genial face turned stern as he turned toward Armand. "And just what are you investigating?"

Armand stood up. "The new Friedrich painting you sold to the museum. I'm curious to know how and where you found it."

Dmitri gazed at Hilda, then at Karl. "Is this necessary? We went through all of this. You inspected the painting and confirmed it as an original. So why does the flimsy assumption of one man turn a masterpiece into mush?"

Karl stepped forward. "Mr. Beldakov, Mr. Arnolfini is a world-class expert. His appraisals are lauded and legendary. So if he says the painting is not by Caspar David Friedrich, I believe him. So, just tell him, how and where did you come across this painting?"

Dmitri seethed under his breath as his piercing eyes practically burned holes in Armand's face. "As an expert, you must be aware that many paintings were looted during both World Wars. Many found their way into Russia, especially when Stalin temporarily occupied Germany, Austria, Poland and other European countries. So the fact that a Friedrich painting made its way into Russia should come as no surprise."

"True," Armand replied. "Looted paintings smuggled from Germany into Russia do not come as a surprise, Dmitri. What I'm suggesting is the opposite. I believe this is a Russian painting by Ivan Aivazovsky that is now being deceptively smuggled into Germany as a Friedrich."

Dmitri's left eye twitched, as he said, "That's ludicrous!" He looked at Karl. "Do you hear what this lunatic is suggesting?" He laughed, yet not so convincingly, as Armand said, "If I'm such a lunatic…" he looked at Karl. "I'll even pay for comprehensive scientific testing. In essence, I'll put my money where my mouth is."

Beads of sweat materialized along Dmitri's receding hairline. He wiped his forehead and said, "Fine! Do all the testing you like. But I know I sold an original Friedrich."

Armand looked deep into Dmitri's shifty eyes. "And how do you know its an original Friedrich?"

Dmitri pointed at Hilda. "Because *she's* the one who told me it was."

All eyes veered toward Hilda, as she swallowed hard. Her face started to turn into a sickly shade of alabaster, like that of an old porcelain doll. "That's true," she mumbled. Regaining her vigor, she added, "But know this, I still believe it's an original Friedrich."

"You see!" Dmitri blurted. "There you have it. Now, I'll admit, I'm not an art dealer per se. I just sell artifacts that I come across at my pawnshop in St. Petersburg. Recently, however, I opened a shop here in Hamburg, because the items I have are generally unknown here in Germany, and are very rare and valuable." He sighed, and added, "I had no idea the painting I had was by Friedrich. So when Hilda saw it in my shop, she informed me of its author and value. That being two hundred thousand dollars."

Dmitri looked at Armand and Karl with nervous eyes. "I had no intention to cheat the museum, I swear. But when I heard how much it was worth, naturally I jumped at the opportunity to sell it."

Armand looked at Hilda. "So, when did you become an expert on Friedrich's work?"

Hilda stood up, now indignant. "I've been looking at Friedrich's work here in our museum for three decades! How is it that only the great Armand Arnolfini is capable of being an art expert?"

"I never claimed to be the only art expert, Hilda. But my expertise comes with decades of not just looking at paintings superficially but also analyzing them. I spent many years testing the various minerals and oils that make up different oil paints at various ages, deciphering and charting the craquelure in different oil and tempera paints and learning how particular artists handle their brushes."

Hilda stared at the wall, speechless, as Armand continued, "And I don't doubt that you've obtained some degree of precision in judging Caspar Friedrich's works, since as you say, you've been around them for decades. But look me in the eye, Hilda, and tell me..." As she did so, he continued, "Did you truly believe that painting was by Friedrich? Or did you see an opportunity to fill the vacancy on the wall left by the stolen *Wanderer Above a Sea of Fog*? And by doing so, attract viewers to flock back here to see an unknown work of his to regenerate your slump in ticket sales?"

Karl and Dmitri looked on with bated breath, as Hilda sighed, heavily. A tear welled in her eye.

Armand shook his head, as he walked over and placed his hand on Hilda's shoulder. "Look, I don't think you're an evil person for trying to rejuvenate business here. Misguided, yes. There are legitimate ways to draw audiences. And this was certainly not one of them. Knowingly presenting artwork by another artist as an original by an old master, however, is reprehensible."

Karl looked at Dmitri. "With this new development, some actions must be taken. However, rather than press legal charges, perhaps we can simply renegotiate the sale. I'm sorry you won't get two hundred thousand for it, but I do like the painting, and I'm sure our viewers will, too. Adding a Russian artist to our inventory is also a wise and valuable commodity to have."

As Dmitri acknowledged Karl with a nod, Hilda looked at them with a sullen face. "I'm truly sorry. I only had everyone's interests at heart. Bear in mind, I didn't reap any rewards, *you* did, Dmitri, and *you*, too, Karl, if it went on display as intended." She glanced at Armand. "But I didn't anticipate *you* visiting us and revealing it as a fake."

She looked up at Karl. "You won't report me, will you?"

"Perhaps not," Karl said. "If we can settle this here I'm fine with letting this slide."

Armand interjected, "Don't be so quick to be the Good Samaritan, Karl."

As their heads snapped in his direction, Armand went on, "We still have the question of the missing *Wanderer Above a Sea of Fog*."

Karl squinted. "What about it? It has nothing to do with this matter." He paused, then uttered concernedly, "Does it?"

"I'm afraid it does," Armand said.

He looked at Hilda. "A moment ago I heard you mention the name Boris Valdoff. And I know he's an infamous black market dealer. In fact, I had him arrested twice. I can't believe that rat is out again. So I suspect that it was you who told Caspar Hein to move the *Wanderer* painting to the rear of the museum, where there's a blind spot on the security cameras." As everyone listened intently, Armand continued, "Caspar was in a grave state of melancholy, so he aimlessly conceded to the domineering side of your personality."

Hilda gazed at Armand with an unsettling mixture of surprise and befuddlement, as he went on, "But the end game of you stealing the famous painting was not personal greed, but rather the loving generosity of a doting mother."

As Dmitri and Karl recoiled, shocked and baffled, Hilda bit her lips as she squinted, turning her gaze down at the floor, then back up at Armand and his astounding revelations.

Armand continued, "The fact is, I know that you are the mother to Caspar's three surviving children." As jaws dropped, he went on, "Caspar confided in me just weeks before his passing. Helmut was his only legitimate child with his wife Mary, who humbly accepted your children into her house to avoid a public scandal. One that probably would have cost Caspar his job and their family's financial security."

Hilda's eyes pinched tightly closed as tears squeezed out of her lids and streamed down her devastated face.

Armand sighed. "It pains me to say this, Hilda, but

your children have all struggled through life. Caspar told me you always gave them money to pay their bills, making them dependent on you. They never grew up to be self-sufficient adults. Your big heart and domineering ways backfired, and this time, in a most gargantuan and lucrative way. So, how much did you sell *Wanderer Above a Sea of Fog* for?"

Hilda opened her glazed eyes and looked meekly up at Armand. "Sixty-million." Pulling a tissue out of her pocket, she wiped her tears and said, "Each of my children received twenty million. But they're loving children, I tell you. They were kind enough to give me twenty million out of their share. So, I did a fine job as a mother."

Karl and Dmitri stood dumbfounded, not only by the astounding confession but by Armand Arnolfini's amazing skills of deduction.

Karl shook his head and sat down at his desk. He looked over at Hilda. "You must have known that painting is worth at least a hundred-and-forty million."

Armand looked at Karl. "Yes, and perhaps even more. However, that's the bane of dealing on the black market." He looked back at Hilda. "Moreover, many paintings on the black market disappear into private collections and never see the light of day again, robbing millions of people the beauty of precious works of art." He sighed, heavily. "However, the real problem now is getting it back."

Over the next four months much had happened. Hilda found herself in prison with her three children while Armand tracked down Boris Valdoff. As Armand arrived in Kiev, Boris fled to Minsk, then from Minsk on to Istanbul, and the leapfrogging continued until Armand finally burst into Boris's hotel room in Vienna. After a brief but bitter scuffle, Armand forced Boris to reveal where he stored the masterpiece.

Valdoff's transaction with the Saudi buyer was duly thwarted and Armand returned the masterpiece to the Hamburg Art Museum. Along with Caspar David Friedrich's masterwork was a new work by Ivan Aivazovsky, a Russian master relatively unknown throughout Europe. Amid several days of fanfare, the museum had tripled their earnings, a precedent that continued for untold months.

During that time, Armand had attended the gala, then eventually arrived home in Westport, Connecticut. He embraced his wife and children with even greater affection. He was grateful for the choices he had made in life, having chosen Andrea as his loving wife and appreciative of the way they both raised their children, namely with equal doses of love and logic, whereby cultivating admirable young citizens, ones dedicated to learning and self sufficiency, as well as to helping others and striving for peace and progress.

Armand put on his headphones and turned up *The Gates of Delirium* once again, as he knew life was akin to war and peace. Storms are a perpetual occurrence, and as such, it's incumbent upon those of sound mind to actively confront the darkness so that humankind can bask in the luminous serenity of peace and sing the glorious tune:

Soon oh soon the light
Ours to shape for all time, ours the right
The sun will lead us
Our reason to be here

The Author

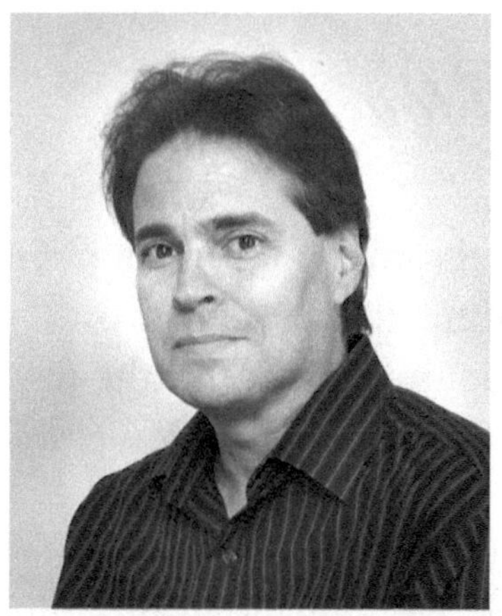

Rich DiSilvio is an award-winning author of thrillers, mysteries, historical fiction and nonfiction. He has written books, historical articles, and commentaries for magazines and online resources. His passion for history, art, music, and architecture has yielded contributions in each discipline in his professional careers.

DiSilvio's work in the entertainment industry includes projects for historical documentaries, including James Cameron's *The Lost Tomb of Jesus, Killing Hitler, The War Zone* series, *Return to Kirkuk, Operation Valkyrie,* and cable TV shows and films such as *Tracey Ullman's State of the Union, Celebrity Mole, Blood Ties, Monty Python: Almost the Truth,* and many others.

He has written commentaries on the great composers (such as the top-rated Franz Liszt Site), and conceived and designed the Pantheon of Composers porcelain collection for the Metropolitan Opera, which also retailed throughout the USA and Europe.

His artwork and new media projects have graced the album covers and animated advertisements for numerous super-groups and celebrities, including, Pink Floyd, Yes, The Moody Blues, Cher, Madonna, Jay-Z, Willie Nelson, Miles Davis, the Rolling Stones, Alice Cooper, Queen, and many more.

As a software designer/developer, Rich pioneered the first interactive CD-ROM for educating staff and parents about Applied Behavioral Analysis (ABA) for training individuals with autism.

Rich lives in New York with his wife and has four children.

Thank You

Thanks to all my readers for expressing your enjoyment with the character Armand Arnolfini. It was this show of support that inspired me to continue the series after the first two episodes, which appeared in *Short Stories II: Mysteries, Thrillers & Historical.*

This completes the third full volume of art crime cases that Armand Arnolfini investigates, and includes his wife and two children, who are now older and become involved in some of his cases.

As mentioned before, I am indebted to all the great artists who have influenced me over the years and made these fictional adventures possible. Their contributions to Western civilization are indeed to be cherished, and I feel couching them in entertaining mysteries brings their names and talents to a broader public not acquainted with their work.

To my dear family and friends who have supported my creative endeavors, along with my editors, marketers, and to all the contest judges who have voted several of my books as award winners, I am most grateful. *Thank you!*

— Rich DiSilvio

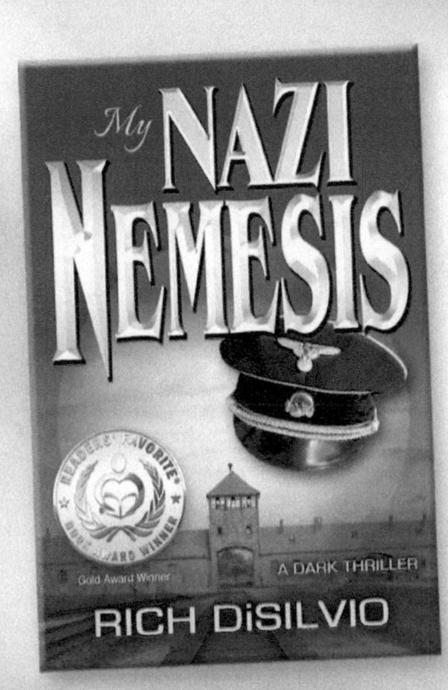

My Nazi Nemesis

GOLD AWARD WINNER

★★★★★ **"DiSilvio's plot is cunning and ingenious!"**
-- Jack Magnus for Readers' Favorite

A deadly love triangle launches a father and daughter team to hunt down a nefarious Nazi. Yet twists and turns abound, leading to a shocking climax.

Hardcover: 9780981762586
Paperback: 9780981762579
eBook: 9780981762593

A Blazing Gilded Age

INTERNATIONAL AWARD WINNER
AND BEST COVER DESIGN

A riveting rags-to-riches saga about a poor family's struggle to survive amid a nation burning with ambition yet bleeding with injustice. Features, Teddy Roosevelt, JP Morgan, Mark Twain, Tesla and more.

Lauded by HISTORY/A+E and noted biographer Roger DiSilvestro.

Hardcover: 9780981762562
Paperback: 9780981762555
eBook: 9780997680720

Tales of Titans Series

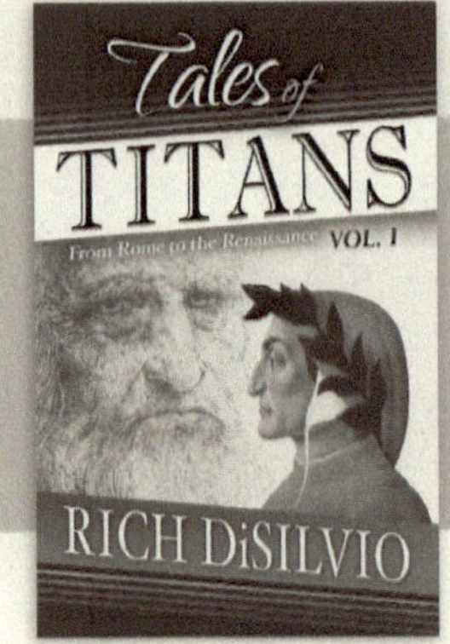

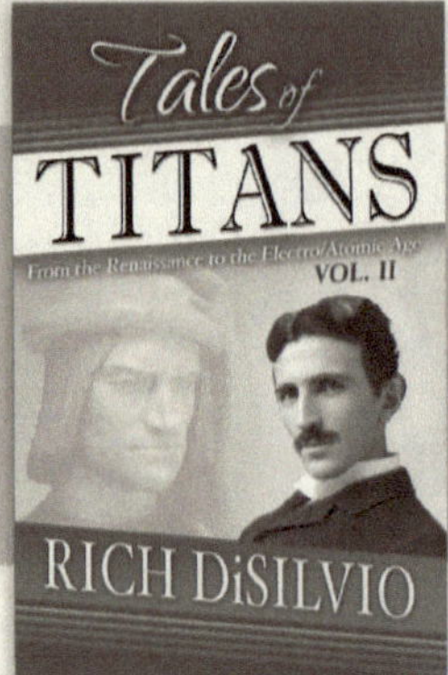

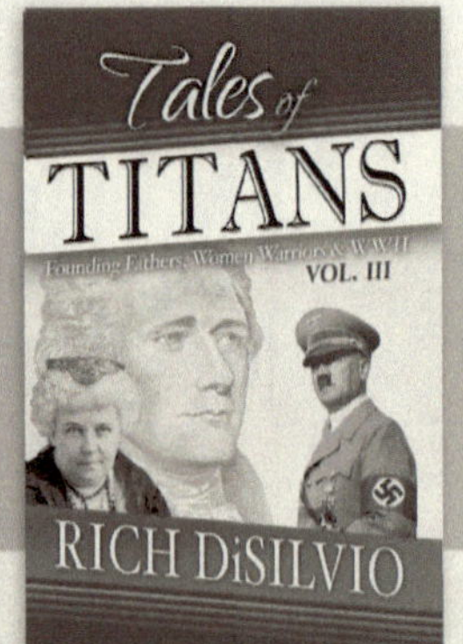

Tales of Titans brings great historical figures to life with concise yet compelling essays, coupled with engaging narratives that enlighten readers to their miraculous deeds, and misdeeds, that have significantly shaped Western civilization.

This handsomely illustrated series offers readers brief biographical overviews and cogent analysis, while the quasi-fictional scenarios transport readers into a fascinating past, whereby putting flesh on the bones of several titans and offering glimpses into their hearts, minds, and actions.

Tales of Titans, Vol. I : From Rome to the Renaissance
Augustus & Livia, Vespasian & Titus, Hadrian, Constantine, Dante, Brunelleschi, Columbus, Vespucci, King Ferdinand, Pope Alexander VI & Cesare Borgia, and Leonardo da Vinci.

Tales of Titans, Vol. II: Renaissance to the Electro/Atomic Age
The Medicis, Gutenberg, Lorenzo de Medici, Savonarola, Leonardo & Machiavelli, Martin Luther, Queen Elizabeth I, Shakespeare, Galileo, Darwin, Marx, Stalin, Freud, Marconi, Edison, Tesla, Westinghouse, Einstein, Fermi and von Braun.

Tales of Titans, Vol. III: Founding Fathers, Women Warriors & WWII
Samuel Adams, Thomas Paine, George Washington, John Adams, Thomas Jefferson, James Madison, Alexander Hamilton, Ben Franklin, Sybil Ludington, James Armistead Lafayette, Elizabeth Cady Stanton, Susan B. Anthony, Harriet Tubman, Adolf Hitler, FDR & Churchill

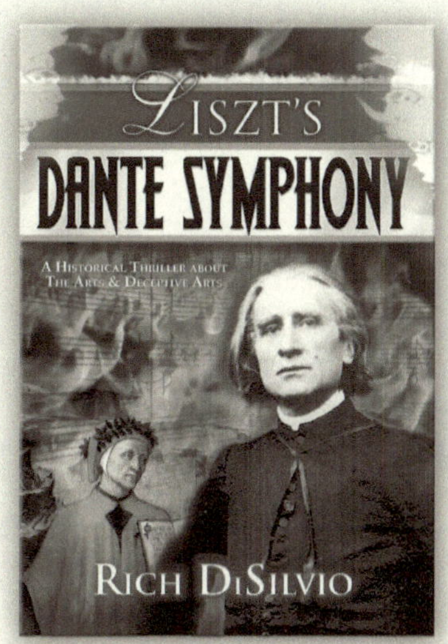

Liszt's *Dante Symphony*

A historical mystery/thriller highlighting the belligerent rise of Nazi Germany from its Prussian roots, replete with ciphers, spies, murder and a stellar cast, including Albert Einstein, Rossini, Liszt, Nazi officers and Adolf Hitler.

Hardcover: 9780981762548
Paperback: 9780981762531
eBook: 9780997680713

The Winds of Time

The Winds of Time is a historical tour de force of Western civilization by Rich DiSilvio.

With masterful style, DiSilvio paints a fascinating historical canvas with the flare of a consummate artist. Key figures and the primary cultures that literally shaped the Western world are candidly analyzed, revealing both the dark and luminous sides of mankind. Moreover, DiSilvio's insightful essays add intriguing new dimensions to the historical record.

Hardcover: 9780981762524
eBook: 9780997680706

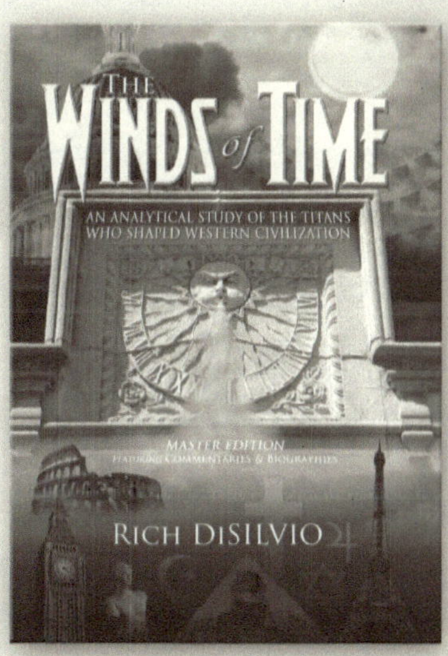

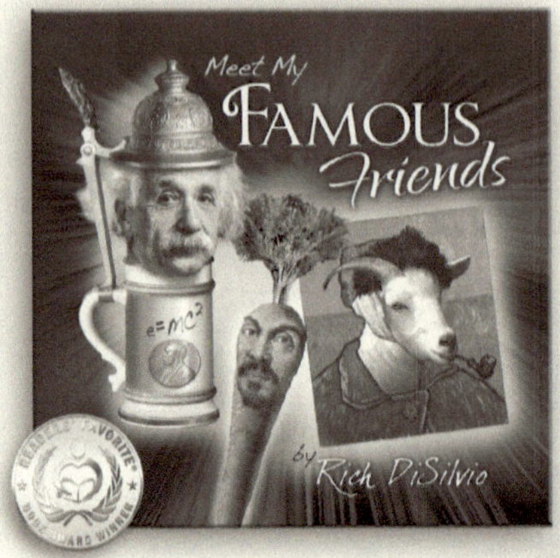

SILVER MEDAL WINNER

Meet My Famous Friends

Inspiring kids with Humor!
A whimsical picture book that pays homage to great historical figures in imaginative ways.

Author/Illustrator Rich DiSilvio presents a broad array of geniuses and heroes in a humorous and compelling fashion by altering their names and appearances, whereby making us see very familiar people in very different ways.

While children will get a kick out of looking at the comical artwork, teens and even adults will appreciate the witty play on words, inventive creations, and perhaps glean a thing or two about some of these iconic people who had a great influence on society in one form or another. Their lives and contributions have uplifted humanity in various ways, thus being great role models for young and old alike.

Hardcover: 9780997680751 Paperback: 9780997680768 eBook: 9780997680775

PURPLE DRAGONFLY WINNER

Danny and the DreamWeaver

A MS novelette by Mark Poe (aka Rich DiSilvio) about the power of dreams and the imagination.

When Danny meets Nostrildamus in his dream a bizarre journey begins!

Packed with dry humor, a mystery, and zany-looking artists, like Michelanjello & Hippopotamus Bosch, *Danny and the DreamWeaver* is an imaginative adventure of criminal intrigue and art history that demonstrates the importance of looking at life differently.

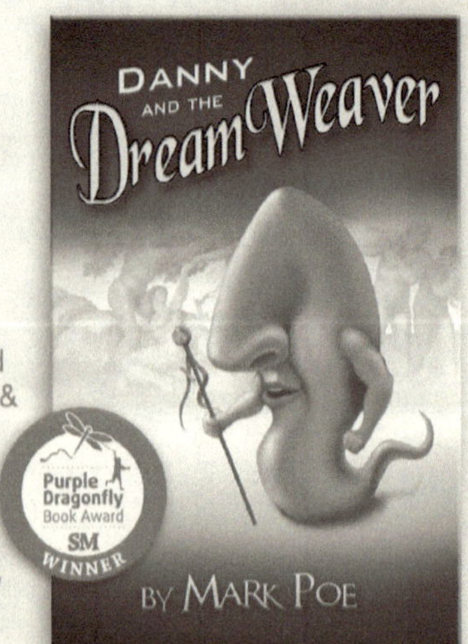

Paperback: 9780997680737
eBook: 9780997680744

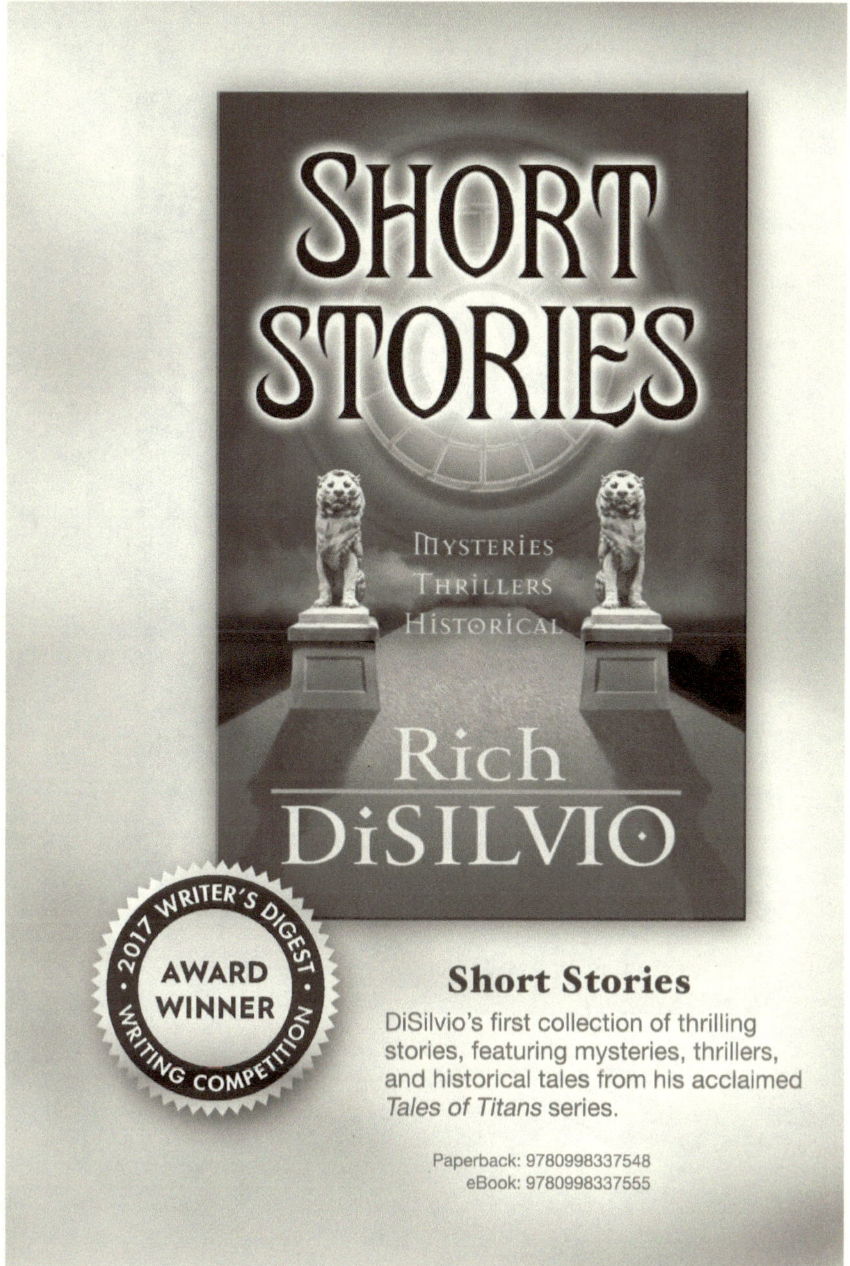

Short Stories

DiSilvio's first collection of thrilling stories, featuring mysteries, thrillers, and historical tales from his acclaimed *Tales of Titans* series.

Paperback: 9780998337548
eBook: 9780998337555

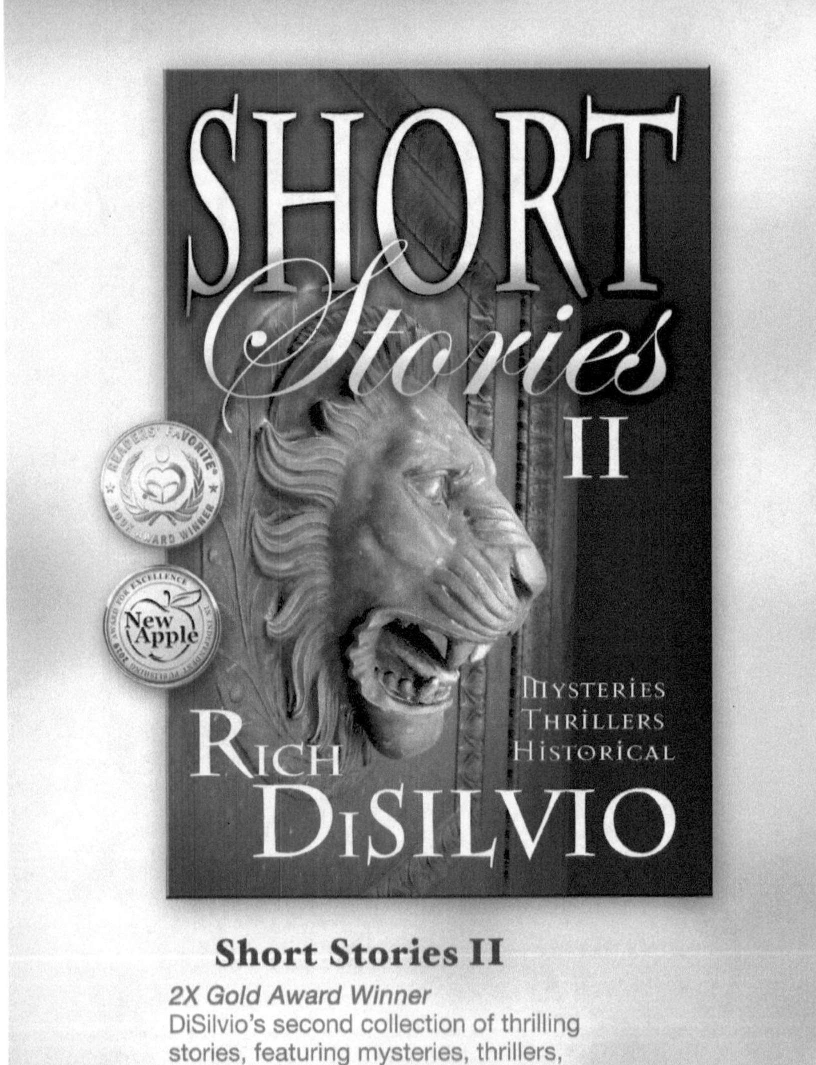

Short Stories II

2X Gold Award Winner
DiSilvio's second collection of thrilling stories, featuring mysteries, thrillers, and historical tales from his acclaimed *Tales of Titans* series.

Paperback: 9780998337562
eBook: 9780998337579

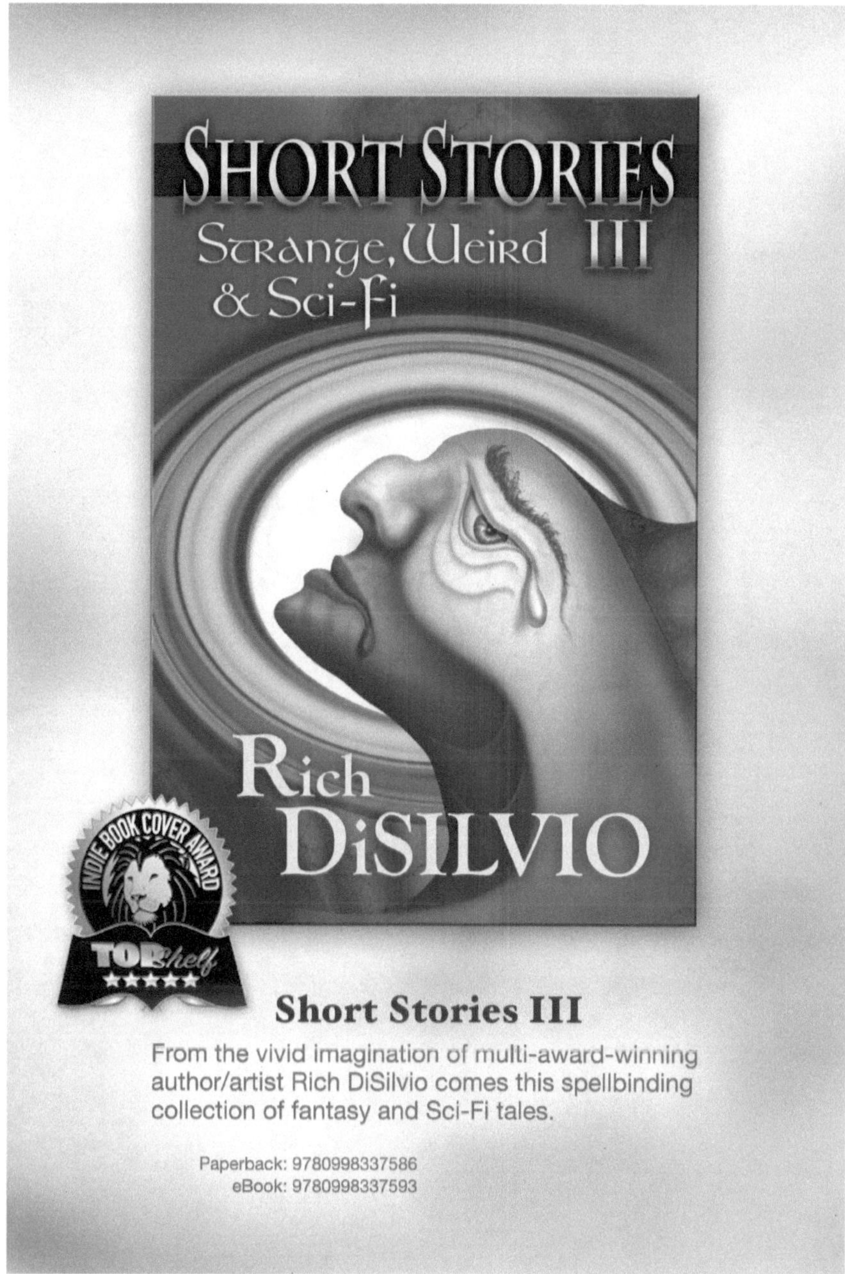

Short Stories III

From the vivid imagination of multi-award-winning author/artist Rich DiSilvio comes this spellbinding collection of fantasy and Sci-Fi tales.

Paperback: 9780998337586
eBook: 9780998337593

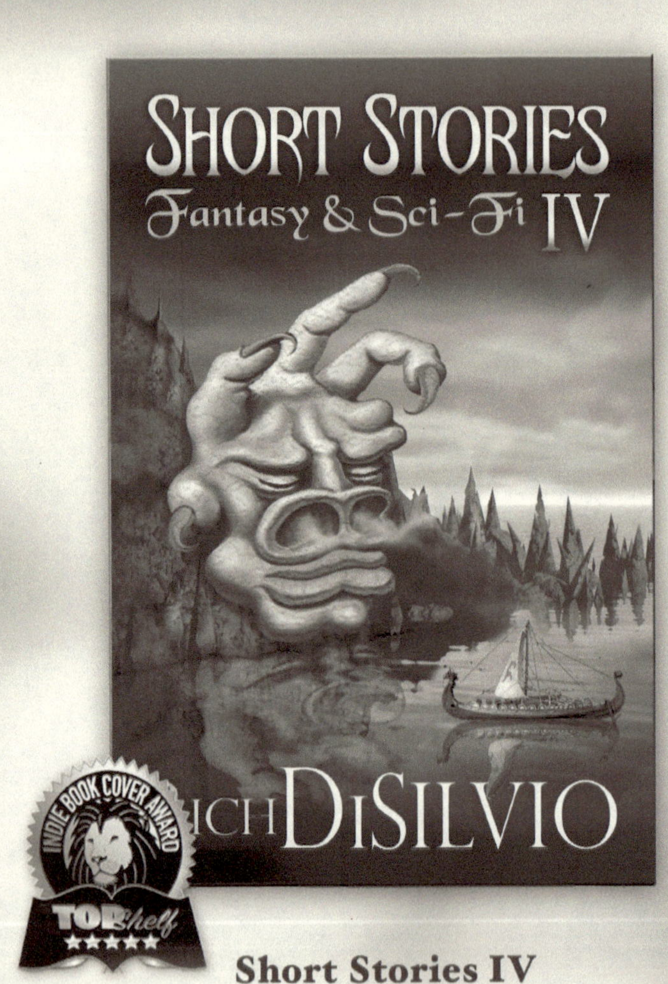
SHORT STORIES
Fantasy & Sci-Fi IV
RICH DISILVIO
INDIE BOOK COVER AWARD
TOP shelf

www.ingramcontent.com/pod-product-compliance
Lightning Source LLC
LaVergne TN
LVHW091040080826
845145LV00002B/563

* 9 7 8 1 9 5 0 0 5 2 1 5 8 *